THE FORGOTTEN GIRLS

ALSO BY OWEN LAUKKANEN

The Professionals

Criminal Enterprise

Kill Fee

The Stolen Ones

The Watcher in the Wall

THE FORGOTTEN GIRLS

OWEN LAUKKANEN

G. P. PUTNAM'S SONS | NEW YORK

PUTNAM

G. P. PUTNAM'S SONS
Publishers Since 1838
An imprint of Penguin Random House LLC
375 Hudson Street
New York, New York 10014

Library of Congress Cataloging-in-Publication Data

Names: Laukkanen, Owen, author.
Title: The forgotten girls / Owen Laukkanen.
Description: New York : G. P. Putnam's Sons, 2017.
Identifiers: LCCN 2016036563 | ISBN 9780399174551 (hardback)
Subjects: | BISAC: FICTION / Crime. | FICTION / Suspense. | GSAFD: Suspense fiction.
Classification: LCC PR9199.4.L384 F67 2017 | DDC 813/.6—dc23
LC record available at https://lccn.loc.gov/2016036563
p. cm.

Printed in the United States of America
1 3 5 7 9 10 8 6 4 2

Book design by Gretchen Achilles

To the memory of the missing and murdered women

of Vancouver's Downtown Eastside.

You are not forgotten.

PROLOGUE

You don't ever surf trains on the High Line.

The wind howled like a creature. Screamed. Steel shrieked against steel. The night was a dark blur: pine trees by the thousands, Douglas firs looming out of the darkness, the occasional red smear as a signal tower whizzed past. And above, the night sky, the stars, so many and so bright.

Ash pulled her coat tight around her thin frame. Clutched her pack and ducked low behind the shipping container to ward off the cold. Couldn't escape the bite in the air, late October in mountain country, the wind like icy fingers through her worn, ragged clothing.

She'd been riding this train for two days, all the way from Chicago. Figured she'd make the coast sometime midday tomorrow. The hotshot was Ronda's idea, a solid mile of containers on flatbed stack cars, three locomotives up front, the fastest train on the railroad, a string of green *go* signals pointing the way west.

"Seeing as you're so damn set to risk your ass out there," Ronda told Ash, "you might as well make it fast."

Ronda wasn't sold on the High Line idea. Ronda said what they all said, what Ash herself had told other girls more times than she could remember. *You don't ever surf trains on the High Line.* Not alone. Not at all, if you could help it. Bad things happened to women up here.

And yet here Ash was, bundled up by her lonesome, fifteen to twenty cars from the back of the train, the sun long set, the weather already bad and fixing to get worse. The last weather report Ash had seen called for snow flurries through the passes, maybe worse. You could take cover on the slow trains, tuck into the little cubbyhole on the end of a grain car, find an empty boxcar and curl up, build a fire. The hotshots were open-air, though—and they *moved*. Ash had been near hypothermic since the last crew-change point, and it didn't stand to get warmer anytime soon.

Mark this down on your long list of bad ideas. It was always her mother's voice Ash heard in situations like this. *You'll screw around and die of hypothermia and have no one to blame but yourself.*

Not like Ash had a choice. Time was of the essence. Ronda had let slip about Texas Johnny the last time they'd talked, said he was holed up at Ronda's place, the last round of tests at the hospital pretty well sealing his deal. And Ash had spent enough time with Texas Johnny, eaten enough of his food by the campfire and borrowed enough of his money, that she figured she owed the old rider a visit before the end came.

"That's noble of you, kiddo," Ronda'd said when Ash told her. "Only thing, this is a limited-time offer. Poor guy'll be lucky to last out the week."

Three days, Ash told her. *Keep him alive until Tuesday. I'll catch out on the next thing smoking.*

Three days. No time to dip south, take the warmer, safer route. No choice but the hotshot, the High Line. Bogeyman stories and the constant threat of hypothermia.

The train was slowing now. The wheels beneath her flatbed shrieked in protest, a shrill, deafening wail, the containers shuddering and swaying above Ash like ships in a storm. Ash peeked over the stack car's sidewall, looked out into the night. Saw a cluster of lights through the trees, a couple of storage tracks branching off from the main line.

A town—small, from the look of it, a few houses and some railroad outbuildings, maybe a store or two. The train slowed and then jarred to a stop beneath a roadway overpass. The air was suddenly quiet, still, the silence ringing in Ash's ears. A few flakes of snow drifted down, then a few more. Even without the wind, the night was bitterly cold.

Nothing moved in the town, but up the tracks, toward the engines, she could see other trains on the sidetracks. Headlights and shadows, flashlights and voices. Men, railroad men.

The hotshot just waited there. None of the other trains moved, either. This wasn't a crew-change point; Ash was pretty certain. There was no reason for the train to be stopped.

But they weren't going anywhere. And the low wall of the stack car didn't provide much protection. Ash huddled against the container, trying to block out the wind. Glanced across the tracks and caught a glow flickering under the roadway bridge.

A fire.

A fifty-five-gallon oil drum, a weak flame stoked by garbage and scrap wood. The fire meant warmth. It meant real food, something cooked, maybe even hot coffee. It also meant other riders. And other riders meant danger to a girl traveling alone.

Ash was sick of being cold. She was sick of eating trail mix and granola bars, all of it gritty with road grime and diesel fumes. She could handle other riders, she'd proved that already—been out here six years, some puny punk rock chick from the ass end of Wisconsin, a hundred pounds tops, and no other rider, man or woman, had ever laid a hand on her. Damned if they were going to start now.

Ash shouldered her pack. Found her knife in her coat, her grandmother's knife, rubbed the hilt for good luck. Pulled herself to her feet, climbed up out of the stack car, and dropped down to the trackside. Picked her way across the storage tracks to the edge of the right-of-way, a rutted mud road, and followed it back toward the bridge and the fire.

There was only one person, as far as Ash could see. A bundle of filthy coats and an old sleeping bag, age and gender unclear, just a vaguely human form leaned up against the concrete wall of the overpass, close enough to the fire to keep warm.

Ash hesitated, heard Ronda's admonitions. But the promise of warmth got the best of her, and she squared her shoulders and walked closer.

"You mind if I join you?" she asked the pile of coats.

The other rider stirred and peered out at her, met her eyes and looked away. "Make yourself at home," he said, shifting slightly. "Looks like we're in for a wait."

Ash nodded her thanks, crossed in close to the fire. Held her hands to the flame. "You know why they're all stopped?" she asked. "I figured my hotshot would roll all the way through."

"Derailment in the mountains west of here," the rider told her. "Shut down the main line. They're holding all trains."

Ash looked up the tracks: three trains stranded, her chances of making Seattle tomorrow dwindling fast. More snow was falling now, gusting around the wind, and Ash shivered. "It's cold out there."

"Only getting colder," the rider said. "It's fixing to be one hell of a winter."

He looked at her again, bolder now, and Ash could see hunger in his eyes—and something else, too, something darker. She glanced up the line again, the railroad men in the distance, too far away to be any comfort.

Forget this. Better freezing cold than dead, right?

Behind her, the coats rustled. Ash turned back, ready to tell the rider she was going to take a rain check, take her chances on the hotshot, but discovered as she did that he'd shrugged the coats off and was standing now, bigger and taller and *meaner* than she'd imagined.

"Don't you try anything," she told him, watching the way his lip curled as he circled the drum toward her, a predator stalking prey, moving in for the kill. "Don't you fucking dare."

The rider didn't flinch, didn't slow. Ash reached for the knife as he came for her. Closed her fingers over the handle, struggled to pull the blade out. And then he was on her, and she was fighting for her life.

1

Tanya Sears had to admit the guy was cute, anyway. It was just that she couldn't remember his name.

Mike something, maybe. Mitch. Matt. He'd told Tanya three times already, not that it mattered. It wasn't like she was going to marry the guy. Still, as a matter of self-respect, Tanya figured she'd better get his name sorted out before they wound up in bed together.

As it was, they were huddled in close outside Mike/Mitch/Matt's front door, swearing and stamping and shivering as Mike/Mitch/Matt fumbled with his keys while the frigid subzero wind tore into them both.

Minnesota in January. Heaven on earth.

"Hurry *up*." Tanya snuggled in closer to the guy. "I'm freaking *freezing* out here. And the colder I am, the more work you're going to have to put in warming me up again."

Mike/Mitch/Matt glanced down at her and turned on that smile again, that thousand-watt stunner that had more or less melted her into a pool of Jell-O after he'd nearly taken out her eye with that pool cue back at the Lamplighter. That smile was the main reason Tanya was here—that and the tequila. And Mike/Mitch/Matt knew it, too.

"I'm working on it," he told her. "Just a little hard to concentrate when you're all up in my business."

Tanya arched an eyebrow. "Performance anxiety?"

Mike/Mitch/Matt slid a key into the lock. Twisted it and pushed the door open. Turned that smile on her again and stepped back so she could enter. "Not on your life."

His place was kind of small, but clean, neat and tidy, no dirty dishes in the kitchen, no clothes lying around, all the furniture tasteful and modern—hell, even the books on the bookshelf were arranged alphabetically. The place was almost *too* tidy, Tanya thought, like, might-not-really-like-girls tidy. And wouldn't that be her luck, to finally meet a decent guy and he's gay. Or he happens to keep a stock of severed heads in his freezer.

Mike/Mitch/Matt took her coat and showed her to the living room. Dimmed the lights and played with his phone until music started up from some speakers somewhere, something moody and instrumental, sexy but not cheesy, didn't scream *one-night stand*, but didn't quite say *You're the love of my life*, either.

Mike/Mitch/Matt disappeared into the kitchen, said something about fixing drinks. Left Tanya sitting on the sofa with nothing to do, and she was just about giving in to the urge to rearrange the books on the dude's bookshelf when she saw he'd left his phone on the coffee table and decided it was time she sorted out the name situation once and for all.

She picked up the phone, sly as she could. Slid her finger across the unlock screen, entered Mike/Mitch/Matt's passcode—eight-eight-nine-three; she'd watched him type the code back at the bar—and *presto*—she was in, a background picture of some Twins player and a handful of apps. Tanya opened Facebook and tapped through to Mike/Mitch/Matt's profile. Squinted at the screen, everything kind of fuzzy.

Mark, the guy's name was. *Mark, Mark, Mark.* Thirty years old, single. Worked for the Marsh Implement Company, the local John

Deere retailer. A tractor salesman. Okay, boring, but he still had that smile. Tanya could live with it.

She crept on Mark's Facebook profile for a bit. Sent herself a friend request. Closed Facebook and opened the photo library. Chose a picture at random and started scrolling through.

Most of the pictures were boring stuff: Mark on a hunting trip, Mark in a fishing boat, Mark with some buddies in Minneapolis somewhere. Then a couple landscape shots, real artsy stuff, soulful. Looked like the desert; it definitely wasn't *here*.

Tanya kept scrolling. Found a picture with a road sign. SANTA FE. "Why were you in New Mexico?" she asked before she could stop herself. Mark poked his head through the doorway, and Tanya held up the phone. "I spied on you when you typed in your passcode. Total invasion of privacy, I know, but these pictures are really beautiful. When did you take them?"

Mark frowned a little, confused. Then he laughed. "That's a funny story, actually," he said. "Hold on."

He disappeared back into the kitchen. Tanya scrolled some more. A few more landscape shots, a few more pictures of Mark. Mark standing proud in front of a new combine, handing over the keys to some wizened old farmer. A picture of a mountain valley, pristine, no sign of human life, a stunning picture. Tanya admired it for a moment. Then she scrolled right again, to the last picture, the newest.

This picture was different from the others. Tanya stared at it, her mind not comprehending. Couldn't look away.

"What's the matter?" Mark came back, holding a cocktail glass in each hand. "Don't tell me you found that stupid selfie from the Kenny Chesney show."

Tanya didn't answer. *Run,* her mind hollered. *Run as fast as you can.* But she didn't move. Couldn't. She couldn't tear her eyes from the screen.

"Tammy?" Mark set down the drinks. "Uh, what's going on?"

Tanya didn't say anything. Didn't do anything, either, not until Mark sat down beside her and reached for the phone. His fingers brushed her wrist, and that jolted her alive, broke the spell.

Tanya let Mark take the phone from her hand. Then she screamed. She screamed, and she didn't stop screaming until the police came.

2

I'll warn you now: this will be intense."

Special Agent in Charge Drew Harris slid a slim folder across his desk. On the other side, Kirk Stevens and Carla Windermere swapped glances.

It was early January in what was already turning into a frigid new year. Outside, a blizzard raged, blanketing the Twin Cities in another heavy layer of snow. Inside the FBI's Minnesota regional headquarters, the SAC had his heater cranked high, but Stevens could still feel the chill on his skin from the morning commute. He'd been in the Criminal Investigative Division for all of five minutes before Harris had summoned him and Windermere to his office—a new assignment.

Stevens and Windermere had been working cases together for going on four years now. Their partnership had begun by chance, Stevens an agent with the state's Bureau of Criminal Apprehension, Windermere a hotshot with the feds, an interstate kidnapping ring the catalyst. In the years since, the BCA agent and his FBI counterpart had chased bank robbers, contract killers, human traffickers, and one truly sick online predator, and somewhere along the way, Stevens had switched offices from the state police hangout in Saint Paul to the FBI's new HQ in Brooklyn Center, northwest of Minneapolis. He and Windermere now formed a joint BCA-FBI violent crimes task force and, to this point at least, they hadn't exactly been hurting for work.

Stevens could feel Windermere watching him as he reached for the folder. A beautiful, often brilliant thirtysomething from Mississippi, Carla Windermere exuded tough, take-no-prisoners and all kinds of attitude, but Stevens had learned that his partner's prickly outward persona was mostly a defense mechanism. The real Carla Windermere was infinitely more complex.

She'd taken the last case hard, a suicide fetishist with a preference for vulnerable teens, and Stevens still wasn't exactly sure how deep she'd been hurt. Stevens himself was no stranger to tough assignments; the case before last had involved human traffickers importing young women as sex slaves, and Stevens, father to a teenage daughter, had struggled throughout the investigation to keep his emotions in check.

He and Windermere had faced their share of intense situations already, and Drew Harris knew it. Agent Stevens hesitated before he opened the folder, wondering what new awful crime could have prompted the SAC's warning.

There was a picture of a woman, a close-up of her face. She might have been young, but Stevens couldn't be sure; her face and neck were badly bruised and partially decomposed, and her skin had been mutilated besides, though by what or by whom wasn't immediately obvious.

She was dead, though, that was obvious, and whoever she was, she hadn't died peacefully. She lay on a background of pristine white snow, her black hair spilling out around her, a stark contrast. Stevens's gut churned as he studied the picture.

"Ouch. You weren't lying." Windermere craned her neck to look over Stevens's shoulder. "Who is she?"

"Nobody knows," Harris replied. "What we *do* know is that she was murdered. The sheriff's department in Boundary County, Idaho, recovered her body last week. A railroad maintenance crew found her in a snowdrift by the tracks. Sheriff's and coroner's reports are attached."

Stevens flipped the pages, scanned the reports. Both were brief: the woman had been sexually assaulted and beaten, brutally. The Boundary County coroner had determined she'd been strangled to death, though exactly *when* was still a mystery. It was bitterly cold in the Idaho panhandle this time of year, and the low temperatures had arrested the decomposition process, essentially mummifying the woman.

"Terrible," Windermere said, reading. "Horrible. Awful. But, I'm sorry." She looked across the table at the SAC. "Am I missing something, boss? This all happened in Idaho. Where do we come in?"

Harris nodded, like he'd been expecting the question. Gestured to the folder. "That picture of the victim is a printout of a digital photograph the police department in Willmar, Minnesota, lifted from a personal cell phone. Turn the page."

Stevens did. Found another set of photographs: a youngish man with tired, bloodshot eyes and a deadpan expression.

"Mark Higgins," Harris said. "A tractor salesman, a Willmar native. The picture was on his smartphone. A young woman stumbled on it. Apparently, they met at a local bar and Higgins brought her home. She decided to do a little snooping before they got down to business."

"For real?" Windermere said. "Dude never heard of a lock screen?"

"Most people still don't lock their *doors* out in Willmar," Stevens told her.

"Yeah, but most people don't have pictures of murdered women in their homes."

"The woman, Tanya Sears, freaked out and called the local PD, who booked Higgins," Harris said. "Higgins denies taking the picture, or ever having seen the deceased before."

"So how'd the pic get on his phone?" Windermere asked.

"That's the thing," Harris said. "Higgins hasn't volunteered much to the Willmar PD, and they don't have the resources for a prolonged investigation, anyway. They kicked this up to the BCA, who passed it on to us when they discovered the Idaho connection." He looked at Stevens over his glasses. "Your old boss thought it smelled funny. I'm inclined to agree."

"This Higgins dude's probably the killer," Windermere said. "Look at him. He's a creep."

"I guess you're going to find out." Harris stood. "Willmar PD is expecting you. I told the chief if anyone could unravel this thing, it's you two."

3

Mark Higgins didn't look much better in person. There were bags under his eyes, and his hair was a mess. He looked like the clothes in a suitcase at the end of a three-week vacation: wrinkled, disheveled, starting to smell.

Higgins sat at a table in a sparse interview room in the Willmar Law Enforcement Center, a handsome low-lying complex not far from the town's namesake lake. It had taken Stevens and Windermere nearly three hours to drive the hundred miles, the snow outside falling heavy and fast, obscuring visibility and blanketing the highway.

The Willmar PD's chief was a man named Nordheimer. He shook Stevens's and Windermere's hands, offered them coffee, and showed them to the interview room, where Mark Higgins had company already: his lawyer, a young man in his father's second-best suit who stood up when the agents entered the room.

"I want to reiterate that my client hasn't been formally charged with a crime," he announced. "Mr. Higgins is here of his own accord, as a show of good faith toward the Willmar Police Department, and can exercise his right to leave at any time."

"Good to know," Windermere said, sitting down across from Higgins, "but he's dealing with the FBI now. And good faith or no, he happens to be a man with a picture of a murder victim on his phone. If he chooses to walk, that tells me and my partner that he cares more about saving his own skin than he does about catching the killer. And is that *really* the impression he wants to give to the feds?"

The lawyer colored. "I—I'll need to confer with my client."

Windermere waved him off. "Relax," she said, gesturing to his empty chair. "Sit down. In case you didn't know, it's a blizzard outside. Your client isn't missing out on any big tractor sales."

The lawyer wavered. Higgins didn't say anything.

"Come on," Windermere told them. "The sooner we get this done, the sooner you can exercise your right to quit bothering me."

But Mark Higgins didn't have much to say for himself.

"It's not my picture," he told Stevens and Windermere. "I didn't take the picture, and I don't know the girl. I sure as heck didn't kill her."

Windermere fished a copy of the picture from her briefcase. Dropped it on the table in front of Higgins. "Have another look," she said. "It was dark the other night. You were a few Surlys short of a twelve-pack. Maybe you see it again, it jogs your memory."

But Higgins didn't react. He glanced down at the picture, at the dead, battered woman, shook his head, and pushed the picture away. "Not mine."

"You understand the confusion, right? Your girlfriend did find this pic on your phone."

"She's not my girlfriend," Higgins said, "but yeah. This isn't the first time this has happened."

"What?" Stevens leaned forward on the table. "Pictures of murdered women showing up on your phone?"

"Not murdered women, but pictures, yes. It started, like, five or six months ago. I would turn on my phone and there would be a bunch of new pictures in my photo folder, strange pictures, pictures I hadn't taken."

"Like what, for instance?"

"Landscapes, mostly. A few desert pictures. Very few people. There was some really beautiful stuff, actually."

"But you didn't tell anyone?" Windermere said. "You didn't think that was weird?"

"Of course I thought it was weird." Higgins glared at Windermere like *she* was the killer. "I thought it was just a glitch in the software, and anyway, some of the pictures were kind of neat. Did you look? Whoever did take them was actually pretty good."

Windermere looked back at Nordheimer. "You have the phone handy?" she asked. "I want to see for myself."

Nordheimer produced Higgins's phone in an evidence bag, unsealed it, and handed it to Windermere. She shot Higgins a look as the phone powered up. "If this thing does some crazy self-destruct bullshit, I *will* have you arrested," she told him. "And I don't give a damn what your legal representation has to say about it."

"It's not going to self-destruct," Higgins replied. "But you're going to be scrolling past a lot of tractors."

Higgins wasn't lying; there were a lot of pictures of him selling tractors. Combines, dozers, riding lawn mowers. All kinds of agricultural equipment. There were pictures of a woman, too, farther back on the camera roll, a pretty brunette. She was standing with Higgins by a lake in one. In another, she was wearing combat fatigues. Windermere showed the picture to Higgins, who couldn't meet her eyes.

"She's, uh, a good friend," he said. "Jessie. She's been overseas for, like, six months now."

"Right," Windermere said. "Does Tanya know?"

Higgins didn't answer. Didn't have to, as far as Windermere was concerned. Whatever. Not Windermere's business.

She kept swiping, and she saw what Higgins was talking about. Interspersed with the home life pictures were a handful of arty landscape shots, somewhere hot and barren, no people for miles. Desert landscapes, the American Southwest. Texas ranch land, Louisiana swamps.

"I've never been south of Kansas or west of North Dakota," Higgins told the room. "Haven't had a vacation since Christmas, either. You can ask my boss about that."

There were road signs in a few of the pictures, highway billboards, the back end of an auto-parts yard. Santa Fe. Flagstaff. Abilene, Texas.

There were no people in the pictures. No sign of the photographer, or of anyone else, for that matter. Just landscapes and scenery and lifeless, abandoned buildings.

Windermere reached the end of the photo roll. "This is it?"

"I mean, yeah," Higgins replied. "There were more, but I deleted most of them. I only kept the ones I really liked."

"The ones you deleted," Stevens said, "do you remember anything about them?"

"Not really. They were just kind of mediocre."

"Were there people in any of the others?" Windermere asked.

"Some of them," Higgins told her, "but I deleted all of those. They weren't *my* people, you know? I didn't know them from Adam."

4

He's a tractor salesman," Stevens told his wife over dinner that night. "Swears he never saw the woman before in his life, has no idea how these pictures keep popping up on his phone."

Stevens and Windermere had grilled Higgins for a couple more hours. Pushed him for information about the lost pictures until, finally, the lawyer stepped in. This time, they conceded the point.

"My client is going home, too," the lawyer had told Stevens and Windermere as they packed up to leave. "There's no reason to keep him here. He's committed no crime. I insist—"

"Yeah, yeah." Windermere had waved him off. "Go home if you

want, Mr. Higgins. Maybe call your good friend Jessie—or Tanya, if you prefer. But don't go anywhere, understand? Stay close."

Higgins laughed humorlessly. "Where would I go?"

"That's the spirit. Go home, fire up Netflix, wait for us to call you. Oh." Windermere reached back, took Higgins's phone off the table. "And we're going to be keeping this."

Dinner had been all but cleared from the table when Stevens arrived home in Saint Paul, but Nancy Stevens had a plate in the oven for him, and she sat beside him at the kitchen table and listened as he explained the case between mouthfuls of meat loaf.

"And you're sure he's telling the truth?" she asked as Stevens turned his attention to a pile of steamed broccoli. "Could he be trying to protect someone? It seems weird that these pictures would just show up like that."

"Very weird. We're going to talk to the cell service provider tomorrow, see if they have any answers. Have to call the sheriff in Idaho, too. We—"

Stevens broke off as his daughter entered the kitchen. "What's going on?" she asked as she walked to the fridge.

Stevens and Nancy shared a look. Andrea was seventeen, a high school senior, as smart and stubborn as her mother, who herself was a legal aid lawyer and perennial champion of the underdog. Andrea was mature for her age, almost an adult, but Stevens still didn't feel especially comfortable talking shop with her in earshot.

An awkward silence ensued. Andrea poked her head out from the fridge. "Come on, Dad. How bad could it be?"

Plenty bad, Stevens thought, but he kept that to himself. "It's nothing crazy. Just a guy out in farm country had a bunch of weird pictures show up on his smartphone, one of which happens to be evidence of a crime. But nobody knows how the pictures wound up there."

"Huh." Andrea retreated from the fridge with a carton of milk and poured herself a glass. "Did he lose his phone recently? Like, did he have to replace it?"

Stevens frowned. "I'm not sure. What difference would that make?"

"Well, it's the cloud," Andrea said, as if the answer were obvious. Stevens looked at his wife, but she was mystified, too. Andrea sighed the way only a teenager forced to explain technology to her parents can sigh, and brought her glass of milk to the table. "The *cloud*," she repeated. "You know, like, online storage. So you can access your data from anywhere."

"Sure," Stevens said, though he was already kind of lost. "But what does this have to do with phantom pictures?"

Andrea took a drink. "I was reading about this online, the exact same thing. Some guy in New York had his phone stolen. He replaced it, but then these weird pictures from China started showing up on his new phone. Some guy taking selfies in a bunch of orange trees."

She paused, waiting for her parents to make the connection. When they didn't, she continued. "Because the old phone was still connected to the guy's *cloud*, don't you see? Even though the old phone was, like, in China, the cloud system meant the New York guy was still getting pictures."

She grinned at her parents. "It turned into this huge thing. The guy in New York went over to China and they both became, like, huge celebrities. All because of a stolen phone."

"So if this guy's phone was stolen," Nancy said, "someone else could be taking pictures on his old phone and automatically uploading them to his new one."

Andrea sat back. "Exactly. So does that help?"

Stevens was already standing. "I'll tell you in a minute," he said. "I have to make a phone call."

Replaced my smartphone?"

On the other end of the line, Mark Higgins gave it a beat. Then his voice brightened. "Actually, yeah. I was out at some bar in Minneapolis about six, seven months ago and someone swiped the damn thing. It was a real pain in the ass, too; I had to shell out five hundred bucks to replace it." He laughed a little. "That's all you wanted to know? Does it get me off the hook, or what?"

"I don't know yet," Stevens told him. "I'm still putting this together."

5

It's called the cloud," Stevens told Windermere. "Andrea says it's some new storage thing. Like, you put your files on your phone, and you can access them on your laptop or wherever."

Windermere cocked her head at Stevens, the hint of a smile playing on her lips. "Yeah, Stevens, the cloud. You're telling me this is the first you've ever heard of it?"

Stevens held up his cell phone, which was just about old enough now to qualify for antique status. "I'm not exactly Mr. Technology over here, remember?"

They were back in their shared office in the FBI's Brooklyn Center headquarters. Stevens had called Windermere first thing that morning, told her he'd had an epiphany.

"Great," Windermere had replied, groaning. "You couldn't just text me?"

"Andrea told me about this story," Stevens told Windermere now. "Some guy in New York whose phone was stolen, and somehow it made it all the way to China. The new owner posted, uh, *selfies*, and they showed up on the New York guy's new phone. The old phone was never logged out of his cloud."

"Aha." Windermere sat back in her chair. "And I bet you're going to tell me Higgins had his phone swiped recently."

"Six or seven months ago, from a bar in Minneapolis. A smartphone, just like his current one. Same brand and everything."

"Well, gee whiz, Stevens." Windermere clapped her hands. "Maybe we should hire Andrea onto our task force. That's exactly the kind of fresh thinking we need."

They drove to the Mall of America, Stevens's Cherokee cutting through what slush remained on the roads from yesterday's blizzard. Other drivers, though, weren't so lucky; they passed multiple spinouts and cars run into ditches, more casualties of this merciless winter weather.

The mall, at least, was mostly empty.

"Sure, that could happen," the kid at the phone store told Stevens and Windermere when they'd outlined Stevens's theory. "We don't really like to talk about it, but it happens occasionally."

"Perfect," Windermere said. "So how do we track down who's using the phone now?"

The kid shifted his weight. "Well, that's tricky. If you have a phone tracker app activated, you can just follow the app."

"And if he doesn't have a tracker?"

"Gah." The kid grimaced. "Then you might be out of luck. Whoever's using the phone now probably has a new service provider, so you can't track it through the phone company. I hate to say it, but your best bet is probably to just study the pictures as they come in for clues. It's a long shot, but you never know, right?"

"We tried that," Stevens said. "It didn't get us anywhere."

The kid winced again, like he was passing a kidney stone. "I mean, if you have your guy bring his phone in to one of our technicians, we can adjust his account to make sure this doesn't happen again."

"Thanks," Windermere told him. "We'll pass that along."

The Boundary County sheriff was a man named Chuck Truman. Stevens reached him at his office in Bonners Ferry in the northeast corner of the Idaho panhandle.

"Glad to hear from you," Truman told him. "Word has it you have a man in custody. Some tractor salesman?"

"*Had* in custody," Stevens corrected. "We had to let him go. He swears he didn't take the picture, and we have no other proof that he's ever been to Idaho or ever knew the victim. Frankly, Sheriff, we were hoping you might have some answers."

The sheriff chuckled a little bit. "I suspect we're both going to walk away from this call disappointed, Agent. I told your SAC about all we know. It was a railroad maintenance crew who found her, in Moyie Springs, about ten miles east of here on the Northwestern Railroad's mainline."

"And nobody knows who she is."

"We canvassed the town, the county, the Kootenai tribe," Truman said. "No missing persons reported. Of course, the woman was buried under a deep pile of snow. She could have been there for some time—heck, since October, for all we know."

Stevens made a note in his notebook. "But the body was preserved enough to determine a cause of death?"

"That's right," Truman said. "To be honest with you, I was set to write the poor woman's death off as accidental. It happens more than we'd care to admit in the wintertime in these mountains. You make a mistake out here when the temperature drops, you can wind up dead pretty easily."

"Sure," Stevens said. "We know a thing or two about that ourselves over here."

"Minnesota, yeah. Anyway, Cathy—that's my coroner, Cathy Blake, and she's a crackerjack—Cathy agreed with me that most of the injuries our victim suffered *could* have been accidental, like maybe she fell off a train or something. The girl had been dead too long to really tell."

Stevens put his pen down, intrigued. "But?"

"But," the sheriff continued, "Cathy was damn sure the damage done to the victim's throat was emphatically *not* accidental." He paused, and Stevens could hear him flipping pages.

"'The victim's larynx was crushed, as was her thyroid cartilage,'" Truman read. "'Further, I found numerous petechial hemorrhages when I examined the victim's eyes.'"

"Meaning what, exactly?" Stevens said. "I'm a little rusty on my forensic pathology."

"You and me both," Truman said. "According to Cathy, though, it's a clear sign the victim died by asphyxia. Meaning—"

"She was strangled to death."

"Exactly," Truman said. "We may not know much, Agent Stevens, but we're firm on cause of death. Beyond that, I'm afraid we're stymied."

Stevens leaned back in his chair. Figured he'd about exhausted the sheriff's supply of information. "Cause of death is a start," he said. "We'll keep working the picture angle, see if we can't dredge up the photographer. In the meantime, you let us know if you catch any more leads on this girl's ID."

"Will do," Truman said. "As far as we can tell, she's just another poor transient whose luck happened to run out in our mountains. Sad, but it kind of goes with the territory around here. Although . . ." He trailed off. Didn't finish the thought.

"Yeah?" Stevens prodded.

Truman cleared his throat. Spoke softer. "There are rumors about this part of the country," he said. "Cascades to Glacier Park. Anytime anyone turns up missing, there are people who'll tell you it's the work of a killer—one killer, every dead body." He laughed a little bit, hollowly. "I've looked into the stories, as much as I can, but I don't have the resources to go chasing down bogeymen. It's an old wives' tale, what I figure." He paused. "But that doesn't mean I don't find it all a bit creepy."

6

The rider stepped off the train and down into the snowdrifts. It was near dark already, late afternoon, the night coming fast and mean and long at this latitude. The rider didn't mind. He loved the winter months.

It was the emptiness, mostly. It was the way the tourists cleared out, their camper vans and SUVs all done choking the highways, crowding into towns, pushing out the locals. It was the way the restaurants emptied out, the stores, the parks. It was the stillness, the way the snow muted every sound until it felt like you were the only person in the mountains, and maybe the world.

There was a peace in the winter that didn't exist when the weather warmed. There was a calm, but that calm had an edge to it, a darkness on the fringes. People left the mountains in the winter because the mountains were dangerous. They left for fear of the cold, for fear of the howling-banshee storms that brought snow and wreaked havoc, closing the roads and isolating the towns, sending cars skittering off the highway and into ravines. Only the strong survived in the winter. The weak perished long before spring.

It was true that it was more difficult to find prey in the winter. Every predator knew that. Most viable candidates had learned to migrate or hibernate; anything with any sense left the mountains, and people were no different.

But the rider didn't mind. Those who stayed behind stayed because they had no other choice. They were bound to the mountains by circumstance, lack of resources, lack of opportunity. They were weakened by the cold and the lack of tourist dollars, desperate and vulnerable. The rider liked vulnerable. Vulnerable made for easy targets.

And the snow was damn good at hiding bodies. People disappeared in winter. They turned up in the thaw, dead as could be, and nobody batted an eye. Easy for someone to get lost in a storm. Walk the wrong way coming home from the bar and you'd die in a snowdrift, easy. No one really asked questions. The winter was deadly. People took that as fact.

The rider had come west again, caught on a slow, heavy drag, stepped off when the train slowed at a crew-change point nestled deep within the mountains. The change point was a small town, railroad-dependent, a hotel for the train crews and a bar for them, too; a few houses and a gas station, a sad excuse for a school.

The snow had eased to a few stray flakes, but the roads were still covered, and what little traffic passed the rider passed him slowly and cautiously. He kept to the shadows, turned away when he saw headlights, heard the crunch of tires approaching.

The bar was half full when the rider walked in the door, Bob Seger on the jukebox, a thick cloud of tobacco smoke filling the small room, nobody caring to enforce the state's smoking ban. A few faces turned when the rider walked in, looked him over from behind their bottles, turned away again. Impolite to stare, and anyway, the rider knew he didn't look like much. He fit in, in places like this. He looked like he belonged with this crowd.

What crowd there was consisted of a handful of aging loners propping up the bar, a table of railroad guys in the corner by the jukebox, some truck drivers playing pool, and a couple of women. And the bartender, who wore a look like he was wishing he'd skipped town when he was still young enough to make a go of it.

The rider slid a five on the bar and ordered a Budweiser. Left the change and retreated into the smoke, found a booth in the corner. He kept his eyes on the table as he drank the beer, avoided eye contact with the rest of the crowd, knew mostly everyone would forget he was there.

"Buy me a drink?"

One of the women; she'd watched him come in. She stood at the edge of his table, hip cocked, a short skirt and a beer company tank top, cut low enough to show off the tops of her breasts. She wore heavy makeup, was fighting a losing battle; even in the dim light, the rider could see she was well past middle age.

The rider met her eyes, then looked away fast, a reflex he hated and was powerless to control. He forced himself to look up again, study her face. Made himself see that she was just like the others.

She's just an animal. An ignorant beast, simple and cruel. And she's only here to manipulate you, just like the others.

Like all of them.

"I don't think I've seen you before," the woman continued, smiling everywhere but her eyes. "You work on the trains?"

The rider shook his head. "Just passing through."

"A wanderer, huh? Man after my own heart." The woman shifted on her heels, smiled wider, plastic. "Listen, you're cute and I'm thirsty," she said. "How about we get this thing started?"

The rider swallowed his revulsion. He set the bottle down, lay his left hand flat on the table so she could see the glint of gold on his ring finger. Now wasn't the time. Not yet. Not like this.

"Gee, I'd love to," he told the woman. "But I swore I'd behave."

Disappointment flashed behind the woman's eyes, but just briefly. Then she smiled again, bright as she could fake it, and straightened. "The last honest man," she said, turning to leave. "I guess I can't be mad at that. You have a nice night, anyway."

The rider stayed in the bar, in his corner, all but invisible. He finished his Budweiser and ordered another, left another five on the bar. He drank slow, and he watched the railroad guys play the jukebox. Watched the truckers shoot pool. Watched the woman and a couple more work the room.

Whores. The rider made himself sit still. Watched the women and let the hate burn hot inside him—need and jealousy and envy and desire, a hundred emotions burning together in one searing flame.

After about an hour, the woman found a willing partner, one of the railroad guys. His friends hooted and jeered after him as he took the woman's hand and followed her out of the bar. The rider watched her go. Watched the railroaders laugh and slap one another on the back. He nursed his beer.

The woman and the railroader came back a half hour or so later. His buddies cheered again, and he blushed and bought a beer and sat down, steadfastly refusing to look in the woman's direction.

A couple other women dropped by the rider's table. They made similar pitches for his time. The rider showed them the ring. The women wandered away again.

Fat fucking chance, the rider thought. *Money, that's all you're after. You wouldn't even look at me if you didn't see me as a mark.*

Another hour passed. The rider finished his Budweiser and was about to order another when the woman walked out again, the first woman, with one of the truck drivers this time.

The rider watched her go. Stood and walked through the smoke to the men's room, pissed in the urinal and zipped up again. Opened his coat and checked the handcuffs on his belt, the scarf he'd fashioned into a garrote. And the knife in its sheath on his belt, the bowie with the custom handle, the knife he'd taken from the Indian girl. The rider liked the knife. It was a nice souvenir.

He replaced the knife. Slipped the handcuffs and the scarf into his coat pockets, buttoned his coat closed again, and walked out of the restroom. There was a rear exit to the bar, just beyond the restroom doors. Let the marks walk out the front door with the whores. When a girl disappeared, they'd be the first suspects. The rider slipped out the back door instead, unnoticed.

The snow had picked up a little bit, but not enough to be consequential. The rider circled around the side of the building to the parking area, kept to the edge of the lot, found a stand of pine trees, and waited there.

He surveyed the lot. Found the truck drivers' rides, a couple of logging rigs, Kenworth sleeper cabs towing skeleton trailers. The rider watched the rigs. The snow fell. A car crunched by on the main road in front of the bar. Somewhere in the distance, a diesel engine throbbed.

The cab light came on inside the nearest rig. Then the door opened and the woman climbed down, slipping a little in her heels on the snowy ground. The trucker locked the door to his rig and hurried back into the bar. The rider heard the jukebox again as the driver opened the door, the railroad guys getting rowdier.

Neanderthals.

The whore didn't go back inside right away. She crossed the lot to an old gray Ford Taurus, opened the driver's-side door, and sat down inside. The rider watched her flip the mirror down, check her makeup, apply new lipstick. Perfect. He stepped out of the shadows and walked across to the car. He was shaking again, excitement and fear and anger, an energy that propelled him forward, drowned out his rational brain, replaced it with something urgent, something primal.

The whore didn't see him approach. She didn't look up until he tapped on the window. Then she flinched, gasping, froze up like a scared rabbit. But she relaxed when she saw the rider's face. She put her lipstick away. Rolled down the window, and her smile was back. "Change your mind?"

The rider grinned back. Bounced on his feet. "You're just too pretty," he told her. "I guess I couldn't resist."

7

So we have a pretty good idea how the woman's picture showed up on Higgins's phone," Windermere told SAC Harris. "But we still don't know who took the picture or where he or she disappeared to."

"The pictures should have location tags," Harris said. "When I take pictures on my iPhone, it automatically knows when and where the shot was taken."

"Sure," Stevens said. "True. According to the tag on Mark Higgins's phone, the picture was taken last Sunday—four days after Sheriff Truman and his deputies moved the body."

"And if the location tag's to be believed," Windermere said, "the picture was taken at a roadside diner in Barstow, California. See, the trouble with geotagging is it only works if the phone is connected to a network."

"So the picture could have been taken when the phone was offline and uploaded to the cloud when it came online at that diner," Harris said. "This guy would have had to travel all the way from Idaho to California without turning on his phone."

"We put a call in to Barstow PD, have them canvassing the diner and the rest of the city for anybody who might have seen anything," Stevens told him. "The diner doesn't have any security footage, but at least we have a location."

"We know the photographer hangs around the Southwest," Windermere said. "And we can be certain that whoever's taking those pictures can lead us to the victim's identity. We just have to track him down."

"Perfect," Harris said. "So how are you going to do it?"

Stevens and Windermere looked at each other. Let the question hang there. Then Stevens had a thought, something he'd been playing with all morning.

"I don't know much about this cloud thing," he said, "as we've already established."

"Definitively," Windermere said. "But go on."

Stevens sat forward. "I was just thinking: Higgins deleted the pictures he didn't like from his phone. But if he was hooked up to the cloud and he had, say, a laptop, would the pictures have automatically been deleted there, too?"

"Most likely," Harris said. "But not one hundred percent for certain. It's worth a check."

"Damn right," Windermere said, reaching for Harris's phone. "And even if they were deleted, maybe our friendly tech guru can get them all back. Let's try it."

By midafternoon, they had Mark Higgins's laptop, couriered through the snow from Willmar. Windermere scared up the office's resident computer whiz, a young tech named Nenad with a Superman tattoo on the inside of his wrist, set him loose on the laptop. Nenad looked almost bored when he found out the assignment.

"Pictures," he said. "Old pictures, that's it? You're sure you don't need me to hack anything?"

"Not right now," Windermere told him. "They're *deleted* pictures, if that makes you feel any better."

Nenad cracked his knuckles. "Nothing's ever really deleted," he said. "Give me ten minutes."

It took him five. Windermere was still waiting for the coffee machine when the tech poked his head into the break room. "It's done."

She followed him back to her office, where Stevens was already browsing through a cache of files on Higgins's laptop.

"I did all I could," Nenad told them. "The longer a file stays deleted, the better the odds the computer will write over the data. Anything too old is already gone, but I salvaged everything recent."

Windermere thanked him. Promised the next time she called, she would have a mainframe for him to break into. Then she sat down beside Stevens and clicked open the oldest of the pictures. Scrolled through a couple blurry shots of Mark Higgins until she found what she was looking for.

It was a group shot, four kids around a campfire in gray daylight.

They were teenagers, or just barely past, twenty-two or twenty-three at the oldest. A girl and three boys, piercings and tattoos, punk rock hairstyles. They had the worn-out, grimy look of the panhandlers and squeegee kids who patrolled parts of downtown Minneapolis, but they were smiling at the camera, all of them, and one of the boys was holding up a handle of Old Crow. As far as Windermere could tell, the girl in the picture wasn't the murdered woman. She clicked through.

The next picture was pretty enough that Windermere wondered why Mark Higgins hadn't kept it. It was taken inside an empty boxcar, two kids sitting in the open doorway, a row of trees visible in the daylight beyond. The kids had their backs turned; impossible to identify them.

There were more pictures in a similar vein. Groups of people in ragged clothing clustered around campfires and makeshift shelters, their hair often unkempt, their faces usually dirty. A girl hugging her knees to her chest on an empty container train, the tracks blurred but visible through the steel latticework on which she sat. Then Stevens clicked to the next, and they both sat forward and stared at the screen.

This was the dead woman. Like the others in the pictures, she was young, twenty or so. She was striking, high cheekbones and vivid eyes, a wide, laughing smile. Her black hair was mostly hidden beneath a woolen watch cap; she was walking away from the camera, her head and shoulders half-turned to look back at the photographer. She was pointing to the background, like whoever'd taken the picture had caught her midexplanation, midjoke. She looked young and happy and full of life, completely unaware of the fate that awaited her.

"That's her, right?" Stevens said. "That's our victim."

Windermere nodded. "Yeah." She couldn't look away from the screen.

"Did you notice the background?" Stevens asked.

Windermere hadn't. She blinked, refocused. The pretty woman was pointing at a train, a massive diesel locomotive maybe sixty feet behind her. She was walking toward the locomotive. Windermere frowned. She didn't get it.

Then she did.

"They're train hoppers, these kids," she said, feeling a little jolt of accomplishment as the piece fell into place. "Our girl was surfing those trains."

8

According to the file's metadata, the picture had been uploaded to the cloud in Grafton, West Virginia, in August of last year.

"I didn't even know train hopping was still a thing," Derek Mathers told Stevens and Windermere as he studied the picture over their shoulders. "I kind of imagined it went out of fashion after the Great Depression."

Mathers, another agent in the Bureau's Criminal Investigative Division, was also Windermere's boyfriend—though Windermere herself was still warming to the term. Mathers had dropped by the tiny office at the end of his workday, found Stevens and Windermere poring over the same picture, the victim and the train.

"These kids don't look like the bindle crowd," Windermere said.

"This is something different from just hoboes riding the rails because they can't find jobs."

"Whatever it is, we've found our victim." Stevens clicked to the next picture. "So let's see if we can't learn a little more about her."

"Better yet, let's ID the photographer," Windermere said. "Is it too much to ask for a picture with *his* face?"

Mathers straightened. "I'll leave you to it, I guess," he said. "I assume this means you won't be home for dinner?"

"We'll order something," Windermere told him. "Don't wait up."

They kept scrolling. Followed the photographer—and the victim—as August turned to September, and then to October. They'd headed west as fall approached, through Clarksburg, West Virginia, down to Knoxville, Tennessee, and back up to Louisville.

"God," Windermere said. "*We* were in Louisville in October, Stevens."

They had been, on their previous case, chasing the online suicide fetishist and his latest—and last—victim.

From Louisville, the photographer followed the victim west to Saint Louis, and then beyond, to Kansas City, mid-October now, the riders starting to bundle up a little more. Then, abruptly, the victim vanished from the pictures. The photographer was still taking shots—Fayetteville, Arkansas, then Shreveport, Louisiana, then Dallas, then Abilene, Texas—but the victim was gone.

"So, what?" Windermere said. "Did our photographer take her up to Idaho in secret? Did he meet her up there? Something's not computing here, partner."

They continued to search, on familiar terrain now. The desert, the Southwest. Santa Fe, Flagstaff. More train hoppers, ragged and weary, but seemingly happy. More stunning vistas. But no sign of the pretty young woman.

"By this point, we have to assume Higgins would have recognized her, right?" Stevens said. "He told us he'd never seen the victim before in his life. And *these* pictures are . . ." He checked the metadata. "Less than a month old now."

"We know the photographer saw the victim again, though," Windermere said. "What Higgins remembers is immaterial. And just because the victim isn't in any pictures doesn't automatically mean she's not there."

"The photographer could have erased any evidence of the victim from his phone," Stevens said. "You said the pictures only upload when the phone's connected to Wi-Fi, right?"

"Exactly," Windermere said. "But keep looking. Maybe our friend Higgins missed something."

Stevens was almost at the end of the cache when Windermere grabbed his arm. *"Stop."*

"What?" Stevens drew his hand back from the keyboard. "Do you see her?"

Windermere shook her head. Reached across to the trackpad. *We're not getting that lucky,* she thought, clicking back, *but this might be a lead.*

She scrolled back two pictures. Found the shot she was looking for, a close-up of two faces. A young man with a Mohawk, midtwenties, and a pretty girl with purple hair, a little younger. The girl held a marijuana cigarette. She was laughing.

Stevens scratched his head. "I don't follow. Who are these people?"

Windermere was feeling the adrenaline, but she kept her poker face. "No idea, partner."

"Then why'd you stop at this picture?"

Windermere gave it a beat, didn't say anything, waited for Stevens to get it. Finally, she laughed. "You're such an old man," she told him. "That picture right there is a *selfie.* You remember what a selfie is, Stevens?"

"I think I have the gist of it, sure."

"A selfie is when you take a picture of your*self,* partner," Windermere said. "That's what these kids are doing. And that means there's a good shot one of these pretty punk rockers is our mystery Ansel Adams."

She stood. "We need to get that picture over to the sheriff in Idaho and out to every FBI resident agency west of the Rocky Mountains. State patrols and every local police detachment on a railroad line. The train cops, too, obviously. Roust the hobo encampments and look for these kids; pay particular attention to the rail yards."

Stevens reached for his phone, brought up a map of the Southwest on his computer. Windermere did the same, fingers tapping a beat on her desk.

"We have to move quick, partner," she said. "These kids are mobile. If we don't nail down our photographer fast, we're going to lose him forever."

9

It took another long, anxious day. A couple sleepless nights. Around eleven the second morning, though, the phone rang with good news.

"Looking for Wintermore," the man on the other end of the line said. "Agent Carlos Wintermore?"

"You got Carla Windermere," Windermere told him. "That's as close as you're going to get. Who are you?"

"My apologies, ma'am. My name's Homer Doyle; I'm a detective with the police department down here in Barstow. We got word you were looking for runaways?"

"You saw our picture," Windermere said, scrambling for a pen. "You found the kids?"

"That's correct, ma'am," Doyle said. "One of them, anyway. The, uh, male one. One of our patrol guys nailed him on a possession charge, booked him with nearly an ounce of methamphetamine and the assorted paraphernalia. The kid isn't going anywhere."

"Perfect." Windermere snapped her fingers at Stevens until he looked up. "We're on the next flight."

They caught an afternoon flight to Las Vegas on a Delta 737, three and a half hours gate to gate.

"The part that worries me," Windermere said, fiddling with the in-flight magazine, "is if Doyle only found the boy in the picture, where does that put the girl?"

From the aisle seat, Stevens shrugged. "These kids are itinerant. Maybe she went her own way. Or maybe she saw the police coming and bolted."

"There haven't been any new pictures uploaded to Higgins's cloud, though," Windermere said. "Not since the victim. I just don't think it bodes well."

They transferred in Las Vegas to a shuttle flight to Barstow-Daggett Airport, an eight-passenger Beechcraft King Air. The little plane shuddered and bounced as it took off, a strong desert crosswind, repeated the process on its final approach. The movement did nothing to calm Windermere's nerves.

Detective Doyle was waiting for them outside the airport in a Dodge Charger sedan with Barstow Police markings. He was a friendly-looking guy, the far side of middle-aged, and he visibly winced when Windermere introduced herself.

"Awfully sorry about the Wintermore thing," he said, climbing into the driver's seat. "Ears must be going already."

Windermere smiled, forgave the guy instantly. "Probably just a bad connection."

"You're a kind person to say so." Doyle shifted into gear and drove away from the airport. "I guess you want to meet your runaway, huh?"

The runaway's name was Warren. Doyle had been able to piece that together from what few belongings the kid had on his person. But Doyle hadn't found a smartphone. And Warren wasn't exactly the talkative type.

"Just sits there and scowls at us," Doyle told Stevens and Windermere, nodding at the steel door to the interview room, a little reinforced window at eye level. "Sometimes he spits and sometimes he swears. Nothing original, mind. It's all 'filthy pigs,' and 'dirty fascists,' that old tune."

"We've heard it all before," Windermere said, reaching for the door. "Let's see if he can't show us some new material."

She opened the door and walked into the room. Crossed to the little table where Warren sat looking up at her, baleful. She dropped the picture of the victim—the Grafton picture, when she was still alive and vibrant—on the table in front of him. "Recognize this girl?"

Warren didn't bother to look at the picture. "I don't have to tell you shit," he told Windermere. Then, under his breath, *"Fucking pig."*

Windermere took back the photograph. "Warren, honey," she said, "my colleagues out there are charging you with possession with intent to sell. That's a three-year sentence, minimum—more if they can prove you sold your meth to a minor or trafficked it across state lines. You keep mouthing off like that and I assure you, people around here are going to start looking extra hard for ways to make your life miserable. You understand?"

Warren didn't say anything. Looked down at his hands.

"That's what I thought," Windermere said. "So, tell me." She dropped the victim's second picture, the postmortem shot, on the table. "Do you recognize this girl or not?"

This time, she got a reaction. Warren closed his eyes. Leaned back in his chair and let out a long breath. "Ah, shit," he said. "I fucking *told* her this would happen."

10

Warren wasn't clear on the victim's name—"Amy or Ashley, something like that. We weren't exactly close"—but he knew where she'd come from, and he knew why she'd wound up in Idaho.

"Riding to Seattle," he told Stevens and Windermere. "I think somebody died? Said she had to get up there, like, really quick, bailed on us in Kansas City and that's the last time we saw her."

"'We,'" Windermere said. "Who is 'we'?"

"Me and my friends, you know? We were supposed to go to LA for the winter. Hang out, see some movie stars or whatever." Warren shifted in his seat. "Listen, if you're looking for reasons why that girl's dead, you're totally doing this wrong. I haven't seen her since, like, mid-October, and she was plenty alive back then."

"So you say." Windermere sat down opposite him. Could sense Stevens standing off her shoulder. "But I still think you can help us, honey. See, somebody took those pictures of your friend Amy or Ashley on a smartphone. And they used the *same* smartphone . . ." She fished out the last picture, the selfie of Warren and the purple-haired girl. Showed it to him. "To take *this* picture. So you can see why we would make the connection, right?"

"Yeah, okay." Warren's eyes shifted between Windermere and the pictures. "It's weird, I guess. But I don't have any idea how those pictures wound up together. That's not even my phone."

"You took the picture, didn't you?" Stevens asked.

"Yeah, but only because my arms were longer. You ever tried to let the girl take the selfie?" He shook his head. "It's impossible. She wanted the picture, so I took it. It's *her* phone."

"*Her.* Who is *her*?"

"And where is she now?" Windermere added.

Warren shook his head again. "She has nothing to do with this. Sorry, but you're completely wrong. We *warned* that girl not to go up there. We told her what would happen, but she caught on anyway, like she thought she was invincible. And now she's dead, I guess, but if you're surprised about it, you're crazy."

Windermere and Stevens exchanged looks. "Crazy," Stevens said. "Why's that?"

Warren gave him a withering glare. "Because that's what happens up on the High Line, okay? Single girls, especially. *You don't ever surf trains on the High Line.* There's something evil up there. People just die, or they disappear and never show up where they're headed, and that's just how it is."

Stevens nudged Windermere. "The sheriff I talked to in Idaho, he said he'd heard rumors." He turned back to Warren. "So, what, you're saying it was a serial killer who did this?"

"I don't know what it was," Warren said. "They call him a ghost rider, like he rides back and forth and never gets caught, just looking for women to murder. Everybody knows about it; you just don't go up there. That's why I told Mila she's fucked in the head."

"Mila . . ."

"This girl." Warren pointed to the selfie. "She got a message on that phone a few days ago, probably the same message you guys, like, intercepted. Said her friend was found somewhere up north, and all of a sudden Mila just freaked the fuck out." He laughed a little bit, hollowly. "We were supposed to tramp around California for a while, see the sights. But all of a sudden the only thing she could talk about was hopping the next hotshot northbound."

Stevens and Windermere looked at each other. "So we know she went north," Stevens said. "That narrows the search."

"Yeah," Windermere replied. "Now we just have to search every yard, station, and hobo camp from here to the Canadian border."

"Oh, I can save you the trouble," Warren told them. "That girl was in a hurry, but she was damn clear about where she was going."

He let it hang there. Stevens and Windermere waited. Warren sat forward, studied Mila's picture.

"She had to see what happened, I guess," he said finally. "Had to see where he did it, where that rider killed her friend." He met Windermere's eyes. "She had her heart set on getting up to the High Line, and nothing I could say was going to change her mind."

"The High Line."

Inside the little prefab yard office, the railroad foreman pulled up a map on his computer and turned the screen around so Stevens and Windermere could see.

"It's the northern main of the Northwestern Railroad," he told them. "Chicago to Seattle via the top of the map—North Dakota, Montana, Idaho. Northernmost stretch of long-haul tracks in the country."

Stevens surveyed the Northwestern route on the screen. He'd seen Northwestern trains pulling through the Twin Cities, headed down to

Milwaukee and Chicago or west across the plains to the Rocky Mountains, the coast. The line passed through Minot, North Dakota, and Havre, Montana, stuck to within a hundred miles of the Canadian border, wound through the Rockies at Glacier National Park, cut down to Spokane, and then shot through the Cascades to the Pacific. In the process, it passed right through Moyie Springs, Idaho—the town where the railroad crew had discovered the dead woman.

"What the hell is she thinking?" Windermere said. "She's going to find this guy—this *ghost rider*—herself?"

Stevens stared down at the map, couldn't begin to guess. "The Idaho panhandle," he said to the foreman. "Could she get there from here?"

"I mean, sure," the foreman replied. "If she hopped a train north, like you're thinking, she could make Sacramento and then ride all the way up the coast to Puget Sound. We link up with Northwestern rails just outside Seattle."

"We're going to need a map," Stevens told him. "And a list of station stops on your line up the coast."

"And if you could tell your bulls to look out for a little purple-haired train hopper, we'd be much obliged," Windermere added.

"I can do that," the foreman said. Then he paused. "If your girl's headed for the High Line, she's in for a heck of a rough ride."

"Why's that?"

The foreman pointed to the map again. The stretch of main line through western Montana, Idaho, Washington State. "That's mountain country," he told them. "It gets cold up there this time of year; I mean real cold. Anyone trying to ride would freeze to death within hours." He shook his head. "I'm saying it just can't be done."

11

The rider rode east as the weather turned bad. Another squall, sudden and furious, bitter gusts of wind and blinding, swirling snow. The rider didn't mind. He welcomed the storm. Fresh snow would erase any sign of his visit. It would hide any trace of the prostitute.

He rode until the train slowed for the passing siding and then, as it drifted to a stop, he dropped back onto solid ground again, trackside, the snow breaking his fall. He walked up the tracks to the road crossing, the snow deeper, unplowed, and found the stand of Christmas fir trees and his snowmobile hidden behind it, the Ski-Doo 583 he'd been driving through these mountains for years.

He pulled the cover off the machine, stowed it in the cargo compartment behind the seat. Dug the key from his coat and tried the ignition. The engine started, as usual; it had never failed him, even in the cold. It was a machine made for extreme conditions, reliability. It was a machine for the mountains, and the rider respected it.

He sat on the machine for a few minutes, waiting for the engine to warm. Removed the Indian girl's knife and studied the blade. Removed his newest souvenir, too, held it up to the light, watched it turn.

The prostitute had worn a necklace, a thin chain of silver with a small stone. Amethyst, she'd told him after some prodding. Her birthstone. A gift from her first boyfriend; she didn't know why she still wore it. The rider had his theories, but he hadn't pressed the issue. The woman hadn't been in any frame of mind for contemplation.

The rider dropped the necklace into his pocket, revved the engine, and started up the logging road. Whatever the symbolism, the necklace made for a good token. The prostitute's name had been Kelly-Anne. The rider would remember her whenever he looked at the charm.

12

"*Hey, lady.*"

Mila Scott opened her eyes, peered out from her nest inside the open boxcar, and blinked in the sudden daylight. It had been dark when she'd fallen asleep, rainy, too. Now the rain was gone and the sun was shining, the train was stopped and a man was looking in at her.

Instantly, Mila was awake. She'd learned to sleep light since she'd started riding trains. Too many weirdos out there, on both sides of the law. Too many dangerous situations. You couldn't drop your guard for long, not when you were alone.

But you shouldn't be alone, stupid girl. You're supposed to be with Ash, remember?

Mila shook her head clear, ran her fingers through her hair. Too early for this. She needed a cigarette. What she really needed was a drink of something hard, maybe a bump from Warren's stash. But Mila was out of the hard stuff, and Warren wasn't around anymore, either.

The man outside the boxcar cleared his throat. He was a bull; she'd known that as soon as she'd rubbed the sleep from her eyes. He wore a dark shirt, dark pants, a badge, a radio, and a gun. Mila could see his cruiser parked trackside. Beyond were just a couple sidetracks and then green foliage and farmland, everything lush and dazzling after the earthy monotony of the desert.

"You're her, aren't you?" the bull was saying. "You're the girl they're looking for."

Mila didn't know where she was. She'd caught on a junker in Fresno after the main engine on her hotshot broke down, rode north a full day and night straight, through Sacramento and Northern California and the Oregon line, slept restlessly as the sun set again and the train trundled north, seeing Ash in her dreams, alive-Ash and dead-Ash, the both of them. Now the sun was inching above the horizon again, so it was morning, not exactly early. Mila wondered if they were getting close to Portland yet. Wondered if she was really going to do this.

The bull tapped his nightstick on the doorframe. *"Hey,"* he said again. Waited until she'd looked at him, until he was sure he had her attention. "Whoever you are, you can't be here," he said. "This train has to keep moving, and you can't be on it."

He held out his hand. Reluctantly, Mila pulled herself to her feet. Stretched, her neck feeling twisted as a coat hanger wire. Ignored the bull's hand and dropped down out of the boxcar.

"Good," the bull said, his hand on his radio. "Now step away from the tracks there so I can give them the highball."

Mila obeyed. Ash always said you did what the cops told you, unless it got weird. Most of the time, the worst they would do is give you a ticket. Sometimes they'd want to throw you in jail, but you'd be out in a day or so, and anyway, jail wasn't all bad. The food was warm.

Damn it, she needed a cigarette. A drink. Anything.

The bull spoke into his radio. The train hissed and shuddered and rumbled to life. Slowly, it pulled away from Mila and the bull and his cruiser—a long line of hoppers and boxcars, tankers and lumber flats. When the last car had passed them, Mila could see a little railroad outbuilding across the tracks, a sign on the wall reading SALEM.

The bull was looking at her again. He was smiling slyly, like when you figure out the punch line before the joke's through being told.

"You *are* her," he said. "They said you'd have purple hair. How many purple-haired riders could there be on this line?"

Mila snapped to attention. She'd hardly been listening earlier, figured the bull's chatter was just normal cop crap. Now, though, she realized what he was saying.

"Wait," she said. "Rewind. *Who* said? Who's looking for me?"

"Oh, everyone. Railroad police, city cops, FBI." The bull took her arm, trying to lead her toward his cruiser. "They put out an all points bulletin up and down the line. Said to keep our eyes out for a girl with purple hair."

The FBI. Mila rubbed her face. The *FBI*?

Warren, she thought. *What the hell did you do now?*

As far as Ash was concerned, Warren was the cause of most of Mila's problems. Warren and those little baggies he kept in his packsack.

It was Warren, in the end, who'd lured Mila away from Ash, way back in Kansas City, October, the last time they'd seen each other. Ash about to hop a northbound, telling Mila it wasn't too late, she could come—Texas Johnny would love to see her, too—and Mila smiling and pretending to think about it, pretending that she wasn't hooked on what Warren was holding, just some cheap rider crystal and not even that good, certainly not worth the price Warren wanted—but at that point, Mila was pretty sure she couldn't live without it.

So she'd told Ash she would meet her in a few months, down the road somewhere, told her to keep in touch and be careful. Told Ash she'd love to go, but Warren wanted to see Los Angeles, told Ash she was pretty sure she might love him.

And Ash had said yeah, sure, she would, had the decency to pretend like she believed Mila, like she didn't know it was the high Mila was chasing and not some lowlife rider boy. She told Mila to be careful, too, and then Ash's train was starting to pull out, and she had to run or she would miss it, and they hugged quickly at the edge of the rail yard, and then Mila watched as Ash chased down a grain car, took hold of a handrail, and swung herself aboard, as easy and graceful as always. Like she'd been born to do it. And Mila had watched until that grain car was gone and all that remained of the train was a little flashing red light in the distance—*No cabooses on the trains anymore, girl; you noticed that, right?*—and Mila had watched until the light was gone, too, and then she'd turned around and gone back to find Warren and his stash.

And that was about where everything started to go sideways. And now Ash was dead, and Warren had gone and done something crazy, and the goddamn *FBI* was looking for her.

Shit.

"Why are they looking for me?" Mila asked the bull. "What are they saying I did, exactly?"

The bull just shrugged. They were almost at his cruiser. "Didn't say. Just said to look out for you and hold on to you if we found you. Said to call it in right away."

He stopped beside the cruiser, fiddled with his keys. Mila looked around at the vast expanse of farmland, the town itself in the distance, a half mile or so up the tracks. Couldn't wrap her head around it. *The FBI. Jeez.*

The bull opened the door to his cruiser and reached for her arm again. Mila pulled away, danced free from his grip. She didn't have time for this. She had to get north.

The bull glared at her. "Come on, now," he said. "Don't make this harder than it has to be."

Ronda Sixkill was waiting in Seattle. Mila couldn't afford to be late. She needed to get to the High Line, needed to make things right for Ash. She'd screwed up. Ash was dead. There was no fixing that, but she had to do something. Nobody else was stepping up, were they? And she owed it to Ash, either way.

She owed it to Ash to make things right.

"Nobody's going to hurt you," the bull was saying. "But you have to come with me, understand?"

He grabbed for her again, but he was big and old and slow. Mila ducked away from him. This time, she didn't stop when she was clear of his grasp. This time, she bolted and didn't look back.

13

Montana Fish, Wildlife, and Parks field warden Becky LaTray was at her desk in the agency's office in Libby, thirty miles from the Idaho line, when her phone began to ring.

"Becky." Jim Benson's voice boomed through the receiver when she picked up the handset. "How're you doing down there?"

LaTray felt her eyes drift unconsciously to the clock on her desktop computer. Jim Benson was a rancher in Butcher's Creek, a little railroad town fifty miles to the northeast of Libby, on the edge of the county line—and thus within LaTray's jurisdiction by exactly three miles. She was never more aware of the significance of those miles then when Benson had her on the phone, which was more and more lately, now that his wife had passed.

It was a quarter to one in the afternoon on a workday, and LaTray had a pile of paperwork to get through. She pasted her best smile on her face and tried to hide the impatience in her voice. "Doing fine, Jim. Just about running out of places to put the snow, but that's winter for you. What can I do for you?"

"Been a hell of a winter," Benson said, untroubled by the field warden's prompts. "A new storm every week, it seems like, and cold, too—deathly cold. I've half a mind to bring the horses in to sleep in the main house if the temperature drops any colder overnight."

LaTray picked up the first file on her stack. A possible Canada lynx seen in Troy, near the Idaho line. The lynx were a threatened species; the public was encouraged to report any sightings.

"Whatever it takes, right?" she told Benson. "Long as it gets you through the winter."

"I've been thinking about calling it quits," Benson said. "Move somewhere hot, California maybe. See what this global warming thing is all about."

Maybe you should, LaTray thought. *Bother the wardens down there for a change.* "Listen, Jim, I'm a little busy right now. You mind calling me back in a while?"

Benson sucked his teeth. "I didn't even tell you why I'm calling, Becky." He paused, like he was waiting for her to ask. She didn't. He continued. "I was riding Maverick out back of the property this morning, thought I'd see how deep the snow was getting out there. You remember Maverick; she's my old mare. You would have met her the last time you came out, when I wanted to show you that ferret."

"Right. I remember, Jim. So anyway."

"Right, so anyway." Benson sucked his teeth again. "I was riding Maverick and she shied up about thirty yards from the tree line, wouldn't go any farther. I couldn't figure out why until I looked into the trees, and there was a *wolf* there, a big black sucker. Mean-looking thing."

LaTray sat up a little straighter. A wolf was actually a half-decent reason to call. "Yeah," she said. "Okay?"

"I figured I didn't want this guy sniffing around, so I let off a warning shot with my thirty-ought. Figured to scare him back into the woods. But he didn't go. So . . ." He trailed off.

"Oh, jeez, Jim," LaTray said. "Don't tell me you shot him."

"No! No, no, Becky." Benson laughed. "I tried another warning shot and it still didn't faze him, so I figured I'd better call you."

LaTray exhaled.

"That's what we're supposed to do, right? Call one of you wardens to come take a look?"

LaTray looked at her clock again. Nearly one o'clock, and Butcher's Creek about a two-hour drive, all of it snowed-in two-lane highway and winding back roads. It'd be almost sundown by the time she got out there, and then she'd have to get home in the dark.

Still, you couldn't just slough off a wolf sighting because the guy who called it in was a pesky old man, could you?

LaTray sighed, reached for her hat, her rifle, the keys to her work truck. "Gimme a couple of hours," she told Benson. "I'll come take a look."

It was three thirty by the time LaTray pulled her agency Super Duty pickup to a halt at Jim Benson's front gate, worn out from the drive and about ready for a drink. She'd taken MT-37 north almost to Canada, paralleling Lake Koocanusa above the Libby Dam and turning south again toward Butcher's Creek ten miles shy of the border, the last half hour of road pacing the railroad tracks—the Northwestern main line, big mile-long behemoths thundering past every ten minutes or so, utterly unencumbered by the snow.

Should have taken Amtrak, she thought. *Or should have told Jim just to shoot the damn wolf.*

Benson must have been watching for her from the ranch house, because he was out the front door almost before Becky killed the ignition. He came strutting down the drive, a big smile on his face, like Becky was the prom queen taking him to the dance.

"Roads give you any trouble?" he asked, moving in for a hug that

Becky managed to avoid. "They say it's going to snow again tomorrow, if you can believe it."

"I believe it," Becky replied, reaching back into the Ford for her rifle. "Where's this wolf of yours, Jim?"

"Oh, he took off, finally." Benson shook his head. "Big old train came roaring past the property, must have spooked him. He up and bolted."

For a brief moment, Becky imagined that there hadn't been any wolf, that Benson had called her up here on false pretenses. "You go out there, see what had him so interested?"

Benson just smiled. "No, dear," he said. "I was waiting for you."

They took a couple of Benson's horses out along the fence line, toward the western edge of his property, where a long stand of pine marked the end of the ranch. There was a creek back there, Becky knew, a forestry road, and somewhere down the bottom of a rock cut, the Northwestern mainline. Mostly, though, it was wilderness, like most of this part of the state: rock and trees and water.

And snow. Thirty yards from the fence line, the snowdrifts were almost at the horses' chests. Becky could see the tops of the fence posts, though only barely. But she could see where the wolf had been. The snow wasn't as deep inside the woods proper, and she could see where the marauder had tamped it down farther. She could see something else in there, too, something dark on the ground, the snow around it dirty, mottled. Bloody.

Shit, she thought. *The last thing Jim needs is a big old wolf thinking this is a good place to get dinner.*

"Could be a deer," Becky said, squinting. "Unless you lost an animal lately."

Benson made a negative sound. "They don't want to be out here any more than you or me," he said. "They stay in the barn most of the time, wait for me to feed them."

It took another twenty minutes to cover that last thirty yards. The trees started a couple yards from the fence, and the dead thing, whatever it was, was lying about five yards beyond. Becky shouldered her rifle, slipped from her horse on the other side of the fence. Waded through the snow toward the dead thing.

"You see that wolf coming back, you kill it," she called back to Benson. Then she turned around again, and she could see the dead thing clearly. It wasn't a deer, and it wasn't one of Jim's animals; she could see that now. And she could see also that she was into something a hell of a lot bigger than a marauding wolf.

"Call the sheriff," she said, turning back to Benson. "We're going to need some guys out here, fast as we can get them."

14

I have some bad news, kiddo, *Ronda's email began, and that's as far as Mila got before she slammed the phone down and looked away, fast.*

It was early evening, and the diner was mostly full. People looked over, startled by the noise, and Mila could practically see the judgment on their faces—not that she cared, not now.

The waitress came over, a middle-aged woman with bottle-blond hair. She'd been hovering for a while, kept pretending to check on Mila, asking if she wanted anything else to eat, drink, whatever. The subtext was clear: she wanted Mila to leave, take her purple hair and her packsack and her ripped, dirty clothing somewhere far away from her diner.

Warren was in the parking lot. He and his buddies had made friends with some guy with a beat-up old Aerostar van, and they were driving down to Big Bear tonight, already talking about hotboxing the thing and skinny-dipping in the lake. Mila could see them all through the window, making eyes at her, waving Hurry up. *Every now and then, Warren reached over and leaned on the horn.*

But Mila didn't care about all that. All she cared about was Ronda's email. She took a couple deep breaths, tried to compose herself. Picked up the phone and made herself read.

I have some bad news, kiddo. A friend of a friend found your girl on the High Line. She'd been gone awhile, he says. It wasn't pretty.

Mila closed her eyes. Picked up her phone. **I don't believe it,** *she typed.* **How does he know it was her?**

She waited. The waitress fixed her with the stink eye. Mila ignored her. Hit refresh on her phone, refreshrefreshrefresh. Then Ronda wrote back. **I recognized her. He showed me a picture.**

Show me, *Mila replied.*

A pause. **You don't want to see. Like I said, it's not pretty.**

Mila wrote back immediately. **Show me.**

The door to the diner opened. Warren walked in. He smiled at the waitress, who glowered back at him. Walked to Mila's table and stood across from her.

"We're all waiting," he told her. "Come on. We want to get there before it's too cold to swim."

"I just need a minute," Mila told him.

"They're all, like, impatient. They're talking about leaving without you."

Mila looked at him. Looked back at her phone, torn. Knew she'd lose her connection with Ronda as soon as she left the diner. Knew she'd lose her ready supply if Warren left without her.

But she knew she couldn't bail on Ash again.

"Do what you have to do, I guess," she said finally. "This is serious."

Warren put his hands in his pockets. Glanced out at the van, then back at Mila. "I'll tell them you'll be out in five, okay?"

"Yeah," Mila told him. "Okay."

"Okay," Warren said. And he shuffled out of the diner and crossed the lot to the van. Mila unlocked her phone again and opened Ronda's picture.

15

The phone rang in Windermere's hotel room, a Hampton Inn not far from the railroad yard in Barstow. It was six in the morning, and Windermere was wide awake, thanks both to jet lag and the fact that she couldn't get this case from her mind.

With Crystal Meth Warren's help, Stevens and Windermere had tracked down an ID on their purple-haired person of interest: one Mila Denise Scott, nominally of Massena, New York, way up by the Canadian border. She'd run away from her foster family a year and a half back, when she was seventeen; her foster mom's sister, a woman named Deborah Hood, had filed the missing person's report.

"Not that anybody bothered looking too hard," Hood told Windermere when she'd tracked the woman down. "She'd packed a suitcase, after all, left a dang note. Why expend the resources on somebody who didn't want to be there, right?"

"But you didn't see it that way."

"She was *seventeen*, for God's sake." Hood's voice shook a little, and she trailed off.

"We'll try our best to find her," Windermere told her. "I'll keep you in the loop."

"I guess I just felt guilty," Hood said, her voice softer now. "I know I could have done more for that girl; she was so unhappy. They told me she was gone, and all I could think about was how I never did anything to make her believe it was worth sticking around."

The phone was still ringing. Windermere picked it up. "This is Windermere."

"Agent Windermere? It's Homer Doyle." The Barstow detective. He coughed, self-conscious. "I just heard from the Northwestern bulls. Apparently, they got a hit on your girl."

Windermere sat up. "Yeah? Did they grab her?"

Doyle hesitated. "Well, see, that's the thing. One of their guys found her on a mixed freight in Salem, Oregon, kind of just south of Portland. I guess she was hiding in a boxcar."

"Okay." Windermere was standing now, twisting the phone cord, waiting for the big reveal. "So do they have her or not?"

"Well, no. No, they do not."

Windermere didn't say anything. Rolled her eyes to the ceiling and thought about hanging up.

"I guess the bull got her off the train," Doyle was saying. "He knew it was her from the purple hair, but when he mentioned that you guys were looking for her, she bolted."

"He mentioned *us*? Like, the *FBI*?"

A pause. "Uh, correct."

"Damn it, Doyle." Windermere threw a pillow. It hit a lamp in the corner, which threatened to topple over. The lamp rocked back and forth but stayed upright. "No wonder she bolted."

"Yeah," Doyle said. "I know. They said the bull is really sorry."

"I bet he is."

"At least you know she's in Salem," Doyle said, his voice brightening. "So that's a plus, right?"

"I guess it is." Windermere imagined pitching Drew Harris on more plane tickets, hotel rooms, rental cars. "I guess we'll head up there, check it out."

She hung up the phone. Then she pulled on a pair of sweats, checked her hair, and knocked on the door to the adjoining room. Stevens opened it fast. He was holding his laptop and a handful of printed pages.

"Was just about to go get you," he said. "I think I found something."

"You can tell me about it on the flight," Windermere said. "Pack your bags, partner. Our girl just ducked a railroad bull in northern Oregon."

Stevens held up his laptop, the pages. "I'm thinking we can do better than Oregon, Carla," he said. "Hear me out."

I was thinking about what Warren said about the High Line," Stevens told Windermere as he set his laptop on the duvet and sat down beside it. "How every rider knows there's something evil up there, somebody preying on women. That sheriff I talked to in Idaho, he said something similar, like he'd always heard rumors but never had the resources to really check it out."

He handed her the printouts. "Couldn't sleep last night," he told her. "And the business center downstairs is 24-7, so—"

"So you destroyed half a rain forest instead." Windermere flipped through the pages, found a collection of news reports, blog posts, opinion pieces. Stevens had been productive.

"It's not just the riders who are talking about this," Stevens said. "And it's not just riders going missing, either. I must have found a hundred cases, if these reports are true. That's not just coincidence, Carla."

Windermere thought about Mila Scott, somewhere up in Oregon, slipping away from them. She sifted through the printouts again absently. "So what are you saying, partner? You don't think if there was a serial killer operating up there somebody would have noticed already?"

"Sure," Stevens said. "Except these cases are spread across three states and two mountain ranges, god knows how many counties. And Truman said himself that the winters are killer up there. It would be easy to write off a few missing women and a handful of dead transients if you weren't looking for some kind of pattern."

"Maybe you're right," Windermere said. "I don't really know. But we have a concrete lead on the one person who can shine a light on this case for us, and she's slipping away from us, somewhere in Oregon. We can't afford to go off chasing hunches right now."

She made to stand. Stevens touched her hand lightly, and Windermere was so surprised by the gesture, she sat down again.

"Normally, I'd be with you," Stevens said. He reached for his laptop, turned the screen so she could see. "But it happened again, Carla."

On his screen was an email from Sheriff Chuck Truman. The subject line: LINCOLN COUNTY. The body of the message: a few lines and a picture. A woman's body—or what was left of it—in a bed of snow, her face and body mutilated, her clothes torn to scraps around her.

"Lincoln County Sheriff's Department found the body last night," Stevens told her. "About a hundred and fifty miles east of Boundary County, Idaho, and . . ." He paused. "Less than a mile from the Northwestern main line."

Windermere studied the screen, the picture Truman had sent. She couldn't look at it very long without feeling something wake up inside her, some kind of anger she could barely contain. Suddenly, finding Mila Scott didn't seem like job one anymore.

"A ghost rider," she said, standing. This time, Stevens didn't stop her. "Montana in January. Damn it, partner, I really hope you're wrong."

16

I can't let you do it," Ronda said. "Kiddo, it's insane."

Mila was talking on a pay phone outside of the diner. Ronda had insisted Mila call her, collect, right after she'd sent the picture.

The picture.

Mila couldn't think about the picture without wanting to cry again. Cry or throw up; she'd done plenty of both. It was Ash, all right, in that photo Ronda sent. It was Ash—and it wasn't. It was her face, anyway, her skin and her eyes and her mouth and her hair. It was all the superficial things that made Ash look like Ash, beaten and shattered and broken and torn. Ruined.

The real Ash was gone. She'd been gone long before the picture was taken.

Warren was gone, too, gone forever, his stash along with him, and Mila could already feel the empty gnawing inside her, the need, growing, pushing her to want to chase the van down and pay whatever price Warren wanted, do whatever he asked for a bump.

"Kiddo," Ronda said. "You still there?"

Mila exhaled. "I'm here."

"Did you hear what I said? I can't let you do this. It's a suicide mission."

"Maybe." Mila looked out onto the highway, the train tracks in the distance. "But nobody else is going to do anything. They'll forget about Ash like all the rest."

"Fine," Ronda said, "but Ash is gone, sweetie. You aren't helping anything by getting yourself killed."

"I have to go up there, Ronda."

Ronda started to protest. Mila cut her off. "We can talk about it in person," she said. "I'm coming your way. If the trains work out okay, I'll be there in a couple of days."

She hung up the phone. Surveyed the parking lot again, the lights of a truck-stop town after dark. Then she reached for her phone. She was still close enough to the diner to be connected to the Wi-Fi, and she opened Ronda's email again. Pulled up that picture, even though it hurt to look at it.

I'm sorry, Ash.

Mila saved the picture to her phone. Then she walked across the parking lot and out toward the train tracks, scanning the horizon for her ride.

Now, in Salem, Oregon, Mila snuck one more look at Ash's picture as she crouched in the bushes, ten feet from the tracks. Not the horrible Ash-but-not-Ash picture that Ronda had sent, but the other Ash picture, the happy one, the picture Mila had snapped as they were running to catch that hotshot in Virginia, somewhere in the Alleghenies.

Ash had turned back, seen the phone, and rolled her eyes, laughing. "Come on, girl," she'd said. "Are you a rider or a tourist? We're missing our train."

Click.

The truth was, Mila didn't feel like a rider, even after a year hopping trains. She knew she would have washed out within weeks, turned tail and gone home again—or worse, gotten herself killed—if she hadn't met Ash. If Ash hadn't *found* her.

Ash was a rider.

Mila was a tourist.

Ash had protected Mila, covered her ass. Tried to get her clean again, keep her off the drugs. *Girls have to stick together out here, you know?* But Mila hadn't done the same, and now Ash was gone, and there wasn't much to do but make it right, or as right as these things could be made.

Mila pocketed her phone. She was north of Salem now, had spent the day skulking through town, avoiding the bulls and the local police, looking for a hotshot to get her the heck out of there.

She'd snuck into a sporting goods store on the outskirts of town and swiped a black watch cap from a rack by the door. Pulled it low on her head and cursed Warren and his punk rock peer pressure. Boring brunette Mila wouldn't attract nearly the same attention, but she'd had to be a try-hard, as usual.

Never mind. She could fix her hair color in Seattle, at Ronda's. But first, she had to get out of Salem.

Mila listened for the heavy throb of the big diesel locomotives, peering through the darkness for the first glimmer of headlights. Time passed. Fifteen minutes, maybe. A half hour. The night air was bitterly cold, and Mila knew she'd be even colder if she surfed a hotshot.

Suck it up, girl. It's only going to get worse.

Then she heard the telltale rumble, low at first, but getting louder. Saw the rails light up with a headlight around the bend. She tensed as the train appeared, the engineer giving it throttle as he pulled out of town, the ground shaking like an earthquake as the locomotive approached.

It was a long mixed train—a junker, Ash called them—boxcars and grain hoppers and tank cars and flats. Junkers were slower than hotshots, but if you found an empty boxcar you were riding in style, protected from the wind and the elements and prying eyes. Even the grain cars had little cubbies to hide in.

A cut of hopper cars was approaching. Mila tensed, watching the stepladders on the ends of the cars, looking for her shot. She picked a car and hefted her packsack, ready to throw it aboard.

The hopper approached, wheels squealing. The train was picking up speed. Mila threw her packsack at the hopper's little cubby. Then she grabbed the stepladder and held on for her life.

The train nearly wrenched her arms from their sockets. She squeezed the ladder tight, let the train carry her, pulled herself up, and swung aboard. She curled up in the cubby, watching the city lights fade in the distance as the train thundered north, Ronda somewhere ahead, and then Ash.

17

Just getting to the High Line was a hell of a chore.

Barstow to Los Angeles International Airport was a two-hour drive—an hour and a half with Windermere behind the wheel, the rental Hyundai's little engine screaming in protest the whole way. From LAX, the agents caught a flight to Spokane, landing at Spokane International just in time to learn their connection to Kalispell, Montana, was canceled.

"Weather," the gate agent told them. "Got a heck of a snowstorm running through there right now."

"A snowstorm." Windermere thought of Barstow, the desert, Los Angeles. Thought of Miami, where she'd first joined the Bureau. Warm weather. No snow. No need for winter clothing. "Shoot, Stevens, and I forgot to pack my mittens."

Stevens gave her a smile, then glanced over his shoulder at the long line of passengers rebooking to later flights, no word yet when the airport in Kalispell would reopen.

"So, what now?" Windermere asked him. "I don't relish the thought of waiting in this airport all day. But I'm betting the highways are closed, too."

They were headed for a town called Butcher's Creek, two hundred and fifty miles northeast of Spokane, near the Canadian border. Stevens checked his phone.

"Highway might be closed," he said, "but the railroad isn't."

Truman said it was a rancher who found the latest victim," Stevens told Windermere, reading from his notes as they pulled out of Spokane on Amtrak's *North Coast Limited.* "Some guy named Benson had a wolf lurking around his property, called the warden to come take a look at it. Warden showed up, figured out pretty quick why that wolf wasn't leaving."

Windermere made a face. "Oh no."

"Afraid so," Stevens said. "The body was in rough shape when they found her; no purse or ID, either. But she's a female and probably Native. Lincoln County Sheriff's Department is treating the case as suspicious until they can pin down a cause of death."

"Strangulation," Windermere said. "That's how Truman's Jane Doe died, right?"

"That's right. Boundary County coroner found her larynx crushed."

Windermere shivered. Outside, the train kicked up a gale of snow and ice as it wound through the mountains, obscuring what little could be seen through the windows. It looked cold out there, ice-age cold—and as darkness fell, it looked desolate.

"Pretty crummy place to be a serial killer, if there really is one out here," she said, staring out the window. "This doesn't look like a neighborhood where nature needs the help."

It was long past midnight when the *North Coast Limited* stopped at the little flag station in Butcher's Creek. Stevens and Windermere were the only two passengers to disembark, and as Stevens climbed down to the platform and the bracing, bitter cold, he shivered and hoped someone from the sheriff's department had remembered they were coming. This was frostbite weather, die-of-exposure stuff, even to a native Minnesotan, and Stevens, who'd spent the last couple of days sweltering in the desert, was shocked at how quickly the mountain air chilled him.

"Come on," he told Windermere, shouldering his overnight bag as the train pulled away behind them. "Let's see if we can't find some shelter."

Windermere rubbed her hands together. "Right behind you, partner."

There was a vehicle idling at the other end of the platform, an SUV, and Stevens could see the light bar and sheriff's department markings as he walked closer. The driver's door opened as they approached, and a woman stepped out in a heavy, fur-lined parka. "You must be the feds."

"Sure are," Stevens replied. "Are you the welcoming party?"

"Kerry Finley, Lincoln County sheriff's deputy." Finley looked like she was a few years younger than Windermere. A trim build and a ready smile. She held out her hand. "Glad you all could make it."

18

Ronda's like the den mother for all us riders," Ash told Mila. "Especially the girls. You ever need anything while you're out here—a bed for the night, a job for a couple weeks, bail money—you get in touch with her and she'll make it happen."

Summer on Lake Superior. They'd ridden a drag up through Minnesota for a meetup outside Duluth, a group of riders at a friendly lakeside campsite, cookouts and bonfires and tall tales from the road.

Music, too; some of the riders had instruments, old beat-up guitars and harmonicas, African drums. Someone brought out an accordion. They circled around the fire and played train-hopper classics, traditional hobo tunes. Played some newer stuff, too, Bob Dylan and Neil Young, Johnny Cash.

Mila lingered on the outside of the circle, as close as she could get to the music without being noticed, while Ash pointed out people she knew. Ash had talked Mila off the crystal again a couple weeks back, and Mila was feeling the comedown: depression, paranoia. She didn't want to be here.

She wanted to get high.

"That old drummer, that's Texas Johnny," Ash was saying. "He used to play backup for Waylon Jennings before he started riding trains. Could have been a big star if he hadn't bugged out and hit the rails. They say he hasn't slept in a real bed in forty years."

Mila didn't know who Waylon Jennings was, but Ash had moved on anyway, was talking about the young man with one arm playing the harmonica.

"Lost his left arm to a hotshot," Ash explained. "A rainy day and the train moving fast, he just slipped and . . ." She grimaced. "That was that."

Mila watched the harmonica player, the empty sleeve of his shirt pinned to his shoulder. He played better than she ever would and didn't look too upset about his missing arm. Then the song ended and the music died out and all of the musicians looked across the fire to a big woman in a folding camp chair, like they were waiting for her approval.

The woman gave it. "Well done, boys," she said, smiling. "Now how's your take on 'Oklahoma Hills'?"

Instantly, the band was off and running again, launching into the next song. The woman sat back in her chair, nodded along, satisfied.

"It's her birthday," Ash whispered. "All she wanted was a meet-up and some music."

"Who is she?" Mila asked, and Ash blinked and looked at her like she'd asked who was president.

"Who is she?" Ash repeated. "That's Ronda Sixkill, girl. She's basically the queen of the riders."

Mila's train made Seattle late on a miserable, rainy night. She stepped down from her hopper car in a freight yard near the docks and hurried across the slick ballast to the edge of the yard.

She was cold. It wasn't even below freezing, and she was already shivering. The rain seemed to seep through her clothing and even her skin, chilling her in a way even the snow couldn't.

You'd better toughen up, girl. It's going to be a hell of a lot colder where you're going.

Mila walked down the tracks until she found a road crossing. She could see lights up the road a ways, a half mile or so, shining bright through the rain. She shouldered her packsack and followed the lights.

Civilization turned out to be a couple of pawnshops and a check-cashing joint, all closed. A convenience store that could have been out of business and an all-night diner. Mila turned on her phone, searched for a wireless signal. Found a weak one, still usable, from the bigger of the two pawnshops.

Bingo.

Mila entered the diner, sat at the bar. Ordered a cup of coffee and wrote a message to Ronda.

I'm here.

You ever need help while you're on the road," Ash said, "you get in touch with Ronda. She'll make it happen."

Mila watched Ronda from across the bonfire. The big woman was definitely the center of attention. Every couple minutes, another rider would emerge from the dark with a flask or a bottle outstretched like an offering, and every time Ronda refused, cracked a joke instead, sent each rider away smiling. If there was such a thing as a celebrity among train hoppers, Ronda Sixkill was it.

"Descended from a Cherokee lawman," Ash said. "I heard he was actually a railroad bull, but whatever. Ronda doesn't need to be out here, that's the crazy thing about her. Still goes back to her house every winter, plays host to whoever needs out of the cold."

Mila didn't say anything. She was daunted by the big woman's presence, her charisma, the obvious way the other riders deferred to her. "How am I supposed to get in touch with her?" she asked. "She doesn't even know my name."

Ash grinned. "That's a two-part question. You get ahold of her on the rider message boards. Whenever she's at home, she's online."

"Online?" Mila gestured around at the wilderness, the lake. "This isn't exactly an Internet hotspot. How am I supposed to message her?"

Ash slipped something out of her pocket, pressed it to Mila's hand. A phone, a smartphone. A new one.

"Where did you—"

"Minneapolis," Ash said. "That guy who was bugging me at the bar, the one who kept grabbing my ass? He left his phone on the table, and I swiped it."

Mila stared at the phone. It looked complex. It looked expensive. "Can't he track it?"

"I know a guy who cracks phones," Ash told her. "He owed me a favor. You swipe yourself a phone charger and you'll be set. Even when we're not riding together, we can still keep in touch."

Mila slid her finger over the screen, unlocking the phone. It had a camera, she saw, and a lot of apps she didn't recognize. There were pictures of the phone's old owner, and there was music.

"You could put a new phone card in," Ash was saying, "but you don't have to. You can connect to the Internet through any Wi-Fi signal. Send emails and look up places to go and whatever you need."

"Okay, great," Mila said. "But I don't even know this Ronda person. Why should she care about me?"

"That's the second thing." Ash reached for Mila's hand, pulled her into the light. Circled the bonfire to where Ronda was sitting.

"Ronda Sixkill," Ash said as they approached, "I think you should meet my friend Mila."

Forty minutes and two coffee refills later, a car pulled up outside the diner. It hung there at the curb, long, low, and dark, the driver in shadow, but Mila knew who it was.

She left a few crumpled dollars on the bar beside her coffee cup, picked up her packsack, and went back out into the rain.

The car was big and old, a Buick or an Oldsmobile or something. Its wipers worked fast over the windshield. Mila walked to the passenger door. She opened it and slid inside.

It was warm in the car, and dry. The seat was the softest Mila had ever felt. Ronda Sixkill sat behind the wheel. She was looking at Mila with those motherly eyes.

"I guess you made it after all, kiddo," she said. "Now what do I have to do to convince you to stay?"

19

Stevens and Windermere spent the night in the only hotel in Butcher's Creek, the unimaginatively named Northwestern Hotel. The rooms were army-barracks sparse: twin beds, plywood furniture, and broken TVs. Meant for train crews, Kerry Finley explained. "They don't see many tourists this far off the highway."

"Makes no difference to me," Stevens said, yawning. "I feel like we just about crossed the Rubicon to get here."

He slept fitfully. Woke up to the phone ringing, light shining in through the windows, a blinding glare from the snow that covered the town.

"Deputy Finley is downstairs with the sheriff," Windermere said when he answered the phone. "You want me to tell them you need your beauty sleep?"

"No amount of sleep is going to save me," Stevens replied. "I'll be down in five minutes."

He dressed in a hurry, brushed his teeth, patted down his unruly hair. Found Windermere and Finley in the lobby with an older man who must have been the sheriff. He fit the mold: the mustache and the Stetson, the air of quiet competence, like he'd been bred specifically to keep order in mountains like these.

"Judd Parsons," he said, shaking Stevens's hand. "Sheriff of Lincoln County. I hear you've met Kerry already."

Finley nodded. "Morning, Agent Stevens."

"Well, you sure look like federal agents," Parson said, studying Stevens and Windermere. "And two of you, to boot. If I didn't know any better, I'd say the government doesn't believe I can conduct a real investigation."

"We're looking for a connection between your Jane Doe here and the unknown victim on Sheriff Truman's caseload in Boundary County," Stevens told him. "If we can't find a connection, we'll get out of your hair, let you do your thing the way we're sure you know how. But if there is a connection between your Jane Doe and Sheriff Truman's, it means—"

"You can stop calling her Jane Doe," Parsons said, interrupting. He held up his hands, a peace offering. "All due respect, agents. But we made her ID while you were on your way up here."

The town was tiny, hardly more than a village. There was a big Northwestern tanker train slowing to a stop on the main line; as Windermere watched, two men stepped out of a crew cab pickup and disappeared inside the lead engine. A moment later, two different men emerged from the locomotive and climbed in the backseat of the truck, which drove away from the tracks, across the town's main street, to stop in front of the Northwestern Hotel.

"Kelly-Anne Clairmont," Sheriff Parsons told them, leading them out to his Lincoln County SUV. "She's an Indian girl, lives in the village here. We found her ex-husband's car abandoned on a forestry road behind the Benson property. It's stuck pretty good in the snow back there, three miles or so from town."

Stevens and Windermere followed Parsons into the truck and buckled their seat belts as the sheriff pointed his vehicle down the main road out of Butcher's Creek.

"Your team get a read on the state of the body?" Stevens asked. "You're treating this death as suspicious; must have been some sign of—"

"The state of the body was *bad*," Parsons said. "That old wolf saw to that. I'm treating the death as suspicious because of the carnage, but I'm betting we're going to find what killed Kelly-Anne wasn't so suspicious at all."

"Anyone talk to the ex-husband?"

Parsons gave him a look, like *What kind of backwoods bumpkins do you think you're dealing with?* "Called him as soon as we found the car," the sheriff said. "Asked him if he knew where his car was. He said Kelly-Anne took it to the bar a few nights back, never came home.

Said give him a heads-up if we knew where it was, he could use the damn thing back."

"The bar," Stevens said. "That's the one in town there?"

"The Gold Spike, yessir. Only bar between here and Eureka. Kelly-Anne was a . . ." The sheriff laughed. "You could say she was a local favorite around there."

"Does the ex have a story for the last couple of days?" Windermere asked. "What's he been up to while Ms. Clairmont was missing?"

Parsons found her in the rearview. "You're pretty sure this is a homicide, huh?"

Windermere held his gaze. "We got a young Native woman the next county over, strangled to death and dumped in the snow. Now we have another young woman's body here. I don't know about you, but that sounds like a pattern to me."

"If we started trying to link every dead Indian around here, Agent Windermere, we'd drive ourselves crazy." Parsons chuckled to himself. "Now, I don't know what Sheriff Truman has been telling you, but deaths like these aren't exactly uncommon in winter."

He slowed the truck. They'd reached a snowy forestry road. "These are the mountains, young lady," he said over his shoulder. "You make too many mistakes, it'll cost you your life."

20

There was a cluster of vehicles parked at the foot of the forestry road, another SUV with Lincoln County sheriff markings, a Ford Super Duty with Montana Fish, Wildlife, and Parks. There was a young woman, too, in a different uniform. She carried a rifle slung over her shoulder.

"That's Becky LaTray," Parsons told them as they climbed from the car. "Fish, Wildlife, and Parks warden. She came out when Jim Benson saw the wolf. She found the body."

He called over and the warden looked up, saw Stevens and Windermere, straightened, and came across to them.

"Becky, these are a couple of our friends from the federal government," Parsons said. "They're investigating dead Indians and want to know if Kelly-Anne here was murdered."

LaTray was a pretty, fresh-faced thirtysomething. She bore a passing resemblance to Deputy Finley, if not in appearance then in overall attitude; neither woman looked at all bothered by the chill in the air or the bleakness of their surroundings—or the grisly nature of the case, natch.

These mountain girls, Windermere thought. *Without even trying, they make me look like a slug.*

LaTray shook Windermere's hand, then Stevens's. "I'm hardly the person to talk to about murder," she told them. "All I really know is wildlife, and that wolf had pretty well had his way with the body before I showed up."

"County coroner's taking a look," Parsons said. "Should give us an official cause of death in the next couple of days, if you're sticking around."

"Tell him to put a rush on it," Windermere replied. "Look for signs of strangulation—crushed larynx, thyroid cartilage, petechial hemorrhages. Ligature marks, sexual assault, too. The works."

Parsons didn't look happy about it, but he reached for his radio. Windermere turned back to LaTray.

"I guess you're thinking the wolf came by postmortem," she said. "Found Ms. Clairmont's body and scavenged a meal."

"That's right. They rarely attack people, especially not healthy young women." LaTray pulled out a camera. "The wolf was gone when I got here, but I took a few pictures of the scene."

She handed the camera to Windermere, who scrolled through a couple shots, then handed the camera back. The wolf had clearly been at the body for a while. His teeth had done serious damage; the snow was littered with torn clothing and worse.

"So where is this wolf now?" Windermere asked, scanning the trees that lined the side of the road. "He still out there somewhere?"

LaTray nodded. "We're keeping our eyes open," she said. "Now that he has a taste for people, he'll probably come back sooner or later."

"And then?"

LaTray patted her rifle. "And then we do what we have to do," she said grimly. "Preferably before he does any more damage."

Stevens and Windermere rode up to Kelly-Anne Clairmont's abandoned Taurus in LaTray's Super Duty pickup. *Stick close to the woman with the biggest gun,* Stevens figured. *Especially when there's a hungry wolf in the area.*

The snow was thick on the narrow road, and LaTray drove at a crawl, keeping her tires in the tracks from Sheriff Parsons's Explorer up ahead. The SUV seemed to be cutting a fresh path; any trace of Kelly-Anne Clairmont's passage had been erased by the last snowfall.

"How'd she wind up all the way back here?" Windermere asked. Outside was nothing but thick trees and mountains, and off to the south somewhere, Jim Benson's ranch.

LaTray met her eyes in the rearview. "I mean, people get lost," she said. "Pretty easy to do when it's whiteout conditions. Especially if you have a couple drinks in you."

"You've seen a lot of these," Stevens said.

"In a professional capacity? Not really. The wolves stay away, for the most part—or we hope they do. But as a Montanan in general? Sure." She shrugged. "The winters are hard up here."

"So we've been told," Windermere said.

Parsons's brake lights came on, and LaTray stopped the truck. She looked across the cab at Stevens. "You all are thinking this was a murder, huh?" she said. "I have to say, we don't see too many federal agents around here. Especially not for—"

"Dead Indian girls," Windermere said. "That's what the sheriff said, right?"

LaTray colored. "I was going to say Native Americans. The sheriff has his own way of talking, but he doesn't talk for everyone."

"Yeah, well, the jury's still out on whether this was a homicide." Windermere was reaching for the door handle. "In the meantime, we're just enjoying our Montana vacation."

The little Ford sat in deep snow just ahead of where Sheriff Parsons had pulled his Explorer to the side of the forestry road. It was a tiny thing, mid-eighties, rusted all to hell, the snow almost up to the top of the tires.

"So here's the car," Parsons told them. "Wayne Clairmont's been asking for it back, so as soon as you all have had your look at it, we'll tow the thing back to his yard."

"You mean as soon as you clear Wayne's alibi for the night of his ex-wife's murder," Windermere said. "Right?"

Parsons looked at her hard. Windermere held his stare. Finally, Parsons raised his hands. "I guess we're playing hardball," he said. "Fine, then. You and your colleague can interview every man, woman, and teddy bear in this town, if you like. But you're in charge of telling Wayne he can't have his ride back."

"Duly noted," Windermere said. "You have a fingerprint kit?"

Parsons stared her down for another long beat. Then he turned to Deputy Finley, who was standing by the Explorer. "Kerry, hand me that crime scene kit in the backseat, would you?" he asked. "It seems this here is a homicide scene."

21

Mila remembered being cold.

It had been raining for days, and it would keep raining forever. Her thin jacket, her suitcase, everything she owned was soaked through. She was cold and hungry and wet and miserable. She was starting to feel the withdrawal again; it had been too long since she'd hit. She was starting to feel desperate.

The rider jungle was a terrifying place. It was a society all its own, with rules, laws, and customs she could hardly imagine. Most of the citizens were men, most were older; they watched her walk among the shelters with undisguised hunger.

Mila had intended to lurk on the margins, look for a friendly face, but the jungle was scaring her and she could feel her anxiety welling, the crippling panic. She'd walked to the nearest campfire, a group of furtive-looking riders passing a pipe back and forth, and she'd stood as tall as she could and asked them, all of them, any *of them, if they could spare a bump.*

There had been a pause. She could see the other riders shooting looks at one another. Finally, a man spoke up. "You can have some of my stash," he told her. "But you'll have to trade for it."

She could hear the other riders laughing as she followed the man down the row of encampments to a shelter made of scrap siding and a big orange tarp. It looked dry underneath—a sleeping bag and a pile of odds and ends, room to stretch out, warm up—and she was inside the shelter before she'd had time to think about it.

The man followed her in. He had to crouch to get inside; he filled the small space. It was a single-person shelter, clearly, and Mila could feel the man's warmth, smell his odor.

"So, now," he said, and he was leering at her, "what can you offer?"

The implication was clear. There was no point in pretending otherwise. She'd wondered when this would happen, wondered how long it would take before she was faced with this decision.

How much did she want that fix? Enough to do . . . this?

Probably.

The man came closer, like he was trying to swing the vote. Put his hand on her arm—and then the edge of the tarp flapped open, right above Mila's head, and there was Ash glaring in at them, at the man, though Mila didn't know she was Ash yet, just an angry, beautiful girl with dark hair and a big knife, a knife she was brandishing at the man.

"Let her be, asshole," Ash told him. "There isn't a girl in the world desperate enough for what you're offering."

But I am desperate, *Mila thought.*

The man rocked back on his heels, eyeing Ash, gauging his chances. Ash held up the knife, let him get a good look at the blade. "You really want to test me?" she said. "Do it. Ask Jungle Jim how that worked out for him."

Whoever Jungle Jim was, his name was warning enough. The man stepped back from Mila, muttering something about only having fun. Ash held out her free hand, and Mila climbed up from under the tarp and out of the shelter. Realized as she brushed wet hair from her eyes that Ash was already walking away.

"Jeez, girl, you can't let them think they can just take what they want

from you," Ash called over her shoulder. "They'll never take you serious that way."

Mila didn't say anything. Didn't know what to say. She was still hungry, was the main thing. She was still cold. She still needed that fix.

Ash made it twenty feet. Then she stopped, half turned back. "I have some stew and warm clothes in my tent," she said, beckoning Come on. *"And if you insist on getting high, I know a guy who can front you who isn't a total sleaze. Unless you'd rather, you know, take your chances with these lowlifes."*

Hell no, *Mila thought.* Hell freaking no. *She grabbed her suitcase and hurried to follow.*

Mila jolted upright, disoriented by the sunlight. She'd slept; it was morning. She could hear pots and pans clattering downstairs, the smell of bacon wafting up. She lay in bed, stared up at the ceiling. It was weird to be here.

They'd arrived late last night, soaking wet from the storm. Ronda had fixed Mila a grilled cheese sandwich and a glass of milk when they'd arrived. She'd given Mila a towel and a bathrobe and let her take a shower. And she'd made up the spare bed and turned down the covers. She didn't say much.

"We'll talk in the morning," she told Mila. "It's too late to start up with it now."

Now morning was here, and Mila rolled out of bed, dreading the conversation to come. She rifled through her packsack, found a pair of grimy jeans she hadn't worn since she'd crossed into California with Warren, jeans she'd forgotten she owned. She pulled them over her legs and felt something in the back pocket as she did, slipped her hand in. Pulled the thing out and stared at it.

A baggie, long forgotten, about the size of a quarter. The last dregs of a half gram of crystal inside, not much, but enough. Enough for a little strength, anyway, strength to face Ronda, strength to keep going. Strength to catch on a long freight headed into the snow.

Mila could still hear Ronda moving about in the kitchen. She turned her back to the doorway, opened the baggie. Poured the contents onto the back of her hand, where her thumb started. Studied the little pile of white powder, savoring the moment.

This is the last you'll get of this for a while.

She plugged her nostril with her finger. Leaned down to thc pile. Was just about to inhale, take the trip, crank up, when she heard something behind her and knew it was Ronda.

"I brought coffee," the older woman was saying, pushing into the bedroom with her hip, two steaming mugs in her hands. "And not that campfire crap, either, but *real* stuff. When's the last time you had—" She saw Mila, the crystal, and stopped. "Oh," she said. "Oh, no, kiddo. You can't do that here."

Mila paused, torn between the urge to take the hit right now, in front of Ronda, and the knowledge that Ronda would never help her if she did.

"It's not much," she said lamely. "I just— I need something to get me going."

"Hence the coffee," Ronda said. "Listen, kiddo, you do what you want, but you want my help, you're going to have to trade for it."

She looked at the little pile of powder on Mila's hand. She set down her coffee mug and held out her hand, the implication obvious. *Shit.*

You sold out your best friend for this shit. Now she's dead. Are you really going to do it again?

Mila sighed. She tipped her hand over and poured the little pile of crystal into Ronda's palm. Followed Ronda into the bathroom and watched her flush the drugs, her panic growing as the water whirlpooled away.

"And not just your little stash, either," Ronda said. "You want me to help you on this misguided mission of yours, you're going to get clean and stay clean. For your sake, not your friend's, because whatever it is you're hoping to find in those mountains, you're not bringing her back, understand?"

Mila didn't say anything.

"Swear it, kiddo," Ronda told her. "Or you'll never make it into those mountains."

Mila closed her eyes. *You're probably going to die, anyway. Do something useful with your life before you go. Do something for Ash.*

"I swear," she told Ronda. "I'll get clean."

Ronda handed Mila a mug. "Well, all right," she said. "Come on downstairs. I made breakfast."

22

A railroad lineman found her," Ronda told Mila after Mila had eaten, scarfing down a plate of bacon and three scrambled eggs, orange juice, two more mugs of coffee, the works. "A friend of mine, Roger Domino. When Ash didn't show up last October, I called in some favors on the Northwestern line. You do this long enough, you get to know the train crews. You start to make connections."

Mila nodded. Ash had told her something similar, how most of the train guys didn't really care about riders being on the trains, so long as you stuck to your own business and didn't cause trouble.

"Where did they find her?" she asked.

"Some place called Moyie Springs, Idaho, near the Montana line." Ronda frowned. "The weird thing was, it's not even a division point. But the night before she was supposed to arrive, there was a big train derailment on the High Line, a bunch of chemical tankers. All traffic east and west halted for nearly eight hours. The way I figure, her hotshot must have stopped to wait out the derailment in that little town."

"And the bulls kicked her off?"

"Maybe. Or maybe she just got real cold. She was on a flatcar, remember, and there was the first snow that night. Maybe she just wanted some shelter."

Mila felt a chill. "Ash said the rider always travels in a storm. She said he rides where no normal person could survive."

Ronda stood, taking her coffee mug to the sink. Stared out through the window as she rinsed it. Outside, it was still raining, raining hard, and Mila knew the rain turned into snow the higher in the mountains you went.

"I've heard the bogeyman stuff," Ronda said after a minute. "I don't put any stock in it. Whoever's riding that High Line is flesh and blood, just like you and me. He just happens to be a damned evil soul."

Later, when Ronda left the house for groceries, Mila made herself a hot chocolate and logged on to Ronda's Wi-Fi with her phone. She found a map of the High Line on the Internet. The mountain region, from the Cascades through the Rockies. Found Moyie Springs. Found a bunch of the other towns Ronda had mentioned, places where the police had found bodies.

It was a huge stretch of track, five hundred–plus miles. A lot of ground to cover. She would have to prepare wisely. Mila logged on to the rider message board. Started a thread.

I'm looking for the ghost rider on the High Line, she wrote. I know it's a bad idea, so save your advice. Just point me in the right direction, if you can.

She posted the thread. Fingers crossed. If this didn't work, she would have to pump Ronda for whatever information she had. Or she would have to hope to get lucky.

Mila took a screenshot of the map. Saved it on her phone. Drank her hot chocolate and stared out into the rain.

23

Derek Mathers was packing up for the night when his computer chimed, breaking the silence in the Criminal Investigative bullpen in Brooklyn Center, Minnesota. Most of the other agents were already gone for the night; Mathers was working late, taking advantage of Agent Windermere's absence to clear some paperwork, a few minor cases.

In truth, the paperwork could wait, but Mathers had nothing but a cold home waiting for him once he left the office. He'd made reservations for two at some fancy romantic restaurant for the night, anticipating that Windermere would be home by now, but she was still turning over rocks in that Montana mountain town with Stevens, and Mathers was pretty well resigned to a microwaved meal and the hockey game in her absence.

He slid the last of his files from atop his desk and locked them away. Then he turned back to the computer. The chime had come from a program that mirrored Mark Higgins's cloud; SAC Harris had okayed the return of Higgins's laptop, but he'd instructed Mathers to keep a watch on the cloud regardless, at least until Stevens and Windermere's return.

There'd been no activity since Fresno, three or four days ago. Even Mark Higgins was through uploading tractor pictures, by the look of it. But now Mila Scott had photographed something new.

Mathers clicked through to the program, found the picture. A map of the High Line—well, that was no surprise. Stevens and Windermere were already certain she was headed that way, and the Northwestern Railroad had been asked to watch out for her, but Mila Scott wasn't the Bureau's highest priority at the moment. Someone would intercept her eventually.

Out of curiosity, Mathers clicked through to the picture's metadata—the upload location, date, and time—expecting to see another diner's IP address, or maybe a McDonald's. When he ran the IP address through a tracer, though, he had to stare at the results for a beat before it clicked. Then he reached for his phone.

He tried Windermere first. Went straight to voicemail, didn't even get a ring. Tried again, ditto. Was her phone turned off?

Mathers tried Stevens next, got the same story. No ringing, just Stevens's voice on his mailbox greeting. Mathers left a message—"Please call when you can"—and hung up the phone.

Must be somewhere without service. Way up in those mountains.

He looked around his cubicle, debating what to do next. Windermere's service had been spotty since she'd arrived in the northwest. There was no predicting how long she'd be out of range.

Still, he couldn't just sit on this information. Mathers opened his Internet browser. Found the Bureau's Seattle resident office, placed a call.

"I have a person of interest I need checking up on," Mathers told the agent who answered. "She's at a private address. Got a pen?"

24

It was my grandmother's," Ash said, holding the knife up so the blade caught the firelight. "She gave it to me when I was fourteen. She'd had it since she was a teenager, she told me."

Ash handed Mila the knife, and Mila examined it, the long, dangerous blade, the custom-tooled handle. A woman on horseback, her hair flowing behind her.

"It's total Hollywood Indian bullshit, I know," Ash said, laughing. "But I like to think the woman on the handle is her."

"Your grandmother?"

Ash nodded. Found another piece of scrap wood and laid it on the fire. "She raised my mom and my aunt and uncle on her own after my grandfather died," she said. "Never took a handout from anyone. Even when she got old, she still ran the house. Everyone would always listen when she talked."

She stared into the fire, the flames dancing in her eyes. "She was a tough, strong woman, my grandmother. Nobody fucked with her. Nobody."

Mila turned the knife over one more time. Then she handed it back. "What happened to her?"

"My grandmother?" Ash blinked. "She died," she said. "Cancer. She died and it all went to shit with my family, and I had to get out of there. That's why I'm here."

"Oh, I'm sorry," Mila said. "I didn't mean to—"

Ash waved her off. She gazed at the knife some more. "Nobody fucks with me, either," she said after a while. "Not while I have my grandmother with me, you know?"

Ronda came back with provisions. Heavy winter clothes, a coat, boots, and gloves. Food. Water. A compass. A spare phone charger.

"You find this guy, you contact the police, okay?" she told Mila. "Don't go trying to be a hero on your own."

Mila took the phone charger, the warm clothes. Started packing them into her sack beside her own little knife, the first thing she'd ever stolen. It wasn't as nice as Ash's grandmother's knife, didn't have a story behind it, except for how Ash had flirted with the counter boy at the camping outfitter in Toledo, Ohio, distracting him while Mila pocketed the blade. Maybe that was story enough.

"What about weapons?" Mila asked Ronda. "Do you have, like, a gun?"

Ronda looked at her sideways. "What did I just say? You call the police. You don't confront this guy."

Fine, Mila thought. *But still.*

She was thinking, what if this guy surprised her? What if he got the drop? She was thinking about Ash. Ash took her grandmother's knife to the High Line. It wasn't enough.

Ronda was still looking at Mila, waiting for an answer.

"Okay," Mila said. "I'll call the cops. Promise."

Something was moving outside. Cars. Doors slamming, voices. Lights flashed through the rain and played against the windows, red and blue. The police.

Mila stood quickly. "Did *you* call them?"

Ronda saw the lights. She went to the window and looked out, then came back shaking her head no. "I don't turn people in. I wouldn't have bought you this stuff if I'd known they were coming."

"Well, they're here."

Boots on the front steps, heavy. More voices. A knock at the door. Ronda looked back at Mila, her partially filled packsack. "You ready to go?"

Mila sped up her packing. "Give me, like, five minutes."

"You have two," Ronda said. "The cops don't exactly wait to be invited in this neighborhood."

Mila packed her clothes as quick as she could. The food and the water and the compass. Stuffed it all into her packsack and zipped it closed. "Ready."

Ronda was already leading her toward the back door. "Listen," she said. "You'll never make it through the mountains on an open train car."

"I'm going," Mila replied. "I already told you."

Ronda held up her hand. "Listen to me, kiddo. This is the only way you'll make it. You want to know how the rider gets around in those storms?"

Mila stood silent, hand on the back doorknob. *He's a ghost,* she thought. *He's an evil spirit. Superhuman.*

Ronda shook her head, like she could read Mila's mind. "It's not magic," she said. "Listen close. Those really long trains, the coal draggers and some of the hotshots, they can't make it through the mountains with just a couple of engines at the front. They'll put a couple more in the middle of the train, or maybe at the back, remote-controlled. There're no engineers inside them, but it's warm in the cab anyway. No wind, no snow. You just have to look out, because if the bulls catch you in an engine, they'll throw you in jail."

Remote-controlled engines. That's how he gets around.

Ronda reached out, pressed something into Mila's palm. "Every diesel on the Northwestern line uses the same key. The rider has one. Now you have one, too."

"Ash—" Mila said.

"Never found a key. Didn't think she needed one. She swore she could tough it out a few days on a flat."

The knocking started again. A man was calling Ronda's name. Mila stared at her, her mind struggling to process. Ronda nudged her forward. "Time to go, kiddo," she said. "Stay safe."

Mila opened the back door. It was still pouring rain outside. Cold, and just about dark. She started to leave. Then she stopped.

"The rider," she said. "Has anyone ever survived?"

Ronda glanced over her shoulder. "I don't know for certain," she said. "But I never met anyone who bragged about getting away. Now *go*."

She nudged Mila outside, and Mila turned back to thank her, but the door was already closing, and then it was shut and she could hear the lock engage, and she was alone in the cold and the wet again.

She shouldered her packsack and hurried away from the house.

25

Wayne Clairmont didn't have an alibi.

"Didn't know I needed one," he told Stevens and Windermere when they tracked him down at home in Butcher's Creek. "Probably would have made more of an effort if I'd known she was going to go off and die."

Clairmont's home was small and cluttered, a few blocks from the Northwestern tracks. Between the agents and Sheriff Parsons, his living room was full up.

"When's the last time you saw your ex-wife?" Windermere asked Clairmont.

He took a drag from his cigarette. "Guess it was last week, when she came by to borrow the car."

"You lend her the car often?"

"Sometimes." Clairmont laughed, and the laugh turned into a cough. "Only when she's broke, I guess, but that's often enough."

"Do you know what she was doing at the Gold Spike that night?" Stevens asked.

"Oh, the usual, I expect."

Stevens and Windermere traded looks, and Clairmont stubbed out his cigarette, looked past them to Sheriff Parsons.

"You gotta be smart people, you FBI agents," he said. "Do I really have to spell it out for you?"

The Gold Spike was mostly empty. It got emptier when the sheriff walked in.

The bartender was an older guy with a long white beard, looked like he belonged on the back of a Softail in a Harley-Davidson ad. He watched a bunch of his regulars make for the front door, slipping past Parsons and Stevens and Windermere as they did. A couple of women among them, Stevens saw. They didn't exactly look dressed for the weather.

"Help you, Sheriff?" The bartender didn't bother to hide his distaste. Parsons didn't seem to mind.

"Want you to meet some friends of mine, Hank," the sheriff replied. "These here are a couple of real-life government agents. They want to ask you about Kelly-Anne Clairmont. You know her?"

The bartender reached for a rag, wiped it lazily over the surface of the bar. "Sure, I know her. I know what happened to her, too. But I don't have nothing to say about it."

"And why's that?" Windermere asked.

"Because I don't know a damn thing," he replied. "She was in here that night, doing her thing like always, making friends, the usual. She was here, and then she wasn't, and then she was, and then she was gone for good." He put down the rag. "And I daresay I didn't much care either way."

"You remember any of those friends she was making?"

The bartender didn't even pretend to think about it. "Nope." He flung the rag into a sink behind the bar. Then he pointed across the room. "But she might."

Stevens and Windermere followed his gesture and saw one of the escapees trying to sneak her way from the front door to a booth in the corner, a purse lying forgotten on the vinyl. She walked a couple more steps before she realized every eye in the room was on her. Then she stopped. Regarded the assembled like the raccoon by the trash bins.

"Aw," she said. "What kind of bullshit are you all trying to pin on me now?"

The woman's name was Ramona.

"But I go by Joey," she told Stevens and Windermere. "You know, like the Ramones?"

"You like punk music?" Stevens asked her.

"Yeah, some. It's more Ramona Henry isn't exactly the best name for business."

She was a prostitute. She was probably about forty, wore a faded denim miniskirt and a low-cut top, a high schooler's clumsy makeup. She'd agreed to sit with the agents on the promise that they weren't out to bust her, and maybe a free beer for being such a good sport.

Now she drank her Rainier and fidgeted in the booth, clutching her purse to her chest like she was afraid to lose it again.

"What did Kelly-Anne go by?" Windermere said. "Did she have a business name?"

"Not that I ever knew," Ramona said. She made a face. "Then again, she wasn't named anything as bad as Ramona, either."

"Were you here a couple nights back? Did you see her?"

"Honey, I'm always here." Ramona drank. "And yeah, I saw her. It's a small room, isn't it?"

"Was she working that night?"

Ramona gave them a look, like *Why else would you come to a place like this?* "It was a decent night. Steady crowd, lots of guys." She grinned. "The snow closed the roads, too, so we had a, you know, captive audience."

"Business was good, huh? How'd Kelly-Anne seem to be doing that night?"

Ramona emptied the bottle. "Oh, Kelly-Anne did great. She had a real good fricking night. There were these railroad guys in the corner who were all into her, and a couple of truckers over by the pool table. I think she pulled one of each, right after the other. Bam, bam."

A railroader, Stevens thought. *Wouldn't that be convenient?*

"You remember anything about these guys?" Windermere asked. "Where they were coming from? Where they were going?"

"The railroad guy was an engineer, I think," Ramona said. "Came in on a coal train. But he and Kelly-Anne came back to the bar when they were through. Then she left with the truck driver." She scratched her neck. "He was a logging guy, I think. Had a buddy with him. They were gone ten, fifteen minutes. Then he came back alone."

She was looking at her empty beer bottle. Windermere signaled the bartender for another. Waited until the beer was delivered before she asked her next question.

"You think the truck driver could have done anything to her?"

"What, like drive her out of town and leave her dead in the snow, then come back to the bar in fifteen minutes?" Ramona shrugged. "I mean, I'm no expert, but—"

"Maybe he waited to hide the body," Stevens said. "Stashed her somewhere safe and then came back after the bar closed."

"Mmm, no, I don't think so. Those boys left with us, Carli and me. If he came back to the Gold Spike, it wasn't until morning."

Windermere leaned back in the booth. This wasn't helping. "What else do you remember?" she asked. "Anything about that night strike you as odd? Anything stand out in your mind?"

Ramona looked up at the ceiling. "I mean, it was a normal night, I guess. Mostly all regulars, train guys and truckers. There was this one guy in the corner for a little while, but he didn't want company, so we left him alone."

"Did he talk to Kelly-Anne?"

"Sure he did. She was the first to go over there. He shut her down, you know, a little too fast, like he was nervous or something. Wouldn't make eye contact. He *did* have a wedding ring, not that that ever stopped anyone."

"Was he an old guy? Young guy? You remember anything about his face?"

Ramona took a long pull of her beer. "Honey," she said, "you've been doing this long enough, the faces blur together. I don't remember a damn thing about him."

That was it for Ramona. Stevens gave her his card, asked her to think on it some more. Put twenty bucks on her bar tab and told her to be safe.

He stood and made to follow Windermere to where Parsons waited by the door. Then he stopped at the edge of the booth. "You ever hear any rumors of a killer around here?" he asked, turning back. "Someone preying on Native women, runaways and the like?"

Ramona arched her eyebrows. "What, like a serial killer?"

"That kind of thing, yeah. You ever hear any stories?"

She scoffed. "Honey, we don't need a serial killer around here, not my demographic. The guys in these parts seem to dispose of our kind well enough on their own." She drained her second beer and looked him square in the eye. "You want my opinion, you put that girl's death down to natural causes, whether it was cold that killed her or a man. It's all the same thing on this side of the mountain."

26

The rider had never seen a winter this savage.

Another storm was coming. He stood at the window and watched the clouds roll over the mountains in the distance—leaden gray and ominous, portents of cold and wind and blinding snow.

The chatter in town blamed the extreme weather on La Niña, something to do with cooler ocean temperatures, though the science didn't matter so much to the rider. What mattered was what he could see through his windows. Another storm was coming. He would hunt again.

They'd found the last girl only a few days ago. The rider had heard snippets when he went into town for groceries; a rancher had turned her up on the edge of his property. Nobody had known the girl's name; as far as anyone could tell, she was another drunk Indian. There was speculation she was a prostitute.

The rider knew he should be cautious in the aftermath. He knew even one dead woman would attract attention. People would be more alert. The prey would be wary. He would be better off waiting, letting the interest die down.

But the talk of the dead girl had aroused the rider's instincts. It had reminded him of the way the girl had fought beneath him, the fear in her eyes as she'd died. The way she'd screamed uselessly, her voice drowned by the wind.

The rider had let her scream. Let her struggle, flail, fight, wear herself out. Waited until she was exhausted, staring up at him, the fight gone, and then he'd taken his turn.

The girl didn't die easy, but she died all the same. She'd fought again, at the end, as he choked the life from her. Tried to scream again. Didn't matter.

No one was listening to her.

The rider watched the gathering clouds a few minutes longer before he turned away. He felt stifled, tamed, *gelded*, cooped up in his cabin, nothing to do but pace and imagine, replay how he'd punished the woman, how he'd taught her for teasing, lying, manipulating. He'd waited as long as he was able, but he would explode if he didn't find another kill soon.

There were preparations to make; he would have to leave soon, come down off the mountain before the blizzard hit, catch a train and let chance and the weather decide his next victim. He was eager.

As he crossed the small cabin, the rider's gaze fell on the wooden chest on his table. It was medium-sized, the equivalent of two shoe boxes. Its predecessor had been a woman's jewelry case, but the rider had quickly outgrown it. Inside the chest were the memories he'd accumulated, the souvenirs he'd taken from his prey.

The chest never failed to entice him, no matter his hurry. The rider opened the lid, studied the contents: jewelry, scraps of clothing, photographs. A love letter. The rider preferred objects of obvious value to his victims. He liked to watch their eyes widen as he took their totems from them, and he liked to assure them that he would cherish each item long after its owner was gone.

There were engagement rings in the box, all heartbreakingly modest. Photographs of parents and favorite pets. Kelly-Anne's amethyst pendant. A silver dollar—lucky, its owner had claimed, a gift from her stepfather. The rider hoped his luck would be better than hers.

He kept all but one of his souvenirs in the chest. The girl from the first snow, the train hopper in Moyie Springs, the rider kept her fancy knife with him, as a weapon, and also a reminder. The girl had cut him with her knife. She'd hurt him. But the rider had prevailed in the end, as he always did.

The rider knew it was foolish to hold on to so many incriminating tokens. Anyone who found the chest could easily trace the contents. Still, he couldn't resist. Couldn't help but feel proud of the collection he'd amassed, triumphant.

He could still see the faces of the girls at their lockers, whispering to one another and sneaking looks in his direction, their voices carrying, mocking him, all because he'd had the gall to ask the prettiest of them to the dance. Making fun of his stutter, the tear in his shirt. Standing before him, a buffet in short skirts and tight sweaters, teasing him with their bodies, tempting him, delighting in refusing him.

All the rider had ever wanted was to be loving to women, but their behavior had only ever earned his disgust. He'd been *nice* to women, smiled, listened to them. Opened doors, held out chairs, paid for countless dinners. Tolerated every annoyance, jumped through every hoop placed before him, and still no woman had ever returned his affection. No woman had ever treated him with anything but cruelty.

The storm was moving closer, the distant peaks across the valley now vanished in the clouds. The rider closed the chest, carried it across the cabin to the worn rug by his bed. He pulled up a corner of the rug, loosened a floorboard underneath. Tucked the chest into the cavity below, beside his insurance policies—an unregistered pistol and a thousand dollars in twenty-dollar bills.

The rider took the money. Took the pistol. Replaced the loose floorboard and covered it with the rug. He set the money and the pistol on the bed, walked to his wardrobe, and began choosing his camouflage. He would have to dress warmly, he knew. The storm would bring bitter cold.

27

How about your name?" Mathers asked his computer monitor. "Let's start with that, at least."

On the other end of the Skype connection, the woman rolled her eyes. "I'm sure you can figure that out," she said. "You sent a pack of squad cars to my house already. I hope to hell you knew where you were sending them."

"You're Ronda Sixkill," Mathers said. "Is that right?"

Around Mathers, the Criminal Investigative bullpen was dark and quiet, the rest of the office long departed. He'd stuck around after calling the Seattle resident agency, wanting to see if his lead panned out, if the Bureau agents on the coast could follow Mila Scott's latest

IP address to the runaway herself. He was already hearing Windermere's reaction when he told her the good news.

But the Seattle agents couldn't deliver. They hadn't found Mila Scott at Ronda Sixkill's address, though it was clear that Ms. Sixkill—a widower—hadn't been alone for long.

"Two sets of dirty dishes in the sink," the Seattle agent told Mathers. "Rumpled sheets on the guest bed. The homeowner denies any knowledge, but that's nothing new."

Mathers couldn't decide if that news made it better or worse. If Ronda Sixkill *was* hiding Mila Scott, they'd just barely missed her. And like losing a race by a matter of inches, it was always the close calls that stung the most.

"Get Seattle PD scouring the neighborhood," Mathers told the Seattle agent. "The nearest train yards, too. I don't want this girl leaving the city."

Now Ronda Sixkill scowled at Mathers across the Skype connection. "I can't imagine what good you think you're doing right now," she said. "Hauling me in, wasting your time and mine."

She was an older woman, on the bigger side, kind of reminded Mathers of his aunt Francine, who always had candy to dish out and soft, squishy hugs at Thanksgiving. The difference was, Aunt Francine never stopped smiling, and Ronda Sixkill looked downright angry.

"We connected you to a person of interest in a murder investigation," Mathers told her. "You're refusing to tell us what you know about her. That makes you a problem right there on its own."

Sixkill looked away, muttered something Mathers didn't catch. "I beg your pardon?"

"I said I never knew the federal government to care so much about one runaway girl," Sixkill said. "Who lit the fire under your asses? Is her real dad the president, or what?"

"This has nothing to do with her family," Mathers said. "It has to do with the picture of the dead woman she's carrying around on her phone."

Sixkill stared at the camera, blank-faced. "I don't know anything about that."

"No?" Mathers unlocked his desk, flipped through the papers inside until he found what he was looking for, a printout of the dead woman's photograph. He held it up to the monitor so that Ronda Sixkill could see. "Mila Scott has this picture on her phone. The Bureau would really like to know why."

Sixkill's brow creased. "Mila didn't take that picture," she told Mathers. "She had nothing to do with what happened."

"We know that," Mathers told her. "We're ahead of you there. What we don't know, and what we're hoping she can tell us, is *who* the victim is, and who might have done this to her. But we just can't seem to catch up to her long enough to get her to talk to us."

Sixkill was silent a moment. She pursed her lips, seemed to be thinking this over. Finally, she shifted in her seat. Spoke softly, too softly for the microphone to pick up.

Mathers leaned closer. "Say again?"

"I said her name was Ashlyn," Sixkill said. "Ashlyn Southernwood."

28

Windermere checked her phone.

"Damn it, partner," she said. "Still no reception. I feel like I'm back in the Stone Age."

Across the table, Stevens checked his phone, too. No dice. Tried to remember the last time he'd had bars, figured it was somewhere near the state line on the train last night. Wondered if they'd missed anything, out there in the world. Wondered when he'd get a chance to reconnect.

It wasn't likely to be soon, not with this storm moving in. The snow had begun falling in earnest just as night fell in Butcher's Creek, and though Stevens and Windermere had hoped to follow Sheriff Parsons back to the county seat in Libby, ninety miles to the southeast, the worsening weather had changed their minds fast.

"Can't make the drive down in the dark," Deputy Finley told Stevens and Windermere. "Not in this weather."

Which was fine, Stevens thought. He'd white-knuckled the ride out to Jim Benson's ranch, in daylight and sans flying snow. Driving those roads in the dark sounded like a suicide mission, and the weather was only going to get worse. Another foot of snow was coming with this new storm, and from what Stevens could tell, that meant they'd missed their window. He and Windermere would be stuck in Butcher's Creek until the storm passed and the roads cleared, however long that took.

In the meantime, they would have to live without cell service, though from the sound of the wind picking up outside, they'd be lucky to have *power* through the rest of the night.

Stevens and Windermere had holed up at the Gold Spike in a corner booth, Hank the bartender casting shade in their direction from the taps. He'd grudgingly cooked up a handful of chicken fingers and a pile of lukewarm fries and brought them both bottles of Rainier, but it was clear he wasn't enthused about the idea of a couple of federal agents moving in. As far as Stevens was concerned, the feeling was mutual.

It was maddening, being stuck here, the snow all but arresting what little progress they'd made. For all the locals' bleak pronouncements about weather and nature and Sheriff Parsons's "drunk Indians," women were dying here, and Stevens wanted to know why.

Windermere set her bottle down. "What's on your mind? You're zoning out on me."

Stevens blinked back to the here and now. "Sorry," he told her. "It's this storm, I guess. I don't like sitting around when we could be on the job."

"I feel you." Windermere looked around the bar. "I don't know if it's just Hank over there or what, but this whole situation is giving me the creeps."

"You feel it, too, huh?"

"Like there's something weird going on around here," Windermere said. "And we don't know the half of it yet."

Stevens picked at his fries. Didn't reply. Figured they would talk themselves into hysteria if they kept at this tack. He was just about to ask Windermere if she thought they should head back to the hotel when the front door to the Gold Spike swung open and Kerry Finley walked into the bar, trailing swirling snow and icy wind behind her.

The Lincoln County deputy scanned the empty bar, found Stevens and Windermere in the corner, and walked over. She was carrying a stack of files, and she dropped them on the table beside the remains of their chicken fingers.

"Chuck Truman isn't the only one who pays attention to rumors," she said. "And despite what Sheriff Parsons thinks, not everyone in Lincoln County is willing to write these women off." She gestured to the files. "I took these from the sheriff's detachment when I heard you were coming. Figured you might like a little reading when I dropped you at the hotel in Libby tonight, but I guess this bar will have to do." She gestured around the Gold Spike. "I guess this bar will have to do."

Stevens reached for the top file. It was a plain manila folder, filled with newspaper printouts and photocopied police reports. "What is this stuff?"

"This is every unexplained disappearance along the High Line that I could find," Finley told them. "You want to go hunting bogeymen, here's your material."

Outside, the wind gusted—strong. The lights flickered, and the Gold Spike seemed to shudder on its foundation. The young deputy slid into the booth beside Stevens. "Heck, I might even join you," she said, reaching for a file. "It's not like there's anything else going on in this town tonight."

29

What I don't understand," Agent Mathers said, "is why you didn't just come to us in the first place. I mean, this is what we're here for."

Ronda Sixkill was still on the Skype call with the Minnesota FBI agent. She'd told him about Ashlyn Southernwood, about how her friend on the railroad crew had found the body, sent her the picture. How she'd sent it to Mila when Mila insisted on proof.

And then Ronda Sixkill had told him more. She'd told him about the High Line, how train hoppers steered clear. She told him why.

"Bad things happen there," she said. "Women go missing, year after year. It's a suicide run, riding up there alone. It's an invitation to get yourself murdered."

"So why did Ashlyn go?" Agent Mathers wanted to know. "Surely she must have known."

"She did." Ronda paused, seeing Texas Johnny in her mind—gaunt, pale, dying before her eyes. And Ash, who knew the risks, taking her chances just to say her good-byes. "She knew. She had to get out west, though, and fast. She had no other choice."

Agent Mathers chewed on this. "So, okay," he said. "What I don't understand is why you didn't just come to us in the first place."

Ronda Sixkill took a long time to respond, so long that Mathers was afraid the connection had dropped. He was about to repeat the question when she spoke.

"I was married once," she said. "I was young and I didn't know any better. He was the first man who ever really took notice of me, and I imagined that meant he loved me. And since he loved me, I imagined I should try to love him back."

Her gaze went distant a moment, back in some long-ago memory. Then her eyes hardened and she focused on Mathers again.

"He was a jackass," she said. "A real piece of work. I got used to the name-calling and the black eyes and the bruises. It was the broken bones I couldn't quite reconcile. I was still young enough that I could see my life ahead of me, and I was dumb enough to think that if I spoke, somebody would listen."

Mathers could already see where this was going. "Yeah," he said.

"The police came to the hospital where I was laid up, two of them," Sixkill continued. "Men about my husband's age, much older than me. White men. They asked what had happened, and I told them, every last detail. They didn't write it down. They pretended to listen. Then they asked me if I'd had anything to drink that night." She laughed a little, a hard-edged kind of laugh. "They asked me what I'd done to piss him off."

"I'm sorry," Mathers said.

"Why? You didn't do anything." Sixkill shrugged. "Nobody laid charges. Lovers' quarrel, they said. Domestic spat. Bad luck I fell the way I did, but I'd brought it on myself. They walked out, I went home, and it wasn't two weeks before it happened again."

Sixkill reached offscreen, came back with a glass of water. She drank, and then she looked back into the camera.

"I'm not the only woman with a story like that, Agent Mathers, not where I come from. So you ask why I didn't call the police; I'll tell you. Indian women have been dying in this country for years, and the next time a white policeman lifts a hand to put a stop to it, he'll be the first I've heard about."

"We're trying," Mathers said. "I can't speak for your friends, or for the rest of the women who've disappeared on that High Line—"

"*Murdered.* They were murdered, Agent Mathers. Let's call it how it is."

"Okay. Murdered. I don't know what's being done in those cases, or who's investigating, but I can assure you, the FBI takes Ashlyn Southernwood's murder very seriously. So if you have any information that could help us find the killer, I promise you, we'll put it to use."

"I don't know much but what I've already told you," Sixkill replied. "Except that if there is a rider killing women on that High Line, all the snow and cold don't mean anything to him."

She waited for Mathers to ask why. He did.

"The big trains through the mountains, they have remote-controlled engines in the middle and in back. Nobody rides in them, but they have cabs and seats and windows like any other locomotive. And protection from the elements. If you're looking for the ghost rider, that's where you'll find him. And . . ."

She stopped. Looked at Mathers through the camera, looked at him hard, like she was searching for something in his face. Finally, she continued.

"And if you're looking for Mila Scott, you'll find her there, too. I told her about the remote-controlled engines. Gave her a universal key to every Northwestern locomotive before I sent her on her way."

Mathers was already reaching for his phone, typing with his free hand into an Internet search window, looking for contact information for whomever was in charge of the Northwestern High Line.

"Let me ask you one more thing," Mathers said as his search results loaded. "What happened to your husband in the end?"

On his screen, Sixkill laughed again. "You should know," she said. "You read my file, didn't you?"

Mathers looked back at her and realized she was right. Realized he knew what had happened, wondered how he'd forgotten.

But Sixkill told him anyway.

"I killed him," she said. "I stabbed that old bastard through the chest. Did eight years in the Mission Creek women's pen for it, and you know what, Agent Mathers?"

He met her eyes. "What?"

"I would do it all over again," she said. "I'm not sorry about it at all."

30

They sifted through Kerry Finley's cold cases at the Gold Spike, and when Hank kicked them out—with undisguised relish—they took their act back to the Northwestern Hotel.

Outside, the snow fell thick, the wind bitterly cold and fierce, rocking the windowpanes. Windermere took the bed by the door, spreading her files out on the bedspread and forcing herself not to speculate about the last time the innkeeper changed the sheets. She had other things to think about.

Deputy Finley had brought an encyclopedia of unsolved cases. Every dead or missing woman from the Cascades to the Rockies, suspected foul play or not, for the last decade. Windermere counted sixty-five different files.

"Of course, not all of these are going to be murders," Finley said. "And not every homicide is going to be the work of the same guy. People kill each other up here: domestic disputes, robberies—heck, people come here to escape. It stands to reason you'd have a few bad apples."

"So how do we pare this list down?" Windermere asked.

"Proximity to the railroad, for starters." This was Stevens, who had a map open on his bed of Butcher's Creek and the surrounding environs. He'd been studying it for a while.

"Sheriff Truman's Jane Doe was barely ten feet from the tracks when they found her," Stevens said. "And look here." He held up the map, pointed. "That's the Benson ranch. Behind it, that line there is the forestry road where Kelly-Anne Clairmont was discovered."

Windermere looked at the map, got the point quickly. The forestry road curved away from the Benson ranch, dropped down toward the creek itself—and the Northwestern main line. "I remember," she said. "You think the tracks are the connection?"

"It's not just the tracks. There's a passing siding there, see? It's like a stoplight; trains wait there to let other trains by. Mila's friend Warren mentioned stories about a ghost rider up here, remember?"

"Yeah," Windermere said. "He also said the killer wasn't human."

"Human or ghost, if our unsub *is* a rider, he could have ditched Kelly-Anne Clairmont's car and her body, made it look like she'd wandered off into the woods, and he could have hiked down to the tracks, waited for a train to stop, and climbed aboard and vanished. The storm would have covered up his trail."

"It also would have killed him," Finley said. "Riding a train in that blizzard? There's not much protection on those freight cars. You're exposed to the elements. Below-zero temperatures, and that wind? You wouldn't survive a mile."

Windermere looked at Stevens for an answer. She could tell by his expression he didn't have one. "Sure," he said, "but humor me here. We have sixty-odd cold cases and all night on our hands. If this pattern doesn't fit, we'll look for another."

The wind gusted and the lights flickered momentarily. "What do we have to lose?" Stevens said. "From the looks of that storm, we're going to be here awhile."

31

The train slowed. Then it stopped completely. Inside the locomotive, Mila Scott stirred awake.

They were in a town somewhere, a big town, but Mila couldn't tell where. It was light out again, morning, and the rain had turned to snow outside. She'd been on the train all night.

She'd run from Ronda's house until she was sure she'd left the police behind her. Then she huddled in the rain outside a Starbucks, stole the Wi-Fi, and looked up the Northwestern Railroad's main yard online. It had taken her an hour and a half to walk there. She had to keep ducking under awnings and into shadows whenever police cars drove past.

The Northwestern's train yard was huge. It took her a long time to orient herself. There were no campfires around, no signs of any hobo jungles. Nobody to ask for directions. Mila hiked along the tracks to the north end of the yard. Crouched down in a ditch and watched the trains come and go.

The ditch was muddy. The rain never stopped. She was soaking wet and dirty within ten minutes, and it took another hour before she saw what she was looking for: a long train of coal cars, all of them empty, headed back into the mountains to pick up more coal. Mila waited as the twin engines on the front of the train passed. Watched the endless string of coal cars. You could ride in an empty coal car; she'd done it before. It was a cold ride, even in good weather.

The coal cars seemed to stretch on forever. Then the throb of a diesel engine got louder again, and Mila saw another locomotive in the string, sandwiched between the cars. There was no light on in the cab. Its headlight was off. This was what Ronda was talking about.

Mila stood up from the ditch, slipping in the wet grass. She ran, ducking low, across the empty storage tracks, the locomotive grinding toward her. She reached the train just as the locomotive was passing, caught the grab irons and pulled herself onto a stepladder in front of the wheels. The noise was tremendous.

The metal was slippery. Mila held on tight, afraid to move, until she heard the train's whistle and saw a crossing ahead, cars lined up at the gates. She climbed the steps onto the end platform. There was a door in the nose of the engine, a heavy lock hanging from it. Mila tried her key and felt the lock turn. She pulled the door open and stepped inside.

Suddenly, the air was warm again. The rain was gone, and the noise inside was much quieter. Mila poked around the nose, found a bathroom and a little hot plate. Then she climbed up into the cab itself, where there were seats and big windows and a dry floor to sleep on. She watched the city pass by for a little while. Then she made a bed on the floor of the cab, lit a cigarette, smoked it, and tried to rest.

Now, the next morning, it didn't look like there was a train yard outside. There were no storage tracks beside the train. There was just a road parallel to the tracks and the town on the other side—warehouses, gray and industrial.

The engine was still running. Mila could hear it, feel it rumbling. She could hear something else, too, just faintly. After a moment, she realized she was hearing voices.

Mila peered out the rear window of the locomotive. There was a railroad truck parked in the snow beside the tracks and two men standing beside it. As she watched in horror, one of the men walked to the front steps of Mila's locomotive and swung himself aboard.

They were checking the train. The second man hung around by the truck, staring up into the cab. Mila ducked down instinctively, her heartbeat accelerating. Knew the first man would come in through the nose of the locomotive in seconds.

There were two doors at the rear of the cab, one on either side of the train. As quick as she could, Mila scrambled to the far door. She pushed it open and hurried out onto a narrow walkway along the side of the engine. She pulled her packsack out behind her, praying she hadn't left any signs, and caught the door before it slammed shut. Then she slipped under the guardrails and dropped down to the trackside, a longer drop than she'd expected. She hurried through the snow toward the line of warehouses, hearing the engine spool up again behind her, the coal cars clanking together as the train started to move.

Damn it. Guess I'm staying here awhile.

Twenty minutes later, she found a coffee shop near the train yard, a warm mug of coffee and a seat by the heater. She was in Wenatchee,

Washington, on the other side of the Cascade Mountains from Seattle.

Mila's phone was dead, the battery sapped by the cold, but she charged it in the coffee shop and connected to the Wi-Fi. She found an email from Ronda. Call me. Was about to write back, tell Ronda she'd look for a pay phone, when she noticed another email, a response on the rider forum. *I'm looking for the ghost rider on the High Line,* she'd written. *Point me in the right direction, if you can.*

Someone had written back. I can.

32

You already know this is a bad idea, so I won't try to change your mind, the message began. But you should know that you're probably going to die.

The writer was someone named Lazy Jake, a woman, according to her profile. She'd written Mila a private message after replying to her thread, and Mila had ordered another coffee and sat back down to read.

I saw the rider, Lazy Jake wrote.

Or if he wasn't the rider, he was some other creepy-ass dude. I ran into him last summer in Glacier Park, August sometime. I'd been bumming around in East Glacier Park Village for a couple months and I was headed back to the coast. Caught on an empty boxcar on a junk train headed westbound, and he hopped on in Essex, about midway through the park. I watched him climb onboard a few cars down from mine. He saw me, too; we made eye contact briefly. There were a couple other riders in my boxcar, young guys, but I don't think the rider saw them.

Anyway, the train didn't stop again until Whitefish, in the yard there, and we're all hiding out in the boxcar, keeping our heads down, when I hear something moving outside the doors. I think it's the bulls, so I push as far to the back of the car as I can, and then all of a sudden this face pops in through the open doorway and it's him. It's the rider who caught on in Essex, and he's looking at me like I'm dinner.

The guys were talking about getting off in Whitefish, exploring for a few days, but as soon as this guy climbed into my boxcar, I started begging them to stay around. I didn't want to be left alone with this guy. He just gave me the creeps.

So the guys thought about it and decided to stay, and the train started moving again, the three of us at one end of the boxcar, the weirdo rider at the other. He was just huddled up in a corner, wrapped up in his filthy clothes, stealing glances my way, trying not to let on, but every now and then I would catch him, and his eyes would dart off again, fast, like he was trying to pretend he hadn't just been totally eye-fucking me.

This went on for at least an hour before the train finally slowed down at some siding in the middle of nowhere. Then he gathered his stuff and just stepped off the train; didn't say a word, just disappeared into the forest like a ghost. And me and the guys all watched him go, and then we talked about how weird he was, all the way to Spokane.

Mila lowered the phone. It was a creepy story, sure, but there were lots of creepy riders on the rails. What made Lazy Jake so sure that this creep was *the* creep?

But Lazy Jake had anticipated the question. You're wondering how I know it was him, she'd written. You're thinking I'm probably crazy, or imagining things or just weird. And you might be right. I thought about it later, and I kind of felt stupid. But then I heard about this:

She'd attached a link. It was a news article from the *Flathead Beacon*, dated September 16. BODY FOUND IN ESSEX RAVINE, read the headline. Below was a picture of a dark-haired young woman.

33

Kasha Graham, twenty-three," Windermere read. "Kitchen staff at the Summit Inn, Essex, Montana. Went missing August twenty-fifth of last year, body found in a ravine just outside town on the fifteenth of September. Autopsy inconclusive due to advanced decomposition, but in the absence of any firm signs of foul play, the coroner ruled she'd probably just fallen."

Windermere looked up. "Essex is apparently a big railroad town," she told Stevens and Deputy Finley. "Just about every train going over the Rockies stops there to change crews. Judging from this map, the railroad's about all it's got going for it, that and the Summit Inn."

She passed the file across the bed to Stevens, who flipped it open and examined the picture inside. A candid shot, probably downloaded from Facebook, of Kasha Graham and three other young people posing outside the Summit Inn. They wore kitchen whites and big smiles;

the background was blue sky and high mountains. Kasha had dark hair and fine features. She looked happy.

"Did they question these people?" Stevens asked, more to himself than to Windermere. "Her coworkers?" He flipped through the thin file, the missing persons report, the results of a rather cursory autopsy. The Flathead County sheriff's department *had* questioned the staff at the Summit Inn, but nobody knew anything. Kasha had disappeared on her day off. She'd told her coworkers she was going for a walk, which wasn't abnormal; it was a beautiful day, and there really wasn't much to do besides walk. She hadn't come back.

Stevens put down the file. Rubbed his eyes. Outside, the blizzard continued, blowing snow and howling wind. It was morning now; Stevens, Windermere, and Finley had been sorting through the stack of files for hours. They'd pared the stack down to twenty-five or so cases that looked like they might fit the pattern.

Young women, many—but not all—of Native American descent, all gone missing or found dead within a mile of the Northwestern main line. Roughly half of the women had never been found. Of the rest, five or six of the deaths had been ruled homicides. The remainder were deemed accidental.

Kasha Graham. Kelly-Anne Clairmont. Lucy Baker. Gale Fowler. Alberta Chipman. Nicole Germain. They were waitresses, gas station clerks, runaways. Some were unemployed. Some had criminal records; some were reportedly prostitutes. Some of the women hadn't been identified. They were itinerants, vagrants, some of them train hoppers. None of their disappearances had raised much of a fuss.

Stevens had forced himself to be cautious as he reviewed the cases, knew he was already biased. Knew the deaths of Kelly-Anne Clairmont and Mila Scott's rider friend had colored his opinion, had him looking for ghosts. Now, though, armed with this stack of twenty-five dead or missing women, Stevens was ready to believe there was something afoot.

It was just a damn shame they couldn't do anything about it. The phone lines in Butcher's Creek had gone down in the night. Cell service was still a pipe dream, ditto an Internet connection. Until the storm abated, Stevens and Windermere were stuck in dark territory and it didn't sit well with Stevens.

He stood. Paced to the window, looked out at the storm, a Northwestern coal train grinding eastbound just barely visible in the flying snow. Stevens watched until the last car was gone. Then he turned back to the others.

"Let's figure this out. Sooner or later, this storm is going to blow over, and I want to be ready when it does. We need to get in contact with every sheriff's department responsible for those cases," he said, pointing to the stack. "We're going to need to reopen every investigation, take it from the top. See if we can't put together a profile on this guy."

"We're working blind," Windermere said. "If there's really one killer, we don't know a damn thing about him except he likes vulnerable women and apparently hops freights."

"That's a start," Stevens said. "We'll run the fingerprints Sheriff Parsons lifted from Kelly-Anne Clairmont's car and work through the coroner's reports for any DNA evidence, signs of sexual assault, or a preferred murder weapon, whether he's strangling them all or otherwise."

"This is going to be tough," Finley said. "Some of these cases are three, four years old. I get what you're trying to do, but trails run cold, don't they? Memories fade, evidence disappears. Heck, some of the sheriffs you'll want to talk to have probably been voted out by now."

"We'll talk to them anyway," Windermere said. "We're the FBI,

Deputy. You all like to play up this bumpkin routine, but I'm not buying it. I refuse to believe there aren't competent investigators in these mountains and that they won't want to help us solve this thing."

Finley looked her in the eye. "I'll help you," she said. "We'll get it done."

"Good." Windermere gestured out the window, the snow nowhere near slowing. "Now all we have to do is hope Mother Nature cuts us a break sometime soon."

34

Ashlyn Southernwood.

Mathers couldn't get through to Windermere or Stevens. He'd tried through the night after ending the Skype conversation with Ronda Sixkill, and he'd tried Carla's number in the morning, as soon as he woke up. Still nothing. Straight to voicemail. Wherever they were, they were deep out of range.

Mathers watched the Weather Channel as he prepared for work. Turned up the volume when the national forecast came on—the Pacific Northwest, the Rocky Mountains. The meteorologist was talking about cold ocean temperatures, the jet stream. He was saying that this was a significant weather event, this frigid, snowy winter; how global warming, paradoxically, was only going to make it worse. There was another storm in northern Montana and the Idaho panhandle, he said, the second big blast in just over a week.

Mathers watched the weather map, the news footage from northern Idaho. The mountain passes closed, the towns inundated. The blizzard expected to rage another day, at least.

And Stevens and Windermere were somewhere in the middle of it. Mathers turned off the TV. The thought of Carla out there was unsettling.

He kept trying Windermere's cell. Tried the sheriff's department in Libby, Montana, but could only find out that the FBI agents were holed up with a deputy in some place called Butcher's Creek, so small it didn't have a police force. When Mathers tried the hotel there, he couldn't get a connection.

The goddamn storm. Mathers forced himself to switch focus. Ronda Sixkill had given him plenty to work with; no sense sitting around waiting for Stevens and Windermere to solve the case by themselves. He set out to find Ashlyn Southernwood.

The search took most of the morning, and when Mathers finally tracked down Ashlyn Southernwood, he found she wasn't a Southernwood at all. She was a Corbine, Ashlyn Corbine, from the Bad River Reservation in northern Wisconsin.

"Southernwood was my mother's last name," Nicole Corbine told Mathers when he reached her by phone. "That girl was crazy about her grandmother, I'll say that about her. It was just after she died that Ash took off out of here."

If Nicole Corbine was upset by the news of her daughter's death, she wasn't showing it. "It's not like I'm *happy* about it, mind you," she said, sighing. "It's just not all that unexpected. That girl's been gone a long time, and we weren't all that close to begin with."

"When did she run away?"

"Just after my mother died, like I said. That would have been, what, five or six years ago. Ash was fifteen."

Fifteen, Mathers thought. *And you didn't lose your mind looking for her?*

Nicole Corbine must have interpreted his silence as a question. "I had four other kids to raise," she said, though not defensively. "Ash was her own girl, bright and stubborn as hell. She wanted off the reservation, and there wasn't anything I could do to stop her. It was only her gran keeping her around. When she died, like I said . . ."

"You ever hear from her?"

"Oh, sure. She sent a couple letters to her brothers, a postcard or two. Sometimes she called, if it was a big holiday. Sometimes she didn't. She seemed happy, so I tried not to worry. Wasn't much good worrying would have done, you know?"

"Yeah," Mathers said, "I guess I do. You mind if I send you some pictures of her? You can confirm it's your daughter?"

"Go ahead, if you have to. I guess it's standard procedure in something like this, huh?" She paused, and when she continued, her voice hitched, just a little. "It was bad, wasn't it? What they did to her, was it bad?"

"It was bad," Mathers said, suddenly feeling like he had an anvil on his chest. "I'm sorry."

Nicole Corbine was quiet for another beat. When she spoke again, her voice was small. "Do they know who killed . . . who did it?"

"We're working on it," Mathers told her. "Two of our best agents are on the case."

"So you don't know."

"Not yet, but we'll find him. I'm sure we will."

"I guess you have to say that," Corbine said. "These kinds of situations."

"No, I don't," Mathers replied. "I mean it."

The line went silent again. Then Corbine cleared her throat. "I wish she hadn't gone, you know? Like, I know I couldn't have kept her here with a team of horses, but it's still . . ." She trailed off. "I miss her."

"I'm sorry." The words seemed insignificant, minuscule. "I really am."

"Yeah. Well, send those pictures if you have to." Corbine's voice was stronger again. "And good luck finding whoever did it."

"I'll keep you posted," Mathers told her. "We'll get him."

"Yeah," Corbine said. "Okay." Then the line went dead, and she was gone.

35

It was supposed to be like a vision quest," Ash said. She laughed. "Not that I believe in that shit, but, you know, it's supposed to be like an Anishinaabe tradition, a rite of passage or whatever. So I kind of told myself that's what I was doing when I left, trying to find *myself."*

Mila gripped the grab irons, dangled her feet off the side of the reefer car. Watched the Everglades pass, miles of endless swamp. The reefer car was like a boxcar, except it had a little cubby on the end for the freezer unit. Ash and Mila had climbed inside the cubby somewhere in southern Florida. They were headed north.

Sometimes the reefer unit would kick on, every half hour or so, drowning out the rest of the noise and making it impossible to talk. Then they would just laugh and sit at the edge of the cubbyhole and stare out at the world as it passed.

But the reefer had shut off again, and Ash was talking, and Mila was asking questions she'd asked a hundred times before, but that she asked again anyway because, well, there was nothing else to do. And Mila liked to hear Ash talk.

"My grandmother died and my mom was busy with my brothers," Ash said. "And I looked around at my friends and they all seemed, you know, happy *to be stuck in Diaperville—no joke, that's the name of the town—for the rest of their lives. And I didn't want that. I wanted to be like my grandmother. I wanted to travel and see things and actually* be *somebody. So I climbed on a freight train headed for Duluth, and I haven't really stopped for long ever since."*

"So was it worth it?"

"Was it worth it?" Ash gave Mila a look. Smacked her on the shoulder a little. "Look around, girl. We're freaking free. *No responsibilities. Nothing to do. We can go where we want, and nobody can stop us."*

Mila followed Ash's gaze, out the cubbyhole and across the passing scenery. She still felt cowed by this life, like she didn't quite belong, like sooner or later she would screw up and do something awful, something she would regret forever. But Ash didn't seem to care about any of that. Ash seemed born to hop trains.

"Do you ever miss home?" Mila asked her.

"I miss my grandmother, sure. I miss her stories and I always *miss her cooking. I wish she wasn't gone, but at the same time, I don't. If she was alive, I wouldn't be here right now." She cocked her head. "And you'd probably be dead, girl. Nobody to show you how to survive in the jungle."*

"I would have survived," Mila said, though she knew it wasn't true. "But do you ever miss your family? Like your mom and your brothers?"

Ash's smile disappeared. She watched the scenery pass, her eyes distant. "I mean, of course I do. They're my family, aren't they?"

"Would you ever go back?"

Ash didn't answer right away. "I don't know. I think about it sometimes."

"And?"

"And?" Ash blinked back to the present. Smiled, but kind of sad. Started to say something else, but then the reefer unit kicked on, drowning her out, and there was nothing to do but laugh and ride on in silence.

Mila awoke suddenly, out of breath, her heart pounding. Sat up and looked around the cab of the locomotive, tensed, sure she'd heard voices. Sure someone was coming to find her.

But there weren't any voices. The train rumbled on. Mila pulled herself up to the driver's seat and looked out the window. The snow was still falling, but it had eased up a little bit. She could see the moon above the mountains—or a bright patch through the clouds, at least.

She was back in a remote-controlled engine. She'd caught on at the outskirts of Wenatchee, resolved to stay alert, watch out for bulls and other train people, cover as much ground as she could and hope she didn't get caught.

The woman on the forum, Lazy Jake, had given Mila a destination. **The siding where he jumped, she'd written. It was just north of some town called Anchor Falls, a ways north of Whitefish. Mountain country. We passed the little post office, and I remember one of the guys saying the name. Anyway, the siding was north of there, in the middle of nowhere. I**

have no idea why he chose to jump off the train at that spot, but he sure looked like he knew where he was going.

Mila rubbed the sleep from her eyes and watched out the window. Waited for a town, a siding, some kind of sign. Brought up the map on her phone and tried to estimate how far the train had gone while she'd slept. Outside was just forest, never-ending trees.

And then the train slowed at another small town, another crew-change point, someplace called Bonners Ferry, a railroad truck waiting by the tracks. Mila had just enough time to look across at the town—a gas station, a handful of restaurants and a couple dingy bars, a few houses and railroad buildings—before she had to duck away so the railroad men wouldn't see her.

Five minutes later, the engine loaded up again and the train inched back out onto the main line. Mila stayed low until she was sure the town was behind her. Then she climbed up into the driver's seat again and closed her eyes, tried to sleep, as she waited to make Anchor Falls.

36

The man wasn't much to look at, when Pamela Moody first saw him. He was crammed into a booth at the back of the Hungry Horse Saloon, an unfamiliar face among a fair crowd of regulars, the bar pretty well packed, everyone looking for a place to wait out the storm. He was dressed for the weather, bundled up in an old army coat, a heavy wool watch cap. Her eyes had been drawn to the way the bar lights caught the snowmelt on his clothing, in his beard, tiny water droplets gleaming like crystal, unexpectedly bright.

He'd been watching her. That was the next thing she noticed, how he turned away quickly as soon as she made eye contact, his gaze darting down to the table, furtive. When he looked up at her again, it was like he was forcing himself to meet her eyes, like everything in his being was trying to pull him away.

"Something to drink?" she asked him.

"Rainier," he replied, too loud, abruptly, like he wasn't used to talking—or maybe he wasn't used to being taken seriously. There was defiance in his voice, a challenge. He wasn't comfortable here. She could feel his eyes on her as she went for his beer, tracking her movements across the bar.

When she turned around, though, the bottle in her hand, he *wasn't* looking at her, but down at the table, hunched into himself and drawn into the shadows, and she felt a brief burst of pity for him, a quiet, wilting man in a room full of blue-collar beer swiggers, macho-man types.

She set the bottle in front of him, and the man put a five-dollar bill on the table and looked up at her again, something desperate in his expression, some kind of yearning, like there was something he wanted to say but just couldn't. She waited a beat, but he couldn't find the nerve, and she took the money and left him to his beer, feeling his eyes on her every time she crossed the room.

He didn't move much the rest of the night. She brought him two more Rainiers, and he paid and tipped well again, and when she went back to his booth a while later to see about a fourth, he was gone, no trace of him but the puddle of snowmelt where his hat had lain on the booth's vinyl seat.

But now he'd showed up again, surprised her in the parking lot outside the saloon, the bar closed and quiet, the lot all but empty, only her boss's Silverado and her man's F-150 left in the snow. The storm was still howling, wind gusting, the air white, and she'd slogged through at least a foot of new powder on her way to the truck, could hardly see back to the saloon when she reached it.

She was standing at the driver's-side door, fumbling with her keys, when she felt him behind her. Couldn't have heard him over the wind, couldn't have seen him through the snow. She was alone one minute, and the next he was there, ten feet from the truck when she turned around.

"Car won't start," he said. Still wouldn't look her in the eye. "Battery, I guess. You wouldn't happen to have jumper cables?"

Pamela glanced back toward the saloon, a reflex, Reg still inside, finishing the count. The way the snow was blowing, he wouldn't see her truck from the door. Wouldn't hear her calling over the wind. *Shit.*

She *did* have jumper cables, stashed under the back bench, could help the guy out if she wanted, but everything about this situation was screaming that something was wrong. Telling Pamela to get in the truck, lock the doors, haul ass for home. Leave this creepy guy here and let Reg deal with him.

The man tried a smile, but it came off as awkward as the rest of his act. "I've been out here an hour," he said. "Pretty well stranded. Think you could help me out?"

Shit, shit, shit. But just being awkward wasn't a crime, was it? And what the hell, he'd tipped her decent. What kind of Montanan would she be to abandon a guy in a snowstorm?

Of all the men in that bar for you to worry about, she thought, *this guy is the* least *likely.*

"Yeah, I have cables," she said finally. "Back of my truck. Where are you parked?"

The man waved into the blizzard somewhere. "Across that way. Won't take more than a minute of your time, I promise."

"Well, all right." She took her keys from her purse, turned to unlock the truck. *Felt* him move again, saw him, too, this time, a shadow in the corner of her eye. Then something jarred her head and she was falling, and then she was down in the snow and he was standing above her, looking down at her, his lip curled up again, but this wasn't a smile. This was something mean, hateful, *hungry*.

Pamela tried to speak, but she couldn't, and then her vision started to go dark at the edges, and she fought it, or tried to, but the dark came on too strong. Then she was out, for minutes or hours or days, and she awoke with a fierce headache and a need to throw up. The man was there, watching her, and he wasn't looking away anymore, didn't look nearly so shy, and all Pamela Moody wanted in the world was to go back to the darkness again.

37

The rider stepped out of the locomotive's cab as the train slowed for the siding. He climbed down the ladder and watched the forest for the telltale break in the trees. The train drifted to a stop, a red signal in the distance. The rider dropped off the locomotive and into the snow. Hurried across the main track toward the forest on the other side.

His snowmobile lay hidden where he'd left it, as always. It was covered in snow, a foot at least, fresh. The rider pulled the cover off of the machine and turned the key in the ignition. The engine rumbled to life, reliable as always. The rider liked reliable. He liked trucks that never failed, trains that ran through freak storms. He liked law enforcement that never bothered to look too hard at a dead woman's body.

And the law in the mountains was nothing if not reliable. The rider chose drug addicts, prostitutes, the homeless, and runaways. He chose women for whom an early death wasn't an *if* question, but a *when*. He chose women the mountains wouldn't miss, women who died easy. Women who nobody saw.

The rider had been careful when he took Pamela Moody. He'd worn a condom, as always. He'd wiped her truck for fingerprints, tried to avoid touching her body with his bare skin as much as he could. He'd tried his best; sometimes his anger took over when he was punishing these women. Sometimes he blacked out and couldn't help what he did.

The odds were almost certain that nobody would find Pamela Moody's body, at least not until spring thaw. The snow would bury her until the weather warmed, and then the animals would have their way with what remained. Maybe a hiker would stumble onto her bones sometime in the summer. Someone would find her truck. What story would they tell themselves?

She was a bar waitress. Maybe she turned tricks on the side. Maybe it was drugs, alcohol. She got drunk one night and drove off in a storm. It's a miracle she made it as far as she did before . . .

Before the inevitable happened.

The rider sat astride his snowmobile, letting the engine warm. Dug into his pocket for his latest souvenir. He'd been creative this time. He'd been bold.

PAMELA MOODY, read the label on the inhaler. FOR ORAL INHALATION. TAKE AS DIRECTED.

The rider had waited until Pamela Moody was disposed of before he'd claimed the inhaler. He'd taken it from the floor of her truck, carried it with him to the train, studied it in the cab of the locomotive as the train rumbled westward. He saw Pamela Moody's panicked eyes. Heard her frantic gasps for air. The memory pleased him. He would cherish it for a very long time.

The rider pocketed the inhaler. Reversed the snowmobile from its hiding place. Aimed it up the mountain, through the fresh snow. He was tired. He was eager to get home.

38

The blizzard raged through Butcher's Creek all day and another night, stranding Stevens and Windermere in the railroad hotel with Deputy Finley's stack of files and the Gold Spike's dwindling supply of food and drink.

But on the morning of the second day, just when Windermere was starting to worry that old Hank would run out of chicken fingers—or beer—the storm showed signs of calming. By nine o'clock or thereabouts, the snow had slowed to just a scattering of flakes, and Windermere could look from the hotel window clear across the train tracks to the creek on the other side, a marked improvement from the zero-visibility conditions the day before. By eleven, a snowplow had rolled through town, cleaning up the main road. And by eleven fifteen, Stevens and Windermere were packed up in Finley's Lincoln County SUV, headed east.

"Closest cell service is probably in Eureka, about thirty miles from here," the deputy told them as she drove. "I figure we'll head up there, check in with our respective people, get this investigation rolling."

Damn right, Windermere thought. *And step on it.* She'd been stewing in that crummy hotel for far too long, reviewing the twenty-five probable cases with Stevens until she was sure they could recite the details of each one back to front. Now Windermere was sick of planning. They'd been groping in the dark for far too long on this thing already. The weather had cleared; it was time to execute.

The drive to Eureka took nearly an hour. Windermere watched her phone the whole way. Finally found bars on the outskirts of town, and as soon as the bars came, so did the messages.

Forty missed calls, roughly half of them from Mathers. Another ten from Drew Harris, and one or two from the cable company trying to sell her on the HBO package. One look at Stevens in the backseat and Windermere knew he was seeing the same action.

"Mathers called," he said when he caught her watching him. "He called a lot."

"Yeah, no kidding." Windermere punched redial. "Let's hope he had more to say than just he misses us."

"*Carla.*"

Mathers sounded relieved, and as loath as Windermere was to admit it, she was kind of glad. It was good to hear his voice—nothing against Kirk Stevens and Kerry Finley, but Windermere was starting to get lonely for her big, dumb boyfriend. Not that she'd ever tell him that.

"Ran into a bit of snow, Mathers," she said. "You getting separation anxiety already?"

"A little bit, I won't lie," Mathers replied. "But mostly I wanted to catch you up on your case."

"Catch *me* up?" Windermere snorted. "You think you know something I don't?"

"I'd bet on it."

Finley pulled the SUV off the highway and parked in front of a small sheriff's detachment. The deputy held up five fingers—*five minutes*—at Windermere, who nodded *Go ahead*. She turned her attention back to the phone as Finley climbed from the car.

"Okay, Mathers," she said, switching her phone to speaker. "I have Stevens listening in, so don't get kinky on me. Just give us the facts."

"The facts." Mathers inhaled, like he was about to run down a list. "Okay, first of all, your Jane Doe is an Anishinaabe woman from Wisconsin named Ashlyn Corbine, aka Ashlyn Southernwood. She ran away from home after the death of her grandmother six years ago and had apparently been riding trains ever since. Her mother didn't put out a search for her because she figured her daughter was happier on the rails."

Windermere swapped glances with Stevens. "Huh. How'd you ID her?"

"Easy. A woman named Ronda Sixkill gave me her name."

"Ronda . . . Sixkill. Okay?"

"Mila Scott uploaded a picture from an IP address associated with Ms. Sixkill's personal Internet connection, in Seattle. I put the Seattle office on the case, and they got me Ronda Sixkill."

"What about Mila Scott?" Stevens asked.

"I'll get to that," Mathers said. "Ronda Sixkill knew Ashlyn, and she knows Mila, too. She believes Ashlyn was murdered by a serial killer who haunts the Northwestern Railroad's High Line, and apparently Mila feels the same."

"Yeah, we're kind of feeling that way ourselves," Windermere replied. "Last we heard, Mila was trying to get out to the High Line to do some amateur sleuthing."

"But she couldn't ride a freight train out here in this weather," Stevens said. "Too cold."

"Yeah," Mathers said. "That's what everyone I talked to thought, too. But apparently we just missed Mila Scott at Ms. Sixkill's house, and she was headed east on the next available train."

"That can't be right. She'll die."

"Not so much." Mathers let it hang, and Windermere knew this was the punch line. "Those big coal trains through the mountains, they use multiple engines, but only one crew. Sometimes they put a remote-controlled engine in the middle of the train."

Windermere flashed back to the freight trains they'd seen on the Northwestern main line. She could remember seeing engines in the middle and on the rear of the trains. "Yeah, okay. Aren't they all locked up?"

"They are, but they all use the same key. You get a Northwestern key, you can ride any locomotive on the railroad. They're heated; they have bathrooms and kitchen facilities. Ronda Sixkill had a Northwestern key. She gave it to Mila."

Windermere stared at her phone. "So you're saying this girl is looking for our serial killer, riding toward us right now, in a freaking *heated train engine*, Derek?"

"I assume so. I have Northwestern Railroad police checking every remote engine that comes through the Cascade Mountains, but so far they haven't turned up any sign of her. So it could be I'm totally wrong about this." He coughed. "But that's not the only thing about these remote engines, Carla."

He waited. Windermere waited. Stevens got it first. "Those trains run in any weather," he said. "Even storms like yesterday, those trains were running."

"Yep," Mathers said. "Exactly."

Through the SUV's windshield, Windermere watched Kerry Finley come out of the sheriff's detachment and cross toward the vehicle, her mouth a thin line, her brow creased with worry. But Stevens was still talking.

"If Mila Scott could get her hands on a key, it's safe to say she's not the only one," he was saying. "We've been wondering how our killer could get around in these storms. Prevailing opinion has been it's impossible."

"Yeah, well," Mathers said. "It sounds like prevailing opinion is wrong."

Finley opened the driver's door of the SUV. Looked in at Stevens and Windermere, then noticed the phone. Opened her mouth like she had something important to say.

"One second, Derek," Windermere said. She turned to Finley. "What's up?"

"Sheriff's department just heard from our counterparts in Flathead County," she said. "They had a young woman go missing last night down in Hungry Horse. Haven't turned up any sign of her."

Windermere felt her body go numb. Last night, while they'd been stuck in that shitty hotel in that nothing town, believing there was no way the killer could be anything but stuck just as bad. Damn it all.

Stevens was already buckling his seat belt. So was Finley. "He did it again," Windermere said, though they all knew it already. "He got another one."

39

She was alive.

Pam Moody woke up in a monochrome wasteland. Flat, lifeless white and dull, dirty gray. Hard, jagged black. And red, too; there was plenty of red. But even the red seemed devoid of color.

Her head buzzed. She was groggy. She thought she'd been dreaming. Then the pain came back, sudden and unrelenting—hurt like a thousand knives stabbing into her body—and she could feel the man's hands on her throat again, remembered very clearly what he'd done.

She kept trying to block out what was happening. Shield her mind, retreat into some kind of fantasy world, ignore the awful reality, the man and his anger and the back of Darryl's truck.

She'd done it before. This wasn't the first time a man had tried to take from her. She'd been younger the last time, still stupid and naive. She'd tried to fight, kicked and clawed, and it was only after she'd exhausted herself and couldn't fight anymore that she forced her mind to drift away from her body.

Pam was older now. She saw no reason to fool herself. She was smaller than the man who'd knocked her out in the parking lot. She wasn't nearly as strong. She was still dazed from how he'd hit her; there was no point in fighting.

She wanted to go away. That's all. She wanted to disappear back into her fantasy world, Christmas morning in Columbia Falls, horseback riding with her dad—her happy place. She could go there, go back, and when she returned, the man would be finished. The hard part would be over. She could pull herself together, go home. She would try to decide what to tell Darryl.

You were probably asking for it, teasing those men at the bar again. Flirting with them all night; what did you think would happen?

Maybe she wouldn't tell Darryl. She would shower and climb into bed and try to forget this had ever happened.

But the man wouldn't let her escape. His eyes, they stared down at her in the backseat of Darryl's truck, glinting in the dim glow from the instrument panel as he whispered to her, cursed her out—vile, awful, profane things.

He finished quickly. That was her mercy. He'd been unable to function until he'd wrapped his hand around her throat, the smooth leather glove choking the breath from her lungs. Then, panting heavily, muttering, swearing, he'd lifted her skirt and torn off her underwear and done what he'd wanted, crude and rough and violent, single-minded.

She couldn't breathe. Even when he finished, when he released his grip on her throat, she was strangling. Wheezing, coughing, gasping for air and not getting any, she twisted and fought beneath him, reaching for her purse and the inhaler inside, cursing herself, her body, the man who kept her pinned beneath him.

The man followed her eyes. He saw the desperation and seemed to glean its meaning. He reached into the front seat of the truck, pulled her purse into the back. Rummaged inside until he found what she wanted.

Pamela fought to breathe, her body betraying her, her panic increasing. The man held the inhaler aloft. Then he tossed it to the floor beside her. Laughed as she scrambled for it, as she held it to her mouth greedily. Watched her. Those eyes. He pulled his gloves tight, slow and deliberate. Smoothed the leather, flexed his fingers.

"Relax," he said. "It will be over soon."

But it hadn't been over.

He'd meant to kill her. He'd dragged her from the truck, dropped her in the snow, and knelt over her, hands on her throat again. Choked the breath from her, savage and unyielding, until her lungs screamed for air and her vision went dark.

Then he'd dragged her. She watched him through lidded eyes, semiconscious. He took her to the edge of a long drop, and she felt the snow, the biting wind swirl up from the abyss. He wasn't looking at her now. Those eyes were dull, his jaw set, an automaton fulfilling a task. He'd rolled her to the edge. Then he'd shoved her over, and she'd been too weak to stop him, too weak to do anything but fall.

She fell. She hit rock and bounced and hit rock again, and the pain came, everywhere, piercing and hot. Somewhere in the distance, she heard Darryl's truck come to life. She lay there and watched the snow and waited for her body to shut down.

He'd meant to kill her, she knew. She'd imagined he would. But here, now, she'd woken up. It was daylight, and she was alive. Barely.

Pamela Moody lay on her back and stared up at her surroundings, snow and rock and flat leaden sky, and wondered how long it would take for nature to finish the job.

40

Pamela Moody," Finley read from her notes. "Waitress at the Hungry Horse Saloon, twenty-five years old. Didn't come home from her shift last night; boyfriend called the deputies this morning. No sign of her truck at the saloon, and her boss swears he saw her leave."

The deputy had driven Stevens and Windermere down to Hungry Horse, a tiny village on the banks of the Flathead River at the fringe of Glacier National Park, sixty miles to the southeast of Butcher's Creek. The Northwestern Railroad's main line through the Rockies skirted the village on the northern side of the river; Stevens could see a passing siding and a parked junk train as Finley drove them into town. He searched down the line of freight cars for a remote engine, didn't see one—but that didn't make him feel any better.

They'd ordered a stop to all Northwestern trains in the area before they'd left Eureka, instructing the engine crews and railroad bulls to search every remote-controlled unit before proceeding. There'd been pushback from the railroad, but not much; if riders were breaking into the railroad's multimillion-dollar locomotives, the Northwestern management wanted it stopped as much as anyone. So far, nobody had reported anything suspicious, and Stevens feared that trend would continue. If the person responsible for Pamela Moody's disappearance had indeed hopped a freight, he'd had hours to escape before Stevens and Windermere sounded the alarm.

Finley had parked her SUV outside the bar where Pamela Moody had worked, the parking lot plowed down to the hard-packed snow, the rest piled in huge eight-foot piles along the fringes. The Flathead County deputy was waiting there to fill them in on the search efforts so far.

The deputy looked like he was a few years older than Stevens. A weathered face, a genuine smile. His name was Michael Dillman, and he shook each of their hands in turn before gesturing across the lot to the saloon.

"Pam Moody worked the night shift at the Horse last night. Closed up at two and was out around quarter to three, according to her boss. He watched her walk out the door, and he swears that's the last he saw of her."

The Hungry Horse Saloon was a modest affair, low-lying, few windows, a backlit sign above the door with more bulbs burned out than functional. It was the only bar in town, but given the size of the town, that wasn't saying much.

"Her boyfriend called it in," Stevens said. "Is that right?"

Dillman cocked his head a little. "He didn't so much call it in as he created a ruckus," he said. "Turned up at Ms. Moody's boss's place around eight thirty this morning, pistol in hand, demanding Reg Winter—that's the boss—let him in. Apparently, Winter had been making passes at Ms. Moody for a while now, and Greer—that's the boyfriend, Darryl Greer—figured she must have finally given in. Winter called me, and I managed to calm Greer down, disarm him, put the story together."

"And you didn't find Pamela Moody at Winter's house, obviously," Windermere said.

"No, ma'am. Mr. Winter was adamant he hadn't seen Ms. Moody since she left the bar."

"So what's the boyfriend's background?"

Dillman pulled out a notepad. "Darryl Greer, thirty years old. Works at the aluminum plant down the road in Conkelley—or he did, until the plant closed. He says he usually falls asleep before Ms. Moody gets home. Usually wakes up when she climbs into bed after her shift, but he woke up to sunlight this morning and knew something was wrong."

"He have an alibi for last night?"

"No, ma'am. He watched a hockey game until the cable gave out. Then he fell asleep."

Stevens surveyed the lot. The Hungry Horse Saloon sat on the main drag, across from a couple gas stations and a strip of fast-food restaurants, the highway running right through the middle of town, parallel to the river and the train tracks. There were a couple of bridges over the river, access roads to the tracks and the mountains beyond. Neither of the bridges were more than a mile from the saloon, though in a storm, Stevens knew, even a mile would have seemed like a marathon.

Easy, he thought. *Don't go chasing bogeymen yet.*

He turned back to Dillman. "Winter and Greer, where are they now?"

Dillman pointed down the street. "At the station," he said. "I heard you all were coming, so I brought them in, made them promise to behave themselves. Told them it'd be a hell of a lot easier for both of them if they just cooperated."

"You know this town," Windermere said. "Do you have any theories?"

"Ma'am?"

"Any idea what happened last night. In your professional opinion."

Dillman thought for a minute. "I wouldn't want to make any assumptions. But Reg Winter's well known for making passes at his waitresses, supposedly fired a few of them for not playing along." His face darkened. "He's a creep, that's for sure. But he swears he kept his hands off Ms. Moody, so I just don't know what to tell you."

"That's fine," Windermere said, turning back to Finley's truck. "Which way is the jailhouse? I want to talk to these boys myself."

41

Darryl Greer and Reg Winter sat on opposite sides of the holding cell in the sheriff's detachment in Hungry Horse, glaring out through the bars, refusing to look at each other.

There was another deputy in the office, a middle-aged woman named Renner, and she stood as Dillman led Stevens and Windermere into the office, Kerry Finley bringing up the rear.

"They tried to fight, Mike," Renner reported. "But I told them the first to throw a punch had to eat your cooking for lunch, and they calmed down some."

"Good," Dillman said, walking past Renner to the holding cell. "So let's see if they're ready to talk this thing through."

Stevens took Darryl Greer into Dillman's office. Brought Deputy Renner with him, closed the door. He left Reg Winter for Windermere, Dillman, and Finley, figuring the barman would be more receptive to Windermere's brand of tough love.

Greer, for his part, looked more scared than anything. He accepted a seat opposite Stevens at Finley's desk, glanced back to where Renner guarded the door, and then settled in and looked at Stevens again.

"Any sight of her?" he asked. His voice was raw, his eyes hollow. "I mean, if she wasn't with that asshole, then . . ." He let it trail off.

"We're still looking," Stevens told him. "She have any friends we could talk to? Anyone she might have gone home with last night?"

"She was supposed to come home to *me*," Greer said. "I mean, she got off at three in the morning. In a blizzard. Where would she go?"

Still, he gave Stevens a handful of names, three or four local women he claimed were Pam Moody's closest friends. Stevens wrote them down and made a note to follow up when he was finished with Greer.

"What about men?" Stevens asked him. "I'm sorry, but, you know—"

"Yeah," Greer said. "I know. I guess I made it seem like she's some kind of big slut, running over to Reg Winter's like I did." He sighed. "It's just, he's been sniffing around her since he gave her the job, and I know he's the kind to fire a girl for not putting out, you know? I thought maybe he'd finally worn her down."

"We heard about his reputation," Stevens said. "No other men you can think of? Nobody has a crush on her, anything like that?"

Greer made a *No* sound. "She's kind of a homebody, really. We're saving to get the hell out of here, together. Soon as we have the money scraped up, we're gone."

"Where to? Could she have decided to leave without you?"

"In that blizzard?" Greer made a face. "Maybe if she was crazy. Anyway, she didn't have near enough money. And I told you, we're going together." He paused. "Look, I know you have to ask these questions, but I just want to find her. I'll answer whatever you want, just—time's wasting, you know? A storm like last night, it doesn't leave survivors for long."

He talked about her in the present tense, Stevens noticed, like he believed she was still alive. And he seemed genuinely concerned about his girlfriend's whereabouts. He might have been acting, but Stevens didn't think so. He was thinking about the train tracks across the river, about Kelly-Anne Clairmont and Ashlyn Southernwood.

He was thinking this case fit the pattern.

In the holding cell, Windermere and Kerry Finley went to work on Reg Winter.

"I hear you're a sleazeball," Windermere told him. "Not too bright on workplace harassment laws, either."

Winter scowled at her. He was a tall, skinny guy, late thirties, balding. He looked like he'd been the kid in tenth grade who dreamed of owning a bar, drinking all night and meeting chicks. He looked like he'd never grown out of that phase.

"I didn't have anything to do with that broad disappearing," he said. He tilted his chin up at Dillman. "I told this one all that already."

"You're the last to see 'that broad' alive." Windermere hunched down in front of him until she was looking in his eyes. "And rumor has it you had a little crush. Put it together, and you're the FBI's number one suspect. So you want to tell me something to get you off my shit list, Reginald?"

Winter held her gaze. Hard, like he was working through his chances of throwing a punch before Finley could draw down. Windermere tensed for it, ready to react in case the barman tried anything dumb.

But he didn't. He spat on the floor instead.

"Look," he said. "Here's what I know: we closed around two. Pam tidied up while I did the count. When I was finished, I poured us a couple shots, Fireball, to celebrate. Was a hell of a night, and we'd both made it through. She shut me down. Said she had to go and walked out the door without so much as a wave good-bye." He scratched his head, as if he couldn't believe anyone would turn down the offer. "I figured, hell, can't let a couple shots go to waste, so I disposed of them. And then I disposed of a couple more. And by the time I got out into the parking lot, her truck was gone."

"What time was that?"

"Shit, I don't know. Three thirty, maybe. It was real fucking late, is all I know. I wasn't too worried about the exact time."

"Anyone see you leave?"

"If they did, they were hiding real well."

"Anyone waiting for you at home?"

Winter gave her a look. "Probably wouldn't have been pouring Pam shots if I had an old lady," he said. Then he rubbed his face. "No one to vouch for me, got no alibi. I know where you're going with these questions, but you're chasing the wrong tail. I didn't have nothing to do with Pam disappearing."

Windermere shuffled her notes. She didn't like Reg Winter, figured he was probably the town asshole, figured he'd been sniffing around after Pam Moody last night, no question about that. But the thing was, she kind of believed him when he said he didn't know where she'd gone. Winter seemed like the type to make a pass at a woman. He didn't strike Windermere as smart enough to dispose of a body and make it back to bed before dawn, especially in a storm like last night's.

But he was the last person to see Pam Moody alive, and that made him pretty damn valuable.

"Did Pam seem distracted last night, unhappy?" Windermere asked. "She give any indication she was planning anything unusual?"

"She seemed *tired*," Winter replied. "Seemed like she was itching to get home and go to bed. I assume that's why she turned down her shot and hightailed it out of there so fast."

"She look worried?"

"No more than usual, I'd say. But what the hell do I know?"

"Okay," Windermere said. "Can you think of anyone she might have come into contact with last night? Any customers who seemed a little too into her?"

Winter at least pretended to think about it. Then he spat again. "Look, it was a busy night," he said. "I was swamped, barely had time to take a leak, much less babysit my waitress. If she had someone hitting on her, I didn't see it. I didn't see much but the fridge and the cash register all night long."

42

She was in a ravine.

Pamela Moody lay on her back and stared up at the sky beyond the rocky walls of the canyon. She was cold. She hurt bad. She was sick of waiting to die.

She wasn't dead yet.

The air around her was quiet. Nothing moved. Even the sky seemed static, just a blank wall, a paint swatch, "chronic-depression gray." The snow had stopped falling. The wind had died down. What few trees she could see around her were still. She couldn't hear any sounds; she might have been the last woman on earth.

She'd heard a train whistle a while back. Distant, though, like she was imagining things, like she might not have heard it at all. She remembered the man pulling her from the truck, but she didn't hear any traffic from the top of the ravine. She didn't hear anything.

She could see rocks and snow and sky, the walls of the ravine rising jagged around her, a few hardy, stunted conifers clinging to the terrain. The man had obviously meant to hide her here, likely somewhere far away from town, somewhere no one would think to look for her. He'd probably counted on the snow covering her body. It was smart, she decided. More snow would fall soon enough.

Her head ached. The rest of her ached, too. She'd broken her body when she fell, when she'd bounced off the knife-sharp rocks; she'd bled through her clothes here and there. Every time she shifted position, she could feel the pain again.

She had expected to die fairly quickly. It was a miracle she'd woken up at all, she knew, but the miracle wouldn't last forever. She had imagined she would fall asleep again, drift off, and that would be that. It wouldn't be the worst way to go. Might be kind of pleasant, actually.

But Pam hadn't drifted off. She'd just lain there and stared up at the walls of the canyon, unable to turn her mind off, even with the cold and the pain. She kept seeing the man's face, hearing his awful voice. The memory didn't scare her; it made her really freaking mad.

She should have known better. She *did* know better. She'd had a weird feeling about the guy since she took his drink order, and when he'd shown up by Darryl's truck, she should have raked out his eyes with her car keys. Instead, she'd let the creep get the drop on her, let him use her and hurt her and, damn it, toy with her, the way he'd dangled her puffer just out of her reach. That made Pam angry. It made her mad that he'd *won*, that she was going to die because of some dickhead who needed to play rough to get laid.

Shit.

Pam wasn't ready to die, no matter how she tried to will her mind into accepting the inevitable. Her body wouldn't let her go. Her brain wouldn't shut off. She kept seeing the guy's face as he teased her with the puffer. She kept thinking how much she'd like to turn the tables on him.

Well, hell. She was probably going to die regardless, but lying around waiting was getting old. Pam tilted her head back, gritted her teeth, the pain as fresh as if the bastard were right above her with a knife. She craned her neck until she could see all the way from the bottom of the ravine to the top, the lip where the man had kicked her over, the rocks she must have hit on her way to the bottom.

The lip was maybe sixty feet above her. The ravine rose at an angle; the wall was mostly fresh snow, punctuated by bare rock. She couldn't see any easy path to the top, even if she'd been in peak physical form. Right now she wasn't even sure she could walk.

But she could move a little bit at a time, if she could block out the pain and just roll herself over. She could pull herself forward; inches she could cover, excruciatingly slowly, and if she could just get her legs working somehow, make herself crawl, she might be able to actually *get* somewhere.

It beat waiting to die. And if the pain got unbearable or she wore herself out, well, heck, death was always the fallback plan, anyway.

43

Stevens met Windermere coming out of the holding cell, Deputy Finley and Mike Dillman behind her. "Nothing doing," he told them. "Unless Darryl Greer's a heck of a good actor, he doesn't know a thing about where Pam Moody might have gone. He seems pretty concerned that we're not looking hard enough for her."

"No luck with the sleazy boss, either," Windermere said, hooking a thumb back to the holding cell. "He's as greasy as advertised, but he swears he watched Moody leave last night, and I just don't think he has the brainpower to pull this off and lie about it."

"He would have had to dispose of Pam Moody's truck in the blizzard and then come back for his own," Deputy Finley said. "Would have been a tall order last night, unless he was working with a partner."

Windermere looked over Stevens's shoulder, where Deputy Renner was escorting Darryl Greer from Mike Dillman's office. She pursed her lips. "Look, we can't just write these guys off yet. I know you're thinking serial killer, Stevens, but we can't let that cloud our judgment. We have to investigate Greer and Winter like they're our prime suspects."

"Time's wasting," Stevens said. "If Pam Moody's still alive out there, her clock is ticking."

"All the more reason to discount Winter and Greer as soon as possible. We can't just go charging off into the mountains after ghosts, not without evidence."

"I can work on the local boys," Dillman interjected. "Won't be much trouble to take a look through their houses, their cars, see if anything's out of order. Missing suitcase in Greer's closet, bloodstains on Winter's carpet."

"You'll need backup," Windermere said. "More eyes are always better."

"So come with me. Your partner can look into the serial killer angle while Renner phones around to Pam Moody's friends."

"Works for me," Stevens said. "Deputy Finley can help me out with the legwork. And if I can't find anything concrete, we'll jump on board with you two."

Windermere thought about it. Figured she saw some merit in the serial killer angle herself; it was a sexier theory, anyway. Was wondering if she and Stevens were seeing what they wanted to see, though, to avoid going home, to avoid copping to the fact that this entire case could be a waste of time, a ghost in the mountains, rumors and conjecture. Better to cover their asses in case the truth turned out to be as mundane as everyone else seemed to think.

"I'll call you if I need you, partner," Windermere told Stevens. "Assuming the phones don't cut out again. You want to take a bet on who strikes pay dirt first?"

Stevens didn't smile. "Only bet I want to make is that Pam Moody's still alive," he said. "And one of us had damn well better find her."

Stevens and Finley took an empty desk in the detachment office while Windermere and Dillman rode out with Reg Winter. Winter had given the law permission to take a look through his place, just insisted he be there to supervise.

"Probably got some things you don't want to see," he told Windermere. "And I don't mean of the criminal variety."

Dillman made a face. Windermere didn't. "I'm not worried about your stack of pornos, Mr. Winter," she said. "You got a flesh-and-blood girl in your closet, we're going to have a problem."

Stevens watched them walk out. Wondered if he was being premature, jumping into the serial killer thing right away. Figured he'd find out either way, soon enough.

"Just heard from Sheriff Parsons up in Libby," Finley told him. "He had the coroner put a rush through on Kelly-Anne Clairmont's autopsy, look for signs of assault, rape, the gamut."

Stevens looked up. "And?"

"And . . ." Finley coughed. "Well, the state of the body being what it was, they couldn't run every test in the book. But they did seem to think that she'd had sex of a rough nature shortly before she died."

"So she'd been raped," Stevens said.

Finley didn't meet his eyes. "They didn't say that. Said since she was a prostitute and all, it was impossible to determine whether it was rape."

"The hell—" Stevens started to argue, but thought better of it. "What about cause of death? Don't tell me they're blaming that on her job, too."

"No," Finley said. "It's better news, there—in a manner of speaking. The coroner checked out what was left of Kelly-Anne's neck and throat—and there wasn't much of it, not enough that he could pin down an exact cause of death. But he did find that her larynx had been crushed and her hyoid bone fractured, in a way that he figured would have been tough for the wolf to accomplish. Said it looked to him like she'd been throttled, though he couldn't swear to it."

Stevens felt a burst of adrenaline, validation. "Just like Ashlyn Southernwood in Boundary County."

"Just like Boundary County," Finley said.

"So we can call it a homicide," Stevens said. "And we can call it a pattern. What about the car? Did his team run the prints?"

"Ran 'em. Got the phone book, most of them smudged or otherwise unidentifiable. No prints on the steering wheel, though. Sheriff Parsons thinks Clairmont drove with her gloves on."

"She wasn't wearing gloves when the warden found her."

"No, but that wolf scattered clothing all over the place, so . . ." Finley shrugged. "Parsons and the boys didn't find any blood in the car, anyway. No bodily fluids. Nothing that pointed to the killer."

"Maybe not," Stevens said. "But we know he's out there. And I'll be damn surprised if he didn't take Pam Moody, too."

"Well, let's see about that." Finley looked around the small detachment. "What are we doing to track this girl down?"

Stevens gave her a slight smile. "Chasing ghosts," he said. "I need a topographical map of the area and a direct line to the Northwestern Railroad dispatcher. Let's see what kind of half-cocked theory we can cook up."

44

Just moving had been torture. Crawling was worse. Pam Moody had no way to tell time, but she imagined she was lucky if she'd covered ten feet in the span of an hour.

She'd made it to the base of the rock wall, the slope that climbed steeply to the lip of the ravine. She'd left a trail behind her, a slug's path through the snow, dragging her lower body as she pulled herself forward with her hands, her legs screaming every time they struck something, some bones definitely broken.

At least you're not paralyzed, you wuss. Keep it moving.

The snow where she'd lain was a horror show. She must have landed hard when she'd fallen, and bled, because patches of ground were stained with her blood. Pam had forced herself not to consider the implications. Focused on the black rock rising up from the snow and pulled herself toward it. Now she was at the base of the wall, and she rested, exhausted, her hands numb from digging through the snow.

You might lose your fingers, even if you do make it out of this.

But the thought was so absurd that Pam had to laugh. She was marooned at the bottom of a six-story Rocky Mountain ravine in January. Every inch she moved felt like a set of large, jagged teeth were tearing her in half. She would never make it out of this canyon, much less to safety. Her fingers were the least of her problems.

She rested at the bottom of the wall. Warmed her hands inside her torn clothing, searching her body for a place that didn't hurt. It wasn't much warmer inside her coat than out, but maybe she could save a thumb, at least.

Pam cleared the cold and the hurt away. Made herself focus on the man, the hate in his eyes, the way he'd laughed as he'd held her puffer out of her reach. Slowly, she pulled herself up the slope of the wall, wincing as the rocks cut into the flesh of her palms. She shook the pain off. She'd been hurt worse. And it wasn't like there was anyone to hear her cry.

45

We had six trains through Hungry Horse last night," the Northwestern dispatcher told Stevens over the phone. "Four eastbound and two westbound."

Stevens wrote this down in his notebook. "How many stopped in town?"

"At the siding? Let's see." The dispatcher hummed to herself. "One of the eastbounds and both westbounds. The eastbound didn't stop for long; it was a hotshot, containers to Chicago."

"And the westbounds?"

"Coal trains. Headed for the coast."

Stevens wrote this down, too. "Remote-controlled engines?"

"Yessir, on both of them. We can pack on more tonnage if we cut them into the middle of the train."

"Sure." Stevens drummed his pen on the desktop, thinking. Windermere had called the Northwestern Railroad from Eureka that morning, as soon as word of Pam Moody's disappearance had reached them. The railroad had checked all trains running through Hungry Horse. They hadn't found any riders.

"What time did those westbounds come through?" he asked the dispatcher.

More humming. "Um," she replied, "the first one was around midnight, the next at four in the morning. Stopped for about an hour, both of them."

Stevens underlined the second train in his notebook. Underlined it again, for good measure. "That's our train," he said. "If our rider's involved in this thing, he left on one of those engines."

"You want to stop it again?" The dispatcher sounded skeptical. "My boss said we can't just keep stopping trains without any proof—"

"Don't sweat it," Stevens told her. "He's long gone anyhow. Can you get me a list of where else that train stopped last night and this morning?"

"I could, but it might take a little time."

"That's no problem." Stevens read off the sheriff's detachment's phone number. "Call me back, would you please?"

He ended the call. Turned to where Kerry Finley was leaning over a topographical map of the region, spread out on Deputy Renner's desk. Finley looked up as Stevens hung up the phone. "So what are we looking for?"

Stevens joined her at the desk. "Hiding places," he said, studying the map. "Anywhere the ghost rider could have dumped Pamela Moody."

There were two roads heading north out of Hungry Horse, across the Flathead River and the Northwestern main line. They were forestry roads, twisting and winding up into the mountains, rough gravel at the best of times—and in January, unplowed snow.

One of the roads crossed the tracks near the Northwestern passing siding, where the coal train would have been sitting at four o'clock that morning. The second crossed the tracks just before the tracks crossed the river; there was only the main line and the long, narrow bridge.

"We'll start with this one," Stevens told Finley, pointing at the road nearest to the passing track. "Easier to hop a train when it's standing still, right?"

They took Finley's SUV across the Flathead River. The bridge was low, and the river was mostly snow and ice, but in the middle, where the current was strongest, the water hadn't frozen over. It ran deadly black, cold just to look at it, and Stevens felt a chill as Finley piloted the truck toward the north shore.

If Pam Moody wound up in that river, she's a Popsicle. No chance she'd survive. And that current could take her body anywhere.

No sense worrying about that now. For all Stevens knew, Windermere had stumbled onto Pam Moody, alive and in chains in Reg Winter's basement. He checked his phone: one bar, and flickering. If they went any farther, he'd be out of contact again.

The road bisected the Northwestern main line at the west end of the siding. There was a path to the switch and an equipment locker, and then the road branched off and split away from the tracks, climbing into the mountains from two different directions, curving up the undulating terrain before disappearing around curves of thick stands of fir trees. Finley stopped the truck. "Which way?" she asked.

Stevens scanned the two roads. The snow had fallen thick here, and apparently uniformly; he couldn't see any telltale tire tracks in either direction.

"He can't have gone far," Stevens told Finley. "He had to dump Moody's truck and then hike back to the siding—"

"In a hell of a blizzard," Finley said.

"Exactly. He wouldn't need to do a big expedition. Just get deep enough that it'll look like she got herself stuck. That truck's going to be close, if it's out here."

"It'd better be." Finley gestured out the window, gestured up, where the sun was already closing in on the tops of the western mountains, a lonely bright patch against the lifeless gray sky. "We're losing light already. Night comes on quick this time of year."

"I don't want to be out here at night," Stevens said, pulling open the passenger door and stepping down into the snow. "But I sure as hell don't want to go to bed without knowing, either. Let's split up."

So they split. Finley took the west road, Stevens the east, slogging up the grade, searching the snow for any sign of human life. It was cold in the forest, bitterly cold; he'd grabbed a spare winter coat from the Hungry Horse detachment, bundled it tight around himself. The Hungry Horse deputies couldn't do anything about Stevens's boots, though; his socks were soaked through, his toes numb, before he'd made it thirty feet from the truck.

It was quiet in the forest, too, nearly silent. Stevens breathed hard as he plowed ahead, every breath sounding like an avalanche in the stillness. He scanned the trees, the road ahead, searching for the gleam of metal, the glint of light reflected against glass, that would signal he'd found what he was looking for.

But Stevens didn't see anything. And when he'd walked five minutes or so, the sun setting at his back, he stopped to catch his breath and turned around and couldn't see the SUV anymore, couldn't see Finley, could see only forest and snow and the gray sky above, the shadows growing long all around him.

The stillness was eerie. This was not a friendly place, not now, with the light fading and the temperature dropping. This was a place that didn't need help to kill you. But the rider was out here, somewhere in these mountains. And that made it eerier still.

Stevens drew his service pistol from its holster, gripped it through his gloves. Knew he was being silly, knew the rider was long gone, if he'd been here at all. Knew any other predator in these woods would require significantly more stopping power than his .40 Smith & Wesson could provide.

The pistol made him feel better, though, so he kept it drawn as he pushed ahead, searching the darkness in between the trees, watching the shadows grow longer. He wasn't scared, exactly; Stevens was a rational man, an experienced outdoorsman and a competent cop, and he wasn't going to freak out over a walk in the woods.

All the same, Stevens felt a definite surge of relief when Finley's voice broke the stillness, hollering out from behind him, down the western road somewhere, calling Stevens to come take a look at what she'd found.

46

It would be dark again soon. It would be dark again, and then it would get colder, and then Pam Moody knew she really *would* die, whether she was on board with the idea or not.

She'd barely made it twenty feet up the ravine wall, and she'd been wriggling and pulling herself across the rocks for what felt like hours. Her palms bled from fresh wounds, bright red on white snow. Her whole body screamed as she dragged it up the makeshift path. She'd given up crawling; the pain in her legs was too much. She just tried not to scrape them against the rocks as she pulled herself along with her hands.

Her hands had gone numb again. She knew she had to stop, warm them up; she could use a break. But she could see a little more above the ravine walls now, see the bright spot in the low clouds that must have been the sun, alarmingly close to the ravine's western wall. Night would come quickly. She didn't have much time left.

It was foolish, what she was putting herself through. What was she hoping to achieve? Why couldn't she just rest, get comfortable while she waited? Even if she made the top of the ravine, then what?

Then nothing. It would get dark, and she would still be far away from anything, anybody. She would still die out here, alone and freezing cold. Maybe someone would find her body eventually; that was a plus. Maybe she would die easier after she'd exhausted herself.

Still. This was torture. Why keep going?

Because of the man, that's why. Because of the man and his smirk and his hateful words. And because Reg was probably down at the saloon right now, telling everyone how Pam Moody was a slut and she'd probably skipped town, and Darryl was probably propping up the end of the bar, commiserating, and even if he knew she'd been dragged away and lay dying, he would probably tell her it was partially her fault, that she'd flirted too much with the guy when she brought him his beer, smiled at him a little too long, gave him the wrong idea. He'd think she'd deserved it when someone finally *did* find her body. He would crack open a beer and sit back and tell whoever would listen how his girl had gotten her own damn fool self killed, and it was nobody's fault but her own.

Or maybe he would be sympathetic. Maybe he was tearing his hair out right now, going crazy looking for her.

Or maybe he was right.

Maybe Darryl was right and she'd led the man on. He'd chosen her, hadn't he? She must have *done* something. Maybe her skirt was too short and he liked her legs so much that he just had to put his hands on them. Maybe she'd done something dumb unconsciously, like lick her lips, and it had given the man a huge raging hard-on and he couldn't think straight again until he'd had her. Maybe she really *had been* flirting with him. Maybe she really did deserve this.

Pam pulled herself over to the side of her little path. Tilted her head to the sky, eyes closed, caught her breath. Decided she might just stay here, like this, until night fell. It was as good a place to give up as any.

Then she opened her eyes and she knew, immediately, that she had to keep moving.

The ravine must have been a riverbed during the spring thaw and into the summer. It snaked down from in between the mountains, a V shape, narrow at the bottom and open at the top. Pam could see up the ravine, north, more snow and rock, and then trees and jagged cliff faces. To the south, the ravine descended, winding around boulders and more stands of conifers until it dipped out of sight. Eventually, it would reach the Flathead River, she expected, though she couldn't see the river from here. What mattered was the ravine ran north–south. Pam was climbing up the east wall. And skirting the west wall, coming up from the south, Pam could see something moving, half-hidden by the rocks.

She watched, the cold forgotten. The thing, whatever it was, was about a hundred yards distant, too quick to be a bear, too big to be a rodent. It was black, a living shadow, tracing the riverbed toward her. It wasn't a deer. It sure as heck wasn't a human.

The thing disappeared behind a snow-covered boulder. Pam waited. Realized she was holding her breath. Then the thing reappeared again on the near side of the boulder, and she let that breath out in one long, resigned sigh.

The thing was a wolf, low and black and malevolent. It was a large wolf, a male probably, a hundred pounds, easy. It jogged up through the ravine, its nose to the snow, following some invisible scent. Pam watched it approach with mounting horror. It was still on the other side of the ravine, hadn't seen her, but it would *smell* her soon enough. She'd left blood at the bottom of the ravine. If the wolf wasn't onto her now, he soon would be.

As Pam watched, the wolf lifted his head to survey his surroundings. She saw him see the patch of snow where she'd lain, watched him approach it cautiously. He nosed up to where she'd bled, the white snow turned crimson, sniffed at it, tasted it. He was huge, might have weighed more than she did. He looked healthy, well-fed. He looked dangerous.

He would come for her soon. And as much as Pam thought she was ready to die, she damn sure wasn't ready to be eaten alive.

As stealthily as she could, Pam felt around in the snow for a couple of decent-sized rocks. Stuffed them in her pockets to use as weapons, when the time came. Knew it was a hopeless case, fending off a full-grown wolf with a couple of stones, but what the hell. She armed herself anyway. Then, as quietly as she could, she resumed her struggle to the top.

47

There was no trace of Pam Moody anywhere.

Finley had found Moody's truck, an old brown F-150, stuck in a stand of alders at the base of a sharp rise. The truck was facing *down* the mountain, back toward town; had driven headlong into the trees, from the look of it, lodged itself good and firm. But there was no sign of the driver, nobody inside.

The sun had dipped behind the western mountains by the time Stevens caught up with Finley at the wreck. There were no footprints in the shadows around the truck, not that Stevens could see. The forest beyond the front bumper was dense and impassable, and the road to the west was narrow, cut between stands of trees and sheer rock. But the truck had come down from the west, apparently, and that was a bit of a head-scratcher.

Pam Moody wasn't here. They'd called her name, loud as they could, from the site of the wreck. Scanned the forest with the weak beams from their flashlights. Hadn't seen anything but encroaching darkness and snowy underbrush; hadn't heard any reply but their echoes.

But this was Pam Moody's truck, and that all but confirmed Stevens's suspicions. Moody wouldn't have driven out here by herself, not in that blizzard. She'd have realized her mistake as soon as she hit the bridge, turned around before she crossed the tracks. If the truck was out here, this close to the Northwestern line, the ghost rider had to have driven it. That meant he must have dumped Pamela Moody somewhere close—somewhere farther up the logging road, Stevens figured.

He pulled out his cell phone. Held it up just to see, then put the phone back. "No bars," he told Finley. "We need to call in a helicopter, search party, but I can't do it with my phone."

"Nearest helicopter's a couple towns over," Finley replied. "I'll call it in from the truck, but there isn't going to be much a search party can do before morning."

Stevens backed away from Pam Moody's truck. Slogged back to the middle of the forestry road. "I'm not ready to give up just yet," he told Finley. "He had to leave her somewhere nearby. And he wouldn't have left her any closer to the tracks."

Finley hooked a thumb in the direction of the truck, the dense forest beyond. "Probably wouldn't have ventured any farther into those trees, either," she said. "Or if she did, she isn't in any position to be yelling back at us."

Stevens tried not to consider the implications of the statement. "The way that truck's facing, it came down from the mountain. Only reason the rider would go up there is to hide a body."

Finley followed his gaze up the logging road. "I'll get my truck," she said, starting back through the snow. "We'll cover as much ground as we can before nightfall."

48

Pamela Moody heard the engine as the truck approached. Thought she was dreaming it at first, hearing things in the wind, which was starting to gust again. She was weak and probably delirious, inventing things. There'd been no noise on that road above her all day. Why should anyone show up now?

But it was an engine all right, low and steady, and Pam listened to it get louder above her, heading up and into the mountains. She'd made it another twenty, twenty-five feet up the side of the ravine, numbingly slow and excruciatingly painful, checking back down on the wolf every few inches, hoping he hadn't noticed her yet.

He hadn't. But the lip of the ravine was still fifteen feet above her, and night was closing in fast. If the wolf didn't get her, the cold would, and Pam knew if she didn't make the top of the ravine, whoever was behind the wheel of that truck would drive right past her, keep going, one last, cruel joke at her expense, one last *Fuck you! Sincerely, The World.*

Pam climbed. The engine approached, its sound a crescendo. She could hear the snow crunching under the truck's tires, could even see the beams from the headlights above her, where they passed over the lip of the ravine and into the abyss beyond.

She was ten feet from the top. She might as well have been a mile.

The truck didn't see her. The headlights didn't catch her. The truck drove right past, and it didn't slow down.

She wanted to call out. Get the driver's attention somehow. Scream. She crawled faster, as fast as her body would let her. She wasn't fast enough. Wasn't close enough. Even if she cried for help, the driver would never hear her.

Pam listened as the truck's engine dwindled to silence. Wiped the blood from her palms, warmed her hands in her coat. So close; she'd been *so* close. She'd been stupid to even get her hopes up.

Then Pam heard something behind her. *Felt* something, more like, some primal instinct. She rolled over slightly, turned to look back down the ravine, where the wolf was still prowling around at the bottom, nearly invisible now in the shadows.

But he'd stopped moving. He was standing stock-still, his nose in the air, and Pam knew he'd picked up her trail. She watched, paralyzed with horror, as he scanned the wall of the ravine with his eyes, as those eyes fell on her, huddled against the rock.

Pam didn't breathe. Didn't move. It didn't matter. The wolf eyed her for an eternity. Then he put his nose down, sniffed at her trail, and started across the ravine toward her little path.

49

It was nearly full dark.

They'd climbed the mountain road for twenty minutes, the tires slipping and scrabbling in four-wheel drive, high beams on, moving slowly, both Stevens and Finley searching the roadside for anything that might have been their missing woman.

The road narrowed, hugged cliff faces and flirted with steep drops, and Finley's jaw was set as she drove, her mouth a thin line. The sun was long disappeared; the last light was waning. It would be a hell of a drive back down in the dark.

"We can't go much farther," Finley told Stevens, the truck struggling for traction, the back end slipping out. "They'll have a search party out for us if we don't show up in town soon."

Stevens didn't answer. Stared out at the gloom. Felt the truck slow, and knew Finley was looking across at him.

"Not much chance that girl's still alive anyway, Kirk," the deputy said after a beat. "Not if our killer's the one who brought her up here."

Stevens didn't meet her eyes. "No," he said, numb. "I guess she wouldn't have survived the storm."

"Won't make much difference if we get the body back tonight or tomorrow, except it'll be easier in the daylight, right? Less chance of anyone else getting hurt. But at least we know where to look."

Stevens lowered his window. Shone his flashlight out at the night:

snow and ice and not much else. Knew Finley was right. Pam Moody was probably dead already. They would find her body tomorrow. In the meantime, he and Windermere could start homing in on the ghost rider.

It was an awful feeling, turning back with the missing woman somewhere nearby. And Stevens figured he'd be kicking his own ass all night wondering if they'd made the right call.

"Hell," he said, rolling his window back up. "Okay. But I'll need a stiff drink when we get down off this mountain."

Finley gave the truck some gas, searched through the windshield for somewhere to turn around. "You and me both," she said. "And make mine a double."

50

The truck was coming back.

Pam was dimly aware of the sound of the engine over the thudding of her heart in her ears and the scrabbling of the rocks beneath her. Her mind registered the noise, but she didn't consciously notice it. She was too busy trying to get away from the wolf.

He'd seen her now, and he knew she was injured. Knew she was weak, struggling. Knew she was easy prey.

She'd pulled herself to within five feet of the lip of the ravine, but the wolf had closed the distance. He was maybe ten feet below her, a shadow in the darkness, a pair of glinting eyes. She'd staved him off by throwing rocks; he'd shied back a step or two, but not far. He just watched her, nose down, tail wagging slightly, paced her up the wall, and Pam knew if she turned her back, he'd be on her. The end. Good night.

But the engine was getting louder again, and here were the headlights, cutting a swath through the darkness. The truck was coming back. It was moving slow, Pam could tell, picking its way down the mountain, but it was coming, and if she didn't get up to the road within a minute or two, the truck would be gone.

She backed up the mountain, her eyes on the wolf, as fast as she could. The pain was unbearable. It tore at her, like fire, brought tears to her eyes and streamed down her face. She growled, screamed, clawed at the rocks. Pushed up the ravine wall, inch by inch. The wolf matched her pace. The truck rumbled closer.

She could hear the tires now. The headlights were bright. She wasn't moving fast enough, not on her back. She was going to miss the truck; she would miss it, and then the goddamn fucking wolf would eat her alive.

No way.

Pam threw more rocks at the wolf, whatever she could grab. Then she turned onto her stomach. Pushed herself to a crawl, willed her legs to work, scrabbled with her hands. Pulled herself up three feet from the lip, two feet, her head over the lip now, the truck bearing down on her, blinding headlights.

She wasn't worried about the wolf hearing her, not anymore. She forced herself to keep climbing. Screamed at the truck.

"Help me." It was hardly a scream. A croak, maybe. A scratch in her throat. *"Help me, God, please!"*

The woman came out of nowhere.

Stevens was white-knuckling it down the mountain as Finley picked her route, the truck sliding even worse on the downgrade, the road seeming narrower, the drop-offs seeming even steeper than on the drive up. They were rounding a sharp curve, a ravine on the right, the road hugging space between a cliff face and the drop. Stevens was wondering if he could expense a doubleshot of whiskey. Wondering if he'd even get the chance.

Then the woman appeared.

"Whoa." Stevens reached for Finley's arm, a reflex, as the woman threw herself into the path of the SUV. *"Watch out!"*

Finley had seen the woman, was braking already, fighting the wheel as the truck threatened to spin. The stop seemed to take miles, hours, the woman far behind. Stevens was out in the snow before Finley could shift out of drive.

The woman was trying to scream. She had to be Pam Moody. Stevens could barely see her in the glow of Finley's brake lights, but he'd seen her face, her bloody hands, like a horror movie haunting. He was running back toward her, fumbling with his flashlight. She was trying to yell something. He could only see shadows. He couldn't make out her words.

She looked desperate.

Stevens finally got his flashlight working. Shone it up at the woman. She was crawling down the road, stumbling, falling, trying desperately to run. One look behind her and Stevens could see why.

A wolf, black, huge, sleek fur and taut muscles and deadly sharp teeth. It came up from the ravine snarling, set its eyes on Pam Moody, and made a break for her. Stevens drew his pistol. Had no chance to use it. Shots rang out behind him, four of them, quick succession—*BANG BANG BANG BANG*—deafening at close range, earth shaking, the muzzle flash lighting up the night better than Stevens's flashlight ever could.

The wolf disappeared from Stevens's beam. Finley kept firing, over Pam Moody's head and into the darkness. She emptied her magazine and the gunshots echoed forever, but when Stevens swept his beam across the road, the wolf was gone.

"Scared him off," Finley said, reloading her pistol. "Might have even hurt him a little bit, too."

"Saved the day, Deputy," Stevens said, breathless. "Hell of a job."

Then he hurried across to Pam Moody.

Pam threw herself into the man's arms as he came to her. Didn't matter who he was, what he was doing on the mountain; he and his lady friend had just saved her ass. No damn wolf was going to eat her alive, anyway.

She was probably still going to die, though. She was one hundred percent spent. Felt like she was getting stabbed all over, and she couldn't stand any longer. She went limp in the man's arms, felt him sag under her weight.

"She's hurt, Deputy," he called back to the woman. "I mean, she's hurt bad."

Deputy. So they were cops.

The man lifted Pam and carried her to the truck, his boots sliding on the slippery road. Pam pitched, yawed, thought she might bail, but the man kept her upright, and together they made the truck.

Sure enough, the truck said SHERIFF on the side of it. It also said LINCOLN COUNTY, which confused her. Lincoln County was west of here, wasn't it? How far had the man taken her?

The deputy's buddy laid Pam down in the backseat of the truck. Circled around to the other side and slipped in beside her as the deputy climbed behind the wheel. Pam opened her mouth, tried to ask them where, exactly, they were. She couldn't get the words out. Couldn't get *any* words out. As the truck rumbled down the bumpy, snowy road, Pam closed her eyes and, finally, lost consciousness.

51

Mila Scott woke up with a start. The train wasn't moving. The sun shone through the cab window. Mila stood and rubbed her eyes and looked around for a station sign or a highway marker, something to tell her where she was. Her stomach was rumbling. She was hungry. She was anxious, jittery. She needed a cigarette.

What she needed was some goddamn crystal.

She hadn't meant to fall asleep. She hoped she hadn't slept through her stop; it would be a royal pain in the ass to have to hop another train northbound. But there was a sign by the tracks a couple cars back of the engine. STRYKER.

Mila brought up her map on her phone—running perilously low on battery life. Stryker was north of Anchor Falls, fifteen miles or so.

The railroad branched off here, one line running north into Canada, the other southeast through the Rocky Mountains. Mila's train was stopped to let an oil tanker train roll through toward the border. As soon as it passed, the coal drag resumed its journey.

Mila watched the tracks between Stryker and Anchor Falls, a nervous energy taking hold in her stomach. *The siding where he jumped,* Lazy Jake had written. *It was just north of Anchor Falls, the middle of nowhere.*

Mila figured she'd found the siding, about forty minutes after the train left Stryker. It really *was* the middle of nowhere, just endless green-black forest and the mountains rising high to the east. Mila scanned through the trees, looking for a house or something, some sign of human life. But she didn't see anything, just a little path across the tracks that was probably a dirt road, winding off through the woods toward the peaks to her left and disappearing into forest to her right.

If I get off here, I'll be stuck, Mila thought, staring out at the road until the train drifted past. *No idea which way to go, no food, no way to find this guy. I need more information. And I really need to eat.*

But the drag didn't stop at the siding. It continued south to Anchor Falls, another fifteen minutes or so. There, Mila was ready when the engines eased to a stop. She ducked down into the nose of the cab, pushed out the front door. Gasped a little bit as the sudden cold hit her, gathered her coat around herself, shouldered her pack, and climbed down from the train.

Nobody saw her. There were no railroad men watching, no bulls, and nobody else seemed to care. Mila hurried across the tracks toward the little town, barely more than a tiny post office, a gas station, a couple of stores. Behind her, the coal drag rumbled to life again, pulled out, a long line of gondola cars and her temporary train-engine home. Within a couple of minutes it was gone, the sound of the diesel engines fading into the distance, the air suddenly very quiet, very still.

So this was Anchor Falls. Mila stood on the main street and surveyed the town. A couple trucks passed her, pickups, coated in slush and road grime. They didn't slow down for her. The drivers barely looked her way.

A wireless signal. She would need to find Wi-Fi, Internet access, try to zero in on the ghost rider. Charge her phone, too. She would do that right away, just as soon as she'd eaten breakfast.

52

Pamela Moody survived the night. Barely.

Stevens had called Windermere as soon as his phone showed service. It had been a long, maddeningly slow drive down the mountain, Finley balancing the need to get Moody to help with the risk of losing control and crashing the truck. They'd be no help to Pam Moody if they all ended up in a ravine, Stevens knew, but that didn't make the crawl back to civilization pass any faster.

Windermere had a helicopter on the way when they rolled across the Flathead River and back into Hungry Horse—a medevac unit from the North Valley Hospital in Whitefish. Stevens watched the technicians unload Moody from the back of Finley's SUV, then he hurried alongside her stretcher to where the helicopter was coming in to land. Moody was still unconscious, her pulse very weak and her breathing slow. The techs didn't waste time with pleasantries. They strapped her into the back of the chopper and took to the sky, fast.

As the sound of the rotors disappeared into the night, Stevens walked back to Finley's SUV, where Windermere and Mike Dillman had joined the Lincoln County deputy.

"Guess it won't surprise you that we found nothing at either Winter's or Greer's houses," Windermere told her partner. "And I'm betting you two found that poor girl near some train tracks."

They'd crossed the Northwestern line on their way back into town, a couple miles from where they'd found Pam Moody—or rather, where Pam Moody had found them. Stevens relayed the story of the wolf, of Finley's heroics. Windermere smirked. "Always letting your partner do the dirty work, Stevens, while you waltz away with the girl."

Stevens managed a smile. He was beat, had started the day early in Butcher's Creek, long before he even knew Pam Moody existed. Now all he wanted was to climb into a bed somewhere, somewhere *warm*, let his brain process all that had transpired.

But there wasn't much chance of that happening. Not yet.

"What do you want to do now?" Kerry Finley asked them.

Stevens pushed the fatigue away. "Now?" he said. "Now we haul ass to Whitefish. Follow that helicopter, and cross our fingers that girl pulls through."

By morning, Moody's prognosis was optimistic—although it sure didn't sound that way.

"Hypothermia, frostbite, dehydration, exhaustion." The physician ticked off Moody's ailments on her fingers. "And we haven't even talked about her broken bones yet. Or the sexual trauma." She'd broken both legs and a couple of ribs and fractured her pelvis, though her larynx and hyoid bone were intact; she was still drawing breath, which was probably a miracle in itself.

"I guess he didn't care if he killed her," Windermere said. "He knew if he didn't strangle her all the way dead, the cold would finish the job."

But the cold hadn't. Somehow, Pam Moody had fought off the effects of hypothermia, the pain from her wounds—hell, even that monster wolf. The emergency room doctor told Stevens and Windermere that Moody had busted her hands good trying to escape that ravine.

"I'm talking she clawed her way up those rocks with her fingernails," the doctor told the agents. "Her palms look like she shoved them in a meat grinder."

Stevens saw Moody by the side of the road again, bloody and pale. "Whatever it takes, huh?"

"You said it. You don't survive out there for as long as she did unless you really want it," the doctor said. "And that girl wanted to live."

"So when can we talk to her?" Windermere asked. "We need to debrief her, find out what she knows about the man who did this to her."

"She's going to need some time," the doctor replied. "We're still in the danger zone with her injuries. Recovery has to be the priority."

"I get it. But we kind of have a window here, Doc."

The doctor frowned. "I need the morning, at least," she told Windermere. "Talk to me around lunchtime and I'll let you know."

Windermere started to complain. Behind her, Stevens watched Kerry Finley walk in through the hospital doors, holding a tray full of coffee and a couple of printouts.

"Deputy Dillman said this came for you," she told Stevens, handing him the papers and a cup of coffee. "While we were out on our little misadventure."

Stevens drank the coffee, desperate for the caffeine fix. Set the cup down and scanned through the printouts. Reports from the Northwestern Railroad, train movements.

"Never mind, Carla," he said, touching Windermere's arm. "Let's give Pam her space for a while. I have an idea what we can do in the meantime."

53

The Northwestern Railroad sent a coal train through Hungry Horse at four in the morning on the night Pam Moody was kidnapped," Stevens told Windermere.

He had the printouts open on his lap and Windermere beside him, both of them crammed into the orange plastic seats in a corner of the North Valley Hospital's waiting room.

Windermere peered over his shoulder. "Yeah, so what's the payoff?" she said. "This is your theory, partner. Walk me through it."

"That train was a westbound," Stevens said. "Headed to the coast. It passed through Whitefish and then north up the Stillwater River Valley toward Butcher's Creek and down to Libby. We called the dispatcher at roughly three o'clock the next afternoon. At that point, the coal train was in Davenport, Washington. The crew checked the engines and found no riders."

"Okaaay," Windermere said. "I can see what you're getting at, but what does this tell us? Assuming the rider was even on that train, we know he got off somewhere between here and eastern Washington. How does that help us?"

Stevens held up a printout. "We know more than that. This is a list of where the train stopped and for how long."

He gave it to her. Windermere took it, scanned it. Someplace called Anchor Falls, then Butcher's Creek, then Libby, then Bonners Ferry, Sandpoint, Idaho, and Spokane.

"Six stops," Windermere said. "Spread across hundreds of miles. You want to search every one?"

"Not necessarily," Stevens said, taking the papers back. "But we get people looking in each of those areas. Train crews, especially. We've already seen kills in Bonners Ferry and Butcher's Creek. Chances are he won't kill where he sleeps."

"Fine, so four stops."

But Stevens had more printouts for show-and-tell. "This is a table of every one of the kills we suspect might be his. Spread across the entire High Line, right?"

"Right. Cascades to the Rockies. No rhyme or reason."

"Except this." Now he had a map out. "I had Kerry make this when we were in Hungry Horse. It's a location map of every kill we pin on this guy. Check it out."

Windermere looked. Saw a cluster around the Idaho panhandle, northwestern Montana. Another cluster around Glacier National Park, Whitefish to the eastern slope. Then outliers, all the way west to Skykomish, Washington, east to Havre, Montana.

"We have kills in Libby," Stevens said. "We have one near Sandpoint, and a couple just outside Spokane. But check out Anchor Falls."

Anchor Falls had nothing. No kills on the Northwestern line until Butcher's Creek to the north, and Whitefish to the south, a span of fifty miles.

"That's right in the middle of his prime hunting area," Stevens said. "But there's nothing there, Carla."

"Maybe because there's *nothing* there," Windermere replied. "As in, nobody to hunt. Anchor Falls doesn't exactly look like a booming metropolis, Stevens. And as much as I respect what you're saying here, I'm not ready to point the cavalry at some Podunk little town just based on some dots on a map and a train schedule."

Stevens took the papers back. "I'm not asking for cavalry. I'm just suggesting we keep this place in the back of our minds."

Windermere glanced at the clock on the wall opposite. Quarter to ten. Two more hours to wait for access to Pam Moody. Minimum.

"Damn it," she said, standing. "I'm really not digging this whole *waiting* thing, the doctor be damned." She started across the waiting area to the emergency room doors. "If that girl can break our case open, I'm not waiting till lunch."

54

Scrambled eggs. Bacon. Orange juice. Toast. All of it gone within minutes.

"Wow." The waitress smiled at Mila as she picked up the empty plate. "Guess you were hungry, huh?"

Mila wiped her mouth with her napkin. "Breakfast is the most important meal of the day."

"So they say. You need anything else?"

She was *still* hungry, could have eaten another meal. According to Ash, your appetite was supposed to increase as you came down from crystal, and Mila could testify to it. But she wasn't exactly flush with cash, and who knew how long she would have to stake out this town?

"Maybe just some more orange juice," Mila said. "And also, like, a map?"

The waitress shook her head. "Orange juice I can do. For a map, you'll have to go over to Big Al's across the highway. He'll sort you out."

"Okay," Mila told her. "Thanks."

"You looking for anything in particular?"

Anyone, Mila thought. *Yes, I am. I just don't know a damn thing about him.* "Not really," she told the waitress. "Just trying to get a feel for the area."

The diner didn't have Wi-Fi, not officially. But it did have an unprotected router. Mila found the signal on her phone, connected to it. It was weak, but it would do. But her battery was at six percent.

Crap.

She looked around the restaurant, the walls beneath the booths. Couldn't find an outlet anywhere.

"Do you have anywhere I could charge this?" she asked the waitress, who'd just returned with her orange juice.

"I can charge it in the office in back," the waitress replied. "Tell you what: you leave your phone with me, go over to Big Al's and buy your map. You can spread that map out here when you get back, get a feel for the area while you wait on your phone. I'll even keep you in orange juice."

Mila dug into her packsack. Came out with her charger. "Thank you so much," she said, handing the phone to the waitress. "I'll be right back."

Big Al's Gas Stop was a little two-pump operation with a single mechanic's stall. A little bell chimed as Mila walked in through the doors. There was a man at the cash register, a large guy with a mustache whom Mila assumed was Big Al. She smiled quickly at him, then took in the store: magazines, beef jerky, a cooler of beer and soda in the back. Cigarettes behind the counter and a rack of map books in the corner. A couple of aisles of overripe fruit, stale bread, candy bars, and toilet paper. Judging from the look of the place, it functioned as the sole source of groceries within a fifteen-mile radius, though it wasn't exactly a booming business.

The rack of map books, Mila discovered, had everything from the continent down to the county—Glacier National Park, the Pacific Northwest, even a map of Canada. As Mila turned the rack, the little doorbell chimed again and someone walked into the store.

It was a man, middle-aged, in an army parka and snow boots. He'd come out of a truck parked at the curb, an old Chevy Suburban, white and blue. Mila watched him stamp the snow off his boots, watched him nod to Big Al. Watched as he started through the aisles, as he studied a bunch of black bananas nearby.

Desperate times, Mila thought. *Man, it would suck to live here.*

She picked up the map of Flathead County and brought it up to Big Al's cash counter. "Do you have anything with more detail than this?" she asked.

Big Al shifted in his chair slowly, like the effort required was nearly more than he could handle. He picked up the map as if testing its weight. "What are you looking for?"

"A map of the region," Mila told him. "Anchor Falls and the surrounding area, I guess. Just something with a lot of detail."

"Like a topographical map."

"*Yes.* Exactly. Do you have any of those?"

Big Al slid the map back across the counter. Rearranged himself in his chair. "We don't stock topographical maps," he told her. "Only maps I have are on that rack over there."

Mila spread the map open on the counter. Found Anchor Falls, a little dot on the railroad tracks, the highway a thin line. You couldn't even see the intersecting roads in town. Shit.

Someone coughed, and Mila turned to find the guy in the army parka standing behind her. He had an armload of groceries—including those black bananas—and he looked like he was waiting to pay.

"Sorry," Mila told him, folding the map up again. "I guess I'll take this. How much?"

Big Al shifted again. Peered down at the map. "Says six ninety-five."

"Six ninety-five." Mila dug into her pockets for her wallet. Remembered she wanted a pack of cigarettes, too, but caught a sudden funny feeling before she could get the words out, a feeling like she should be scared of something, but she had no idea what.

She found a ten, stuffed the rest of her money away. Slid the ten across to Big Al, who took forever to ring up the sale. Mila tucked the map under her arm, stuffed her change into her pocket. Turned to go, and as she turned, she caught sight of the man behind her again, and then she knew why she was scared.

The man had his parka unbuttoned to reach his wallet. He was wearing a plaid flannel shirt underneath, tucked into a pair of blue jeans. But it wasn't his clothes that stopped Mila short. It was the knife on his belt.

It was a bowie knife, a long one, hanging at his side. A beautiful, custom-tooled handle, an Indian woman on horseback. Mila stared at the knife, felt her stomach turn over. She knew that knife. She'd seen it before.

That was Ash's knife on that man's belt.

55

Mila stood frozen, halfway to the door. Behind her, the man with Ash's knife was paying for his groceries. He and Big Al were saying something about the weather. He hadn't noticed Mila yet.

Her thoughts careened through her head like a pinball. She wasn't ready for this yet. She'd expected to have time, to sort out a strategy. She wanted to ambush Ash's killer, not the other way around.

Heck, you don't even know if this is the right guy. Maybe he, like, found *her knife.*

But Mila knew he was the killer. Couldn't explain it, but she knew. She unzipped her coat. Slipped her hand to her belt line, found her own knife where it sat in its sheath. She gripped the hilt, let out her breath, closed her eyes, and pulled it out.

This is for you, Ash.

But before she could act, the man was beside her. "Sorry," he said, meeting her eyes, then quickly looking away. "I need to get past you."

She was blocking the door. Big Al was watching. Big Al's country music was playing, and there was somebody else outside the door, a woman, waiting to get in, and Mila was holding everything up and being weird, and all of a sudden she knew she wasn't going to kill this man, not here and not now. Her blade was too small, for one thing.

For another, she didn't have the guts.

Mila stepped aside, let the man pass. Watched him walk to his truck and put his groceries in the back. Watched him climb inside and start the engine. Figured that was it, she'd missed her chance.

Useless. You're completely useless.

But the man was just driving over to the gas pumps. Mila watched him step out of the Suburban and lift the hose and start to pump gas. She hadn't missed her chance after all. She could go out there and stab him right now.

But that wasn't going to happen. She wasn't a killer. Who was she kidding? She wasn't going to stab anyone. What she *needed* to do was get evidence on this guy, something to show the police so they would believe her. They would have to listen, if she could prove he was the killer.

Mila pushed open the door. Hurried across the street to the diner, ignoring the man as he continued pumping his gas. She burst into the restaurant and scanned the room until she found the waitress, setting down plates of breakfast in front of an elderly couple.

"I need my phone back," Mila told her. "Can I have my phone, please?"

The waitress frowned at her. "Sure, hon. Just one second."

Across the street, the man was still putting gas in his Suburban. But he would be finished soon. And then he would be gone.

The waitress was asking the old couple if they needed anything else. Mila interrupted. "I need it now, please," she said. "I'm sorry. It's just really important."

The waitress shot Mila a look. "I'm so sorry," she told the old couple. "This will just take a second."

Then she turned and, wordlessly, led Mila across the restaurant to the kitchen. "Wait here," she said, her expression stone. Mila waited. Watched the man out the window. He was finished pumping gas now. He was replacing the nozzle. The waitress was taking *forever.*

"Here's your phone." The waitress was back. "What's the big rush?"

"No time." Mila snatched the phone out of the waitress's hand. Hurried across the diner to the front windows, aiming the phone through the glass at the man. He was cleaning his windows with a squeegee. Mila snapped a picture of him as he replaced the squeegee. As he climbed into the Suburban. She tried to zoom in on his plate, but she couldn't get a good angle.

Crap.

Mila hurried over to the diner's front door. Pushed it open and ran out to the parking lot, the snowy pavement and the slush. The Suburban was pulling away now, driving out of Big Al's lot and north on the highway. Mila ran to follow him. The man drove slow, like he hadn't noticed her. She gained a little ground, got a better angle on his license plate. Lifted her phone to snap another picture—and then she dropped it.

She dropped her phone onto the hard-packed snow. Heard a crack as it landed. Heard another, louder crack as her momentum carried her over the phone, as her left foot landed square on the screen. The phone slipped out from under her like a clown's banana peel and Mila lost her balance, tumbled down, landed hard. Watched the Suburban chug away, in no hurry at all.

Mila picked herself up slowly. Her phone lay a few feet away, and she slid over to it. She knew immediately she was screwed.

The screen was cracked. Shattered. It looked like a store window after someone threw a brick. Wouldn't even power on. Of freaking course.

Mila looked around the tiny town, fought the urge to start screaming. Trudged back toward the diner instead.

56

Twelve hundred miles away from Mila Scott, Derek Mathers's computer chimed. Even as he swiveled in his chair, he recognized the sound.

Mark Higgins's cloud. Mila Scott's phone.

Mathers brought up the cloud on his desktop. Three new pictures, just added. An old SUV, white and blue, at a gas station. A man cleaning his windshield. Climbing into the truck. Driving away. The man wore an army parka, the hood up. Mathers couldn't make out much of his face save for a dark beard, couldn't get a read on the truck's license plate. Still, something about the man had piqued Mila Scott's interest. But what?

Mathers opened the first picture, brought up the metadata. Uploaded to the cloud just minutes ago, he knew that already. But from where?

Mathers keyed the IP address into his search tool. Sat back and contemplated the results. Someplace called Norma's Diner, Route 93, Anchor Falls, Montana.

"Anchor Falls." Mathers brought up Google Maps. "Now where in the heck is *that*?"

57

Pam Moody's story was a hard one to hear.

She'd been awake, but just barely, when Windermere walked into her room in the hospital's critical care unit, Stevens right behind her. She lay propped up in her bed, her face bruised and bandaged, her hands—both of them—wrapped completely in white gauze. She'd been hooked up to an IV and wore monitoring diodes beneath her gown. She was hazy, the doctor told them, from the medication she'd been given.

But hazy or not, Moody remembered. In a slow, dreamlike voice, she told the agents about the night she'd been attacked, from her shift at the Hungry Horse Saloon all the way to the rescue—Stevens and Finley driving past in the gloaming, the wolf right behind her, snapping at her feet as she climbed.

"He was, I don't know, maybe forty?" she said when Windermere asked about her attacker. "White guy, kind of plain. Big, thick beard, really shifty eyes. Every time we made eye contact, he'd look away fast, like he was really shy or something."

"This was at the bar?" Windermere asked. "Sometime during your shift?"

"That's right. He had a booth in the very back, by himself. Drank a couple of Rainiers, tipped me pretty good, and then split."

"Just like Butcher's Creek," Stevens said. "The woman at the Gold Spike said Kelly-Anne Clairmont was talking to a solitary guy in a booth. He left midway through the evening, and in the morning—"

"Clairmont was dead. But nobody at the Gold Spike could remember much about that guy, either."

"He was just some normal-looking guy," Moody said again. "Like, he could have been *you* with a beard, for all I really noticed. He could have been anyone."

"What about his clothes?"

Moody thought. "He was dressed for the weather. Like, a big army parka and a woolen watch cap." Then she blinked. "And his knife. He had a bowie knife, a nice one. There was a picture on the handle, someone riding a horse. A woman, I think. I'm not sure."

Windermere felt her phone buzzing in her pocket. "We can work with that, definitely." She pulled her phone out. Checked the screen. Mathers. "Excuse me for one second."

She ducked out into the hall, swiped her screen to answer. "Mathers. Did you hear the good news?"

"The Hungry Horse woman?" Mathers replied. "I heard you guys saved her life."

"That's right." Windermere tried not to sound deflated. She'd been looking forward to bragging a little. "Stevens did most of it.

Followed her trail all the way up the mountain. Even had to fend off a wolf."

Mathers whistled. "Wow. Where were you?"

"Searching the boyfriend's house back in town. I figured I should follow protocol, go by the book while Stevens chased his bogeyman."

"And now Stevens gets to be the hero. Well, I'm sure you'll get your chance to one-up him."

"Maybe." Windermere walked a couple steps down the hall. Dodged an orderly with a stretcher barreling the other way. "Anyway, what's up? You have something you want to talk about?"

"Got an updated location on that runaway," Mathers told her. "I know you're not focusing on her right now, but I figured you'd want to be updated."

"Can't hurt. Where is she?"

"Real close to you guys, actually. Some place called Anchor Falls. It's, like, twenty miles north of Whitefish. She logged on to the cloud from some roadside diner this morning. Uploaded three pictures of some dude and his truck."

Windermere didn't say anything. Turned back toward Pam Moody's door, only half-aware she was doing it.

Anchor Falls, she thought. *Stevens, you're a freaking savant.*

"Carla?"

Windermere refocused. "Anchor Falls, yeah, Derek. You alert the local cops?"

"It's Flathead County, same as Hungry Horse. Same sheriff's department. I figured you might want to liaise."

"I'm no good at liaising. You do it." Windermere walked quickly back into Pam Moody's room, already plotting the drive north. "Tell them to get some deputies on the ground, stat. Tell them the feds will be there in thirty minutes. And send me those pictures, got it?"

She ended the call. Ducked her head into Pam Moody's room. "Mila Scott just showed up in Anchor Falls, partner," she told Stevens. "Did anyone ever tell you you'd make a pretty good cop?"

58

The waitress glared as Mila entered the diner again. Mila ignored her. Dragged herself to a booth by the windows and heaved herself onto the vinyl seat.

"And she's back again." The waitress had followed her, was standing over the table. "Listen, I don't know how they do it wherever you're from, but around here, we think it's pretty rude to just barge in and interrupt—"

Mila put her ruined phone on the table. Didn't meet the waitress's eye. "I'll get out of here in a minute," she said. "I just need to think."

She could ask Big Al who the man was. Ask him where he lived, how to get there. But Big Al might not tell her, some strange girl he'd never seen before today. Big Al might get suspicious. Heck, he might tell the man she'd been asking after him.

It was worth a shot, at least. Somebody in this little town would know who the man was. Someone would know where to find him. Mila just had to hope she found that person before the man figured out she was after him.

The waitress still hadn't moved. "You broke your phone."

"I sure did," Mila said. "Guess I got what was coming to me. For being so rude, hey?"

The waitress frowned. Then her expression softened. "What was the big hurry, anyway? You came bursting in here like you just saw Bigfoot."

"It wasn't anything like that," Mila told her. "It was just some guy."

"Hurley, yeah. I saw you chasing his truck."

Mila looked up. "You know him?"

"Leland? I mean, I don't know that I *know* him, but I know who he is. Aren't too many strangers in a town this small."

"But you know his name is Leland Hurley." Mila could feel her pulse quickening again.

The waitress shifted her weight. "Sure I do. Leland's what you'd call a real hermit, lives up there in the mountains, but he comes into town every week or so, gets his groceries. Sometimes he comes across to the diner for lunch, never says much. I get the feeling he's kind of shy." She narrowed her eyes at Mila. "Why? What's got you so interested? He's a little old for you, girl."

"He took something from a friend of mine. I want to get it back."

"Something important."

"Very."

"And you can't go to the police?"

Mila looked her in the eye. Shook her head no.

"You're thinking you're just going to walk up into those mountains and tell Leland Hurley he's got to give back what he took?"

"Something like that," Mila said. "Do you know where he lives?"

The waitress hesitated. "I don't suppose there's any way I can convince you this is a bad idea."

"I rode a freight train from California to get here," Mila said. "What that man Hurley took, he had no right to. I'll find him, I promise, with or without you."

The waitress glanced out the window, almost involuntarily, her eyes tracing the slopes of the mountains east of town. She chewed her lip like she was thinking it over. Finally, she sighed and sat down opposite Mila. "You still have that map?"

According to the waitress, Leland Hurley lived up Trail Creek way, about five miles north of town and another ten east.

"Way up in the mountains," the waitress said. "It's wilderness up there. Just a logging road along the creek side winding through the Trail Valley. He lives in a cabin up the head of the valley somewhere, old loggers' land, the middle of nowhere. You can't just walk up to his front door and knock."

Mila studied the map. Trail Creek crossed the railroad tracks about the same place as the siding. The logging road followed the creek into the mountains. The man had disappeared into the forest there, Lazy Jake said. He must have gone east.

"I can find my way out there," Mila told the waitress. "I just need directions."

"Take the highway north until you hit Loggers' Pass." The waitress traced her finger over the map. "Take a right on the second logging road; it won't be marked, but you'll see the creek just before it. Then you follow that road until you get to Hurley's cabin—or until the snow gets too deep and you get yourself stuck."

Mila followed the waitress's finger on the map. Retraced the route until she was sure she had it down. "I don't want to go out there with all my stuff," she said, motioning to her heavy packsack. "Do you mind if I leave it here until I get back?"

The waitress started to reply. Looked like a no. Mila cut her off.

"I won't be very long. There and back. I just can't make it all the way out there carrying all of this weight."

The waitress mulled it over. Still didn't look convinced. "There's a room where we all keep our stuff in the back," she said finally. "Come on."

Mila followed the waitress through the restaurant. There was one cook at work in the kitchen, a young Hispanic man sweating over a grill. He looked up as Mila and the waitress walked in, smiled at Mila, confused, then turned back to the grill.

The waitress was already out of the kitchen. Mila found her in a little break room about the size of a closet. Hooks on the wall for coat hangers, coats hanging from them. A pink snowmobile jacket that would have been the waitress's and a black down jacket that must have belonged to the cook.

"Just leave the pack here," the waitress told Mila. "I'll make sure Ramon knows it's yours."

Mila set the pack down beneath the waitress's coat. Patted herself down, checking for her knife and feeling it through her coat. "Is there a bathroom I could use?" she asked.

"Next door down." The waitress pointed. "Listen, I have to get back out front."

"I'll find my way back." Mila ducked into the bathroom. Stayed there a believable length of time, then crept out again. Made a quick stop in the break room on her way to the front and another short stop in the kitchen, Ramon cooking up some bacon, completely oblivious.

The waitress was at the cash register when Mila emerged. "I'll be back soon," Mila told her. "Thank you for everything."

The waitress looked like she wanted to say something, like she knew she should. But the elderly couple was at the counter, waiting to pay, and Mila slipped past while the waitress was distracted, pushed open the front door and slipped out into the cold. Hurried around the side of the diner, away from the windows, and stopped to take inventory.

She'd found the key ring in Ramon's coat pocket, a house key and the key to some kind of Dodge. There was an old Ram pickup parked behind the diner, a big silver diesel with significant rust. Mila tried the key in the door, but the door was already unlocked.

She climbed up into the driver's seat and took the second item from her coat pocket: a meat tenderizer, a heavy, spiked mallet. She'd been hoping for a butcher's knife when she ducked into the kitchen, something big and scary, but all the knives were over by Ramon. The tenderizer was the closest item at hand.

A meat tenderizer and a small camping knife. A rusty pickup truck. No phone. No plan. Just a name waiting at the end of a long logging road.

Mila turned the key in the ignition, and the truck rumbled to life. She shifted into drive and steered out onto the highway.

59

Forty minutes after Agent Mathers's phone call, Stevens and Windermere pulled into Anchor Falls, Montana, in Kerry Finley's Lincoln County SUV.

Anchor Falls was tiny, little more than a couple of buildings spread out along Route 93, and as Finley piloted the truck across a bridge over the town's namesake waterfalls, Windermere could pick out a post office, a gas station, and the roadside diner where Mila Scott had uploaded more photographs to Mark Higgins's cloud.

Mathers had emailed Mila's latest pictures to Windermere, three blurry shots of a man in an army parka gassing up an old blue-and-white truck. Pamela Moody had recognized the army parka; it was the same as her attacker had worn. And as Windermere scanned the town from Finley's passenger window, she spotted the gas pump from the picture immediately, at the gas station across the highway from Norma's Diner, in the middle of downtown Anchor Falls.

He was here. This morning. And Mila Scott found him.

So where's Mila?

There was no sign of the Flathead County deputies. They were based in Whitefish, Finley was pretty sure, and that meant they'd be coming up the same stretch of highway as Stevens and Windermere. But the deputies were taking their sweet time.

Windermere wasn't about to wait around for them. She climbed from Finley's truck and strode up to the front door of the diner, crossing her fingers they'd find Mila Scott sitting pretty in a booth, chowing down on a cheeseburger, maybe coloring on her place mat or something. No such luck.

The diner was deserted, save for a couple men in a booth at the far end and the waitress, a pretty woman with blond curls, probably in her early thirties. Windermere wondered briefly if she was the eponymous Norma, but the woman's name tag read SHELLY, so there went that theory.

But even if she didn't run the joint, Shelly the waitress knew what was up. One glimpse of the two agents and the sheriff alongside them and she cursed softly, gave them a look like the kid whose dog ate her homework. "You're here about the girl, aren't you?"

Windermere showed Shelly her badge. "We sure are," she said. "You want to tell us where she went?"

60

"Well, she can't have gone far," Windermere said, following Stevens and Finley back out to the truck. "She's a twenty-year-old girl trying to cover fifteen miles on foot. We'll catch up to her quick, talk some sense into her. Then *we* chase down the mystery man."

Windermere was feeling good, confident, for a change. Figured the end was in sight, the hard work just about done. Shelly at the diner had given them the full story, how Mila had showed up in time for breakfast, how she'd asked for a map. How she'd bugged out when she saw the man with the Suburban.

"Leland Hurley," Shelly'd told them. "He lives up the far end of the Trail Valley, northeast of town. Keeps to himself mostly, only comes to town to stock up on provisions. Your girl said he stole something from her friend, that's why she was looking for him."

"The Trail Valley," Stevens said. "How close is that to the railroad tracks?"

"It's close. There's a logging road into the valley, pretty much Leland's driveway. It crosses the Northwestern line about five miles north of here."

Five miles north. The coal train on which Pam Moody's attacker had fled Hungry Horse had stopped at a passing siding north of Anchor Falls. Might as well have been Leland Hurley's private train station.

Windermere had called in Hurley's name to Mathers back in Minnesota, and a couple of minutes later, Mathers had emailed Hurley's NCIC file to her phone.

"Born in Missoula, Montana, 1970," Windermere read. Then she went silent. Scrolled through the file. "Shit."

Stevens glanced at her.

"This dude's ex-army," she said. "And he has a rap sheet a mile long. Sexual assault and attempted rape charges from here to Tacoma, dating back to the mid-nineties. Even one for attempted murder, some place called Rock Springs, Wyoming. Trespassing and vagrancy charges, too. This guy is a bad boy."

"So why didn't we know about him?" Stevens asked.

Windermere kept reading. "Looks like he never did any major time. Pled out, paroled, time served, good behavior. Guess he was going for quantity, not quality."

"Until now."

Windermere met his eyes. "Yeah," she said. "Until now."

Windermere figured they would track down Mila Scott somewhere on Route 93. Bundle her back to the diner for safekeeping, wait on those Flathead County deputies, and prepare a raid on Leland Hurley's cabin. Figured they could take their time as soon as they found Mila. Figured she couldn't have walked far, not in an hour or so, not in this snow.

But as Finley fired up her SUV, Windermere looked across at the diner again, spotted the waitress coming out the front doors, *fast*. Caught sight of the guy behind her, a young Hispanic man in chef's whites, the dude looking agitated, pacing, hands in his hair.

Shelly hurried across to the SUV. "She isn't on foot," she told the agents.

Windermere stiffened. "I beg your pardon?"

"Your girl isn't walking to Leland Hurley's place." Shelly exhaled. "She's driving."

"I thought you said she didn't have a car."

"She didn't, but Ramon does." Shelly gestured to the young man behind her. "A Dodge Ram pickup. I let your girl leave her backpack in the break room when she left. She must have swiped his keys while she was in there."

Windermere felt a sudden numbness. Realized her confidence had been premature, realized the hard work was nowhere near finished.

"We have to get up there," she told Stevens and Finley. "That girl's heading into a death trap—if she isn't already there."

61

Mila kept her foot planted and the pickup's engine roaring. It had been a while since she'd driven, six months at least, and she'd never driven a big truck like this, not in the snow. But the highway was mostly clear, and there wasn't any traffic. She made Loggers' Pass in good time, slowed down a shade and scanned the roadside for the creek.

She nearly missed it. The bridge was barely more than a culvert, and the creek itself was snowed over, a narrow gap in the endless forest, almost indistinguishable. But here was the second logging road, like the waitress said, and Mila braked the truck to as quick a stop as she dared, turned the wheel hard over, and steered off the highway.

The road had been used recently. Mila could see track marks in the snow, and she shadowed the tracks with the tires of the Dodge, or tried to; the thing steered like a barge. The road curved and climbed through the forest—more trees, a green so deep they were almost black, thousands of them in every direction. After a while, the road widened slightly, straightened out, and Mila saw the warning signs for the railroad crossing ahead. A junker train sat waiting on the siding track, two big engines and a mishmash of freight cars. Mila guided the truck over the crossing and back into the forest again.

After the tracks disappeared in her rearview mirror, the road began to climb at a quicker pace, the mountains rising on either side of the truck, funneling the creek into a narrow valley. The curves came sharper, the road swerving around forbidding rock faces, twisting and winding to gain elevation.

The truck began to slip in the snow. The back wheels spun and growled when Mila pushed the gas pedal, and she had to press carefully to avoid losing control. As the mountains closed in and the grade got steeper, though, the truck seemed to rebel against her efforts, slowing to a near stop if she didn't give enough gas, swinging around nearly sideways if she gave too much.

It's like it knows, Mila thought. *It knows where we're going, and it doesn't want to get there.*

She was sweating. She was nervous. She covered the miles slowly, gripped the steering wheel tight. She couldn't even turn around if she wanted now; there wasn't enough room. And anyway, she didn't trust her ability to pull off the maneuver. She was all in. Somewhere at the end of the road, Leland Hurley waited with Ash's knife. Mila pointed the truck up the mountains, kept her foot on the gas. Wondered if Hurley would know who she was when he saw her. Wondered if he would know why she'd come.

62

Leland Hurley was up the mountain a ways when he heard the engine in the distance. He maintained a trapline in the valley, augmenting Big Al's meager grocery offerings with food he could catch—and kill—himself. Hurley wasn't choosy. He ate whatever he found in his traps, from red fox to snowshoe hare to the occasional deer, and on one memorable occasion, a bobcat.

Some hunters caught wolves, but Hurley never had. He wasn't sure what he would do if he did catch one. He felt a kinship with the animals, wild and cunning, pariahs on their native land. The gray wolf was a hated species in Montana, hunted by everyone from farmers and ranchers to sportsmen who wanted to shoot elk and couldn't stand the competition. But the wolf was an intelligent predator; it thrived in the mountains despite civilization's best efforts. Hurley figured the parallels were obvious.

There were no wolves in Hurley's traps today, only a couple of rabbits and an unlucky red fox. But Hurley wasn't thinking about catching wolves at the moment. He was listening to the sound of an engine, a diesel, chugging its way up the valley.

Hurley tensed instinctively. The truck was still miles away, far down the grade, but it would arrive at the cabin eventually. There was nowhere else for it to go. And that meant trouble.

Hurley could count on one hand the visitors he received to his patch of mountain in the span of a year. Strange faces just didn't come out this far; anyone who knew this land existed knew, also, that it belonged to Leland Hurley. And that was usually enough to keep people away, Montanans being nothing if not respectful of one another's desire for privacy.

At times, the odd warden would trek up the valley, though rarely in the winter. And somehow, Hurley knew this wasn't a game warden making the climb.

Slinging his catch over his shoulder, he turned back down the trail. Hurried through the woods on snowshoes, the engine a constant now, chug-chug-chugging ever louder, breaking the stillness. Hurley walked through the forest until he reached his snowmobile, parked at the side of a trail he'd cut through the mountain, painstakingly, over the span of three summers. He'd wanted an escape route from the cabin, a back way through the mountains. The trail was nowhere near finished, but it provided him comfort all the same.

Hurley stowed his catch on the back of his snowmobile and stood in the clearing, listening to the engine approach. It would be a mile out now, maybe even less. The driver would beat him to the cabin quite easily. They could break in, if they wanted. They could search the cabin. They could find his box of souvenirs, if they knew where to look.

Hurley strapped on his snowshoes, left the snowmobile behind.

Shouldered his rifle, an autoloading Browning Safari .30-06 with a sniper scope and a five-round capacity. He'd bought the weapon to hunt, but he'd always suspected he might need it for home defense someday as well. Maybe today was the day.

The visitor was close now, the engine note reverberating through the forest. *Let him come,* Hurley thought, setting out toward the cabin on foot. *Let him look around, even.*

Let him try to run, if he means to do me harm.

63

Mila crashed the truck a few hundred yards from the end of the road. She misjudged her speed heading into a switchback, hit the brakes too hard and locked the tires, lost her steering. Plowed straight ahead into a thick stand of pine trees, branches everywhere, rocky terrain and deep snow. She swore and shifted into reverse, trying to back the truck out. She couldn't. The rear wheels spun, the truck rocked, the engine revved. But the big Dodge didn't go anywhere. Damn it.

Mila punched the steering wheel. Looked around. She could see the logging road in the rearview, winding back down the mountain. She was near the summit, she could tell, had been watching the odometer and knew she'd gone nearly ten miles into the forest. Knew Hurley's camp had to be close.

Close or not, the Dodge was stuck, and Mila didn't know enough about trucks to get it unstuck. She would have to climb the last couple switchbacks on foot.

At least you'll surprise him. He won't hear you coming.

Then she thought, *Yeah, but what happens when you have to get out of here?*

Never mind. She would steal Hurley's truck. Or she would call for help. Or she would hike out. She would sort that out when she needed to. Until then, she needed to find evidence to tie Hurley to the murders.

Mila climbed out of the Dodge and dropped into the snow. Shoved the meat tenderizer in her pocket with her little folding knife, closed the cab door, and left the truck where she'd marooned it. Waded back to the logging road and resumed the climb.

The road was steep here. If Mila looked back, she could see the Trail Valley spread out before her, a vast, empty carpet of tiny green trees, the mountains rising on either side like guards. She couldn't see Anchor Falls; it was hidden by the southern wall of the valley. Even the highway and the train tracks were invisible. She was completely alone out here. She pushed that thought from her mind.

The climb was intense. Her boots slipped in the snow, and she nearly fell, twice. She was panting, heart racing, and she stopped at another hairpin switchback to catch her breath. Looked up the road and saw the clearing.

The road had been zigzagging up the side of the mountain, north and south. Now it turned east, climbed over one last rise, and then leveled out. The lane between the trees widened. Slowly, the scene revealed itself. The trees fell back and the road petered out into a wide, empty space, the mountain falling back on three sides. Directly ahead of Mila, on the far side of the clearing, the forest closed in again and the mountain continued to rise, high into the clouds. But Mila was finished climbing. She didn't need to go higher. Because at the edge of the clearing, nestled into the trees, was a cabin.

It was small and simple, made of thick logs, rough-hewn. A tidy porch and a couple of picture windows that looked out on the clearing and the valley beyond. Mila stuck close to the trees, hid herself in the shadows. Surveyed the house, the outbuildings behind.

The windows were dark. Nothing moved. There weren't any vehicles parked where she could see, though the clearing was crisscrossed with tire tracks and some of them led around behind the cabin.

Mila watched the cabin until she was sure nobody had seen her. Then she crept across the clearing, as stealthily as she could, toward the front porch.

64

Finley hauled ass up Route 93. Windermere rode shotgun, relaying instructions to Mathers through her cell phone.

"I need you in touch with the Bureau's resident agency in Kalispell," she told her boyfriend. "Get every available agent up to Anchor Falls, now. Tactical teams, a helicopter if they have one. This is a serial killer and his potential next victim. You call them and you tell them to move."

She listened. Heard nothing. Took her phone from her ear and checked the screen. Shit. Call dropped. No freaking service.

"For God's sake, partner," she said, twisting in her seat toward Stevens. "We might as well be on the dark side of the moon."

Stevens gave her a look of commiseration, not that his sympathy did any good. There was no telling how much Mathers had heard, no way to know if Kalispell would get the message. The Bureau office was thirty miles south; even if Mathers did manage to muster the troops, the backup would need time to get to the scene.

"We need more men," Windermere told Finley, who was swinging her SUV off the highway and onto the rough surface of the Trail Valley logging road. "I don't care who you have to call, but we need everybody. And they'd all better bring guns."

Finley reached down with her right hand, unhooked her radio. Handed it to Windermere. "You can put out a call, but I can't guarantee you'll reach anyone," she said. "Unless you want me to slow down and wait until we can muster a raiding party."

"No chance." Windermere watched the forest fly by, the truck bumping and jostling over uneven terrain. "We can't afford to waste time."

"Then I hate to say it, but it might be just us," Finley told her. "Until those Flathead deputies get up here, anyway." Then she exhaled, eyes up the road. "Although maybe they'll catch up to us after all."

Windermere felt the truck slowing. "What are you doing? Why are we stopping?"

"Don't have a choice," Finley said, gesturing out through the windshield. "I can't exactly drive this rig through a train."

Windermere followed her eyes. Muttered a curse under her breath, then another, then a whole string of them. They'd reached the Northwestern main line, the end of the passing siding where Leland Hurley would have climbed off his train after attacking Pam Moody, and wouldn't you know it, there was a train at the crossing, a long, slow string of coal cars, lumbering along at no more than ten miles per hour.

Windermere peered up the track. Saw the engines in the distance, disappearing around a corner. Looked the other way and saw an endless stretch of coal cars emerging from the trees.

"Hell," Stevens said. "We could be here a while. These coal trains tend to be about a hundred cars long."

Windermere watched the train slowly pass. Pictured Mila Scott on the other side, up the mountain somewhere, driving straight into Leland Hurley's hands.

"Come *on*, train," she said, drumming her fingers on the dash. "Some of us have places to be."

65

The sound of the engine was gone.

Hurley had listened to it grow louder as he trekked through the forest, heard the big diesel rev higher as it struggled to mount the grade. The driver was inexperienced, he could tell, attacked the mountain without rhythm, as if he wasn't sure how much power he needed to make the climb. The engine roared, then diminished, then roared again. Hurley wondered how the driver had made it this far.

Then the engine revved three or four times, in quick succession, before it went silent. Hurley stopped walking, stood still on his snowshoes. Listened for any sound through the trees.

He heard nothing. He might have heard a door close, but he couldn't be sure. Regardless, the truck had stopped. The engine had cut out. The driver was close.

Hurley hurried to meet him.

66

The cabin was unlocked.

Mila pushed the door open slowly. The air was quiet up here, eerily so. It was even more muted inside.

The cabin was dark. The light from the picture windows seemed to die on the glass. The rest of the little building was all shadows and hanging dust. It was a single room, a bed and a table and a kitchen in the corner. A heavy rug by the bed, worn, its colors faded. The cabin was empty.

Leland Hurley wasn't here, but Mila felt his presence nonetheless, as if he remained in the air and the dust particles, the clothes in the wardrobe and the covers on the bed. He was *here*, all around her, an evil so palpable that Mila looked back into the clearing to make sure he wasn't behind her.

But he wasn't there. The clearing was empty, and so was the cabin. Mila crept inside, closed the door softly behind her. She relaxed her grip on the meat tenderizer. Set about searching the place.

She hoped to find Ash's knife. That was her first objective, even if she suspected that Hurley still had it with him, on his belt. But Ash's knife wouldn't prove that Hurley had killed anyone; at best, it was circumstantial evidence. Mila knew she needed to find something else, something better.

She started with the wardrobe by the bed. Pulled open both doors and rifled through the shirts and sweaters that hung within. Found nothing incriminating, nothing but a man's musty old clothes.

Nor was he hiding anything in the kitchen, though Mila did swipe a carving knife from the block on the counter. The blade was long and wicked sharp, much scarier than her little pocketknife. She could do damage with this blade if she needed to. She really, really hoped she wouldn't need to.

There was nothing unusual in the cabin. Nothing at all, that Mila could find. The man was an outdoorsman. He had heavy winter clothes, boots and coats and army surplus sweaters and hats. He had four or five books, nonfiction. Survival techniques, mountain guides. Dry reading, education, not entertainment. He didn't even have any pictures on his walls.

Hurley didn't have any tools, either, not even an axe, though there was a woodstove along the far wall. The man lived out here in the wilderness; he would have to be self-sufficient. So where was the rest of his stuff?

Through the kitchen window at the back of the cabin, Mila could see an outhouse, Hurley's Suburban, and another building in the trees. A storage shed, it looked like. Hurley would keep his equipment in there, the electric generator. Maybe that's where she would find evidence.

Mila crossed from the kitchen area toward the front door, already buttoning her coat again. As she passed the bed, her path took her over the rug on the floor, and as she stepped in the center, she felt something give. Not a lot, just slightly, but enough that she noticed. Enough that she started to think.

Mila stepped off of the rug. Pulled it away from the bed. Saw nothing but rough wood floorboards, same as the rest of the cabin. She walked to about the middle again. Stepped down and felt a board move.

One of the floorboards was loose. A small one, only a couple feet long. Mila bent over and pried it up from the floor. Looked in at the darkness below and knew she'd found what she'd been looking for.

There was money, first of all, bound up in stacks and stuffed into a cookie tin. There was a gun beside the money, a pistol. Some spare ammunition. And there was a box.

The box was heavy when Mila picked it up. She pulled it from the hole and set it on the floor and looked at it and didn't open it. Something about the box made her wary. Leland Hurley had made an effort to hide the box. She could have guessed why. But Mila realized she didn't want to know for sure.

Do it. Do it now, before he comes back and finds you.

Quickly, before she could change her mind, Mila opened the box. Saw what she'd expected to find. What she'd really hoped that she wouldn't. She looked in at the contents, and what she saw hit her hard, a sledgehammer to the chest.

They were right. Ronda was right. Ash was right.

This is a monster's lair.

67

An amethyst necklace. A small diamond ring. A slim ladies' watch, nothing special, the kind you found in the jewelry case at Walmart. A silver dollar. Women's underwear. Leland Hurley had stashed it all in his box.

He'd kept photographs, too, creased and well-worn, of dogs and smiling older couples, the pictures yellowed with age. There was a love letter to someone named Alberta from someone named Dave. The ink had smudged in a few spots, and the paper was stained in the corner. The stain looked like it might have been blood.

Hurley had even kept an asthma inhaler. It had been prescribed to someone named Pamela Moody, from a doctor in Columbia Falls, Montana. Mila's stomach churned. She tried not to think about Pamela Moody, whoever she was, and what Hurley had done to her before he'd taken her inhaler.

Mila picked through Hurley's macabre collection of souvenirs, looking for something she would recognize as Ash's. She didn't see anything; Ash didn't wear rings, and she didn't carry pictures. She wore her grandmother on her belt, and that was all she'd needed.

Something made a sound outside in the forest. It sounded like a branch snapping, and it sent a jolt of fear like electricity down Mila's spine. She'd been here too long. She had to leave while she could still get away. Take what she could carry and get back to the highway fast, however she could.

Quickly, Mila stuffed her pockets. Took the love letter, the photographs, Pamela Moody's inhaler. She left the jewelry and the watch; too impersonal. The police would never believe her if she brought back a handful of rings. But they would have to pay attention if she showed them things that had clearly belonged to the murdered women.

Mila stuffed the box back down the hole. Took the pistol, left the cash. Took a spare magazine for good measure. Replaced the floorboard and dragged the rug back. Tried to remember how it had looked when she walked in, put everything back as close as she could remember, and hurried for the door.

She stole a glance through the picture window before she walked out of the cabin. Scanned the clearing for any sign of life. Didn't see Leland Hurley, or anyone else for that matter. Maybe she'd panicked for nothing. There was probably nobody out there.

Still, it was time to get back down the mountain. She'd spent more than enough time in this awful place.

Mila pushed open the front door and stepped onto the porch. She'd started across the steps, toward the snow beyond, and that's when she heard the *CRACK* of the rifle as, simultaneously, the roof of the porch exploded above her head.

Mila stopped cold, struck dumb, a raccoon on the highway at midnight. She looked up at the hole in the wood above her head. Her brain struggled to process.

Leland Hurley was out there. He was somewhere in the forest, and he was shooting at her.

CRACK.

The rifle fired again.

Leland Hurley watched the girl through the scope of the rifle. The first shot had stunned her. The second spurred her to action.

She turned back to the door and seemed to hesitate, torn between ducking for cover and running away. Hurley watched her, his finger on the trigger, poised to fire again if she made the wrong choice.

She was the girl from the gas station. He'd noticed her staring at the knife on his belt, caught the way she watched him from the gas station doorway, like she was trying to work up the nerve to approach him.

Hurley hadn't recognized her, but that didn't mean anything. She had the look of a train hopper, some vagabond runaway, and she'd stared at the knife like she'd seen it before. And now she was here.

She knows who you are.

Through the scope of the rifle, Hurley saw the moment the girl's flight instinct took over. She bolted, ran down the length of the porch, away from Hurley, threw herself over the side. Landed in the snow and kept running, slogging through the drifts, headed for the trees opposite.

Hurley tracked her through the scope. Waited until she'd neared the edge of the clearing, then pulled the trigger again. Smiled with satisfaction as the girl disappeared from sight.

Damn it, but this was fun.

68

Finley stood on the gas the second the last coal car passed the crossing. The SUV's wheels chirped and spun, and then the truck launched forward over the tracks. Caught air as it crossed them, bouncing Stevens and Windermere around in their seats, came down hard on the other side, the logging road stretching out ahead of them again, nothing but forest and hard, jagged mountains, Trail Creek to the right and the valley rising ahead.

From her vantage point in the shotgun seat, Windermere searched the terrain for any sign of Leland Hurley's cabin, any trace of Mila Scott. Saw nothing. Wherever Hurley was, he was well camouflaged. The whole area looked completely uninhabited.

Finley slowed the truck as the road curved sharply. Windermere gripped the armrest. "Come on," she said. "We have to *move*, Deputy."

Finley guided the truck around the curve. "Won't do us much good if we wind up in the ditch," she said. "Slow and steady, right?"

"Won't do us much good if Mila Scott's dead when we get there," Windermere retorted. "No time for slow and steady, Deputy. Right now it's *fast as you can*."

Finley started to argue. Thought better of it. The truck's engine surged, and Windermere felt the speed pick up. She held on to the panic bar above her head, bounced her knee on the floor. Stared up at the mountains ahead and wondered which one hid Leland Hurley.

69

Mila pulled herself out of the snow. Checked her body for damage as she crawled out of the clearing. She'd heard the rifle shot, Hurley's third. She could swear she'd heard the bullet as she threw herself to the ground, figured this was it, third time unlucky. Figured he'd put a hole in her back.

But she wasn't hurt. She could crawl. She could stand up and run through the trees—or wade; the snow was too deep for anything faster. She wasn't bleeding and she didn't feel any pain. In fact, she could see the tree trunk the bullet *had* struck. Hurley had missed her again. She was still alive.

Somehow.

Mila didn't expect Hurley to keep missing. She pushed farther into the forest as the ground began to drop away ahead of her, a steep, perilous declination, cliffs and jagged rock and fallen tree trunks. She would break her neck if she tried to run the drop; the mountain was too steep here. She didn't have a choice. She would have to push deeper into the trees, hope she could lose Hurley in the wilderness. Hope she could survive long enough to double back toward the road.

Mila caught her breath. Took the pistol from her pocket and started into the forest.

Hurley shouldered his rifle. Grinned to himself as he stepped into the clearing on his snowshoes.

This *was* fun.

He'd never seen the point in a quick, easy kill. Enjoyed the drama of the hunt, the suspense. He was a man who savored his kills, made the most of his efforts. He worked hard to secure his prey. Why shouldn't he enjoy himself a little?

Hurley could have killed the girl the moment she stepped out of his cabin. He'd had her lined up in his scope, and he never missed with his rifle, not from that range.

The rifle shot would have felled her. Probably killed her instantly. She would have died on his doorstep, never seeing his face. Would have died before he could touch her. Smell her. Punish her.

He'd fired to spook her. To jolt her into action, send her running, start the chase. She'd obliged him, though he'd had to fire twice to scare her out of her stupor. Did she know how lucky she was, that he'd spared her life? Admittedly not for long, but still. The girl was terrified now, thinking of nothing but survival. She would die exhilarated, her mind pure. She would die like the animal that she was.

Hurley started across the clearing toward where the girl had disappeared. He took his time; the girl had left footprints, deep, flailing gouges in the snow. He would follow them to her, as simple as if she'd drawn him a map.

Hell, it was easy.

It was almost unfair.

70

There was nowhere to hide.

Mila felt her strength flagging as she pushed through the deep snow. The mountainside was steep, the forest floor uneven, and the snow came up past her knees. She scrambled forward, clutching at trees to pull herself up the incline, away from the cabin, deeper into the wilderness. She was sweating through her clothing, panting for breath. Her legs screamed for rest, but she couldn't rest here. Not while every step left a trail for Hurley to follow.

She would have to press on.

Mila tried not to think about the killer behind her. Couldn't help it. He had a big gun. He knew the mountain better than she did. He could follow her footprints until she collapsed from exhaustion, and then he could do what he wanted to her. Or he could wait and let nature do the job for him. There was nothing back here, beyond Hurley's cabin. Nothing but forest and high, desolate mountains.

She would have to surprise him. She would have to lure him into a trap and shoot him before he shot her. Kill him. Then she could follow her footprints back to the cabin. She could find her way back down the mountain.

Mila stopped moving. Leaned against a tree as she surveyed the forest, looking for somewhere she could mount an ambush. She could hear something behind her—an engine. Was Hurley *driving* to meet her?

No time to think about that now. There was light through the branches, about thirty yards ahead and ten yards or so down the mountain. A clearing. She could lead Hurley there, watch from the trees until he was out in the open. Then she would empty the pistol at him and pray her shots hit.

Mila pushed off the tree. Forced her legs to keep slogging through the snow, checked back to make sure she was still leaving a trail. She was.

She'd fired a gun before, once, at Ronda Sixkill's birthday on Lake Superior. Ash had disappeared in the dark, come back with some rider's old .38 Special.

"Traded a fifth of Old Crow for an hour with this bad boy," she told Mila. "So let's make it count."

They'd disappeared down to the lakeshore, walked along the water until they found an overturned log, a patch of empty space. Ash set up a couple beer cans on the log, paced back to the edge of the woods, took aim, and knocked down both cans, just like that. The sound was deafening, left Mila's ears ringing. Seemed to echo out over the dark lake forever.

Ash brought a couple more cans of beer from her backpack. Cracked one and handed the other to Mila. Downed her own and waited until Mila had done the same. Then she took the can back and set it up on the log.

"Okay, cowboy," she said, handing the revolver to Mila. "Your turn."

Mila had hesitated. Guns made her nervous, even more than her knife did. But Ash was giving her that look, that We both know you're going to do what I say *look, and Mila couldn't think of a way out that didn't make her sound like a wimp. She took the gun, and the grip was warm where Ash had been holding it. She stepped out of the trees, leveled the revolver at the cans the way Ash had done. Took a deep breath and pulled the trigger.*

The trigger was heavier than she'd expected. She had to pull twice to get the gun to fire, and when it did, it fired wide and wild, high above the beer cans. Mila took aim, pulled the trigger again. More assertive this time. Missed again.

"Focus on the front sight," Ash told her. "Inhale deep and then let out half your breath and squeeze the trigger back, one continuous motion. But forget about the target. Focus on the sight."

Mila focused on the front sight. Let out half her breath. Tried to squeeze the trigger. Missed her shot again.

And again.

Missed every shot until they'd run through all the bullets, and Mila's cheeks were red from failing so hard.

"Well, whatever," Ash said, taking the revolver back. "Probably just a shitty gun, you know?"

Now, as Mila struggled through the snow toward the clearing, she gripped the pistol in her hand and knew Ash had been lying. Ash had knocked off both cans with her first try, after all. It wasn't the weapon. It was the shooter.

Still, Leland Hurley was bigger than a beer can. And the pistol had plenty of bullets.

The clearing was close, just a few yards down the mountain from where she was standing. Mila couldn't see beyond the trees at the edge, just the gray daylight shining through the branches, but it was bright enough that she could tell the trees stopped there. She scrambled down the incline, made it almost to the light. Then she caught her foot on a root hidden in the snow.

She stumbled. Felt her balance slipping, nearly fell. Stayed upright, but careened forward, her boots sliding, toppling her toward the tree line. She reached for branches, grabbed them, and felt them give way. She was too heavy. She was moving too fast. She fell through the tree line and saw nothing but thin air beyond.

It wasn't a clearing through the branches. It was a cliff.

She was moving too fast to avoid the edge. Couldn't find a handhold to stop the fall. Burst out of the trees and onto the rocky ledge, had a brief, split-second view of a carpet of forest spread out for miles, distant snow-covered mountains, and then she was tumbling over the edge, arms pinwheeling in front of her, grabbing at air and then bracing for protection as the ground rushed up to meet her—snow and black, angry rock—and she was closing her eyes and praying she survived.

71

Hurley followed the girl's footsteps into the forest. Smiled as her trail traced the slope of the mountain. She had nowhere to run in this direction, he knew. She had nowhere to hide. He would find her eventually, sure as the sunrise. And in the meantime, he would enjoy the hunt.

Hurley's snowshoes made light work of the terrain. He could cover the ground quicker than the girl, catch up with her before long. And then? Hurley was undecided. He could shoot her with the rifle; that would be the quickest way to deal with her, the easiest way. But quick and easy wasn't fun. Hurley wanted to hurt this girl, whoever she was.

He had his knife with him, the Indian girl's knife. He could incapacitate her, bring her back to the cabin. Discuss her motives for coming here, explore her mind a little. There was nothing that said he had to kill her tonight.

Hurley followed the trail through the trees, along the mountainside, around fallen logs and rocky outcroppings. The girl's footprints were rushed, indistinct; Hurley could see where she'd scrabbled at the snow with her hands, where she'd stumbled. He could see where she'd slowed to rest.

She would tire easily. Her legs would give out from under her, and she would have to stop, whether she wanted to or not. The cold would overwhelm her. She would close her eyes to rest—just for a minute, she would tell herself, seduced by her fatigue. She would lose the battle.

He would surprise her. Rouse her. And then the real fun would begin.

The girl's trail leveled out, and Hurley could see where she'd stopped under a tall fir tree. He imagined her looking around, gasping for breath and listening for him behind her. He followed her trail with his eyes, saw the gap in the trees, saw her trail dip toward it. He took his rifle from his shoulder and followed her prints, slower now.

Hurley suspected he knew what was beyond the trees. He was certain the girl didn't. But he could also imagine the girl plotting to trap him, lead him somewhere vulnerable and ambush him. He advanced on the edge of the forest slowly, scanning the ground for any sign of trickery.

The girl's trail became muddled above the gap in the trees. Her footprints coalesced into one erratic track, as if she'd slipped and fallen—or deliberately tried to obscure her trail.

Hurley studied the snow closely, looking for clues. She might have tried to misdirect him, but she couldn't hide her own tracks, not so effectively that he couldn't find her. But Hurley could see no sign of any ambush. What he did see was a scrap of paper on the ground, a few feet from her footprints.

Hurley picked up the paper. It was blue-lined and folded, torn from a notebook, and Hurley felt a twinge of recognition as he studied it. He'd folded and unfolded that paper many times in the past, replaying the night he'd shared with its owner. Alberta, her name was, and her boyfriend was Dave, some jacked-up rig pig who'd run off to the oil fields. She'd cried when he'd read the note aloud to her, Dave's promises and half-literate professions of love.

Alberta. The note had been in his treasure chest. The girl had found his souvenirs, and she'd taken this one with her. That was a bad sign. That meant she knew everything.

Hurley stuffed the note in his pocket. Looked around for any more of his treasures. Couldn't see any. Satisfied, he cradled his rifle again. Picked his way down the snow toward the light through the trees, followed the girl's messy trail through the branches to where the snow stopped and the rock ledge began, just as he'd expected.

There was a cliff here, not a tall one, maybe fifteen feet high. There was a stunning view from the top, the next valley over, Anchor Creek almost all the way down to town. The mountains on the other side of the valley, the Flathead National Forest. Hurley had taken the view before, on his hunts. He'd learned to be wary of the rocks.

But the girl hadn't been as prudent. Hurley could see the impression in the snow at the base of the cliff where she'd fallen. He could see the trail where she'd dragged herself to cover in the forest, a few yards away. He lifted his rifle, scanned the tree line for any sign of her. Didn't see anything. Then he put the rifle down. Cocked his head and listened.

Another engine. Somewhere back through the forest, on the other side of the mountain. It must be close, if he could hear it from here. It must be almost at the cabin.

Damn.

Hurley looked out over the forest, the valley. Scanned the trees for the girl, still didn't see her. But he could still hear the engine, loud and clear. Hurley listened. He waited.

Then the engine stopped.

Damn.

72

Mila Scott's stolen pickup was blocking the road.

Kerry Finley climbed from her SUV and walked up to the hairpin where Mila must have lost control, locked the steering, and slid the truck into a stand of pine trees just beyond the edge. The front wheels lay in deep snow, but the pickup's ass end hung out over the road, its back tires barely touching ground. The road was too narrow for Finley's Explorer to squeeze by. And from what Stevens could see, Mila Scott hadn't stuck around by her wreck.

On the mountain above, there was nothing but silence, eerie and foreboding. Behind them, the sun was already settling down toward the mountains on the other side of the Stillwater River Valley. Night would be here before long. Mila Scott was up the road somewhere. And Stevens, Finley, and Windermere had no way through but on foot.

"Let's just ram it," Windermere said, pointing at the pickup. "Pardon the pun, but why can't we just muscle that damn truck out of the way?"

Finley scratched her head. "I don't like it."

"Why? Afraid you'll mess up your paint job?"

"Heck, the county will cover that. No." Finley gestured at the truck, the snowy road. "It just won't work, is all. Not enough traction coming up that incline, and that's a half-ton truck we'd be trying to bully. More than likely we'd just end up spinning our wheels."

"Literally and figuratively," Windermere said. "So you want to just hike it?"

"Looks like Mila did." Stevens was up the other side of the hairpin. "I have boot prints leading from the wreck up the road," he said. "Look too small to be Hurley's."

Windermere checked out the wreck again. "Shit," she said, drawing her Glock. "This just gets better and better."

But the road leveled off a few hundred yards farther. Stevens stopped for breath just shy of the summit, hands on his knees, red-faced, panting hard. Not exactly the condition you wanted to find yourself in when you arrived for the big showdown with the killer, but hell, there was no way around it. Even Windermere looked bagged.

"I can see why this guy Hurley got away with it for so long," she was telling Finley. "Nobody wanted to make the trip up here to confront him."

Finley gave her a grim smile. She had her rifle strapped to her shoulder, her service pistol holstered. She wiped the sweat from her brow. "Shall we?"

They stuck to the side of the road, as close to the tree line as the snow would allow. Ducked low, crept fast. Made the last rise and found themselves in a clearing, a cabin at the far end, nobody around, Hurley's old Suburban nowhere to be seen.

"Anybody home?" Windermere whispered.

"Guess we'd better find out." Stevens caught Finley's eye. "Give us some cover, would you? We're sitting ducks once we're out in that clearing."

Finley retreated to the trees. Trained her rifle on the cabin. "Good to go," she told them. "Be careful."

They broke apart and crossed the clearing on either side of the cabin's front door, leaving a clear shot for Finley in between them. Windermere arrived at the porch first. Stevens ducked in behind her, stayed low.

"See the size of those picture windows?" Windermere asked him. "If anyone's in there, they know *we're* out here."

"So either they don't care or they're waiting to trap us," Stevens said. "Whichever it is, let's stay sharp."

Windermere gave a silent count. At three, they dashed up the steps to the doorway. Stevens tried the handle. Unlocked. Windermere stepped back, trained her gun on the entrance. Nodded to Stevens, who pulled the door open, free hand tight on his pistol, ready to react as soon as the shooting started.

But nobody fired on them. Windermere ducked into the cabin. Stevens followed her. It was a single room, small. Nobody inside. No one hiding under the bed.

No sign of a struggle, either, just dust hanging in the air. The bed made, the clothes put away. A rug on the floor. No telling when the last human being had been in here.

"So where the hell are they?" Windermere said.

Stevens didn't have an answer. Couldn't decide if it was a good sign or not that they hadn't found Hurley or Mila yet. Had been counting on finding one of them, at least, up here at the cabin.

Then Kerry Finley called their names from outside, and Stevens and Windermere hurried out. Found the deputy standing in the middle of the clearing, pointing at the snow.

"Tracks," she told them. "Boots from the front door, right there, into the forest. And here." She pointed again. "I could be mistaken, but that looks a lot like snowshoes."

Stevens followed the trail. "I guess they're onto each other. That sure looks like a chase."

"And we're late to the party, as usual," Windermere said, starting for the trees. "Come on, team. Let's see if we can't catch up."

73

Hurley listened.

The sound of the engine had not returned. The air was still again. Below the cliff, in the trees, nothing moved. Hurley listened and tried to work out his options.

It was not a coincidence that another vehicle had come to his cabin. That engine, whatever it was, belonged to friends of the girl. It might even belong to the law. Whoever they were, the new visitors would surely search the cabin. They would find what the girl had found. His treasure chest. His souvenirs.

If they weren't the law, they would call the law soon enough. And if they were the law, they would know who he was. They would know what he'd done.

Hurley scanned the base of the cliff with his rifle's scope again. Searched the trees for the girl. But the trees were thick and provided good cover. Hurley couldn't see more than a few feet into the forest.

He'd been looking forward to capturing the girl. He was enjoying the hunt. He would have liked to have talked to her, coerced her into telling him how she'd come to be here. Now he supposed he might not ever know.

The mountain was quiet. Nothing moved in the forest. Hurley listened and pondered his next move.

Mila hugged her knees to her chest and forced herself to be still. Tried to blend in to the shadows around her.

She'd barely dragged herself from the cliff when Leland Hurley showed up above her. She couldn't walk; she'd busted up her ankle pretty bad in the fall, though she guessed she should be thankful that the snow was deep and she wasn't hurt worse. She'd pulled herself to cover, biting through her lip to keep from crying from the pain. Made the tree line and looked up to see Hurley come onto the ledge.

He was smart enough not to fall, she saw. She'd hoped he would make the same mistake she had, but he'd either known the area or known enough to be careful. Damn.

Mila backed into the forest, where her dark clothes would camouflage her from Hurley and his sniper scope. She found a small break in the tree branches that afforded a view of the cliff, and she watched him, hardly daring to breathe, her ankle throbbing with pain.

Hurley stood there a long time, his head cocked, like he was trying to listen for her. Mila didn't move. Didn't make any noise, even as her muscles began to ache. She fought the pain, felt herself losing. Then, just as she realized she would have to shift position or cry out, Hurley disappeared from her sight.

Mila waited. Searched the break in the branches, but Hurley didn't return. She stretched out her legs, tested her wounded ankle. Couldn't bear any weight. Either broken or badly sprained, she wasn't sure, but it hurt like a mother. Damn it.

There was no noise from up on the cliff. Hurley still hadn't appeared through the break in the trees, but Mila knew he was out there. Knew he was coming for her. And with her ankle messed up as bad as it was, Mila knew, with a sickening certainty, she wasn't ever going to outrun him.

74

Hurley climbed through the forest. Retraced the girl's steps to where she'd turned down toward the cliff, and kept climbing. Cut a branch from a fir tree, used it to brush the snow behind him, clear his tracks as he climbed. It was painstaking work, but Hurley hoped he had time. It would take a while for the girl's friends to discover her trail. It would take longer for them to follow it here.

He climbed up the mountain and across, aiming north, back toward the cabin, but thirty yards up the grade. Climbed until he could no longer see the girl's footprints in the snow below, then continued across the mountain. He was high enough now that the girl's friends wouldn't see him. He could slip past them in secret, make his escape.

That's what this was now, an escape. Hurley had wanted badly to hunt the girl down, but he'd realized on the cliff that to do so would be suicide. The girl's friends would follow her trail. If he continued to track her, he risked giving away his position. The girl could scream for help. She could make noise if she fell again. Or maybe they would just hear him kill her.

Hurley had hunted long enough to know that sometimes the prey got away. He'd learned to weigh the risks, knew when to concede the chase, retreat, and regroup. This girl wasn't worth the risk to his freedom. He could hunt her, and kill her, but she would likely be his last.

And he wasn't through hunting. Not by a long shot.

Hurley kept a smooth, steady pace as he trekked through the forest. Knew he didn't need to overexert himself. The girl's friends would follow her trail to the cliff face. With any luck, they would follow her down.

It would be night soon, anyway. The temperature would drop, and the girl and her friends would find the mountain very uncomfortable. They'd quite likely get lost. They might even die. The mountain wasn't kind to outsiders.

Hurley heard something through the trees, somewhere below. Voices. The girl's friends. He knelt in the snow and took his rifle from his shoulder. Put the scope to his eye and scanned the forest.

The snow was deep. Windermere could feel her boots soaking through as she slogged after Stevens. Could hear Kerry Finley behind her, breathing heavily, the swish of her pants as she trudged down the trail.

Stevens was leading, his pistol drawn, his eyes on the ground in front of him. The trail was an easy one to find, not so easy to follow. Mila Scott's footprints attested to that; they dragged into one another, sloppy, as if she'd lacked the energy to lift her feet fully out of the snow.

Of course, the snowshoes had made easy work of the terrain, Windermere could see. They made a much lighter impression in the snow, seemed to glide through the forest. Leland Hurley would have had little trouble catching up to the young woman.

Windermere stuck close to Stevens. Searched the forest ahead. Prayed they weren't closing in on a murder scene.

Hurley dropped down the mountain as stealthily as he could manage. Dropped as low as he dared, then ducked behind a tree and raised the rifle again. Watched as the intruders came into view.

There were three of them, two women and a man. The man and the black woman stank of government. They wore big dark jackets, hats, and gloves, carried pistols like they knew what to do with them. State cops, Hurley figured, or maybe even feds.

The second woman was local, a sheriff or a sheriff's deputy. She dressed like the law, a well-worn coat with a badge and a fur collar, carried a rifle at her hip. The cops waded through the snow, struggling, the man's face red, all three breathing heavily. Hurley tracked the man in his sight. Followed him through the trees, brought his finger to the trigger.

He could kill this man. Put him down quick, before he knew what was happening. The notion was tempting. The shot was right there. With one squeeze of the trigger, he could rain hell on this interloper.

The man kept marching, oblivious, head down, working the trail. The black woman must have been his partner. The other must have been their guide. Her eyes swung left and right, like she expected an ambush. She was probably quick with that rifle.

There was a fair chance the first two *were* feds, Hurley realized. If the law had followed him up the mountain, the chances were they already knew what he'd done to the women. And that made him a prime target for the FBI and their ilk.

Hurley continued to track the leader. Massaged the trigger with his finger, debated the shot. He could kill the man, sure, and probably his partner, before they cottoned on to what was happening. If he didn't kill all three of them, though, the survivors would take up the chase. They would call for reinforcements. And dead FBI agents would attract major attention.

Just how quick can you be with that rifle, big guy?

Hurley followed the lead fed in his sight. Ached to shoot the bastard, drop all three—*bam bam bam*—in succession. But he didn't pull the trigger. Knew he couldn't take the risk. He tracked the fed until he'd disappeared into the forest. Then he let his breath out, shouldered the rifle. Straightened and continued, reluctantly, back toward the cabin, leaving the law to try to track down the girl, oblivious to the hunter who'd just showed them mercy.

75

The cliff nearly killed Stevens.

He'd been following Mila Scott's trail as it curved sharply down the slope of the mountain. Looked up and saw the bright spot through the trees, daylight making its last stand, saw the way Mila's trail led right for it. Stevens followed, nearly tripped on a root through the snow, barely caught himself before he crashed through the tree branches and into the bright. He *did* catch himself, grabbed on to a trunk and held it for dear life until he was sure he wasn't going anywhere. Then he peeked through the trees and was glad he'd reached out when he had; on the other side of the branches was a rock ledge about three feet wide, and then a sheer drop maybe twenty feet down to more forest.

Windermere poked her head out behind him. Took in the view, then the drop. "Whoa," she said. "Good thing you slowed up, partner. You would have been flying."

Stevens waited for his heart rate to calm. "Looks like someone else wasn't so lucky," he said, pointing down to the base of the cliff. "That's an impact crater in the snow right there."

Windermere followed his finger. "Hell of a drop."

"Sure is. But was it Mila or Leland Hurley who took the leap?"

There was no way to tell. Whoever had fallen had disappeared again, into the trees.

"So how do we get down there?" Windermere asked. "I'm assuming you don't want to jump."

Before Stevens could answer, Finley interrupted. "I hate to be *that* person," she said, "but that sun is setting fast. We keep going with this, we're risking getting caught out here come nightfall."

"The girl's out there," Windermere said. "Leland Hurley's out there. If we let this trail go cold, we might never find either of them."

"You could die out there with them, if you don't turn back now."

"We're not turning back," Windermere said. "Not while there's a chance Mila Scott's still alive. Right, Stevens?"

Stevens looked out over the valley, at the bright spot through the clouds where the sun would be, just about at the top of the mountains in the distance. He realized he could hear something: engines, revving high and getting closer. From the looks on Finley's and Windermere's faces, they heard it, too.

"That'll be the backup," Stevens said. "Flathead County deputies finally."

"Finally," Windermere said.

Stevens listened a moment longer. "Kerry, you go back to Hurley's cabin," he told Finley. "Meet the Flathead deputies, explain the situation. See if you can't get us a helicopter. Barring that, get us some backup. We'll follow the trail until nightfall. Then we'll turn back to this cliff."

Finley studied his face. "And if you get lost?"

"We'll yell as loud as we can," Windermere said. "So keep your ears open. Come on, partner. We're losing daylight. Let's find a way down this cliff."

Finley watched them, concerned. She wasn't happy with this plan, Stevens could tell.

"We'll be back at this cliff before dark," Stevens told her. "Just make sure you have some more deputies waiting for us."

76

The shadows were all-encompassing now. The cold was setting in. Mila could hear movement in the forest somewhere, but she couldn't see Hurley anymore. She couldn't see much of anything.

Hurley's absence didn't give Mila any comfort. She wasn't safe here in the woods, and if she stayed, she would die. The daylight was dwindling. She would freeze overnight. And anyway, Hurley wouldn't give up on her easily. He'd seen her coming out of his cabin. He must have suspected she'd known.

Mila tested her ankle. Collapsed to the snow again, wincing, tears in her eyes. Bit the sleeve of her jacket to keep from crying out. She wasn't going anywhere, not in this state. Not on her feet, at least.

She pushed herself deeper into the forest, sliding on her butt, digging in the snow with her gloves. Her clothes were damp with sweat, her pants soaked through with snowmelt. She was exhausted and hungry. She hadn't eaten since breakfast.

Mila pushed back until she came to a fallen tree, almost as thick around as she was. She leaned against it to rest and realized as she lay there that she couldn't go any farther.

So be it. She couldn't fight the cold, not forever. But she *could* fight

Leland Hurley, if and when he came for her. Mila took the pistol from her coat pocket. With the last of her strength, she pushed herself up and over the fallen tree. Landed hard on the other side, felt that pain in her ankle again, waited for it to dissipate. Turned around, propped herself up on the trunk by her elbows, facing back the way she'd come.

Hurley was coming through those trees. Mila knew it. She gripped the pistol tight. She would be ready when he came.

The going was slow. The grade was steep. Stevens gripped tree branches and bare rocky outcroppings, tried to keep his balance as he led Windermere down through the forest. Knew if he hurt himself here, he would probably die.

As it was, there was a better-than-zero chance they would die out here. A part of Stevens wondered what had possessed him to ignore Kerry Finley's warnings, was thinking, best case, he and Windermere were on the verge of becoming rescue fodder themselves.

Never mind that now. There was a young woman out there, and a killer who'd been loose long enough.

Stevens stepped down off a rocky ledge, landed in about three feet of snow. Turned back to help Windermere down, then together they pushed through the trees to the clearing at the base of the cliff.

The clearing was still empty. They could see the impression in the snow where Hurley or Mila had landed, the trail into the woods where they'd dragged themselves. They could see no other tracks in the snow. They couldn't see Leland Hurley, and they couldn't see Mila Scott.

But that didn't mean they weren't out there.

"Come on." Windermere tugged Stevens's sleeve. Pointed around

the edge of the clearing, a dense ring of trees. "Let's circle around to that trail."

She took the lead now, her Glock drawn. Stevens followed, casting glances out into the clearing, the cliff face, gauging the minutes left until dark.

Hurley was down the cliff. He was getting closer. Mila could hear the trees moving, could see snow falling from the branches. She couldn't see him yet, but he was getting closer. He would follow her trail to the log. And she would be ready.

Mila braced herself against the tree trunk. Leveled the pistol, followed the branches as they rustled in the gloom. She could hear engines in the distance, getting louder. Coming up the mountain. They belonged to the police, hopefully. Maybe the waitress at the diner had sent them.

Either way, Mila realized she wasn't alone on this mountain with Leland Hurley. There was a chance she wouldn't die in the cold.

She just had to survive Hurley first.

Mila could see movement now, just a silhouette through the tree trunks. Couldn't make out his face, but she knew it was Hurley. Mila tracked him with the pistol, her finger tensed on the trigger. Tried to remember what Ash had told her, about exhaling partway. Squeezing the trigger. She waited until the silhouette was standing directly in front of her, fifteen yards away. She took a breath, let it out.

Then she pulled the trigger.

77

Nothing happened.

The gun didn't go off. Mila pulled the trigger again. Nothing. Maybe the gun wasn't loaded. That had to be it. She fumbled in her pocket for the spare magazine, couldn't make it work. Hurley was closing in, and she couldn't even figure out how to load the damn gun. There wasn't any way she could stop him.

She crouched against the tree, as still as she could manage, praying that Hurley wouldn't see her in the dark. Maybe he would walk right past her. Totally miss her. But that wasn't freaking likely.

Mila watched the silhouette get closer. Tried to resign herself to the inevitable. She'd brought the police here. They would find Hurley and arrest him. She had done right by Ash.

But had she?

Would they arrest Leland Hurley?

She had replaced Hurley's box of keepsakes underneath his rug. She'd covered the evidence that would prove to the police what he'd done, and what she hadn't hidden she'd brought into the woods. Hurley could hide her body, bury his mementos. The police would never know it was him.

Mila felt sick with disgust. Fear. She'd come all this way, come so close. And she'd fucked up again.

She would never be like Ash.

Then it came to her. The freaking *safety* was on. She'd seen enough action movies to know about that. Mila turned the pistol. Found the little lever on the grip of the gun. Slipped it into fire mode. Braced herself again, found the attacker in her front sight, ten yards distant. Held the gun steady. Let off her breath. Squeezed the trigger back.

This time, the gun roared.

78

Windermere threw herself to the ground as the gun exploded out of nowhere, everywhere, about ten yards ahead, point-blank. The muzzle flare lit up the forest for a split second, showed her nothing but trees and an overturned log, and then she was diving for cover.

The snow cushioned her fall. Swallowed her up, face and all, and she rolled away from the gunfire, spitting out ice chips and wiping her eyes. Hurley had missed her, she realized; she wasn't hit and she prayed Stevens wasn't, either. Prayed he had the good sense to get down and stay there.

Bang bang bang!

More shots. Windermere heard them ricochet off rock behind her, splinter trees. Couldn't tell how close they were coming to her head, didn't really want to find out. She crawled out of the firing line until she found a tree stump. Rolled behind it, flipped onto her stomach, raised her Glock in front of her, and waited for Hurley to fire again. He didn't disappoint.

Bang bang bang bang!

Found him.

Windermere swung her pistol toward the source of the gunfire. Squeezed off four shots of her own, saw wood chips flying. Heard more shots somewhere else, realized it was Stevens, across the other side of the log. Surrounding the bastard, moving in slow.

Good work, partner. We got this asshole.

Windermere pushed out from the snow as Hurley returned fire in Stevens's direction. Ran forward five feet or so, took cover behind a tree. Ducked out, looked for the muzzle flare. Couldn't get a good shot from here.

"Drop your weapon!" Stevens was shouting. *"FBI, Hurley. Give it up now!"*

Windermere inched left. Saw another stump a couple yards over, good cover, good line of sight. She counted to three, made a dash for it. Heard Hurley open up behind her, heard bullets whiz past. But she made it. Landed safe. Could just make out the log in the last of the daylight. Trained her Glock on the middle of it, an unmissable shot, and waited for Hurley to pop his head up again.

Mila was out of bullets. The gun had clicked empty, and she still couldn't figure out how to reload. Hurley was yelling something, but she couldn't make out the words. Her ears were ringing from the gunshots. Hurley seemed to be firing at her from everywhere.

She was going to die out here in the snow.

Mila crouched low. Fumbled with the pistol. Hurley was right on top of her now. She was almost out of time.

Then she pressed a button by the trigger and heard the magazine fall into the snow. *Bingo.* Mila dug the other mag from her pocket. Stuffed it into the gun, heard the satisfying *chunk* just as she saw a shadow move to her left, five yards from the log. She swung around, racked the slide, finger back on the trigger. Was about to let fly when a woman called out from behind her.

"FBI, Hurley, we have you surrounded. Put. The gun. Down."

A second shooter. A woman. Mila couldn't be sure, but she swore she'd heard *FBI.* These were the freaking *cops* shooting at her.

Her mind struggled to process. Couldn't make it work. Why were the cops trying to kill her? Did Hurley have the FBI in his pocket?

No.

Impossible.

"It doesn't get any easier, Hurley, I promise. Put the gun down and let's end this thing peacefully."

They thought *she* was Hurley. They thought she was the ghost rider. They thought they were shooting the bad guy.

And the FBI knew Leland Hurley was the bad guy.

Mila called out, as loud as she could, *"I'm not Hurley. Please don't shoot me!"*

There was a pause. A long pause. Then the woman called back.

"I'm a special agent with the FBI, hon," she said. "My partner's here with me. We'll show you our badges if you promise not to shoot us."

"I won't shoot you," Mila told her. "I thought you were Hurley. I thought—"

"Put the gun down," the woman said, her voice calm. "Stand up, nice and slow. Keep your hands up until we can figure this out, okay?"

Mila leaned against the log, tall as she could. "I can't stand up. My ankle . . . I fell off the cliff."

From out in the gloaming, a flashlight appeared. It shone over the snow until it found Mila's log. Mila raised her hands. Squinted into the beam. To her left, another flashlight. Footsteps. The agents lowered their lights as they approached the log, and Mila could see a black woman and a middle-aged white man.

"I'm so sorry I shot at you," Mila said. Her heart was still pounding. "I thought you were Hurley."

"We thought *you* were Hurley," the man said. "Glad we sorted things out before . . ."

He didn't have to finish. Mila let her body relax a little bit. Then she thought of something. "Wait a second," she said. "If you guys didn't catch Hurley, then where is he?"

79

Hurley was nearly at the cabin when the cavalry arrived, three Flathead County deputies in souped-up Dodge Durango off-road vehicles, lights blazing, men piling out with rifles drawn, faces flushed with excitement and pent-up adrenaline.

Hurley stuck to the forest at the back of his property. Circled the cabin, watching the men as they secured the clearing, as a couple of them entered the cabin.

It was time to leave. It was time to set out from this place and get far, far away. Whether the FBI found the girl or not, Hurley knew he was made. This was what manhunts looked like before they got off the ground. This was a goddamn situation.

He kept calm. Pushed the anger down in his gut, the frustration that flashed when he thought of the girl in the forest, the three cops behind her. Two of them women, as if it weren't bad enough already.

He chased the thought from his mind. Stole away through the trees until he'd found his hand-hewn road, followed it along the ridgeline, moving fast through the snow, ignoring the chaos behind him.

Night fell as he walked, had fallen completely by the time he arrived at his snowmobile, the forest dark and silent this far from the cabin. Hurley started the engine, tensed as it rumbled to life, fearing the law would hear it and know immediately where he'd gone.

But the forest remained mute. No lawmen appeared to challenge Hurley. He straddled the machine and drove farther into the mountain range, the road narrowing now, progress slow.

Then he reached the end of the road, a wall of trees where he'd been forced to halt his efforts at the end of the summer season. Hurley killed the engine, strapped on his snowshoes again. He kept survival gear in a cargo box on the back of the machine, spare rations and fresh water, a bivouac sack and a lightweight subzero sleeping bag, a compact shovel to dig into the snow for shelter. He kept spare ammunition for the rifle, too, and a pair of night-vision goggles he'd found at the military surplus store in Kalispell.

Hurley abandoned the snowmobile. Double-checked his supplies, shouldered his rifle, and adjusted his goggles. He set off into the dense woods beyond his crude road and didn't look back.

80

"A shootout with the victim herself." Windermere cast an arched eye at her partner. "That's a new one."

Across the booth, Stevens didn't know whether to laugh or have a heart attack. He was still trying to process the events on the mountain, still struggling with how close they'd come to shooting Mila Scott dead.

"Good thing she's a lousy shot." Windermere drank her coffee. "Otherwise, you and I would be full of holes, partner."

"I guess we're pretty lousy shots ourselves," Stevens replied. "And I've never been so thankful to say it."

It was nearly midnight. They'd helped Mila out of the woods and back to the base of the cliff. The Flathead deputies, spurred on by the sounds of gunfire, had arrived shortly thereafter. They'd dropped blankets and food down the cliff to the agents, informed them that a helicopter was on its way up from Whitefish.

Stevens and Windermere had kept Mila warm as they waited for the helicopter. Mila told them her story, about her friendship with Ashlyn Southernwood and Ronda Sixkill, how Mila had risked the High Line even though she knew better, how Mila had leaned on her network of train hoppers to track down Leland Hurley.

"He was wearing Ash's knife when he came into the store," Mila had told them. "Back in Anchor Falls. Ash always carried that knife. She loved it. It belonged to her grandmother."

"And you saw it and decided you *had* to hunt this guy down," Windermere said.

Mila hadn't answered right away. Avoided Windermere's eyes. "No offense, but it's not like the cops ever did anything," she said. "Leland Hurley's been riding forever, and nobody cares. I don't even know how many women he got before Ash."

"At least twenty-five," Stevens told her. "But we don't have an exact number."

"See? Everyone just takes it for granted that the cops don't give a shit. We have to solve these problems on our own."

"*We* give a shit," Windermere said. "I don't know about the local law enforcement, but the Federal Bureau of Investigation takes killers like Leland Hurley serious as cancer."

Mila didn't say anything. Stevens wondered if she was trying to reconcile the FBI's definition of justice with her own. Or maybe she was just in shock, or simply scared. Leland Hurley was still out there, after all, somewhere in the forest. It was an eerie feeling. The woods were dark now, visibility minimal, and Stevens kept his gun handy. Windermere did the same.

The sound of helicopter rotors had filled the valley. To the west, down toward Anchor Falls, the lights of a police chopper swung up out of the darkness. Stevens and Windermere watched it approach. Mila, too.

"He had a little box hidden under the floorboards," Mila said. She kept her eye on the approaching helicopter. "That's where I found the gun, under the rug. He had the gun and some money, and his creepy little box."

She'd pulled her coat around herself. She was still watching the sky, and her eyes were inscrutable. "He kept mementos in the box. Like, he took Ash's knife, but I guess he kept other things, too." She dug around in her pocket. "Some of them fell out of my coat in the forest, but I kept this." She held something out to them. Stevens shined his flashlight on it: an asthma inhaler. "It belonged to someone named Pamela Moody."

There it was. If Stevens and Windermere had been looking for conclusive proof that Leland Hurley was their killer, the inhaler in Mila's hands sealed the deal.

"Pamela Moody," Mila repeated. She pursed her lips. "I guess she's dead now, whoever she was."

Stevens met Windermere's eyes. There was a hint of a smile on his partner's face, just a little. Leland Hurley was still at large, sure, but Mila Scott was safe. Pamela Moody was safe. The tide was starting to turn.

"Let's get you out of here," Windermere told Mila as the helicopter descended into a hover above the cliff. "We can talk more when we've all warmed up a little."

They'd flown back to Anchor Falls and commandeered Norma's Diner, fashioning it into a base of operations, county deputies everywhere—Flathead, Lincoln—even Judd Parsons, sheriff of Lincoln County, had showed up to pitch in. Agents from the Bureau's Kalispell resident agency were en route, too, another helicopter. Until Leland Hurley was captured, Anchor Falls was in manhunt mode.

Stevens and Windermere had taken a corner booth, a couple cups of coffee and two slices of damn good cherry pie. They sat across from each other and watched county SUVs and pickups jockey for space in the parking lot, watched Northwestern Railroad trains stack up on the tracks on the other side of the highway. All traffic was halted, both rail and road, at least for the time being, though just how long that would last nobody was quite sure. Given Leland Hurley's seeming ability to vanish into the snow, it was imperative that they pick up his trail quickly.

But it was too dark for any hunting now. The mountains were a black void against a black sky, the only light in the Anchor Valley coming from helicopter spotlights. Mila Scott hadn't been sure where Hurley had gone; he'd been up on the cliff, the last she'd seen him.

"You didn't hear anyone come down before us?" Windermere had asked while they waited for the helicopter. "No way he beat us down?"

"If he did, he would have found me," Mila replied. "Sure seemed easy enough for you guys."

Stevens mulled this over as he finished his pie. He remembered hearing the sounds of the deputies' engines as they raced up the logging road toward Hurley's cabin. The sound had come clear as he stood on the cliff. Hurley would have heard Kerry Finley's truck if he'd been in the same place. Maybe he'd realized it was time to start running.

Wherever he'd gone, Hurley was still out there, somewhere in the millions of square acres of forest and rock. He was armed, he had snowshoes, and he knew the terrain. Stevens knew he wasn't going to go down easy.

The *thump thump thump* of an approaching helicopter rattled the diner's windows. Stevens looked out across the parking lot in time to watch the Flathead County's Bell 429 Search and Rescue chopper touch down on a blocked-off stretch of highway. The helicopter was equipped with night vision, 3-D terrain mapping, and the rescue hoist that had already lifted Mila Scott to safety. It would be a valuable tool in the hunt for Leland Hurley—but it hadn't found him yet.

A Flathead County deputy climbed from the rear of the chopper and, ducking away from the rotor wash, hurried across the parking lot to the diner. Stevens turned as he burst in through the front doors, watched the man's eyes search the room, settle on him and Windermere.

"Just heard from the Lincoln County deputy up at the cabin," he called across the diner. "She found something she thinks you should see."

81

Five minutes later, they were back in the helicopter, lifting off from the chopper's makeshift landing pad and speeding back through the night toward the eastern end of the Trail Valley. Kerry Finley was riding herd on more deputies up there, jurisdictional issues be damned, locking down the cabin and looking for any evidence they could use against Hurley—or any indication of where he might want to escape to.

Stevens leaned in between the front seats of the helicopter. Watched the ground pass below on the night-vision screen, courtesy of the infrared camera mounted underneath the chopper's nose. If Hurley was down there, he would show up as a heat signature, a beacon of light against the murky terrain. But the ground was as dark on the infrared screen as it was through the windows. They were going to have to look harder to find their fugitive.

The helicopter touched down in the center of the clearing in front of Hurley's cabin. The deputies who'd arrived as backup had moved Mila's stolen pickup truck from the logging road below, and the fringes of the clearing were lined with more law enforcement vehicles. Someone had set up portable lights; they illuminated the cabin and the surrounding forest as if it were midday. The scene bustled with deputies, none of whom seemed concerned by the sudden arrival of a noisy SAR helicopter.

Finley was standing beside her Explorer, a pensive look on her face. She hustled over to the helicopter, climbed in beside Stevens, slammed the door.

"This might be something, it might not," she told the agents as the helicopter lifted off again. "But I think we should have a look regardless."

She gestured out the side window, down to Hurley's cabin, and Stevens looked where he was told, saw a couple smaller buildings behind the main cabin, a shed and an outhouse, Hurley's Suburban parked nearby.

"He keeps his generator in there," Finley said. "Hookup for his vehicle, too, keep the battery charged when the weather drops. The truck's still there, as you can see. But I found something else, too."

Beside the shed was a cut through the trees, a winding path farther into the wilderness. From above, it looked narrow, hardly wide enough for a vehicle, but Stevens could see tracks in the snow.

"Snowmobile," Finley told the agents. "Can't have been recent, or the deputies would have heard."

"But someone's been down there," Windermere said.

"Yup," Finley said. "I believe they have been."

The pilot switched on his spotlight. Traced the narrow road up the side of the mountain until it leveled off and skirted around the back. They flew ten minutes at low altitude, barely above the treetops, the narrow road getting narrower as it wound deeper into the backcountry, almost invisible through the trees.

"I couldn't make it a hundred feet from camp in my Explorer," Finley told the agents. "Trail was just too damned rough."

Stevens couldn't tell from the air, but it sure looked like he'd have his hands full in his old Jeep, even. Figured even a Ski-Doo would have a rough ride.

"He would have to know the road like he built it himself," Finley said, reading Stevens's mind. "Which he probably did. It's no logging road, isn't on any maps. Looks like he cut it through the forest by hand."

"My god," Windermere said. "That would take forever."

"He's had the place for ten years. Guess he had enough time."

"So how far does it go?" Stevens asked.

"Your guess is as good as mine," Finley said. "I was waiting on the helicopter."

Stevens stared down at the road, lit bright in the chopper's spotlight, the forest a suffocating dark on all sides. If Finley's instincts were right and Hurley had indeed escaped this way, he would have had to turn back toward the cabin at precisely the same time Stevens and Windermere were heading to intercept him. It was an unsettling notion, the thought of Hurley passing them, unseen, in the forest.

To this point, the searchers had focused their efforts on the Anchor Valley, to the south, where Mila Scott had been found. But if Hurley had come this way . . .

"What's back here?" Stevens asked Finley. "Where could Hurley be going?"

Finley looked through the front seats and out the helicopter's windshield. "Out there? Heck, a whole lot of nothing. You got the Whitefish Range, then the north fork of the Flathead River, then Glacier Park, the Lewis Range of the Rockies. No settlements for fifty miles, barely any people at all. Canada to the north, and nothing there, either. Nothing but the park to the south."

"A whole lot of nothing," Windermere said. "And our man wandered into it."

"It's nothing for us," Finley replied. "You and me. The way this guy Hurley moves, I'm guessing he sees all that empty space as his God-given backyard."

"Let's not get ahead of ourselves," Windermere said. "We still don't know he came this way."

But even as she was speaking, the helicopter banked and slowed. The pilot pointed through the windshield, angled his spotlight down to where the road petered out, ending unceremoniously at a wall of fir trees. And at the edge of the tree line sat a snowmobile, parked facing the forest like a car at a stoplight. It had been abandoned.

The pilot swiveled in his seat. "You want to drop down, check it out?"

Stevens met Windermere's eyes. "Guess we have to make sure," Windermere said, but from the tone of her voice, Stevens knew she was thinking the same thoughts he was: *Hurley's gone. He's somewhere in that backcountry. And whether he dies out there or not, we may never find him.*

82

Hurley could hear the helicopters in the distance. They were far away, still out of sight. No cause for concern. He would have plenty of time to hide, if they did turn his way.

The local newspaper had made a big deal when the sheriff's

department bought their helicopter. State-of-the-art, the articles gushed. Took more than a year to construct. Every toy and gadget that search and rescue could ever need. Law enforcement, too.

Hurley had read with interest. He'd made a note of the helicopter's features, the infrared camera most of all. If the helicopter flew over him, the occupants would spy his heat signature easily. He would have to find cover before the choppers approached.

The odds were slim they would find him. This was the backcountry, thousands of square miles of nothing but forest and rock. The FBI would find the snowmobile, realize he'd gone east into the Whitefish Range and not south, the way the girl had been leading him. They would focus their search efforts into the mountains, but Hurley wasn't concerned. He was one man in a vast expanse of wilderness. He knew these mountains like nobody else.

It was late now. Early morning. Hurley estimated he'd covered five miles since he'd abandoned the snowmobile. The going was slow. The snow was soft, and the forest dense with fallen trees and thick underbrush. The mountain rose and fell beneath him. He'd been moving almost continuously since he'd heard the girl approach and his muscles ached for rest. But there was no time.

The first night would be the most important. The more ground Hurley could cover before dawn, the better his chances at escape. He didn't doubt he could survive in these woods. He didn't doubt he could outwit the FBI. He'd been a ghost for the better part of a decade. He could disappear again, with a little bit of work, and the law would never find him.

Hurley trudged on. Picked his trail through the forest, brushing back snowy branches, climbing over broken trunks, the environment ghostly green through his night-vision lenses. He'd been waiting for this day, he realized, even looking forward to it. He'd preyed on the weak and the stupid for a long time. He relished the opportunity to test his skills against a tougher adversary.

Time would tell whether the FBI agents would prove to be any match. In the meantime, Hurley would test his wits against the mountain.

83

Stevens and Windermere rode the Flathead County's SAR chopper through the night, flying a grid pattern over the mountains until the pilot glanced back at them, pointing at the fuel gauges.

"Gotta head back," he told the agents through their headsets. "Otherwise, we're going to need rescuing ourselves."

Hurley's snowmobile hadn't provided them much. They'd found a mess of dead animals, a couple rabbits and a fox. A couple empty boxes of Golden Bear rounds for a .30-06 in a cargo box on the back, a wholesale-sized carton of Mayday survival bars stacked up alongside. Some cold-weather gear, army stuff, folded up neat. But Leland Hurley was gone, somewhere in the forest. Even his snowshoe trail was indistinct, impossible to follow with any semblance of speed.

"He'd be in Aruba before we made it out of the woods," Windermere had said. "What about dogs? Can we bring K9s out here?"

Stevens had shaken his head. "Not in wolf country. You're only asking for trouble. Anyway, it's a hell of a distance to track someone."

They'd signaled for the hoist, rode back up to the chopper. Flew tracks over the Whitefish Range into the early-morning hours, searching the helicopter's infrared screen for any kind of heat signature. They'd had a close call, something white and moving, something clearly alive, but when they'd hovered down for a closer look, whatever they were tracking had bugged out and bolted—on four legs.

"Mountain lion, maybe," the pilot said. "They're active at night."

"Maybe he's hunting Hurley," Windermere said. "We should be so lucky."

They'd tracked the creature for a couple miles, just to be sure, but whatever it was, it hadn't led them to Hurley. They'd turned away, the screen dark again, and continued combing the forest for any sign of the killer.

But now the fuel reserves were running low, and the pilot needed to get back to base.

"Don't sweat it," he called back through his headset. "Bureau's sending another chopper from Kalispell, right? They can take up the search where we left off."

Stevens looked out the window, though he couldn't see anything but night sky and the dark, undulating silhouette of the land below.

Damn it, time's wasting, he thought. *We can't afford to take a break.*

But it was either peel off or crash-land in the wilderness, so Stevens, Finley, and Windermere rode back in the chopper to Anchor Falls, had the pilot drop them off outside Norma's Diner, the lights inside still burning bright, long after midnight.

"What do you say, partner?" Windermere asked as the helicopter took flight again. "You up for another slice of pie?"

Stevens yawned. "I could use some more coffee, at least. Maybe it'll wake us up long enough to sort out a plan."

He was bushed. They'd been running nonstop since the last storm had blown over—from Butcher's Creek to Hungry Horse for the Pam Moody rescue and then back up to Anchor Falls, fast as they could, to track Mila Scott to Leland Hurley's cabin. Two solid days, straight adrenaline, and Stevens was pretty well used up.

Can't quit now. Hurley's still out there. Gotta stay on this until you lock him down.

"We'll run helicopter searches all night tonight and all day tomorrow," Windermere was saying across the booth. "Get boots on the ground, too, as many as we can muster. Put men on every logging road on both sides of the mountain range, get Northwestern bulls checking their trains, too."

"The Mounties as well," Stevens said, tracing a line on the map. "And Customs. Canadian border's only forty miles north of here. Could be he tries to make a run for it."

"True." Windermere wrote something in her notebook. "We'll cover every angle. Nothing leaves the county without our say-so, right?"

Stevens sipped his coffee. Studied a topographical map—a hell of a lot of land and not much humanity, a million places a man could disappear.

"Right," he said.

"Let's brief the deputies on our plan. Call the Bureau office in Kalispell, get an ETA on their men. See if we can't scrounge up a third helicopter." Windermere rubbed her eyes. "And then let's get some sleep, partner. It's going to be dawn soon enough."

84

There were no hotels in Anchor Falls. They slept in the back of Norma's Diner instead, a couple of booths toward the rear of the restaurant, the lights turned down low.

Windermere slept fitfully, curled up on the vinyl, her coat for a pillow. Woke at dawn to someone clearing his throat, opened her eyes and saw a couple of new faces, young men in heavy black FBI winter coats. They looked apologetic as she sat up wincing, massaging the back of her neck, blinking sleep away. It was a quarter after eight and the sun just rising.

"Sorry to wake you, Agent Windermere." The agent on the left was the taller of the two, a heavier build and close-cropped hair. "They said we should talk to you as soon as we got here."

Their names were Mundall and Wasserman. They shook hands with Windermere, with Stevens, told them they'd brought a helicopter crew, told them the Salt Lake City office would have a team in Whitefish by lunchtime.

"This guy was killing hookers, right?" Wasserman asked as Shelly brought them four cups of coffee. He was smaller than Mundall, keen eyes and a head of red hair.

"Not just hookers." Windermere stood, stretched. "Transients, runaways, train hoppers. Drug addicts and bar waitresses. Anyone the public wouldn't miss."

"How'd he get away with it for so long?"

"Were you listening? This guy chooses nobodies. People figured the victims skipped town, ran off. Got drunk in snowstorms and froze to death. Hell, even the clear-cut homicides weren't exactly priorities. Who really cares if a junkie gets popped, right?"

Mundall and Wassermann swapped looks, like they weren't sure if the question was rhetorical.

"*We* care," Windermere told them. "We don't like murderers no matter who's getting killed. And we're going to expend every ounce of energy we have in finding this guy and bringing him in, clear?"

"Of course," Mundall said. "Yeah. But how are we going to do it?"

Stevens shifted beside Windermere. "I had an idea." He leaned forward, spread out his topographical map. Made a mark on it with his pen.

"This is about where Hurley's road ended." He traced the topography east, into the mountains. "There are two chains of mountains in the Whitefish Range," he said. "Hurley's cabin lies on the western slope of the range. Beyond the western chain, in the general direction of his trail, there's this plateau here"—he pointed—"and then the eastern slope. And beyond the eastern slope—"

"Roads," Windermere said, leaning over his shoulder.

Stevens nodded. "Logging roads. Campsites. The north fork of the Flathead River, running down from Canada all the way to the interstate. If Hurley can get through the eastern mountains, his escape options increase dramatically."

"Okay," Wasserman said. "So how does he get through?"

Stevens circled an area on the map, the central plateau and the eastern slope of the Whitefish Range. "There's water here, Nicola Creek. Seems like it runs down from the plateau all the way to the

North Fork Flathead. Makes a nice pass through the mountains, wide enough to traverse, from the look of it."

He circled the spot again. "Nicola Creek," he said. "If I were Leland Hurley, that's where I'd be headed."

85

Hurley hiked until dawn. Then, as the sun rose over the eastern edge of the Whitefish Range, he dug a snow cave for himself beneath a rocky overhang, set out his bivouac sack and unrolled his sleeping bag.

The forest was silent around him, even the drone of the helicopters so far off as to be nearly inaudible. He would wake if they got close, he knew, but he wasn't afraid. Their infrared cameras would be hard-pressed to find him under his rock, anyway.

Hurley slept fitfully, seeing the intruding girl in his dreams. It wasn't so much that she'd lived. She hadn't outwitted him; he'd allowed her to survive.

Still, the girl's escape gnawed at him. She would go home, wherever home was. She would likely be famous. She wouldn't be humbled by her experience; rather, she'd be emboldened. Her escape would give her confidence. She would poison more men.

He had failed. The notion stuck with him, stubborn, like a piece of gristle in his teeth. That stupid girl would believe she had *won*.

By midafternoon, Hurley had made it through the first barrier mountains on the west slope of the Whitefish Range. There was a plateau here, long and narrow, and then the taller eastern mountains that blocked the way to the north fork of the Flathead River. There were roads in the valley. The terrain would be easier and quicker to traverse.

Hurley knew an easy way to the North Fork Flathead Valley from here. There was a pass to the southeast where Nicola Creek wound down from the plateau. It cut between the eastern mountains and emptied into the North Fork, a day's hike. From the North Fork, he could move south, following the river to the interstate and the Northwestern main line at the Glacier Park boundary. He could hop a freight train, steal a car. In a week's time, maybe less, he could be in Florida.

It was the easiest route through the mountains. The simplest escape. But though Hurley trusted his ability to outmaneuver the federal agents on his tail, he wasn't foolhardy enough to assume they didn't know how to read a topographical map. They would see Nicola Creek and they would notice the pass. They would expect him to take the easiest path and, therefore, they would concentrate their resources on the eastern slope of the range.

So Hurley turned north as the shadows grew long around him. The plateau continued in that direction, narrowing as the western and eastern mountain chains came together. Hurley knew he didn't need to go far. The law wouldn't expect him to turn north or south so quickly, not while he was in the middle of the range. They would assume he would wait until he'd come through to the North Fork before he deviated. But Hurley figured to outwit them all.

He kept moving, his snowshoes covering the ground quickly, his body settling into a rhythm as night settled in around him. His goggles would run out of batteries soon, maybe even by morning, and that would complicate things. He would begin to run low on ration bars, would soon have to start boiling snow to make water. And the weather could turn foul again in an instant, which would hinder his ability to navigate.

But Hurley wasn't worried. He hiked north up the plateau, through thick stands of fir trees and along the edges of long-dormant clear-cuts. There were old logging roads here, decades abandoned, now choked with thick stands of alder trees and impassible by any vehicle. The roads made a nice break from the density of the forest, though, and Hurley followed them as far as they suited his purpose. He hiked steadily, his mind clear, his breath chuffing out in clouds ahead of him, the air bracing. He didn't think about the FBI behind him. He pushed the girl from his mind. He didn't even think about where he was going and what he would do when he arrived at his destination.

Leland Hurley simply hiked.

86

By lunchtime, the backup from Salt Lake City had arrived, three dark SUVs and a tactical van, a complement of young, hardy agents with grim looks on their faces.

Windermere called a team meeting in the diner, brought the Bureau newcomers in with Kerry Finley, Agents Wasserman and Mundall, the Flathead County deputies. She and Stevens outlined the situation, the rest of the terrain. Sent a couple of the younger deputies to establish a checkpoint ten miles up the highway to Stryker, a couple more down to Lupfer, ten miles south. Dispatched most of the agents and the rest of the deputies east to the North Fork Flathead Valley, the Nicola Creek area in particular.

"Focus on the creek, but spread up and down the valley," Stevens told them. "Stay out of sight as best you can. Keep your eyes open, and we'll try to flush him out to you."

"And stay warm. Stay dry," Windermere added. "It gets a little nippy when the sun goes down."

Finley lingered behind. "I thought I should say my good-byes now," she said, kind of sheepish. "Seeing as how there's a lull in the storm."

Windermere frowned, and Finley caught her expression, explained: "Feds are here. Flathead County's on scene, and according to Sheriff Parsons, we're out of our jurisdiction. My boss seems to think you all have this case under control."

"The problem with bosses," Windermere said. "Sometimes they don't know their head from their ass. Unbelievable."

"I can stick around for the rest of the day," Finley told them. "But the sheriff wants me working a drug case in Eureka first thing tomorrow morning, and he's strongly suggesting I sleep on Lincoln County soil tonight. So . . ." She held up her hands. "You feds have something to keep me busy until nightfall?"

Stevens gestured down to his map. "Have a seat, Deputy," he said. "I want to run something by you."

They set Finley running patrol on US-93, the highway south to Whitefish and north to the Canadian border.

"I'm almost certain Hurley's headed east," Stevens told the deputy, "but he's doubled back on us before."

Finley rubbed her chin. "I see where you're going. Hate to get caught with our pants down."

"We have checkpoints on the highway north, here, at Stryker," Windermere said, pointing, "and south, here, at Lupfer. But we're shorthanded at the southern end. We need an experienced hand to keep an eye on things."

"I can do that." Finley studied the map a moment longer. Then she stood. "I'll check in with you both if anything comes our way. If not . . ." She held out her hand. "Agents, it's been a pleasure. Good luck the rest of the way."

Stevens and Windermere shook hands with the deputy, bid her good travels back to Lincoln County. Promised they'd keep in touch, watched her Explorer drive off until it disappeared.

"Feels weird to be working this case without her," Windermere said. "For a while, she was the only thing keeping us alive."

Stevens knew his partner was right. He'd always considered himself an outdoorsman, but Kerry Finley and the rest of the folks he'd met in this part of the world had showed him how badly he'd been fooling himself.

Do you really trust yourself to track Hurley through this terrain? You think you can survive out there when the weather turns ugly?

Stevens wasn't sure. He felt a heck of a lot better with Finley around, but Finley was gone, and there was a case to work. Stevens turned from the highway and met Windermere's eyes.

"Let's get a chopper back here again," he said. "I want to check out that plateau."

They flew reconnaissance over the Nicola Pass for the rest of the afternoon. Alternated looking down at the terrain from the window and through the infrared screen in the cockpit. Saw heat below, animals here and there, but nothing that resembled a man.

Finally, the light waning and the chopper's fuel reserves again dwindling, Stevens asked the pilot to fly a pass over the North Fork Flathead Valley, where the Salt Lake agents and county deputies were on scene. The task force had spread out over about twenty miles along the eastern slope of the mountain chain, a couple agents and/or deputies every few miles, all equipped with night vision, warm vehicles, and all heavily armed.

"Stay alert," Stevens radioed down to the units. "We don't know how much ground this guy's covered, but chances are he's close. So keep your eyes open and try to stay hidden. He's a very small needle in a very large haystack."

The agents radioed back the affirmative, and Stevens nodded to the pilot, who turned the helicopter back toward Anchor Falls. Windermere caught Stevens's eye as the chopper swung around, another day slipping away, the sunset a glint in her eye.

"We're going to drink that town out of coffee if we keep this up, partner," she said, and Stevens could tell she was trying to keep the frustration from her voice. "How do you feel about another sleepless night in a cracked vinyl booth?"

Damn discouraged, Stevens thought. *That's how I feel.*

But there was no sense admitting defeat, not yet. He forced a smile. "I'll take a cramped booth over that hotel in Butcher's Creek any day," he said. "At least Norma's Diner has pie."

Then the pilot twisted around in his seat again. "You all might be stuck in that diner a while yet," he said. "You hear the latest weather report?"

The way he asked the question gave Stevens a bad feeling. "Not yet," he replied. "You want to fill us in?"

"Snow." The pilot shuddered. "Lots and lots of snow. Midnight, maybe sooner, these mountains get hit hard."

"How hard?" Windermere asked.

"*Hard.* Like, zero visibility, ground-the-chopper type weather." The pilot turned back to the controls. "Let's just say I'm hoping we find this guy quickly. Come tomorrow, these joyrides are going to get ugly."

87

Hurley made the Northwestern main line by midnight. He'd turned westward when he left the plateau, doubled back, dropped down the Whitefish Range in the same direction he'd come, roughly twenty miles north of the Trail Valley on another old, half-overgrown logging road.

The snow was falling now. Light, but it was bound to pick up. The railroad tracks were silent, empty, the line dark in both directions. A single track here, no passing sidings within ten miles. The trains would roll past at speed, if they rolled past at all. Hurley suspected the FBI would have alerted the railroad, maybe even shut down the line. Everyone on the Northwestern payroll would be on the lookout. He would have to keep moving before he thought about catching on.

Hurley was exhausted. His muscles ached all over, and his legs felt like concrete. He was still having fun, but the fun was diminishing. And when the next storm hit, this backcountry adventure would start to smell an awful lot like work.

The snow continued to pick up as he moved westward, following the logging road that had brought him down from the mountains to where it intersected with the highway, US-93, one lane north to Canada and one south to Whitefish. The snow stuck on the highway, accumulated, muted every sound but the wind. The highway was as empty as the Northwestern main.

Here was where Hurley would find out if he'd gambled correctly. He'd assumed the FBI agents would peg him to head east, had based his entire strategy on that notion. If he was right, the law would have concentrated their efforts on the North Fork Flathead River. They'd have left him an opportunity here.

He'd made the highway. Now Hurley settled down at the roadside to wait. Switched off his night vision to save what was left of the batteries, searched through the darkness for the first sign of a headlight, some unsuspecting traveler foolish enough to be out on the roads on such a miserable night.

88

Hurley waited a solid forty minutes before he saw the first headlights, a tractor-trailer headed southbound, back toward Anchor Falls. He crouched in the snow and watched the truck pass. Pulled his coat around him and huddled up to keep warm, loading and reloading his rifle to pass the time.

A half hour later, maybe, the first northbound headlights appeared. Dim through the flurries at first, barely more than a glow. But Hurley heard the engine, and he knew. He stood, brushing the snow off his clothes. Hid his bivvy sack and snowshoes in the snowbank. Clambered up the shoulder and out into the northbound lane.

The engine grew louder. The light neared. Separated into twin headlights, an SUV or a truck. Hurley drew his coat around him, pulled his hat low, made himself as big as possible, and flagged the truck down.

It was only when the truck was upon him that he noticed the light bar, the Lincoln County markings.

Judd Parsons's instructions notwithstanding, Kerry Finley was having a hard time keeping the Hurley case off her mind.

She'd dawdled in Lupfer until well after dark. The deputies at the checkpoint were young guys, barely twenty, likely their first taste of action. Finley told herself she was hanging around to keep tabs on them, make sure the kids knew what they were up against. Make sure they kept their eyes open.

She was thinking, too, that Leland Hurley would want to cover as much ground as he could after dark. She was thinking Stevens and Windermere had a better chance of stumbling into the guy during the night than during the daylight hours. Told herself she wanted to make sure, wanted to drive up to Eureka knowing she'd left the job done right, knowing Hurley hadn't slipped the net on her watch.

These were both valid points. But really, it was the victims who kept Kerry Finley hanging around. Kelly-Anne Clairmont, murdered in Lincoln County and thrown away like she was garbage, when maybe if she and Parsons and the rest had just dug a little deeper into those bogeyman stories, they could have done something to keep her alive.

Finley didn't like the idea that she was giving up on the case. Felt like it meant she was giving up on Kelly-Anne Clairmont and the rest of the victims, like she was giving up on Stevens and Windermere, too.

So she'd stuck around the checkpoint, helped out the deputies processing traffic, even took a run back up to Norma's Diner to pick up dinner for the boys. And now it was late, real late, and here she was just starting north, sipping from a thermos of Shelly's coffee, trying to focus on the drive as the snow came down around her.

And then Leland Hurley walked calmly out of the drifts and parked himself square in her Explorer's path, looking like some kind of arctic mirage.

It *had* to be Hurley. Same clothes as the pictures Mila Scott had taken, same height, same carriage, same *beard*. And who else would be out on a night like tonight?

Finley hit the brakes. Felt the truck shudder, the tires slipping and screaming as the Explorer stopped hard. Watched Hurley through the windshield as the truck got closer, the fugitive's hand raised, his whole body stock-still—until he must have realized it was law enforcement he was flagging down and not some hapless civilian.

Then Hurley raised the rifle he'd kept hidden by his side. Stepped out of the path of the Explorer, the big Ford still sliding, out of control, sliding right up to Hurley and then sliding past him, and Hurley shouldered the rifle and took aim at the truck, and just as Finley got the truck back under control, got the brakes responding again, the truck finally slowing—well, that's when Leland Hurley pulled the trigger.

The shot blew out the Explorer's driver's-side window. Punched whoever was inside clear out of his seat. Hurley kept his rifle trained on the door as he approached the truck. Scanned the cab for signs of life, saw the driver slumped against the passenger seat, blood—and worse—everywhere.

The driver was a woman. The same woman deputy he'd seen escorting the feds through the forest, judging from the look of her. Hurley opened the door and dragged her out of the truck and onto the road. The deputy hadn't even had time to reach for her service pistol. Hurley spared her the trouble, removed it from its holster.

There was no time to waste. There would be others, this woman's colleagues, more lawmen with guns. Hurley returned to the shoulder, retrieved his belongings from the drifts. Hurried to the Explorer and chucked the bag and the snowshoes inside, his rifle, too. Then he walked back to the deputy. Nudged her over with his boot so she was lying on her back, staring up at Hurley, mouth gasping, no words coming out.

"Didn't expect you'd be a woman," Hurley told her, aiming down with the deputy's pistol. "Makes me wish we had a little more time together."

He shot the deputy twice and dragged her body to the embankment beside the highway, thinking he'd hide the woman in a patch of fresh snow.

Hurley paused. Realized he hadn't heard the deputy's radio when he'd dumped his stuff in the Explorer. No dispatcher coordinating backup, no units advising the woman they were coming. The deputy had been as surprised as he was, Hurley figured. He looked down at the body.

"Did you tell them you found me?" he asked. "Do they know I'm here, Deputy?"

But the woman was in no position to answer. Hurley looked up and down the road again, knew sooner or later another vehicle would come, knew he didn't want to be standing here trying to dispose of a body.

Time to go, he thought, but an idea was forming in his head.

He picked up the body again. Dragged the dead deputy back to the

Explorer, opened the rear lift gate, and hefted the woman inside. There was no sense leaving a body for someone to discover, he decided. And anyway . . .

Hurley reached in, relieved the lawman of her coat. Lincoln County Sheriff's Department. A little bit of blood spatter, but Hurley could hide that.

The coat was tight on Hurley. He peeled off his survival gear and pulled it on as much as he could, buttoned it as much as he could. Walked back to the driver's side of the Explorer, climbed behind the wheel. Found the deputy's Stetson sitting half-crushed on the passenger seat, still upright; punched it back into shape and set it on top of his own head, fit it low as it would go, hoped it obscured his face.

The highway was still empty. The radio was still silent. The truck's windshield wipers made a rhythmic progression across the front glass, barely keeping up with the snow. Hurley adjusted the rearview mirror, turned the heater up high. Shifted the truck into gear and tested the gas pedal.

The Explorer's tires must have been brand-new. They gripped the snowy pavement just fine. Hurley brought the truck up to speed and drove north.

89

Leland Hurley," Windermere said, reading. "Joined the army at the end of Desert Storm, missed his shot at combat by a couple of months, signed up for Ranger School instead. Made it all the way to the third phase of training before he washed out, left the service. Dishonorable discharge."

Outside Norma's Diner, the snow had picked up again. Windermere had her shoes off, stocking feet on the vinyl, her phone plugged in to an extension cord running back to the cash register. Stevens sat opposite, nursing another cup of coffee. Watching the storm build, every few minutes the diner door swinging open, bringing a fresh blast of cold air and more exhausted law enforcement, driven inside by the oncoming storm.

"A waitress in Valparaiso, Florida," Windermere continued. "I guess Hurley had a crush on her, but she'd shut him down more than once. So he waited for her to finish her shift one night, rolled up on her in the parking lot, made his pitch again. Wasn't ready to take no for an answer this time, and probably wouldn't have, if a couple guys from the air force base hadn't happened onto the scene, intervened."

"Intervened," Stevens said. "And I imagine their intervention spelled the end of Leland Hurley's career as a Ranger."

"And you'd be correct. After the flyboys kicked the shit out of Hurley, they reported the incident to the chain of command, and it looks like everybody just decided the United States military would be better off without someone of Leland Hurley's ilk."

"So off he went."

"Off he went." Windermere put her phone down. "Though if the army thought a discharge would scare our boy straight, I'd say they were sadly mistaken."

She'd been reading up on Leland Hurley for a couple solid hours now. There was nothing else to do, just read and feel inadequate, watch the snow accumulate and try to imagine where Hurley would turn up.

He hadn't appeared at the Nicola Pass, due east through the mountains from his compound. The agents from Salt Lake City and the Flathead County deputies they'd posted at the head of the pass had scoured the area until the storm hit, by foot, truck, and air, and hadn't seen him. And then the snow started, and the helicopters couldn't fly, and the agents in the field reported zero visibility, so even if Hurley *was* out there, he'd pretty much have to walk right into Norma's Diner and order a slice of pie before anyone realized it was him.

They had Hurley's picture on the wire, every law enforcement agency and TV news station from Cheyenne to Calgary. They had presence on every road and railroad track out of northwestern Montana—FBI, sheriff's departments, and border patrol. Stevens, playing optimist, told Windermere it was only a matter of time before Hurley came out somewhere and someone recognized his face, but Stevens wasn't a very good actor. There was a lot of country out here, a lot of hiding places, and Hurley was clearly resourceful. Windermere could feel their chances dropping with every minute the man remained at large.

But there was no way to look for him, not in this storm. So Windermere sat on her hands and drank Shelly out of coffee, read from the reams of material she'd had Mathers dig up on their subject.

"Ranger training," Stevens said from across the table, breaking her out of her doldrums. "You said Hurley washed out at phase three?"

Windermere checked her phone. "Yup. Eglin Air Force Base, northern Florida."

"How many phases do these guys have to go through?"

"Three, apparently," Windermere told him. "Hurley flunked out early in the final phase."

"So he only finished two-thirds of his training."

"Right. Not that that helps us any. He finished top of his class in the second phase of training."

"What's the second phase?"

Windermere looked up. "Mountain training," she said. "Rugged terrain. Severe weather. Combat and survival."

"So, everything we're dealing with out here."

"Everything," Windermere said. "He's just about tailor-made for this."

90

Hurley drove north through steady snowfall. New tires or not, he drove cautiously. The last thing he needed was to wreck the Explorer; if the law wasn't appraised of his position already, they certainly would be once they found the truck.

The town of Stryker was ten miles up the road. Hurley made it in twenty-five minutes. There wasn't much there: a post office, a passing siding on the Northwestern main. The tracks branched off here, and so did the highway. To the west lay Butcher's Creek and the tracks to the coast. To the north lay Eureka, the Canadian border.

The pavement ended well before Butcher's Creek. Nothing but forestry roads all the way to the Libby Dam, fifty miles through the mountains and impassible in this weather. The border was only thirty miles north, and beyond that, not much but open terrain.

Hurley figured he had one shot before the storm cleared again and the FBI agents realized he'd pulled an end around on them. Figured, FBI or not, they'd get hung up at the border, jurisdictional issues, confusion. Figured he could buy himself some time while they sorted things out with the Mounties. Figured Canada was so big, so *empty*, they might never find him up there. He could get all the way to Alaska if he wanted.

Hurley had liked his chances alone and on snowshoes in the middle of the mountains. In a truck, though? With the snow still falling?

Heck, he was practically home free already.

The law had a checkpoint set up at the south end of town, two Flathead County cruisers angled to block the highway, cherry-red and blues blazing.

Hurley slowed the Ford as soon as he saw the roadblock, scanned the highway for an alternate route, but it was too late; he was already made. As Hurley watched, a deputy climbed from the cruiser in the southbound lane, started down the highway toward Hurley, waved him forward with one hand, the other lingering at his hip by his holster.

Hurley swore under his breath, inched the Explorer forward. Reached across to the passenger seat and the dead deputy's pistol, lay it on his lap as he approached the checkpoint. Pulled the deputy's Stetson low as it could go, adjusted the heavy coat to hide the bullet holes, tried to wipe as much blood as he could from the passenger seat, the dashboard. He crept the truck up to meet the deputy, held the pistol in his left hand, hard up against the door as the lawman approached. Figured he had about a one-in-four shot of pulling this thing off, but then, hell, he'd never been scared of long odds.

The deputy was a young kid. Couldn't have been on the job long. He was shivering as he ran the beam of his flashlight over the Explorer, looked downright miserable to be out in this weather. He lowered his flashlight as Hurley stopped the truck beside him.

"How're you doing tonight?" he asked. Squinted at Hurley's jacket. "Deputy . . . Finley?"

"That's right," Hurley told him. "Hell of a night."

The deputy looked up and down the highway, his teeth all but chattering. "Only getting worse, what I hear," he said. "Got you burning the midnight oil tonight, huh?"

"Until we catch this asshole," Hurley said. Kept his voice calm, steady. Looked the deputy in the eye, long as he could. Felt his insides quaking, forced his body to still. "Lot of people watching this one. Lots of pressure from higher up to solve it in a hurry."

"Oh, I hear that." The deputy turned his attention to the truck again, to Hurley. "Where're you headed tonight? They told us Stryker's the northern perimeter when they briefed us. They thinking this guy's headed north?"

"Can't be sure," Hurley told him. "They're sending me up Butcher's Creek way, make sure the train crews know what they're looking for. Night like this, it's a perfect time for a guy to try to make an escape."

"It sure is rotten out here," the deputy said. He took a couple steps toward the rear of the Explorer, shone his flashlight over the rear door. Hurley gripped the pistol tighter, watched the guy in his side mirror, ready to make a move if he went to look in the back.

"Any luck, they'll find this guy soon," Hurley said. "Send us all home to our families."

"You said it." The deputy looked at the back of the Explorer again. Looked longingly back at his cruiser and seemed to make a decision.

"You drive safe," he said, waving to his buddy in the second cruiser. "Hate to see this guy cause any more mayhem."

Hurley shifted into drive as the cruiser backed off the highway, opening the northbound lane.

"Take care of yourself," he told the deputy. "Stay warm."

"You too, buddy." The kid was already turning back to his car.

Hurley idled the Ford through the checkpoint. Waved thanks to the deputy in the second cruiser, another young guy. Nudged the gas pedal again, rolled through downtown Stryker in all of two minutes, the lights of the county cruisers receding in his rearview.

He drove a mile out of town before he let himself breathe. Pulled over, set the pistol down on the passenger seat, his hand sweaty where he'd held it. Exhaled, long and ragged, closed his eyes, calmed his nerves.

Then he pulled back onto the highway, drove on, saw nothing in his headlights but blowing snow and the dark edge of the night. Twenty miles to Eureka, and nothing much in between. Another ten miles to the Canada line. He'd take it slow, take it easy. Take all night if he had to. As long as the snow was blowing, Hurley knew he was ahead.

91

"Carla."

Carla Windermere awoke to the smell of fresh coffee and to Kirk Stevens standing above her booth, a strange expression on his face.

Windermere sat up, wiping the sleep from her eyes. Looked around the restaurant. The place was getting a smell to it, like your college dorm halfway through winter exams, a bunch of stressed-out bodies with no time to sleep and no time to shower, everyone starting to go a little funky.

Windermere knew she was as guilty as the rest of them. She'd been in the same clothes for, what, three days now; wondered if she would ever get back to Butcher's Creek, the Northwestern Hotel, her suitcase. Wondered what she would pay for a stick of deodorant, clean underwear, decided she would empty her wallet.

At least the snow had stopped falling. Outside the diner, dawn was still largely theoretical, but already Windermere could see across the highway to the gas station, could even see the mountains to the east of town, the Anchor Valley. There was snow everywhere, obviously, piled up on the vehicles jamming the parking lot outside, heaped in mounds by the snowplows that had waged war with the winter on the highway all night. Windermere figured it would take some time to get cleaned up, dusted off, organized, but the brunt of the storm had passed. And that meant they could get back to work.

Windermere ran her hands through her hair. "I was dreaming about Hawaii, partner," she said. "So whatever it is you have for us, I hope it's worth interrupting my beach time."

Stevens didn't look dissuaded. Didn't change his expression. "I just got off the phone with the deputies in Stryker," he told her. "They had a slow night, they said. Not much traffic but a Lincoln County deputy passing through. Someone named Finley."

"Right. Finley said she was headed up to Eureka, remember? Some drug case or something."

"I remember," Stevens said. "But the Stryker boys seemed to think the deputy had been reassigned to Butcher's Creek, said we'd told her to go up and liaise with the train crews."

Windermere frowned. "We did no such thing, Stevens," she said. "Unless you changed the play while I was catching zees."

Stevens shook his head. "Nope. That's not even the weird part. Those boys at the checkpoint seemed to think Deputy Finley was a *he*."

"What?" Windermere set down her coffee. Didn't need it anymore; she was wide awake. "What the hell does that mean? Where's Finley?"

"Damned if I know," Stevens said. "Those boys in Stryker said they saw a man rolling through in a Lincoln County Explorer. Said they were sure it was a man; they could tell by the beard."

Windermere felt that coffee lurch in her gut, fought the urge to be sick. *Hurley. Shit.*

"Find us a helicopter, partner," she said, already halfway to the door. "We need to go north, and we need to go now."

92

Eureka, Montana, was a town of a thousand, exponentially bigger than tiny Stryker. There was no way the law could mark every road in or out of the community, and they didn't; Hurley passed through without incident in the early-morning hours, and then he was on the highway again, engine humming, the Canadian border a straight shot north.

Here, though, Hurley knew he had to be careful. Nine miles to the border, and the guards would be watching for him. Roosville was the only border crossing between the Idaho state line and the eastern slope of the Rockies, which meant there'd be more than a handful of guards, all on high alert.

But Hurley didn't intend to drive into Canada, in the dead deputy's truck or otherwise. He followed the highway a few miles into flat plain and farmland, and then he turned the Explorer east, caught up with the Whitefish Range again and its network of logging roads. There were roads here that curled so far north, they almost kissed the border. And the border wasn't much to speak of, just a clear-cut through the forest, twenty feet wide, no fence.

Miles and miles of unguarded terrain, impossible to fully manage, stark contrast to the fortress walls that cut the line between Mexico and the southern states. People slipped through from Canada all the time, Hurley knew. Smuggled drugs, other contraband. People. Some were caught. Most weren't. Hurley liked his chances.

But progress slowed to a crawl once he'd driven into the mountains. The Ford's tires scrabbled for purchase on the narrow, uneven road and spun, the engine roaring in vain. He'd made it to within maybe three long, winding miles of the border when he decided he'd be faster on foot. He abandoned the Explorer, the deputy's body. Strapped on his snowshoes and shouldered his rifle, his pack with the last of his supplies, and set off.

He was sweating through his underclothes by the time he reached the border. It was midmorning now, the sun high above the peaks to the east, and he'd followed the road as far as he could, winding north along the side of a low mountain to within a few hundred yards of the border. There he finished the last of his ration bars. Washed it down with water from his canteen and set out through the woods.

The going was slow. The forest was silent, save Hurley's breath and the occasional branch cracking beneath his snowshoes. Snow cascaded from above with every step Hurley took, nudged from the boughs packed tight above and beside him. The forest was dark and cold. Hurley kept his eyes out for cameras and detectors. Didn't see any, and the sky above the treetops was free of helicopters. As far as Hurley could tell, he was alone, with just a twenty-foot swath of undefended snow separating him from Canada.

He stopped when he reached the tree line, waited there for a few minutes, gathering his breath and searching the other side for any sign of the law. It didn't seem like it should be so easy, making the crossing. The woods on the Canadian side looked just like those of Montana. Was this it? Was this all it would take?

Nobody challenged Hurley as he crossed the snowy border. He made the Canadian trees and stepped into the forest and continued walking, and within minutes, the border had vanished behind him.

He settled into a steady rhythm again, ignoring the fatigue in his joints and the ache in his muscles, the numbing exhaustion that deadened his thoughts and would slow his reflexes. He kept marching. Right boot, left boot, one in front of the other, as the sun arced down behind him and the forest grew darker, the shadows longer.

Soon it would be night again. He'd made it into the vast Canadian wilderness, and every hour he kept moving and every mile he put behind him brought him that much closer to escaping the law. There was nothing to do but keep walking, let the terrain swallow him, envelop him, hide him.

So Hurley forced himself onward, unrelenting. Let the FBI follow him here. Let them try to hunt him. In this vast, empty terrain?

Good luck.

93

So, what?" the pilot asked. "Should I put you down at the border, let you hash things out with the Mounties?"

In the back of the helicopter, Windermere shook her head. "No time. We need to find Finley and Leland Hurley before we take any meetings. Which means we're better off in the air."

Beside her, Stevens was studying a topographical map, comparing it to the view out his window. The country at the border was flat, farmland and river valley, bordered to the west by long, narrow Lake Koocanusa, which stretched fifty miles north from the Libby Dam to the border and another forty miles into Canada. This was the Rocky Mountain Trench, the Kootenay River valley, and it was surrounded by mountains on both east and west. North of the border, the highway continued up into Canada, following the lake and the Kootenay River toward civilization.

They'd commandeered the Flathead County chopper, rode north over Stryker and west to Butcher's Creek, searching the roads for any sign of Kerry Finley's Explorer. Hadn't found any trace of her, and turned their search north.

"We can assume Hurley wouldn't try to fool a border guard," Stevens said. "Which means if he's up here, he'll be trying to sneak across."

He was trying to push down the empty feeling in his gut, trying to avoid jumping to any conclusions. They'd maintained a search presence on the east side of the Whitefish Range, the Nicola Pass area. Moved agents to Stryker, Butcher's Creek, the forestry roads between Eureka and Libby. Held out hope they'd hear from Eureka, Kerry Finley's voice on the radio, safe and sound, and they'd all breathe sighs of relief and laugh about the big misunderstanding.

But somehow, Stevens knew that wasn't going to happen.

"So if a person wanted to make it into Canada without showing his passport, how would he do it?" Windermere was asking the pilot. "Or better yet, where?"

"Well, he'd do it in the forest, and he'd do it at night, if he had any sense." The pilot leaned across the cockpit, pointed down. "That land's so flat down near Roosville, you could watch your dog run away for three days, if you care to." He paused. "Or your wife, for that matter."

"Right." Windermere checked her watch again. Noon already,

daylight a limited-time offer. "I see forest to the west, all the way to the lake. And east to the mountains. So what are we thinking?"

"Better roads by the lake," the pilot said. "You go into those eastern mountains, you got a long, tough slog ahead of you."

"Long and tough sounds right up Hurley's alley," Windermere said. "Take us east."

The pilot wasn't joking. To the west, the forest grew gradually out of the flatland at the bottom of the Rocky Mountain Trench, extending to the shore of the lake in a more or less orderly manner. What roads had been cut through the trees followed a vague kind of grid pattern, unencumbered by any major topographical irritations.

To the east, the Rocky Mountains rose in earnest from the valley floor, and the roads were thinner, rougher, and fewer in number. They wound up the sides of steep hillsides, curved and doubled back on one another, arced up toward the border and back down again. Stevens guided the pilot across the terrain, one eye on the map, searching out any path through the wilderness that might have conveyed Leland Hurley north.

"I see three potential entry spots," he told Windermere and the pilot. "Each of these roads loops up to within three hundred yards of the border. Unless Hurley's a total masochist, he would have had to follow one of them."

"Except our guy *is* a masochist," Windermere said. "We've already established that."

"Sure," Stevens said. "But still."

But Hurley *hadn't* followed any of the three roads—at least not in Kerry Finley's Explorer. And if he'd left footprints, they were obscured by the snow. None of the occupants of the Flathead County helicopter could see any evidence that Hurley had passed this way.

"Maybe he ditched the truck farther back," Windermere said. "Hiked through the forest. Or he hid it."

"Or maybe we're wrong and he stayed west, after all," Stevens said. "Or maybe he took a different tack entirely."

The pilot gestured out the window to the west, where the sun had started dropping toward the mountains already. "If you want to check the lake before dark, we're going to have to move," he told the agents. "We're going to start losing daylight faster than you think."

Stevens and Windermere looked at each other, and Stevens felt a gnawing indecision, made worse by the pressure of the situation. If they couldn't track Hurley within the next couple of hours, they would lose him for the night. And giving Hurley another night in these mountains was tantamount to buying him a plane ticket, as far as Stevens was concerned.

Windermere was still waiting. Time was wasting. Stevens rubbed his face with the palm of his hand. "Damn it," he said. "I guess we'd better check out the lake."

And they would have checked the lake, and as many of the logging roads west of Roosville as they could manage before dusk—were headed that way, chasing the sun—when the helicopter's pilot happened to take a pass over a low earthen dam and the snow-covered lake behind it. And Windermere, eyes attracted to the break in the monotony of the tree-covered mountain, happened to glance down at the dam and the lake and the road that ran beside it, and as she followed the road north with her eyes, she caught the glint as the sun's rays landed on something that wasn't rock, snow, or forest, but chrome and steel and glass.

"Hold up." Windermere leaned forward, made to grab the pilot's arm. Decided, on second thought, that wasn't the best idea. Settled for pointing down instead, through the bubble windshield and back toward the truck—Finley's truck, she was sure of it—where it sat a couple hundred yards from the dam and a solid three miles from the border.

"There it is," she told Stevens, her heart starting to pound. "Now, where the heck is Kerry Finley?"

94

Stevens got on the radio to the Canadians—the Border Services Agency and the Royal Canadian Mounted Police—gave them the approximate location of Kerry Finley's truck, told them to keep an eye out on the closest stretch of border.

"We'll get our guys out there," the RCMP officer told Stevens. "But you should know that it's a huge piece of land, and not much in it. Pretty easy for a guy to get himself lost."

The Mountie was a woman named Cronquist. She sounded upbeat, anyway, even as she explained the long odds. "Don't get me wrong, I'm up for a challenge," she told Stevens. "I just don't want you thinking we'll have your man gift-wrapped and waiting for you first thing tomorrow morning."

"We know all about needles and haystacks," Stevens told her. "We've been tracking this guy through these mountains for days, infrared night vision and everything. If getting lost in the woods is an art form, this guy's Picasso."

"I never was that big into art," Cronquist said. "But feel free to bring up those infrared cameras, if they're just lying around. They work just as well on this side of the border."

Stevens told her he'd arrange it. Called down to Wasserman and Mundall, filled them in, told them to bring the hunt north, find someone to start working on the paperwork. Was just saying his goodbyes when the helicopter pilot dropped into a low hover above the earthen dam site, the only place he could find room to get low enough for a drop.

"Come on, partner," Windermere said, sliding the chopper's rear door open. "Let's see if all this helicopter noise hasn't scared the deputy out of hiding."

It might have been the noise of the helicopter's approach. Then again, maybe not. But when Stevens and Windermere had slogged their way off the dam and up the logging road to approach Kerry Finley's Lincoln County Explorer with their pistols drawn, they found the front seat deserted, cold, the only sign of Hurley a faint trail of snowshoe tracks leading north toward the border.

"No sign of her," Windermere said. "Shit."

Stevens squinted up the logging road, daylight slipping away, shadows all-encompassing. Knew they'd never track Hurley fast enough on foot, not in their heavy boots and Hurley in snowshoes, knew he would hear the chopper from miles out, find somewhere to hide.

But Stevens wasn't focusing on Hurley now, not really. Stevens was thinking about how he couldn't see any other footprints in the snow around Finley's Explorer, thinking that meant either the deputy wasn't here or she *was* here, thinking that second option was infinitely worse.

Stevens was turning back to Finley's Explorer, hoping maybe the deputy was in a ditch somewhere back near Stryker—a snowdrift or something, hurt but still alive—he saw Windermere lingering at the back of the truck, peering in through the rear window, and he caught the expression on her face and knew they were done playing make-believe.

"Ah, damn it," he said, walking back toward Windermere, though he really didn't want to. "Damn it, Kerry, *no*."

95

Hurley could hear the helicopters again.

They'd started around dusk, the dull, distant drone of the rotors, one machine at first, then more as night fell. Now it was dark, pitch-dark, in the forest, and Hurley could hear the helicopters above him—at least three, maybe more. They'd mostly stayed south, kept close to the border, but now and then they flew closer, close enough that Hurley had begun to look for places to hide.

But there was no hiding. The terrain here was forest, mountain foothills, not the jagged peaks and cliffs he was used to. Anyway, his night-vision goggles were shot, the batteries dead, and Hurley was having a hard enough time picking his way through the snowy undergrowth, let alone searching for shelter.

There was nowhere to hide, and no time. The helicopters were behind him for now. Ditto the snowmobiles Hurley could hear patrolling what few roads existed on this side of the line. The law hadn't counted on him making it this far north, but they would figure it out soon enough. Hurley had to keep moving.

But he was tired. Exhausted. He'd been a fugitive for days, slept a few hours at most. Hadn't eaten a meal since god knows when, was fully out of ration bars. He was hungry. His muscles ached; his limbs failed him. He fell often, crashed against trees and stumbled into creek beds. Hurley knew he was about at his limit. Knew, suddenly and without doubt, that he couldn't make another night like this. He needed rest. He needed food. He needed to come in from the cold.

Shit.

The highway was west, a few long miles through the forest. It skirted the mountains, followed the lake north. There would be civilization by the roadside. Food. Shelter. He could hide, try to sleep, replenish his energy. Then set out again and get away from this place.

Hurley hated to do it. He'd counted on his survival skills, his self-sufficiency. He hadn't counted on the law catching up to him so fast. And he would die out here if he tried to outrun them.

Hurley stopped in his snowshoes. Leaned against a massive Rocky Mountain fir and caught his breath. Listened to the helicopters behind him, incessant, relentless. They were going to keep coming. They weren't going to stop.

Hurley summoned his strength. Hoisted his rifle. Turned and began to walk west.

96

Staff Sergeant Lynn Cronquist was waiting at the roadside when the Flathead County helicopter touched down at the border checkpoint in Roosville, British Columbia. She'd closed the highway; an RCMP Crown Victoria sat parked across both lanes to the north, its red-and-blues flashing. To the south of the checkpoint, two US Customs and Border Protection Explorers stood guard. Otherwise, the highway—and the tiny town beyond—looked mostly deserted.

Cronquist was a tall, solid woman about Stevens's age. She hurried across the pavement toward the helicopter, ducking the rotor wash, helped Stevens slide the door open and shook his hand, then Windermere's, and led them away as the helicopter took flight again. It was five minutes to midnight. The air was bitterly cold.

"We're mostly set up on the Canadian side," Cronquist told them, leading them toward a small single-story building, a single guardhouse on one end, a Canadian flag atop the roof. She waved at the customs officer in the guardhouse, hurried them past.

"Probably need all kinds of permits to bring you guys over here," she told Stevens and Windermere over her shoulder, "but I figured we'd save the paperwork until we get this guy caught, huh?"

Stevens glanced at Windermere, caught her slight nod, approving. Figured he shared her sentiments, had been afraid the Canadians would get hung up on procedure, wouldn't grasp the importance of timeliness in this chase.

"I guess there's a whole story about why a couple of Minnesota FBI agents are chasing serial killers in Montana," Cronquist continued. "But I imagine that's one more thing we can hash out in the afterglow."

Then the Mountie's face grew serious. "They said you were pretty close with the deputy this guy killed," she said. "I'm sorry to hear it. We'll do everything we can to catch the scumbag, you can be sure of it."

Stevens didn't say anything. He'd been trying to keep Kerry Finley out of his thoughts, trying not to see the Lincoln County deputy how they'd found her, shot all to hell and crammed dead in the back of her truck. He was trying not to feel personally responsible.

Cronquist caught the look on his face. "Well, never mind," she said, pushing open the door to the customshouse. "Let me show you what we've got going on."

The staff sergeant had taken over the sleepy customshouse—"Nobody coming through here this time of night"—and turned it into a makeshift operations center.

"Our closest detachment's about forty miles north," she told them. "So we're leaning on Canada Customs to help out."

She'd amassed a team—customs agents from both sides of the border, what RCMP help she could call in from the surrounding region, the Flathead County and Lincoln County sheriff's departments, and, of course, the FBI.

"We borrowed a Squirrel from the base in Kelowna," she told them. "That's our local helicopter; it's an AS350, European. Kelowna's a couple hundred miles away if you're flying, though, so there was a bit of a lag getting the chopper on line. There's only one for the region, and it's a pretty big region, so . . ."

"Yeah, we've heard all about it," Windermere said. "Limited resources all over the map."

"You said it. I called in as many guys as I could muster, sent them out into the woods on Ski-Doos, but again, lot of space to hide, not many people to look. Like I told you on the radio, this isn't going to be easy."

"It hasn't been easy so far," Stevens said. "Why would it start now?"

He'd been afraid of flying at one point in his life. The concept seemed laughable now. He'd spent most of the last three days in the air, in one law enforcement helicopter or another, too preoccupied by the search to worry about the physics of powered flight. He and Windermere had left Kerry Finley's body in the care of a team of local deputies, climbed back into the helicopter, and searched the woods along the border well into the night, pausing only for a quick dash back to the airport in Eureka for fuel. They'd scanned untold miles of featureless black forest with the chopper's infrared camera and saw a couple of elk, but no Leland Hurley. And none of the other helicopters on scene were reporting any different.

"We're still behind him," Stevens told Cronquist and Windermere. "He passed through Stryker just after midnight last night. Gives him a full day to make that crossing. He could be miles inside the country by now."

"And he probably is," Windermere said. "Given that we've been skunked with every pass we've made close to the line."

"So we need to go deeper. Follow him north."

Cronquist pursed her lips. "You want to bring your helicopters over?" she asked. "I can fudge the script for a couple of agents, but if you're wanting to bring the air force into our space, I should probably wake somebody up to check in."

"Do what you have to do," Windermere replied. "But every minute we hold up those choppers gives Hurley that much more time to scatter."

Cronquist sucked her teeth. Thought about it. Finally, she seemed to come to a decision. "It's a dark night," she said. "Anybody gets ornery, we'll just tell them your choppers got lost."

97

The helicopters were closer by the time Hurley reached the highway. Louder. But Hurley barely heard them. He'd taken nearly three hours to cover the last miles to civilization; his legs felt like cement, and his mind struggled to focus. Right boot, left boot. Try not to fall. Try not to give in to the temptation to quit.

But Hurley wasn't a quitter. He pushed himself forward, stumbled his way through the inky-black forest, down into gulches and over rises, dodging deadfall and frozen streams. And then the trees parted and he was staring at highway again, and beyond it, the railroad. The highway was empty. The tracks were, too. But up the road, maybe a half mile or so, Hurley could see lights: a farmhouse, a porch light, a couple outbuildings. No lights on in the windows, nobody awake. But there would be food inside, and maybe somewhere to rest. Hurley stepped out of his snowshoes, strapped them to his pack. Started up the highway.

The house was large and handsome. Old, but cozy, and as Hurley approached, he felt a pang of envy for the occupants within, warm and well fed and content. He shook the thought from his mind.

Hell, you're getting soft, man.

Beyond the house was a compound, a bright light on a standard illuminating a garage and a modest-sized barn. Tire tracks to the doors of the garage; he could steal the car, maybe. Catch some sleep in the barn, recharge. Be gone before anyone knew he'd been there.

Sanctuary.

But Hurley's stomach was empty. He was weak with hunger, with thirst. And he knew if he didn't eat now, he would lie awake in that barn, wishing for food. He needed to eat. Then he would sleep. Then he would continue his journey.

Hurley stuck to the shadows. Crossed the compound as far from the glare of the bright light as he could, hurried toward the farmhouse, the back door. Crept up the steps to the porch, his boots squeaking on packed snow, and moved as quietly as he could to the door, tried the handle. The handle turned. The door was unlocked.

Oh, Canada.

Hurley pushed the door open and slunk inside the house.

He found himself in the kitchen. It was large, comfortable, spacious, an old stove and a huge, buzzing fridge, a table large enough to seat eight adults comfortably. No bowl for dog food by the door. No leash hanging over a doorknob.

Hurley *did* see car keys dangling from a coat hook just inside the doorway. Three sets: Dodge, Toyota, Volkswagen. This was a bonus. As soon as he'd eaten, he could drive away from this place.

But first, the food. Hurley crossed to the refrigerator, hoping the machine's racket would muffle his boot steps. He pulled the door open, saw tonight's leftovers—roast chicken, potatoes—and a couple cans of Molson beer. Cheese, yogurt, lunch meat. Hurley took the bologna. The cheese. Hesitated a moment, then liberated a drumstick as well, a can of beer for good measure. Closed the fridge and devoured the chicken where he stood, couldn't help it. Finished the drumstick and went back for a thigh.

It was as Hurley was reaching for the refrigerator door again that he glimpsed the girl's photograph. It sat on the fridge at eye level, held in place by a Jiffy Lube magnet. The girl was about sixteen or seventeen. She had dark hair and fine, delicate features. She was smiling at the camera, the mountains behind her. A blue sky, green forest. Perfect white teeth.

Hurley let the fridge door close, feeling the heat rising in his chest as he studied the picture as best he could in the light through the kitchen window. Then he looked around the kitchen, took in the pink snow boots lined up by the door, the matching fur-lined parka above it, by the keys. A backpack slung over a chair at the table. A calendar on the fridge: figure-skating practice, school council. Yes, she was one of *them*, all right. She smiled out from the picture like she was already laughing at him. There was no telling how many boys she'd ruined already.

Hurley was tired. Exhausted. He was hungry, famished, and the FBI was chasing him down. But he was a hunter, too. He'd abandoned his last girl to the forest, and the deputy's death had been fast. It had been too long since Hurley had killed, really killed—and this picture, this girl, had awoken the need.

Hurley set the food aside. Left it on the kitchen counter. Propped the rifle against the fridge, reached into his coat for the Indian girl's knife. This was a bad idea, he knew, but he was doing it anyway. Had to. He couldn't resist. This girl was a gift.

He crossed the kitchen toward the front of the house, a living area, a doorway in shadows that must have been stairs. He crept, easing one foot to the floor, then the other, his whole body tense. Made the base of the stairs and looked up into darkness. Listened to the stillness, heard nothing but his beating heart. The house was asleep.

He began to climb.

98

The landing was carpeted. Hurley stopped at the top of the stairs, let his eyes acclimate, sense his surroundings. A long corridor. Empty doorways. Someone snoring softly at the end of the hall.

The first room was the bathroom. Hurley could hear the faucet dripping. He continued down the hall, slowly, slowly. Eased his foot down, chose the wrong place to do it. The floor creaked beneath carpet, a loud, telltale groan. *Shit.*

Hurley froze, gripping the knife tight. Pressed himself against the wall and waited. Listened. Heard nothing, no movement. The snoring continued.

This was wrong. This was foolish. But it was so goddamn *necessary.*

He continued. The next doorway. The door half ajar, blackness beyond. Hurley pushed the door open wider. Saw posters on the wall, a stuffed animal in the window. Heard the sheets rustle, some muttered dream language.

Here she was. Here she was, waiting for him, and now he would have her. He slipped farther into the room. Felt the back side of the door, found no lock. He would have to be careful. So be it.

He crept closer. He could sense the girl now, could hear her breathing, could *smell* her shampoo, her perfume. He was at the foot of the bed, leaned against it. Looked around the dark room and wished for more light. More time. Wanted the girl to see him, to know why he'd come.

This would have to do.

Hurley began to circle the bed. Trailed his fingers on the edge of the bed frame, the smooth sheet, the comforter. Reached across the blanket, searching with his hand for her, heart pounding, drunk on the thought of what he was about to do.

Then a door opened slowly, somewhere behind him. Hinges protested, so softly as to be almost inaudible. But Hurley heard them. *Felt* the footsteps in the hall, the house so still every movement seemed to reverberate to the foundation. Someone was coming this way.

The footsteps came closer, and Hurley knew he couldn't escape in time. Knew his only hope was to hide. He backed into the shadows beside the girl's bed. Thumbed the hilt of the knife and held his breath as the person in the hallway came closer. Waited.

Keep walking, he thought. *Just keep walking.*

The footsteps stopped outside the girl's door. Hurley could feel the person's presence in the doorway, though he couldn't see anything. He stood still in the shadows, his back pressed against the wall, eyes straight ahead, breathing shallow. Knew if he moved, his hunt would be over.

The figure in the hall stepped into the girl's bedroom. Hurley could see a silhouette, a man's form—her father? He stared in at the girl for what seemed like an eternity. Hurley watched him, prayed he didn't reach for the light switch. Tensed his muscles to fight, to leap at the man with his knife. He would damn well get out of this house.

But the man didn't turn on the light. He shifted his weight, backed out of the room, and Hurley let himself breathe again. Listened to the man's footsteps recede. Heard another door open, close again, firm. Heard a toilet flush, running water. The door opened again.

Nature calls. No big deal. Now go back to bed, Dad.

Go back to bed, and let me teach your daughter the lesson you couldn't.

The footsteps returned. Hurley braced himself. Waited for the man to pass the bedroom, to return to his own room, fall back asleep. Ten minutes, maybe, and all would be still again. Patience, and quiet. Hurley had waited longer for worse.

But the man wasn't coming back down the hall. Hurley heard his feet fall on hardwood, the stairs. Heard the steps diminish again as the man descended to the first floor of the house. Hurley let himself relax, figuring Dad was likely checking the doors and windows, reassuring himself. Figured as soon as the man convinced himself his house was secure, he would come back to bed.

Fifteen minutes, then. Maybe twenty.

It was just as the first light switched on downstairs that Hurley remembered the food he'd left on the counter. The rifle he'd propped up by the fridge.

Damn it.

Hurley pushed off from the bedroom wall. Hurried across to the door, as quiet as he could, made for the stairs.

The man would notice the food. He would find Hurley's rifle. He would know Hurley was here.

99

Light glowed up through the stairwell from some lamp around the corner in the living room. Hurley could hear the man's footsteps, louder now on the hardwood, as he followed him down the stairs.

The man was still in the living room, best as Hurley could figure. He hadn't moved to the kitchen yet. Maybe he wouldn't. Maybe he would turn around and come back up the stairs.

No matter. It was too late. The man's fate was sealed the moment he'd walked down those stairs. Hurley would have to kill him, and he would have to do it quietly.

Hurley reached the bottom of the stairs. Touched down on the first floor, stepping lightly, praying the floorboards wouldn't groan underneath him and give him away. He raised his knife, held it in front of himself, a fighter's stance. Peered around the corner, scanned the living room for the man.

But the living room was empty. And there was a light on now in the kitchen. The man stood in the space between the two rooms, his back to Hurley. He was of medium build, black hair turning gray. He was staring in at the kitchen. Wasn't moving.

Hurley knew that wouldn't last. The man's sleepy brain would wake up fast once he'd realized what Hurley's rifle must mean. He would take action, reach for a weapon or the phone, and Hurley couldn't afford to wait around to see which.

He crossed the living room, knife at the ready, speed the objective now, not silence. The man didn't hear him at first. He just stood there, scratching his head, mind struggling to compute. By the time he heard Hurley coming, and tensed, half turning, he was already too late.

Hurley closed the distance fast. Reached his free hand around the man's head, covered his mouth, wrenched his head back. Brought his knife to the man's throat and cut across, fast. The man struggled. He screamed through Hurley's left hand, wrenched against Hurley's grip, kicked, fought for his life. Hurley held firm as the man's fight diminished, his anger turned to panic. As his arms abandoned Hurley's grip and went to his own throat, trying in vain to stop the bleeding.

Hurley guided the man deeper into the kitchen, his eye on a pantry closet opposite the back door. The man's blood pooled beneath him, lakes on the hardwood. His struggles were weakening. He kicked out uselessly now and then, but Hurley held on. Half pulled, half dragged him to the pantry, opened the door with his knife hand, and backed the man inside. Laid him down gently, the man's fight all but gone. He'd stopped screaming, even, lay back and made dying noises, his eyes wide and staring beyond Hurley, staring at nothing. Hurley waited until he was sure the man was past help. Then he stepped out of the pantry, closed the door behind him. Left the man inside to die in darkness.

The kitchen was an abattoir. Blood spattered the counters, the cabinets, the buzzing fridge. Tracked a grisly trail to the pantry door. There was no hiding this, no cleaning it up. There was only escape before anyone saw.

For the briefest of moments, Hurley indulged the idea of returning to the girl, now that he'd dealt with her father. It was a pleasant idea. But it was foolish as hell. He couldn't afford the temptation.

Time was wasting. Hurley circled around the kitchen table, dodging the pools of blood at his feet, and retrieved his rifle and the food he'd left out. Spared a glance at the pantry door, the bloody trail, wondered if the man had died knowing he'd saved his daughter's life. Wondered if the daughter would ever realize just how much she owed her dad.

He crossed to the back door, the keys hanging on the coat hook—Dodge, Toyota, Volkswagen. Hurley lingered over the keys, thinking. Three cars. Three choices.

He decided on the Dodge. American muscle. Was just lifting the keys from the hook when he sensed something behind him, turned, and there *she* was, in the doorway, the daughter herself, the pretty, wicked beast.

(And she *was* pretty, in her pajamas, her hair mussed. She looked younger than Hurley had expected, innocent—but he knew her innocence was an illusion.)

The girl stared in at him. Took in his presence by the door, his face, his rifle. Took in the blood on the floor, the counters, the fridge.

Hurley stared back, and for a moment, nothing happened. Then the girl screamed, *loud*, and ran.

100

The girl disappeared into the living room, pounded up the stairs, her screams echoing everywhere, bouncing off the walls and straight back at Hurley, until his ears rang and he was sure even the police could hear her crying, miles away.

Hurley chased her, his boots slipping in the dead man's blood. Dropped his rifle. No matter, he still had the deputy's pistol. He still had the Indian girl's knife.

He took the stairs two at a time. Energized now, adrenaline pumping. Made the top of the stairs, the carpet—dark, bloody footprints leading down to the end of the hall. A door slammed. The girl didn't stop screaming.

Hurley drew the pistol. Hurried down the hall to the door at the end. There was screaming behind it. Another voice, too. Hurley tried the handle. Locked. No matter. He stepped back. Aimed his pistol. Fired through the lock, kicked the door open.

"Sorry to disappoint, but I'm not one of your pussy boyfriends," he called through the open doorway. "I don't back down that easy, girl."

Beyond the doorway was darkness, another brief hall. A light at the end in an open room—soft, a night-light. Hurley advanced, carefully now, thinking the girl or her mother might jump out at him, try an ambush, hit him with something heavy. But nobody ambushed him. The girl's screaming had died. In its place, Hurley heard muffled sobbing, someone else whispering.

He reached the end of the short hall, the open room. The master bedroom, a queen-size bed, a dresser, matching bedside tables. The shades drawn on the windows, one lamp by the bed. And in the corner, as far away from the little hall as possible, the girl and her mother, huddled up close together, the girl crying, the mother trying to calm her.

The girl's mother was even prettier than her daughter. Hurley could see the resemblance, but the girl's mother had aged into her looks, outgrown girlish innocence, matured into a woman. She was beautiful, so beautiful that Hurley was instantly suspicious. How had a woman like this wound up with the farmer he'd dispatched so easily downstairs? Why had she settled for such an ordinary man?

Maybe the farmer had inherited wealth, Hurley thought. He hadn't seemed like a brute; he hadn't *tamed* this woman.

The girl and her mother watched Hurley from the floor, the girl's cheeks lined with tears, her nose runny. She looked away when Hurley met her eyes, sobbed again. The girl's mother didn't look away, though. She looked up at Hurley, calm, took in the knife and the gun.

Hurley ran his eyes over her body, his excitement building. He would have this woman, and her daughter, too. He would teach them both lessons. He would work slowly, enjoy himself. And he would ask the woman how her farmer husband had brought her here. He would ask her all sorts of questions, ask them both. And he would keep asking, until they'd run out of answers.

Hurley bound the girl's wrists tight with panty hose. Bound her mother's. Pushed them both onto the bed and bound their ankles, too, hobbling them. Stood back and admired his handiwork, enjoyed how they struggled.

The girl was hysterical; she hadn't stopped crying. Her mother seemed to be fighting to keep calm. "Let her go," she told Hurley. "Please. Do what you want with me, but *please*, let my daughter go."

Hurley grinned down at her. "I don't think so." He was shaking, he was so excited, the thrill of the chase, the triumph. "What I have to teach you applies to her, too."

"She's a *girl*," the mother said. "She doesn't need to—"

"Oh, yes, she's a *girl*," Hurley said. He set the pistol down. Drew the knife. Circled around to the girl and held the blade to her cheek, relished how she squirmed underneath him.

"I bet you're a popular one," he said into her ear. "I bet *all* the boys love you. And I bet you just *love* breaking their hearts."

The girl didn't move. Whispered *no* through her tears.

"Liar." Hurley stood. "What's your name, girl?"

The girl waited until he showed her the knife again. *"Shae,"* she said finally. *"Shae Fontaine."*

"You're a slut, aren't you, Shae?" Hurley said. "You're a slut, just like your mother."

Shae shook her head no. Mom made to speak. Hurley backhanded her, knocked her near off the bed. Sent the girl into another round of hysterics.

"You're a fucking liar." He couldn't help the anger. "You're a liar," he said, forcing himself to calm down. "I'm going to show you what happens to every slut, Shae. And then I'm going to show your mom, too."

But Mom wasn't listening anymore. Wasn't looking at Hurley, her eyes cast back at the bedside table. Hurley followed her gaze to a photograph, a snapshot in a pewter frame. Picked up the picture and caught the meaning immediately.

It was a family picture. Mom and poor, dead Dad, sweet Shae. But there was a fourth family member, too, six or seven years old, and in pigtails, hugging her dad tight as she ate an ice cream cone.

Another girl. A witness.

A goddamn problem.

101

Sadie Fontaine ran through the snow as fast as she was able, barely feeling the cold and the wet seeping through her thin socks. She'd been asleep when her sister screamed, thought she was dreaming at first, then sat up in bed and thought maybe *Shae* was the one dreaming.

But Shae had been running, too; Sadie'd heard her feet on the stairs as she ran up from the living room. Heard the muffled *thump thump thump* as she ran down the hall to Mom and Dad's room. Sadie pushed the covers to the floor, stood. Started to the bedroom door, to follow her sister, to climb into bed with Shae and Mom and Dad and let Shae tell them all what was the matter.

But then she'd heard the other footsteps. Heavier, on the stairs, the whole house shuddering under their weight. Slower down the hallway carpet in the direction Shae had gone. And Sadie had known, instinctively, that this wasn't Mom and this wasn't Dad. This was something else, something bad.

Then she'd heard the gunshot. It was louder than anything she'd ever heard in her life. She heard the bad person kick open the door to Mom and Dad's room, heard his voice as he called in after Shae.

Sorry to disappoint, but I'm not one of your pussy boyfriends. I don't back down that easy, girl.

This was no voice that Sadie had ever heard before. This was a bad man. This was a living nightmare.

So she ran.

She'd waited until the man had disappeared into Mom and Dad's room. She'd listened to Shae crying and Mom trying to comfort her. Then she'd snuck away, as quiet as she could, in the other direction. Skipped the creaky step and padded down to the first floor.

But the first floor was awful, too. There was blood in the kitchen, so much blood, everywhere, and no telling whose. Sadie stopped in the entryway, couldn't make herself walk any farther, couldn't step over the blood, *definitely* couldn't step in it.

There was a phone in the kitchen. Sadie could see it across the bloody pools, on the opposite counter by the microwave. She could make her way over there and call the police. She couldn't remember the number, but she could ask the operator or something, right?

She had to do something. Shae and Mom were upstairs. And maybe Dad, too—though looking at all this blood gave Sadie a bad feeling about Dad, and she instantly wanted to sit down and hide somewhere and cry.

But then Shae had screamed again upstairs, loud and plaintive. And Sadie blacked out. Her instincts took over. She bolted through the kitchen, through the blood. Shoved open the back door and ran into the night.

But the night was cold and empty. Sadie's socks were soaked through times infinity, and her thin pajamas didn't provide much protection from the freezing air. She was at the end of the driveway before she realized she didn't know where she was going; there were no other houses nearby, no one on the highway. There was nobody to save her, and no warmth but back in the house with the man.

She should have phoned the police. She could have found the number somewhere. She should have snuck up on the man and attacked him. She should have done *something*. But every time Sadie slowed, she heard Shae scream again in her head, and she just couldn't make herself turn around.

She ran instead. Ran until her toes were numb and her teeth were chattering, until she'd nearly doubled over from the stitch in her side and her lungs screamed for breath as she gulped down cold air.

She was far away from the farmhouse now. The backyard light was very small behind her. There were no other lights but the glow on the horizon from Roosville, ten miles distant. There was nobody else for miles.

She had to go back.

She had to go back and do something to save her family. Her sister, her mom, and—*please, God*—her dad. She couldn't just leave them, no matter how scared she was.

Sadie turned around. Walked back down the highway until she'd caught her breath. Then she ran again, her mind screaming at her that she was going to get killed. She kept going. Pressed forward.

She'd made it halfway back to the farmhouse when the headlights appeared in the distance.

102

The man and the little girl came into the Roosville customshouse around dawn, woke Stevens from the hard plastic chair he'd turned into his latest excuse for a bed. Across the waiting room, Lynn Cronquist intercepted the man and the girl, but not before the commotion had roused Carla Windermere, too.

Stevens rubbed the sleep from his eyes, his mouth tasting like a garbage fire. He checked the clock on the wall and wondered if he would ever sleep a full night again. He stood and hurried to join Cronquist.

"Found her by the side of the road," the man was saying. "Ten miles from town, the middle of nowhere. Couldn't make sense of what she was talking about, so I thought I should bring her to you folks."

The girl might have been six or seven, maximum. She wore only thin SpongeBob SquarePants pajamas, and her whole body shook—from the cold, Stevens wondered, or from something worse?

"We have to *go*," she told Cronquist. "We have to go back right now. You have to come with me and we have to go, *now*."

"We'll take you, sweetheart," the Mountie replied. "We just have to get the story straight first. What's going on to get you so upset?"

"The *man*," the girl said, as if it should have been obvious. "There's a bad man in my house. He woke me up."

Stevens felt the chill as soon as the girl said it. Figured he'd known it was coming, but it hit him like a punch, regardless.

Hurley.

"What's your name?" he asked the girl. "Where do you live? Where is the man?" He caught the eye of another Mountie, beckoned him over.

"Sadie," the girl said. "My name's Sadie Fontaine." She started to cry again. "My mom and dad are still at my house," she said through her tears. "My sister. There was blood *everywhere.*"

Windermere let out a sharp breath. "Goddamn it, partner."

Hostages, Stevens thought. *Victims. This whole situation is going to get uglier.*

Cronquist was already reaching for her coat. "Come on if you're coming," she told Stevens and Windermere. "Doesn't sound like we have time to spare."

103

"W*here is she?"*

On the bed below Hurley, Shae Fontaine's mother pressed her body in between Hurley and her daughter, an ineffective human shield. Hurley had his pistol pulled again and aimed it down at the women, one after the other. He was frustrated, and these *animals* weren't helping his mood.

Hurley had practically torn the house apart looking for the other girl. He'd found her bedroom easily; he'd stormed past it earlier as he'd chased Shae Fontaine. The younger girl—her name was Sadie, he'd discovered, and Mom was Mona—must have disappeared in a hurry. She'd pushed her covers to the floor and left the mattress warm where she'd lain on it.

But she was gone now, and that pissed Hurley off. He'd searched the house, every bedroom, bathroom, the living room and the kitchen. Even the garage—he'd poked his head inside, promised he would kill the girl's sister slowly if she didn't show herself. Heard nothing, not even a whimper.

He *had* found rope, however, and duct tape, which he'd used to bind Mona and Shae Fontaine more securely as the first light of day appeared through the eastward-facing windows. Then he'd threatened the women, hit them, cajoled them, anything to induce them into giving up the little girl.

But neither Mona Fontaine nor her daughter were talking.

It was dawn now. Soon the sun would appear over the horizon. Soon the day would begin in earnest. Hurley had intended to take his time with these women, but his appetite had changed. Instead of triumph, he felt anger.

"Fuck it." He put the pistol away. Watched Mona Fontaine relax, just slightly. Watched her eyes get wide again when he picked up the knife. "Which of you wants to die first?"

Hurley grabbed for Shae Fontaine. Then he stopped. Cocked his head and listened. He could hear something over the girl's screams and the rush of blood through his ears. Something outside the house, in the distance, low and rhythmic. A helicopter.

Hurley left Shae Fontaine on the floor. Hurried to a window, searched for the chopper. The sky was empty. The helicopter was still far away, but the sound was getting louder.

As he turned away from the window, turned back to the women, he happened to glance up the Fontaines' snowy driveway, and there he saw something just as bad as a helicopter, something that made him forget Shae and Mona Fontaine instantly.

A police car, an RCMP cruiser, had pulled in off the highway. It was idling, motionless, at the top of the driveway, no movement inside, the cops not going anywhere. Waiting, no doubt, for reinforcements to come.

Somewhere in the distance, a train whistle sounded. Hurley stared out the window at the cruiser in the driveway and wished he were anywhere but here.

104

The house must have been eighty years old. It was huge, shabby, peeling paint and missing shingles, stately and imposing and kind of creepy, to boot. It looked like it must have been haunted, like if ghosts did exist, they would surely lurk in places like this.

But right now, Stevens knew, the house didn't need ghosts. If Leland Hurley was still in there, the property was cursed enough as it was.

Cronquist stopped the car at the head of the driveway, and she and Stevens and Windermere all studied the place. Stevens couldn't see movement; most of the windows were dark, the shades drawn upstairs. The house might have been deserted.

Maybe he's gone already. Stole the family car and hit the highway.

They would find out in due time, Stevens supposed, as Cronquist shifted the Crown Vic out of gear. "I know this is my turf, but this is your fugitive," she told the agents. "You tell me what you need, and I'll get it done."

Stevens didn't have to see Windermere's face to know she'd been waiting for this. "We're going to need all you can muster, Staff Sergeant, if Hurley's really in there," she replied. "If you can give me a perimeter and eyes in the air, we'll call it a good start. Throw in a tactical team and I'll love you forever."

"Perimeter won't be a problem," Cronquist said. "You'll have our chopper and your air support, too. Tactical team's a ways out, though; I'm going to need an hour to get them on scene."

"We can get ours here in forty-five minutes," Windermere said. "Assuming you can grease some wheels at the border."

"Anything."

"Perfect. Then we're set." Windermere fixed her eyes on the house again. "Now we just have to find out if he's in there or not."

No sooner had she said the words than the Crown Vic took a bullet. The shot came out of nowhere, missed low, put a hole in the hood in front of Windermere. Rocked the car something scary, set them all ducking, the crack of the rifle echoing through the morning air. And then Cronquist had the cruiser slammed into reverse, her foot on the gas, careening the car out of the driveway and back onto the highway, didn't let up until they'd reached the edge of the Fontaine property, a row of thick bushes a good ten feet high.

"Well, dang," she said, shifting back into park. "I guess we know he's in there."

"I guess we do," Windermere said. "So how about we set up that perimeter?"

105

We're going to do this how they trained us," Windermere told Stevens and Cronquist. "Lock this place down until the tactical guys get here. Stay low, stay covered, keep eyes on the house. Wait until we have numbers and let the guys with the big guns do what they're paid to do."

Ten minutes had passed since Hurley had fired on them, and backup had arrived in the form of a handful of RCMP vehicles, a swarm of Mounties on snowmobiles, and the Flathead County chopper patrolling the air above, scanning the Fontaine property in case Leland Hurley decided to get cute.

More reinforcements were coming—Wasserman and Mundall and the Salt Lake City agents, Flathead and Lincoln County deputies, the whole gamut. In an hour or so, Stevens knew, the Fontaine place would make out like your textbook standoff situation, a ring of law enforcement around the outside, a madman with hostages in the house.

They'd moved Cronquist's Crown Vic back to the head of the driveway, slow and cautious, parked it just beyond, and taken cover behind it. Crouched down below the sheet metal, asses on the snowy pavement, guns drawn, sneaking looks down the Fontaines' front lawn as the rest of the Mounties spread out around the edge of the property line.

The way the bullet had hit the car, Stevens figured the shooter was upstairs somewhere, and he scanned the dark upstairs windows again, looking for a sign. Couldn't see much from this distance, had to squint, but he thought he could make out a thin strip of light peeking out from under a curtain, the far side of the house. The way the curtain was moving looked like it was wind, like whoever was up there had the window open in mid-January.

"Upper left," he told Windermere and Cronquist. "My eyes aren't what they used to be, but is that window open or am I crazy?"

Cronquist had binoculars in the cruiser. She pulled them out, handed them to Windermere. "Not just open," Windermere said after a moment. "Someone smashed that sucker out." Then she stiffened. "And—whoa—there's our boy now."

Stevens followed her eyes. Couldn't see anything. Felt Windermere nudge him with the binoculars, took them. Found the window again, felt something like icy fingers on his neck. There was Leland Hurley, all right, peering out from behind the curtain, the barrel of his rifle propped against the windowsill. He stared out at the front yard, at the Crown Vic, at *Stevens*, for a couple long seconds, seemed to stare right into Stevens's eyes, and then the curtain fell back and Hurley was gone again, though he'd managed to burn his image deep into Stevens's mind.

This guy's a maniac. And he has hostages in there.

"We have to go to work on this guy," Stevens said, handing the binoculars back. "We can't afford to sit around. Soon as he realizes he's cornered, he's going to get desperate. We need to calm him down before he does something bad."

Windermere craned her neck over the hood of the cruiser, snuck another look at the house. Chewed her lip for a second, and Stevens wondered if she was feeling the pressure, too, if she was fighting the urge to go running in there, guns blazing, *force* Hurley to give himself up.

"We've done a lot of reading on this Hurley guy," she said. "Chased him over hell's acre, too, but shit, there's no better way to really *know* someone than to listen to what they have to say for themselves, right?"

She gave Stevens the ghost of a smile. "What do you say we give old Leland a phone call?"

106

The law was everywhere. Hurley had watched from the bedroom window as they surrounded the house—Mounties on Ski-Doos, in cruisers, SUVs, pickup trucks. There had to be twenty of them, maybe more, and that wasn't counting whoever was up there in the helicopter, droning around above the farmhouse, the noise constant, incessant, grating on Hurley's nerves.

He couldn't be sure, but he thought he could hear a second helicopter in the distance. The Mounties were bringing the whole damn hockey team.

Let them come. Let them bring as many cops as they wanted; Hurley still held the trump cards, two of them bound hand and foot, one on the bed and the other on the floor.

"Doesn't look good for you girls," he told the Fontaine women as he watched the law assemble. "This thing's turning into a showdown, and you're about the only leverage I've got."

On the floor, Shae Fontaine looked like she'd cried all her tears. "Let us go," she said. "Please. They'll kill you if you don't, and you know it."

"They're not going to kill me," Hurley told her. "They aren't even going to try. Because the second they do, I'm gutting one of you like the pigs that you are. And they're dumb enough not to want that."

He was wrong about the girl. She found a fresh supply of tears pretty quick.

Now the phone was ringing. Hurley could hear it out in the hall. Had a vague recollection of a table out there, barely a foot wide, a phone sitting on it. He showed the women his pistol.

"Try anything stupid and this is over before it even gets started," he told them. Then he walked out of the bedroom.

The table sat halfway down the hall. The phone was where he remembered it. It was still ringing. Hurley looked back at the master bedroom before he lifted the receiver.

Here goes nothing.

"Sure took you long enough," he told the caller. "I was thinking I'd have to start killing people to make you all pay attention."

There was a pause. Then: "You don't need to kill anyone, Leland." A woman's voice, low, the hint of an accent. The South somewhere. "We're paying attention, I promise."

Now it was Hurley's turn to go quiet. He'd been anticipating a man's voice, expected the Mounties would know better than to trust a woman to this work. But then he remembered how easily women manipulated, how they charmed, and he realized the Mounties knew exactly what they were doing.

"Yeah, well," he said, feeling his collar grow hot despite himself. "You'd better not try anything crazy. I'm loaded for bear and it's a good day to die, if you know what I'm saying."

"Nobody has to die, Leland." Jesus, but she was smooth. Like she did this every day. "And nobody's going to do anything crazy. All these people outside, they're not here to harm you. They're here to make sure nobody else gets hurt."

Yeah fucking right. Any one of those Mounties would shoot me dead given half the chance.

"We're thinking about the family, Leland," the woman continued. "The Fontaines. Can you tell me their status?"

"Their status?" Hurley laughed, his throat gravel. "Dad's dead. Mom and big sister are just hanging out."

"Okay," the cop said slowly. "But they're alive, the two women? Can you put them on the phone so I know for sure?"

"No, I can't," Hurley told her. "The cord don't stretch that far."

"Will you take them to a window when we're done talking, Leland?" the woman asked. "If we know they're okay, it puts us all in a better state of mind, you know?"

"They're okay," Hurley told her. "And they'll *stay* okay, so long as you and your collection of assholes out there slow your roll and respect my position."

"Your position. Okay, Leland. And what *is* your position?"

"I'm trying to get out of here. Isn't that obvious? I'm trying to disappear, like I've *been* trying to do, but you all won't leave me alone."

The woman *tsk*ed. "You know we can't let you do that. There's a couple different endings to this scenario, and neither of them involve you getting out of here scot-free."

"It ends with me walking out of here, or it ends with three body bags," Hurley said. "Take your pick."

Hurley could hear the woman muttering to her partners. Picked up on that accent again and had an epiphany.

"You're the FBI agent," he said. "The black one, aren't you? You're a beautiful woman, but I guess you already knew that."

"Uh, thank you," the woman said, and he could tell he'd thrown her off guard. "Are you looking at me, Leland? Can you see me right now?"

"Not even," Hurley said. "But I saw you before."

"In the car?"

"In the forest, by my camp. You were looking for the girl, and you walked right past me, you and your partners."

Silence.

"I could have killed the three of you," Hurley continued. "*Bang, bang, bang,* easy. I *should* have done it, too; would have saved me a whole lot of hassle."

"But you didn't."

"There's still time. I killed that little deputy, didn't I?"

Silence again.

Hurley checked his watch. "Thirty minutes," he said. "I walk out a free man within the half hour or I kill one of these bitches for fun."

The woman hesitated. Hurley knew he'd beaten her. "You show us they're alive," she said finally. "I'll see what I can do."

107

So?"

Stevens watched Windermere's face as she ended the call. Tried to gauge how she'd fared with the fugitive. From the look on her face, Stevens figured she hadn't won the guy over.

Windermere didn't make eye contact. Stared up at the house with

Cronquist's binoculars until Hurley brought the Fontaine women, first Shae, then her mother, to the bedroom window. She nodded to herself, replaced the binoculars.

"So what did he tell you?" Stevens tried again.

"What did he say?" Windermere let out a sigh. "He said he should have shot us in the forest, partner, by his cabin. Said he should have killed you and me both when he had the chance."

108

Hurley paced the master bedroom. On the bed, Shae and Mona Fontaine huddled together, watched him, said nothing. But Hurley barely noticed them. He wasn't thinking about the Fontaine women right now.

The FBI had sent a *woman* to negotiate with him. She'd sounded so smooth, calm, unflappable at first. But he'd showed her. He'd thrown her off balance, he'd beaten her, he'd *won*.

"That bitch," he told the Fontaine women. "That stupid, stupid cow. Thought she could get one over on me? I don't *think* so."

Neither Shae nor Mona responded. That was fine. He couldn't care less about either one of them, not now.

"Stupid cow," he said again. "Stupid, stupid, stupid cow." He could see her through the scope of his rifle, walking clueless through the forest. He was almost *glad* he hadn't pulled the trigger; this was far more rewarding.

Pity it couldn't last.

Hurley checked his watch. Ten minutes had passed, and no word from the FBI agent yet. Twenty minutes until he could kill and be justified doing it.

Hurley decided he didn't want to wait that long to lord his victory over the FBI cow. He walked out of the master bedroom and to the phone again.

109

"Thirty minutes," Windermere said. "Twenty, now. And then he kills one of the women."

Behind Cronquist's Crown Vic, Stevens and Windermere huddled with the Mountie. Tried to work out a strategy.

"The HRT guys hit a snag getting up here," Stevens reported. "Last night's snow is slowing everyone down. They're still forty minutes out, minimum."

"And my guys are the same," Cronquist added. "I have plenty of corporals, pistols, and shotguns, but you want the big boys, we have to wait."

"We don't have time to wait," Windermere told them. "We're not letting those women die in there because we had to wait for a tactical team. We need to do something."

She peered over the hood of the cruiser, looked across the yard at the house. "I need a plan of the house," she told Stevens and Cronquist. "We need to know where this guy is, where the women are."

"Might take more than twenty minutes to get those plans," Cronquist said.

"Not acceptable. Get the other Fontaine girl down here to draw me a map with her crayons, if you have to. Just get me some kind of intelligence, okay?"

Cronquist pulled out her phone. Ducked away. Made a call.

Stevens met Windermere's eyes. "You thinking of storming this place, partner?" he asked.

"We're good at the cowboy stuff, aren't we?" she replied. "But no. He sees us coming, he pulls the pin on this thing. And we fly home with three more bodies on our hands."

"So what are you thinking?"

"I'm thinking I want to know what it looks like in there," Windermere said. "And then—"

She stopped. Her phone had started to ring in her pocket. She checked the screen, cocked her head at Stevens.

"This is Hurley," she said. "He's twenty minutes early."

Did you miss me?"

Leland Hurley sounded like every asshole Carla Windermere had ever fended off in some shitty bar, some house party, the break room at work. Smug, self-satisfied, convinced of his own unimpeachable awesomeness, looking for romance and willing to steamroll any obstacle to get it. Windermere rolled her eyes.

"Sure, Leland," she told him. "I missed you. You were so charming the last time we spoke."

"You don't have to patronize me. I know what you're doing. I know why they sent *you* to talk to me."

"Why? What is it you think I'm doing?"

Hurley scoffed. "*Please.* Why else would they make me negotiate with a beautiful woman? You're here to do the only thing you bitches do well: manipulate a man into doing what you want."

"*You* called *me*, Leland. I'm not trying to manipulate anyone. I'm trying to figure out a way to end this thing peacefully."

Hurley was quiet, but Windermere could hear him breathing. "You must have been pretty your whole life," he said. "How was that for you? Did you enjoy the power?"

"You want the truth?" Windermere replied. "I was the ugly duckling in high school. Wasn't until college that I came into my own."

"And did you break hearts in college, Agent . . ."

"Windermere," Windermere told him. "And I never broke a heart that didn't have it coming."

"Says you." Hurley's voice had an edge to it all of a sudden. "What gives *you* the right to decide who gets to be loved?"

Windermere would have laughed Hurley off the phone if the stakes weren't so high. "I mean, I wasn't trying to decide all that. But as far as who gets to be loved by *me*? Sure, I was picky. I think I deserve to be."

"You think you *deserve* it. What about *us*? Don't men deserve to be happy?"

"All due respect," Windermere said, "but if you're trying to tell me it's on me to make you happy, you're crazier than I thought, pal."

Beside her, Stevens's eyes goggled.

Hurley went quiet a beat. Breathing harder now. "You're a stupid cow, just like the others. They all thought they were smart, but I showed them, didn't I?"

"Leland," Windermere said. "I'm just trying to get us out of this jam we're in, know what I mean? I'm not trying to keep you from finding true love, or whatever."

"You won't beat me," Hurley said. "You can try, but you'll see, like they all did."

"We don't have to—"

"Fifteen minutes," Hurley said. "Then I kill someone."

Click.

110

Cronquist had Sadie Fontaine waiting in a Dodge Durango a hundred yards from the farmhouse.

"We're keeping her close at hand," Cronquist told Stevens and Windermere as she led them to the truck. "Not, you know, *close* close, but we kind of ran out of guys to keep an eye on her, so . . ."

Someone had found an oversized Calgary Flames sweatshirt for Sadie. It draped over her thin body like a dress, but she looked warmer than she had the first time Stevens had seen her. Still looked scared, though; terrified. Her hands trembled as she drew out a map of her house for the agents.

"Upstairs," Sadie told them. "The man followed Shae into my mom and dad's room. That's when he shot the door open."

"Your mom and dad's room." Stevens studied the girl's map. "The far left side of the house, then?"

Sadie gave him a blank look. "It's down the end of the hall," she explained. "Past my bedroom and Shae's."

From what Stevens could tell, that meant Leland Hurley hadn't moved. He'd brought the women to a window in the parents' bedroom. He'd fired from that room. He'd encamped there, Stevens figured, and he'd kept the girls with him.

"What about the phone?" Windermere asked. "He said the cord wasn't long enough to lead into the bedroom."

Sadie pointed to a spot in the hallway. "It's between my room and Shae's."

"Any windows?"

Sadie shook her head.

"What about downstairs? What's it look like?"

Sadie hesitated. "My dad's down there," she said. Her lower lip trembled. "In the pantry, I think. There was a lot of blood."

"Okay." Windermere reached out, touched the girl's hand. "Forget about downstairs, honey. We can figure it out."

"Is there anything else?" Stevens asked. Time was wasting, Hurley's deadline fast approaching. If Sadie Fontaine had any more information, they needed it now. "Any other way into the house?"

Sadie thought it over. Then she brightened. "The attic," she said. "Mom and Dad never let us go up there, but we sneak up sometimes. Shae boosts me up and then she climbs up on a stool."

Stevens felt a jolt of something, some potential. This was something they could use. "Any windows up there?"

"Yeah," Sadie said. "It opens, too. You can get onto the roof over the garage from there, but we never do that. Only Dad."

Stevens and Windermere exchanged looks. This was gold.

"And where do you get into the attic?" Windermere asked. "Is there a hatch somewhere?"

Sadie pointed to her map, the upstairs hallway. "It's right here," she said. "It's right in front of Shae's room."

111

"There's gotta be a way," Windermere said as she and Stevens walked back to Cronquist's cruiser. "No way Hurley knows about that attic. He's not prepared for any incursion through there."

Stevens held Sadie Fontaine's map in his hands. He'd scrutinized the thing, looking for a way to cheat Hurley. Couldn't figure one.

"Shae's bedroom is at the top of the stairs," he told Windermere. "That puts Hurley between the attic and the parents' bedroom. We come in through the attic, there's no preventing him from barricading himself in Mom and Dad's room and putting Shae and Mona in jeopardy."

Windermere took the map from him. Knew they were living on the razor's edge now, ten minutes and counting to Hurley's deadline, neither tactical team close enough to beat the clock.

"We need to get him away from the phone somehow," she said. "We need to get him downstairs."

"Sure," Stevens said. "But how do you propose we do that?"

Windermere had already considered the question. And she had an answer, a bad one. But she was thinking it was about all they had.

"You're not going to like this," she told Stevens. "But listen up."

112

The phone rang again. Hurley left Mona and Shae in the master bedroom. Went out into the hall and picked up the handset.

"Five minutes," he said. "Do you have something for me, Agent Windermere?"

"I don't have a way out for you yet," Windermere replied. "This over-the-phone thing, it's not working for me. I've always been more of a face-to-face girl."

Hurley told himself to end the call. *Hang up on her, now. This is one of her tricks.* But he didn't hang up. Realized he was listening, waiting on the agent's next words.

"I'm coming in there," Windermere continued. "I'm not bringing my gun. We're going to talk this over like human beings and see if we can't come to some kind of arrangement, understand?"

"No," Hurley said. "You come anywhere near this house, I'll kill those bitches, I swear. I'll—"

"Those girls die, you die, Leland. And there are plenty of women with badges out here who'd love to be the one to pull the trigger." She gave it a beat. "I'm coming in the front door, buddy. Don't shoot anyone."

Hurley ran his hands through his hair. Glanced back at the master bedroom, saw no signs of movement. Picked at his fingernails, a nervous tic. Couldn't help it. This was bad. This was a very bad idea.

"You can't do this," he said, his voice rough. "This is *my* show, understand? I make the rules."

He waited for Windermere to respond, but she didn't. After a moment, Hurley realized she'd hung up on him.

This dude has a hard-on for me, Stevens," Windermere told her partner. "Forgive the language, but it's true. He called me up just to brag that he'd beat me. And he couldn't stand when I stood up to his ass."

"So he's pissed off at you," Stevens replied. "He's a maniac who hates women and has special feelings for you. And you're just going to walk right in there and give yourself up?"

"I'm going to *distract* him. And then you and these Mounties are going to save the day. Hell, bring the tactical guys if they ever show up."

Stevens shook his head. "I don't like it, Carla."

"You don't have to like it, partner. I know what I'm doing." She winked at him. "You think *this* asshole is going to be the one who does me in? Some poor wilted flower who didn't get enough love as a child?" She took her Glock from its holster, held it out to him. "I'm going to eat this guy's lunch, Stevens. You just make sure you take care of those women."

Stevens didn't answer, searching for a way to change Windermere's mind. They'd done this before, a long time ago, and it had almost gotten both of them killed. But he'd been partnered with Windermere long enough to know there was no talking her out of it—heck, the fact that they'd done it before probably spurred her on.

He took the Glock. "Mathers is going to kick my ass when he finds out about this," he said. "Just you watch."

"If he lays a hand on you, you tell me. Then *I'll* kick *his* ass."

Sure, Stevens thought, watching Windermere strap on a Kevlar vest. *But what if you don't make it home to hear about it?*

113

Hurley paced.

She's trying to use you, he thought. *She's going to use her guile to try to trick you, and the second you let your guard down, all those Mounties out there are going to come rushing in here and end this thing.*

You need to take back control. Kill one of those cows in the bedroom. Show that woman out there you're in charge.

Hurley knew the smart play was to assert himself, fast, protect his stronghold and prove to the cops outside he was for real. Knew the smart play was to prevent Windermere from entering the house at all costs. But the FBI agent's words had set an itch in Hurley's mind, and he couldn't resist the urge to scratch it.

Win or lose, you can punish this bitch. If she's offering herself up to you, brother, you should damn well take advantage. What better way to prove you're superior than to face down this dumb beast head-on?

Hurley walked back to the master bedroom. "Got another one of your kind coming over," he told the Fontaine women. "I know she's thinking about trying something foolish, but you'd better hope she behaves. Otherwise . . ."

He drew his finger across his throat. The Fontaines stared back. They were through begging. Through crying. They just looked exhausted.

So be it. They'll be crying again soon enough.

Windermere had done many dumb things in her life. This was probably the dumbest.

She double-checked her Kevlar. Gave Stevens a smile—cocky, like, *Giddyap, partner.* Then she stepped out from behind Lynn Cronquist's Crown Victoria and started down the Fontaines' driveway toward the house.

She could feel eyes on her, every Mountie standing guard along the property line, Stevens and Cronquist behind her. The other officers had been briefed; there'd been more than a few words of protest. But Windermere didn't have time to debate. *Something* had to be done to keep Hurley from hurting those women.

He was watching her, too; she was sure of it. Might even have her lined up with that rifle of his. He could blast her head off right now, she knew, and that would be the end of the Carla Windermere story. But Windermere was reasonably certain he wouldn't. Say, eighty percent certain.

Seventy-five.

Windermere was banking on the fact that Leland Hurley would want a better chance at proving his superiority. He'd want her to look in his eyes as he hurt her. So she walked up the long driveway, the world quiet around her, tense, everyone waiting for Hurley's rifle to crack.

But Hurley didn't shoot her. Windermere made the side of the farmhouse, stepped up onto the porch, paused in front of the door, calmed her heart, and dried her hands on her pants. She was scared, though she would never have admitted it. But she wanted to meet this bastard about as bad as he wanted to meet her, she suspected.

She took a deep breath. Then she knocked on the door.

Hurley unlocked the front door. Pulled it open a couple inches. Then, quickly, he stepped back, raised the dead deputy's pistol, and aimed it at the doorway as the FBI agent pushed the door wide open.

"Get in here," he told her. "Fast. Close the door behind you."

The agent obeyed him. She was attractive, even more so now than in the forest, where her coat had been drawn tight and her hood pulled up, concealing everything but her face. Now, up close, Hurley could see she really was beautiful.

Probably had the whole world given to her, he thought, grabbing her roughly and pushing her against the wall. The agent let him frisk her, didn't tense or fight as he patted her down with his free hand, his gun hand pressing the pistol up against the underside of her jaw. She was as good as her word; she hadn't come armed. But that only made Hurley more suspicious.

What kind of crazy bitch throws herself into a situation like this without protection?

A crazy bitch who thinks she can talk *her way out.*

Satisfied that she wasn't carrying any weapons, Hurley stepped back. Kept the pistol leveled at the back of her head.

"Give me one reason why I shouldn't kill you right now," he said.

"Kill me?" The agent turned around slowly, smoothly. Calm and unflappable, no trace of fear in her eyes. "Leland, honey," she said. "You've only just *met* me."

114

Stevens ducked back to the highway. Circled around behind the bushes that lined the southern bound of the Fontaines' property and hurried through the snow toward the rear of the farmhouse, hoping Hurley was too caught up in Windermere to be paying attention.

Stevens didn't like this idea at all, was already trying to figure out how he was going to tell Derek Mathers and Drew Harris how he'd let Carla walk into Hurley's hands more or less unopposed. Knew there wasn't a damn thing he could have done short of handcuffing her to keep her from doing it, but that didn't make him feel any better.

He made the end of the row of bushes. Found more Mounties back here, snowmobiles, a couple trucks. The helicopter overhead. There was a kind of courtyard back here, the garage jutting out from the rear of the house, the barn just beyond it. Stevens could see a couple of RCMP corporals waiting behind the garage, out of sight of the house. They'd been briefed on the radio that he was coming, but nobody had yet told them why.

Stevens studied the farmhouse, the dark windows. Hoped Hurley wasn't watching and booked his way across the courtyard to the rear of the garage. Caught a glimpse of the attic window Sadie Fontaine had talked about, a narrow thing twenty-five feet from the ground, a solid eight feet above the roof of the garage. They would have to be nimble—and quiet.

The Mounties made space as Stevens approached. There were two of them, a man and a woman, both young, fresh-faced, serious.

"Stevens, FBI," he told them after he'd caught his breath. "You guys ready to be heroes?"

115

Windermere tried not to focus on the gun pointed at her head. Tried to take in what she could about her surroundings instead.

She was in an entryway. Beside her was the living room, and through the living room, toward the back of the house, was the kitchen. Ahead were the stairs leading up to the second floor; as Windermere glanced up, she could see the trapdoor to the attic clearly.

You have to get him away from the stairs. Whatever you can do.

Hurley was watching her like he wasn't sure if he wanted to pull the trigger or make a pass at her. Windermere figured she was set, for the short term. Figured it would take a while for the maniac's thoughts to coalesce around one or the other.

She gave him the hint of a smile. Slipped past him and into the living room. Hurley let her go. She could feel his eyes follow her.

"So here we are," she said, walking to a front window, letting down the curtain. "You and me, Leland, in a hell of a bind."

Hurley watched her. His pistol hand wavered, but he didn't lower the gun. Windermere walked to the next window, closed that curtain, too. The living room was dark now, cut off from the outside. Windermere switched on a table lamp. Sat down in an easy chair. "So how are we going to get out of this mess?"

Hurley looked away as soon as her eyes fell on his. His lip curled. "You're not here to get *me* out of anything," he told her. "You're here to brainwash me into doing what you want."

He looked away again. His eyes were as jumpy as a rabbit on speed. He shifted his weight, then again. He wasn't comfortable. Even though he was pointing a gun at her, the guy still wasn't comfortable.

"That's where your head's at, huh?" she said. "All women are manipulative, like, fundamentally. Like, even if I wasn't a cop and you didn't have hostages, I would still be trying to game you?"

Hurley nodded.

"Why?"

"Because it's your nature." He answered abruptly, blurted it out. "All you're good for is using men to get what you want." He narrowed his eyes at her. "You more than anyone, I bet."

"Because I'm attractive."

Hurley nodded again.

"You think I'm hot, Leland?" Windermere asked. "Are you attracted to me?"

"Don't." Hurley spat. He leveled the gun at her forehead. "Don't you try any of that bullshit. I'll kill you. I swear."

Windermere held her hands up. "I'm just trying to get to know you better, dude. Like, I've been chasing you for a while now, and all I know about you is how you were in the army and you're a pretty good survivalist. But what I *don't* know is how you got into this mess."

Hurley didn't answer. She met his eyes, and his gaze pinballed away.

"Come on," Windermere said. "My partner out there, Stevens—he's the guy you didn't kill in the woods—he has this thing about wanting to know people's *motives* when we're chasing them. And I gotta say, in this case? It's kind of rubbed off on me."

Still nothing. Hurley still twitchy, the gun bobbing up and down in his grip.

"Humor me," Windermere said. "We have time for some bullshit before we cut to the tricky stuff. So why are you so mad at women, Leland? What happened?"

Hurley didn't answer right away. Chewed on his lip. "All I ever wanted was to make women happy." He took a step into the living room. Held the gun steady, looked her dead in the eye. "But none of you *bitches* would let me."

116

Stealthily as he could, Stevens followed the Mounties across the top of the Fontaines' equipment garage. The Mounties, Pelletier and Buckley, were kids, agile and full of energy, both of them. Stevens felt like a dinosaur as he worked to keep up.

He was sweating through his shirt, even in the chill air. Slipping on the icy rooftop, trying to stay silent, fully aware that any inadvertent noise could draw Hurley to the farmhouse window, where he would have no trouble spotting them.

Cronquist had radioed from the front of the house as soon as Windermere was inside. Radioed back a minute or two later to report that the front curtains in the living room were down. This was the sign they were waiting for; it meant Windermere was confident she had the situation under control, confident she could keep Leland Hurley away from the stairs.

The Mounties reached the end of the garage, huddled up against the wall of the farmhouse, Stevens bringing up the rear. He looked up to the attic window, eight feet above them.

"Sadie Fontaine said the window should be unlocked," he whispered. "So let's hope she's right."

Stevens and the other man, Pelletier, set up at the base of the wall. Boosted Corporal Buckley up toward the window. Stevens craned his neck to watch, sticking as close as he could to the farmhouse. Buckley stretched for the window, reached it, tried the windowpane. It slid aside easily. Bingo.

"You want to go next?" Stevens asked Pelletier as Buckley slipped inside the attic. "Or should we flip a coin for it?"

The Mountie colored. "No disrespect, sir, but maybe I should go last."

Stevens smiled at the kid's discomfort. "I'm just joshing you," he said. "There's no way I could make it up there on my own."

He let Pelletier boost him up, fought the urge to kick his legs as he pulled himself through the narrow opening. Knew he must have looked ridiculous, wondered what he was doing here. Knew the smart play was to let the Mounties handle this, sit back with Cronquist and play quarterback.

But Stevens had never been the type to delegate the dirty work. And with Windermere inside risking her life for this case, he wouldn't have felt right hanging back and just watching. So here he was, nearly out of breath and on his knees on the dusty attic floor, pulling Corporal Pelletier through the window. When the Mountie was safely inside, Stevens blinked in the dim light, let his eyes acclimate, saw cardboard boxes and old toys and pink-foam insulation and, across the room to his left, the trapdoor.

Stevens stood as tall as he could beneath the low ceiling. Led the Mounties slowly toward the door, conscious of every footfall, every creaky floorboard. Knew if Hurley heard them, the game was over. Windermere was dead, and probably Mona and Shae Fontaine, too.

But the Mounties were quiet. They made the trap door, and Stevens held up, straining his ears for any sounds from below. But he couldn't hear anything, save the drone of the helicopters above the farmhouse. There was no way to tell if Hurley was beneath them. Nothing to do but to look.

The trapdoor wasn't a door but a panel in the floor. Stevens knelt down, pried it up at the edges. Inched it out of its frame and slid it aside about six inches. Listened. Heard nothing. Saw nothing.

Stevens slid the panel farther. Opened up more room. Gave Hurley one more chance to reveal himself, then carefully lowered his head through the hole in the floor.

He could see the stairs immediately, just as Sadie Fontaine had described. A long hall to his left, carpet and doorways. The door at the end must be the master bedroom. If he and Windermere were correct, the hostages were in there.

At the bottom of the stairs was a door. It would be the front door, the door through which Windermere had entered the house. But there was no sign of Windermere anywhere, Hurley either, and Stevens knew they would never have a better opportunity than now.

He lifted his head from the hole, straightened, and looked at the Mounties. "Down the hall to your left and all the way to the end," he told them. "Let's get these women out of here."

117

I tried everything."

Hurley paced the small living room. Kept the deputy's pistol trained at Agent Windermere, who sat on the couch, as relaxed as if she were watching a movie. Following him with her eyes as he paced. Listening.

"Girls would only notice guys who wore the right clothes," he told her. "So I bought the right clothes. Still couldn't get a girl to look at me. I heard that girls liked men who were funny, so I tried being funny. Couldn't get a date to save my life."

He snorted, disgusted with the memory. "I was a *virgin* when I graduated high school. No girl ever even let me kiss her. I tried everything to get them to notice me. I wanted to die."

"But you joined the army instead," Windermere said.

"I guess you did your research," he said. "I figured out that girls want tough guys. Guys who can fight, fix things, guys who have muscle. They don't want funny, well-dressed, *intelligent* men, they want brutes."

The FBI agent made as if to argue. He waved the gun at her, cutting her off. "You have a boyfriend, I bet? What does he do?"

She hesitated. Then she smiled a little. "He's FBI, too," she said.

"Exactly. He's big and tough and dumb. Probably couldn't string two sentences together."

"He's big and tough. I'll give you that. But dumb he's not."

"Bullshit." Hurley resumed pacing. "How'd you hook up with him, then? You guys worked together and, what?"

Windermere shifted on the couch. Smiled again, like she was enjoying the memory. Like she was getting a kick out of this. "He pestered me for a while. Wore me down, I guess. I was stressed out from a case and we went out and got drunk and the next thing you know—"

"He was in your bed."

"I was in *his* bed, actually, or at least the bed in his hotel room. And I thought it would end there, some one-night thing, but he just kept pestering me, and now here we are." She shrugged. "He wore me down. That's the moral of the story."

Hurley looked away. "You *chose* him," he told her. "*That* is the moral of the story. You didn't have to go chasing anyone. You just had to decide which man you wanted."

"But that's life, Leland. That's how it goes."

"It's *unfair.*" He could feel his frustration rising again, his anger, and fought the urge to turn on her with the gun, the knife, punish her. "It's not fucking fair. Even when I joined the Rangers, I wasn't good enough. I had to *pay* women to sleep with me. *Pay them.* But you know what?" He laughed. "That was even worse."

Windermere said nothing. Seemed to sense the edge he was walking, gave him space.

"I found out the truth about women," he continued. "About the time I got kicked out of Ranger school. You probably read about that, too, didn't you?"

She nodded.

Hurley spat. "Some stupid bar whore. She played me night after night, flirting with me, pretending she was interested. Just so I'd tip her better when she brought me my drinks. And when I finally fell for it? She shut me down cold. Acted like I was crazy for ever thinking I had a chance."

He resumed pacing. "You're all the same," he told her. "You're stupid and cruel, every one of you. You manipulate men to get what you want—money, shelter, protection. Even you, right here, right now. You're pretending to listen to me so I won't kill those women upstairs."

"I'm listening," Windermere said. "I'm trying to get a handle on you, Leland, so we can all get out of here safe."

But Hurley ignored her. "I figured it out that night in Florida. I decided I wasn't ever going to play your game again. I wasn't going to let a pack of animals control me, and I sure as hell wasn't going to beg them to give me what I have a right to have."

"What, sex? You think sex is your God-given right?"

"You're goddamn right," Hurley replied. "Do you know what it's like to go without love your whole life? To have women constantly ignoring your needs? I'm entitled to love, to sex, a decent shot at happiness, and if none of you bitches are going to give it to me willingly, then, hell, I'm just going to man up and take it from you."

He let the words hang there. Let them resonate in the still air. Windermere gave it a beat. Opened her mouth to reply. Never got the words out.

Somewhere upstairs, something *thumped*. Something heavy.

Hurley stiffened. "What was *that*?"

118

From the attic, Stevens cringed as Corporal Pelletier hit the carpet with a thud. The kid froze, his face draining of color. Down the hall, Corporal Buckley did the same.

Nobody moved. Stevens had heard Hurley pacing downstairs, talking. Couldn't make out the words, but he figured it meant Windermere was still alive, at least.

Now, though, even Hurley had stopped moving. The whole house went silent. Waiting. Below Stevens, Pelletier reached for his sidearm.

119

"Those bitches." Hurley glared at Windermere. "I told you your kind couldn't be trusted. Leave them alone for five minutes and they start trying to take advantage."

He gestured up with the pistol. "I'll teach them to get crafty. Stand up. You're coming with me. Try anything funny and I'll empty this clip in your back."

Windermere thought fast, knew Stevens was up there with the

rescue party, didn't want this thing devolving into violence until the hostages were out of the house at least. Figured the minute Hurley knew he had company, he'd start shooting. Figured she'd be the most likely target.

"What's your hurry?" she asked him. Worked to keep her voice calm, conversational. "Where are they going to go, Leland? I saw a map of the house. This is the only way down."

She didn't let on that the map had been drawn by a seven-year-old. Or that she knew at least one other way *up*.

"Windows," Hurley said. "They could unlock them. Climb out."

"How? You must have tied them up, right?"

Hurley didn't say anything.

"So they're banging around a little bit," Windermere said. "They're not going far. You're that sick of me already?"

Hurley still didn't answer. His eyes lingered on the base of the stairs, just barely visible from the living room. Windermere knew she was losing him, knew she had to try another tack.

"I mean, come on," she continued. "We're making progress here, aren't we?" Her eyes scanned the living room, the front door, the stairs, the weathered couch and worn rug. Trailed to the kitchen doorway, saw the blood on the floor, the cabinets.

"Lot of blood in there," she said casually. "I guess that's the man of the house, huh?"

Hurley stared at her blankly. Followed her eyes. Saw what she saw, and a smile crept onto his face, creepy and slow.

"Yeah," he said. "Yeah, that was him all right."

"What did you do to him?"

Hurley didn't answer.

"Come on," she said. "I have you for, like, twenty-five murders and a kidnapping scenario. You're not getting yourself into any more trouble. Besides, I want to know." She looked into his eyes. "How'd you do it?"

Hurley did nothing. Just breathed, a glint in his eyes as he thought things over. Finally, he settled.

"I cut him." He patted his belt, his knife in its sheath. "With this knife I took from some Indian girl. You want to see what I did to him?"

No, Windermere thought. *Hell no, I do not.*

But she stood. "Sure," she said. "Sure, Leland. Why not?"

120

Hurley was talking again. And if Stevens listened hard, he could hear Windermere, too. Hear boot steps on hardwood, hear them diminish, just as Hurley's voice was diminishing. He was moving, but he wasn't coming for the stairs. Whatever Windermere was doing, it was working.

Stevens caught Pelletier's eye. Motioned down the hall, where Buckley was waiting. They got the message: *Game on.* Turned around, resumed the mission. Crept slowly, softly, toward the master bedroom.

From the trapdoor, Stevens let himself breathe. Drew his sidearm from its holster, just in case, and watched the base of the stairs in case Hurley appeared.

Come on, he thought. *Get these women out. Get them safe. Then work on rescuing Carla.*

From where he was situated, it looked like a tall order.

121

I had to do it," Hurley told Windermere. "I did it quick, and I took no pleasure from it. But part of being a man is doing unpleasant things when they have to be done."

As opposed to killing waitresses, prostitutes, and runaways, Windermere thought. *You sure didn't seem to find* that *an unpleasant task.*

She'd let Hurley push her into the kitchen, his pistol at the small of her back. Let him give her the tour, the blood spattered everywhere, the remains of a meal on the kitchen counter.

"He had already seen the food," Hurley said. "And I'd left my rifle, too. He would have known I was in the house. He would have tried to do something."

"Wait, so where were you?" Windermere asked. "You have to use the restroom or something? How'd he get the drop?"

Hurley tensed behind her. Didn't answer. Seemed to be chewing on his words. Finally, he pushed Windermere toward the corner of the kitchen, a closed door, a trail of blood leading to it.

"I took him in there," he said, "once I'd cut his throat. I laid him down, gentle, and I let him die in the pantry."

He told the story like it made him a hero. Windermere didn't mind. She was banking on the serial killer's natural pride for his work, his pathological need to tell someone what he'd done. In Hurley's case, especially, she knew the man would find pleasure in explaining his genius to a *woman*. She let Hurley maneuver her, pretended to be impressed.

"He never saw you coming," she said.

"Never." Hurley gave a grunt of satisfaction. "He was probably still half-asleep when I cut him. Mind couldn't make sense of what was going on."

Through the kitchen windows, Windermere could see the backyard, see Mounties on snowmobiles, a collection of police trucks and cruisers. Knew the tactical squads must be just about here; let herself start to plan how she'd extricate herself from Hurley when the men with the big guns started breaking down doors. Wasn't worried. She could keep Hurley talking, get him drunk on his innate sense of superiority. Figured he might let the tactical guys cuff him, just so long as he could keep bragging.

But then Hurley stiffened behind her, and all of Windermere's plans went to shit.

"There," he said. "What the fuck was *that*, now?"

"What was what?" Windermere replied. "I didn't hear anything."

"Upstairs." Hurley was already turning her, his hand on her shoulders, rough, keeping her close. "I heard movement. Voices."

He shoved her out of the kitchen. Back into the living room, toward the stairs. "Come on," he said. "Sounds like the ladies need a reminder who's boss."

122

Boots on hardwood again. Fast this time. Hurley's angry voice, getting louder. Stevens didn't have to hear much to know they'd blown the mission.

The Mounties had freed Shae Fontaine and her mother, brought them to the top of the stairs. The women came along quickly, their eyes wide. Shae Fontaine was rigid with fear, terrified almost to the point of shock.

They'd boosted Shae up to Stevens, and he'd taken her, pulled her into the attic, nice and easy, whispered something that was supposed to reassure her, but from the looks of it, failed miserably. Stevens made sure she was settled, put his finger to his lips, turned back to the hole, and reached down for Mona Fontaine.

They'd boosted Mona up, too, and she'd gone rigid when Stevens took hold of her arms, stared up at him like all the fight was gone, like all she had left was to go stone-still and let the madness wash over her. Stevens hauled her up, deadweight, set her down beside her daughter, and then the Mounties were coming up.

They got the first Mountie, the female, Buckley, up with no issues. It was Pelletier who'd started the problems. He'd shaken off Stevens's assistance, tried to pull himself through the hole on his own, made it more than halfway—and then he kicked his legs back involuntary. Hit the wall loud enough to make a thud, loud enough for Hurley to hear.

And then Pelletier was up and in the attic, yes, but Hurley was coming. Stevens could hear him, and he was bringing Carla Windermere with him.

They had seconds, maximum, before Hurley reached the stairs. Stevens reached for the trapdoor and slid it back into position, sealing the attic just as Hurley pushed Windermere around the corner, their footsteps audible through the attic floor.

Stevens listened to them climb. Could see them in his head, knew Hurley would have Windermere close at hand, wouldn't trust her anywhere else. Knew, too, that Hurley would take Windermere to the master bedroom, find the women gone. Knew things would get very bad very fast after that.

"Get the women out of here," he whispered to Pelletier and Buckley. "Let the tactical guys know what we're dealing with. Tell them Hurley's upstairs and still has one hostage."

The Mounties gave him grim nods and nudged the Fontaine women toward the attic window. Left Stevens wondering if the tactical teams would have anyone left to save by the time the message was delivered.

123

The trapdoor to the attic was sealed. Windermere tried not to stare at it as Leland Hurley pushed her up the stairs ahead of him. Tried not to fixate on it, give away the game. But the trapdoor was closed. She wondered what that meant.

Where were the hostages? Where was the rescue party? As Windermere reached the top of the stairs, she stole a glance down the hall toward the master bedroom and couldn't see anyone there, either. For a moment, she dared to imagine that the whole crew had come and gone—hostages, Mounties, the works. Then she realized that if they'd left her here, she was alone in the house with a madman. And Windermere figured her chances of escaping up here, with Hurley already on alert, were suddenly much lower.

Hurley was muttering behind her. Variations on a theme, the same *All women are animals* crap he'd been spouting since she'd arrived, and probably much longer. Heck, Windermere figured the guy had probably been spitting that *Poor me, I'm an entitled baby* bullshit since he was a teenager, figured maybe *that* had something to do with the fact that he couldn't ever get laid.

Maybe it's not the women, bro, she thought. *Maybe it's you.*

But Windermere had things to worry about other than why some maniac had never found true love. Namely, the fact that the maniac in question was pushing her at a rapid clip down the hallway toward

Mona Fontaine's master bedroom, and Windermere really didn't want to find out what was waiting in there. So she stalled, as much as she could, but Hurley wasn't having it.

"Move it," he told her, prodding her with the pistol as she dawdled ahead of him. "Or I'll cut you down right here and trample your body on my way to kill those girls."

Always the charmer, Windermere thought. *Gee, Leland, why don't* we *go out?*

Stevens heard Hurley and Windermere reach the top of the stairs. Heard their footsteps suddenly muffle as they reached carpet. Heard Hurley mutter something at Windermere as they walked down the hall. Couldn't make out the words, but that didn't matter.

He pulled the trapdoor up from its mount again. Slid it aside and peered down into the hallway. Caught sight of Hurley's backside; he'd just reached the telephone table. Could just make out Windermere ahead of him. Hurley wasn't holding on to her, just shoving her forward with the barrel of the pistol. That was a positive. That gave Windermere some room to maneuver.

Okay.

Corporals Pelletier and Buckley had Shae and Mona Fontaine out of the house and on their way to safety. Meant job one was accomplished, but it left Stevens alone up here, at least until the tactical teams showed up.

Stevens couldn't afford to wait for help. As soon as Hurley discovered the women were gone, the game was over—and Windermere was probably dead.

No time to waste. Stevens pushed the trapdoor completely open.

Searched the attic for something handy, came back with someone's half-deflated basketball. It would do.

He took the ball, held it over the hole in the attic floor. Sent up a prayer that Hurley's trigger finger wasn't faster than Windermere's reflexes. Then he dropped the ball through the hole.

The ball hit the carpet with a *whump*. And for a moment, the whole farmhouse went still.

124

Hurley heard the noise behind him, thought it was the law coming up the stairs at long last. Turned back, frustration mounting, just about sick of this whole fucking game, ready to put holes in whoever was dumb enough to be the first one to show his face.

But there was nobody coming for him. No footsteps, no voices, no Mounties with guns drawn. There was only a basketball, half-deflated, rolling to a stop on the carpet.

Hurley frowned. "What the—"

And then the bitch FBI agent was making her move.

Windermere glanced back, saw Hurley was distracted. Couldn't tell why, but then it didn't matter.

This was her opportunity.

She torqued her body to the left, away from Hurley's pistol. Reached back with her right arm and slammed Hurley's gun hand to the side, heard the pistol go off beside her, the shot *loud* but harmless, bullet into the floor. Then she was spinning to launch herself at him, ducking under the gun, bear-hugging him into the wall and grabbing for the knife he kept in its sheath.

But she didn't make a clean grab of it, felt Hurley swing back around, hammer down with the butt end of his pistol. He caught her between the shoulder blades, nearly knocking her to the carpet. But she held on. Wrested the knife out and swung it up and into Hurley, catching him in the midsection and jabbing again, and then Hurley hit her again, and this time she *was* falling, down down down to the carpet, hit hard and saw Hurley swing the pistol around toward her, knew in an instant that this was it.

And then Stevens fired. Stevens came out of nowhere, somewhere, wherever he was hiding, fired his pistol once, and Hurley's eyes went wide. Stevens fired again and a third time, and Hurley pitched forward and fell, nearly landed on Windermere. She scrambled out of the way, rolled over top of him, landed on his back, and leapt for his gun hand, pulling Kerry Finley's pistol from his grip. Kept Hurley pinned and reached back for her handcuffs.

And then Stevens was beside her, helping her cuff the bastard, knee on his back, and Hurley was fighting, bucking against them, but Stevens kept him pinned as Windermere put the cuffs on him, and still Hurley struggled, cursing a streak, the same old bullshit, *dumb bitches* this and *stupid whores* that.

Windermere let him rage. Let Stevens help her up, and together they covered Hurley and looked at each other while they caught their breath.

"Shitty deal for the feminist movement," Windermere said.

"Defenseless woman needs big tough man to save her from evil psychopath, details at eleven."

Stevens shook his head. "Big man helps tough woman disarm psychopath. Get your facts straight."

"Sure took you long enough to get here, though. I thought I was going to have to kick his ass all by my lonesome."

"Too busy saving the hostages," Stevens replied. "But I knew you could take him."

Windermere looked down at Hurley, still struggling but calmer now, the fight leaving him, dissolving into frustration, until he resembled nothing more than a toddler having a tantrum.

A toddler who could have killed you. If Stevens didn't have your back.

She was shaking. Hated herself for it, hated Hurley for making her do it. "We got him," she said. "I guess that's all that matters."

"Sure."

She straightened. Put a hand on his shoulder, squeezed. "Thanks for being there when I needed you, partner," she said. "Let's go tell the Mounties it's over."

125

He'll live," Cronquist told Windermere over the phone. "I don't know if that's supposed to be good news or not, but the bastard's going to make a full recovery."

"A full recovery," Windermere said. "Lucky him."

"You said it." The Mountie paused. "I'm sorry. I know I shouldn't hate it, but I do. If this guy is half the piece of work you and your partner say he is, I can't say I'm happy that he survived."

"Yeah," Windermere said. "I'd say he deserves worse."

Cronquist was quiet, and Windermere imagined she was thinking the same as Windermere: all of the damage that Hurley had wrought—Arnold Fontaine, Kerry Finley. And the women, Hurley's victims, the full number of whom Stevens and Windermere were still trying to finalize. The agents' working estimates counted twenty-five, but Windermere figured, given Hurley's past, there were bound to be more. She wondered if the maniac would share his final tally once he was out of that Canadian hospital and back in an American interview room.

After a moment or two, Cronquist cleared her throat, told Windermere she'd keep her updated on Hurley's condition, and asked her to keep in touch. Windermere told her, sure, of course, and they ended the call.

Windermere put down the handset and looked around the FBI office in Kalispell, Montana, headquarters for the next phase of the Leland Hurley investigation. Wasserman and Mundall had set up a bulletin board with pictures of the known victims, were divvying up the task of contacting the families while Stevens and Windermere worked through the paperwork.

And there was a lot of paperwork. The Canadian government had a question or two about the FBI's unauthorized incursion onto their soil, and Windermere had spent more than a couple hours on the phone with an assistant FBI director in Washington, DC, justifying their side of the story. She knew they'd had to cross the border, knew Hurley would be long gone by now if they'd waited for permission, but the bureaucrats didn't see it that way, and Windermere didn't think they ever would.

Anyway, Windermere wasn't worried. Hurley was in custody. The threat was neutralized. But a part of Windermere couldn't help but wish the threat was a little *more* neutralized.

"Not to criticize your work, partner," she said to Stevens, who was sitting beside her in the tiny office they'd commandeered, "but couldn't you have put a few more bullets in that asshole? Cronquist and the Canadians think he's going to live."

Stevens pushed back his chair. Crossed his arms over his head and blew out a long breath. "If the universe has any sense of justice, he'll spend a long, miserable life behind bars," he replied. "And maybe he'll want to brag a bit, tell us all about his crimes. He could help the Bureau close a lot of cold cases, Carla."

"I know," Windermere said. "And you know I don't take any pleasure from killing. It's not something I ever enjoyed."

"But still," Stevens said.

"But still." Windermere motioned to the bulletin board, the cold cases, scores upon scores of missing or murdered women. "All those women are dead. Kerry Finley's dead. And Leland Hurley's still alive." She shook her head. "It just doesn't seem like enough."

126

The feeling stuck around.

It stayed with Windermere as she and Stevens signed off on the Hurley investigation, tossed the keys to the case to Wasserman and Mundall and to Boundary County's Sheriff Truman, who'd been brought aboard to represent local law enforcement. It stayed with Windermere through the drive to the airport and the flight to Minneapolis, the taxi ride to her condo and her first long, sleepless night home.

The feeling stuck around, a maddening anticlimax, like somehow they'd failed all of those women Hurley had victimized, like if they'd done something sooner or just paid more attention, hell, Kerry Finley would be alive. Arnold Fontaine, too, and Kelly-Anne Clairmont.

And maybe Leland Hurley would be in the ground, where he belonged.

"Mila Scott's still alive," Stevens had said. "So's Pamela Moody. We put a stop to him, Carla, about as fast as we could. He'll never be a free man again."

Maybe. But still, Hurley haunted Windermere. His victims lingered with her: twenty-five women (at least) who might still be alive, twenty-five women who deserved better than a killer who would live out his days eating three squares a day on the taxpayers' dime.

It was scary to think about. Unhealthy. Awful. But Windermere knew if she could go back to that farmhouse, that final showdown, she would have stabbed Leland Hurley dead with Ashlyn Southernwood's knife. Maybe then the women Hurley had murdered would find their peace.

And maybe Windermere would, too.

She moped. Shrugged off Mathers's attempts to comfort her, shut down on her shrink, couldn't push past the block Hurley had set in her consciousness.

She moped, and she stayed moping for days, weeks, after her return, until one day Mathers knocked on the door to her office, poked his head in, and told her there was a woman he wanted her to meet.

And that's how Windermere and Mathers wound up in Wisconsin, on the shore of Lake Superior, a cemetery overlooking the water, an icy wind blowing in off the lake. Stevens was there, too; he'd tagged along, said he was bothered himself by what had happened in Canada, hoped he'd find closure here. They'd all bundled up, taken Stevens's old Cherokee, driven four hours to get here. And when they'd arrived, Mila Scott was waiting, and Nicole Corbine, Ashlyn's mother, and Mila had Ronda Sixkill along with her, too.

Sixkill was smaller than Windermere had expected. She'd heard Mathers talk about her, read the woman's file, expected to find some tough broad ex-con waiting at the cemetery gates. And Sixkill was solid, sure, didn't look like she brooked being pushed around, but there was a kindness about her, too, the way she drew Mila closer to her, some protective instinct, as the agents climbed out of the Cherokee and approached the three women.

Mila, for her part, looked more or less unruffled by the whole Leland

Hurley encounter. She wore a cast on her ankle from the fall she'd taken, had suffered some minor frostbite, but Hurley hadn't robbed her of anything more. She shook hands with all three agents, met their gazes directly. She didn't look beaten; rather, she looked relieved.

She was holding a small urn. "Ash," she said when she caught Windermere looking. Smiled just a little. "Ash's ashes. I figured if she had to spend time somewhere, this would be it."

It was a beautiful spot, Windermere had to admit, as she followed Mila and Ronda Sixkill through the small cemetery—the barren trees and their naked branches, brown earth and patchy snow, the lakeshore frozen over, ice piled up into bergs and ridges and fault lines. It was cold, but where wasn't, this far north, this time of year? And anyway, Windermere had a new winter coat, bought it first thing after she stepped off the plane from the mountains.

They searched the cemetery for longer than they'd intended, nobody quite knowing where they were going, Nicole Corbine navigating by memory and a vague sense of direction. But they found it at last on a slight rise facing north, the water, a small weathered headstone in a sea of them: *Southernwood.*

"Ash would have wanted to be here," Mila said as they clustered around the gravesite. "She loved her gran more than anything in the world."

"Sure," Stevens said. "This is a beautiful spot for them both."

"Her gran gave her that old knife," Mila said. "That's how I knew it was Hurley who did it. He stole that knife from her."

"You did a damn good job finding him," Windermere said. "We wouldn't have caught him if it wasn't for you."

"Yeah." Mila studied the headstone. "I just wish I hadn't let her take that ride."

She went silent, Ronda's hand on her back, reassuring, and Windermere was struck again by the senselessness of it, angered by her inability to do, well, *anything* in the face of this grief.

"I'm sorry," she said quickly. "I'm sorry we didn't catch Hurley sooner. And I'm sorry we didn't kill Hurley when we had the chance."

She started to say something else, couldn't decide what. Knew she was babbling, getting emotional. Shut herself off.

"I'm just sorry," she said. "I'm really goddamn sorry."

And then Mathers was beside her, pulling her close, rubbing *her* back, and even sorry didn't seem like enough, not here. Not for what she was feeling.

127

They cast Ashlyn Southernwood's ashes to the wind, let them fall onto her grandmother's headstone, let the wind scatter the rest.

"I think she would have wanted it like that," Nicole Corbine said when the urn was empty and Ash was gone. "She couldn't ever stay in one place, you know?"

"Sure," Stevens said. "Sounds like someone else we know."

Mila smiled at that, a tentative smile, and they stood there a few minutes more, until the chill off the lake became too much to bear, and then they bundled their coats around themselves and started back to the gates.

Windermere hung back, just a couple of steps, stole one last glance at the gravestone, Ashlyn's remains already all but vanished. She felt foolish for making a scene, stupid, knew she was supposed to be the tough cop, the hard-ass, knew a life behind bars was supposed to be punishment enough.

And then Ronda Sixkill was beside her, falling in step, and they were walking together. Ronda didn't say anything for a few steps, and then she did.

"It wouldn't have mattered, you know?" she said. "Even if you'd killed him, you'd still be hurting."

Windermere didn't say anything. She'd read Ronda's file. She knew the woman's history.

"That anger, it doesn't go anywhere," Ronda said. "There's nothing that satisfies it, even after he's dead. It just eats and eats and eats, sends you in circles, fighting the same battles over and over, even though there's no one left to fight. You can't fall for the trap." She touched Windermere's shoulder. "You stopped him, Agent Windermere. You put him away. You did good."

Windermere nodded ahead, toward Mila Scott. "Tell that to her."

"She knows. You saved her life, too, don't forget."

"I just wish we'd done more," Windermere said. She wanted to argue the point, but they were at the cemetery gate, and Mathers and Stevens were there, holding the gate open for them, and besides, Windermere figured she'd said all she could say.

128

So where are you heading now?" Windermere asked Mila once they'd returned to the vehicles and the good-byes were just about taken care of.

Mila looked away shyly. "San Francisco?" she said. "Ronda knows a woman down there. She runs a clinic for . . ." She trailed off, blushing. "I'm going to get myself clean," she said. "Ash was always bugging me about it, so . . ."

"That's good to hear," Windermere said. "And how are you planning to get there?"

Mila didn't answer. Looked down at her feet.

"You aren't planning to ride, are you?"

"I don't have any money," Mila said. "But, it's no big deal. I'm used to it now. As soon as I get to Chicago, it's a straight shot to the coast."

"Cripes," Windermere said, reaching for her wallet. "It's the dead of winter, child." She pulled out a handful of bills. "This should keep you fed, at least."

Then she straightened. *"Ronda."* Mila stepped aside as Ronda looked back from her pickup, met Windermere's eyes. "Take this girl to the bus station," Windermere told her. "Buy her a Greyhound bus ticket anywhere she wants to go. Bill the FBI if you need to, but make sure she gets on a bus, okay?"

Ronda looked at Mila, who stared down at the ground, trying not to smile. "I guess I could take the bus," Mila said.

"You *guess*?" Windermere shook her head. "Get on out of here, kiddo. Go somewhere warm. But be safe, do you hear me? No more playing cop."

"No more, I promise."

"You ever feel like the cops don't care about you, you call me and my partner. We care. I promise."

"I know." Mila chewed on her lip. "Thank you."

"No thanks required, kiddo," Windermere told her. "You did good by your friend. You're a hero."

Mila blushed, still couldn't meet her eyes. "There is one thing I wish," she said. "I wish I could have stolen Ash's knife back. I really hate knowing that asshole got to keep it."

Windermere felt her spirits lift a little. "That, we can help you with." She nudged Mathers, who missed it at first. Nudged him harder and he figured it out, pulled a plastic bag from his pocket.

"Got this back from the Canadians a couple of days ago," Windermere told Mila. "It's not needed as evidence, not anymore. And the damn thing saved my life, so I kind of want to see it wind up in a good home."

She took the bag from Mathers, pulled the knife out from a brand-new sheath. Held it out to Mila. "We thought you would want it," she said. "Something to remember your friend by."

Mila stared at the knife, disbelieving. Took a couple of seconds to process. Then, in an instant, she'd taken the knife and stuffed it into her coat. Wrapped her arms around Windermere before Windermere could react, caught her in an inescapable bear hug. And it was all Windermere could do to hold on, stay upright. Let the girl hug her, and try to feel like she deserved it.

AUTHOR'S NOTE

I've never been interested in writing serial killer novels. I don't quite have the stomach for it. But a couple of years ago, I moved to a neighborhood in Vancouver, Canada, known as the Downtown Eastside. It's a notoriously seedy part of the city, rampant with drug use and extreme poverty—and it's a neighborhood where, in the 1980s and '90s, a man named Robert Pickton murdered as many as forty-nine women, most of them prostitutes, many of Native descent.

For years, Pickton's activities were something of an open secret in the Downtown Eastside. Women disappeared, simply vanished, their absences marked by neglected doctors' appointments and uncashed welfare checks, by missed phone calls to families on Christmas and birthdays. Rumors abounded—a serial killer on the loose. But these women were streetwalkers; they were junkies, society's flotsam and jetsam. And the police response to each case was shockingly apathetic.

The Downtown Eastside is a scary place, on its surface. It's easy to write off the whole neighborhood, to look past the people and see only the grime and the garbage, the discarded needles and broken pipes, the dingy, rent-stabilized, single-room hotels. And for years—decades—the police, and the city at large, did just that, while the community's women continued to die at an appalling rate.

The details of the Pickton murders are horrifying in their brutality. I'll spare you the details, but if you're interested in the case, I recommend Stevie Cameron's excellent book *On The Farm*. It's a devastating read—but it's well worth your time, if you can handle it.

I walk my dog through the Downtown Eastside every day. There's a memorial rock that we pass, by the water's edge, installed in the memory of the community's lost women. On it is carved:

The heart has its own memory. In honor of the spirit of the people murdered in the Downtown Eastside. Many were women and many were Native Aboriginal women. Many of these cases remain unsolved. All my relations.

It's a beautiful, terrible, sacred place. It's a reminder that these women were daughters, mothers, sisters. That they loved, and were loved, that they are missed. It's a reminder that they mattered, they *all* mattered, no matter their circumstances.

This is the background to *The Forgotten Girls*.

ACKNOWLEDGMENTS

I'm grateful as always to my agent, Stacia Decker, for her support and encouragement. And to Neil Nyren, Alexis Sattler, Katie Grinch, and everyone at Putnam. It's a privilege to work with such a wonderful team, and I'm so proud of what we've accomplished together. (A special thanks to the copy editors and production staff who are perennially saving me from making a fool of myself. Heroes, every one of you.)

There are many, many booksellers who've championed my stuff, and I'd like to single out a few of them: McKenna Jordan, John Kwiatkowski, and Sally Woods at Murder By The Book in Houston, Texas; Lynn Riehl at Nicola's in Ann Arbor, Michigan; Barbara Peters and Patrick Millikin and everyone at the Poisoned Pen in Scottsdale, Arizona; Fran, Adele, and JB at Seattle Mystery Books; Anne Saller at Book Carnival in Orange, California; Maryelizabeth Hart at Mysterious Galaxy in San Diego, California; Walter Sinclair and Jill Sanagan at Dead Write Books in Vancouver, British Columbia; and, with all my heart, Pat Frovarp and the late Gary Shulze at Once Upon a Crime in Minneapolis, Minnesota. Thanks to you all.

Thanks also to Becky Stewart and Tim Hedges; you make the road just a little less lonely.

Thanks to Alexis Tanner, Kristi Belcamino, Lynn Cronquist, Alex Kent, the Malmons (Dan and Kate), the DoJos (Aaron, Mellissa, Felicity, and Vera), the Parents (Jason, Angele, Josh, Ben, Al, and

Denise), the Thompsons (B.J., Vicki, Owen, Jake, and Ava), Jesse Cope, Brianna Coughlin, Timothy O'Brien and Jennifer Hogan, Jon McGoran, Jon Stern, Steve Shadow, Keith Rawson, Michele Lewis, Michelle Isler, Dayne Cody, Arthur Crowson and Megan Elias, Brandon Colby Cook, Robert Johnstone, the Beetner family (Eric, Marie, Molly, and Gracie), Sarah Husmann, Sarah White, Bill Gordon, Bill Bride, Kyle Shipps, Robin Spano and Keith Whybrow, Steve Weddle, Court Harrington, Chris La Tray, Dietrich Kalteis, Alma Lee, Lonnie Propas, Cathy Ace, Tricia Barker, Wayne Arthurson, Peggy Blair, "Diamond" Phill Gribben, and Tara Imlay.

And thanks to my partner, Shannon Kyla, and to my family—Andrew, Terry, Mom, Dad, Phil, and Laura. You make everything possible, and you make it all worthwhile.